Endorsements

What readers have said about *Through the Crystal Snow*:

———⟡⟡⟡———

Brilliant! I couldn't put it down.

———⟡⟡⟡———

Can anyone to be as good as Robert Tyler, or as evil as Alexander Johnston? O'Keef makes us believe that both are possible.

———⟡⟡⟡———

Wonderful characters and great story come together in *Through the Crystal Snow*! You will love this book.

THROUGH THE
Crystal
SN❄W

Through the
Crystal
SN❄W

A NOVEL

ROBERT D. O'KEEF

For Gary & Linda

Robert D. O'Keef

TATE PUBLISHING
AND ENTERPRISES, LLC

Published by Tate Publishing & Enterprises, LLC
127 E. Trade Center Terrace | Mustang, Oklahoma 73064 USA
1.888.361.9473 | www.tatepublishing.com

Tate Publishing is committed to excellence in the publishing industry. The company reflects the philosophy established by the founders, based on Psalm 68:11,
"The Lord gave the word and great was the company of those who published it."

Book design copyright © 2013 by Tate Publishing, LLC. All rights reserved.
Cover design by Caypeeline Casas
Interior design by Jomel Pepito

Published in the United States of America

ISBN: 978-1-62746-220-4
1. Fiction / General
2. Fiction / Christian / General
13.06.28

Dedication

TO PHYLLIS, LEIGH ANNA, ANDREEA, ELEANOR,
MARY ELEANOR, LYNNLEIGH—
the special women in my life.

Names Are Important

I AM PROUD OF HOW I GOT MY name. My father was a slave on a plantation in Chowan County right on the Albemarle Sound in the eastern part of North Carolina. He had been trained as a blacksmith, but mostly, he was used as a field hand. He hated working in the fields. One tobacco priming season, when he got to the end of a row, he just put his armload of tobacco down, stepped into the woods, and kept on going. He hadn't planned to run away, but at the time it seemed like the right thing to do.

My father had heard the talk of the other slaves as they gathered around the fire at night. To get to freedom, he had to go north. He had to cross a state called Virginia and another called Maryland. He had to climb some mountains and then get to the other side. When he did, he might be in the land of freedom— some place called Pennsylvania. But if he wanted to be really assured of his freedom, he'd have to go all the way to some place called Canada.

Being smart, my father decided to travel only at night. He also decided to hide "in plain sight." So he mostly slept in barns. Around five each morning, just as the morning light was coming, he would find a barn or some other outbuilding to hide in. Every farm and plantation had them. He preferred barns to the other outbuildings because they were bigger and had more places to hide. He would crawl to the tallest part of a barn and snuggle up in the hay for a good day's sleep.

He didn't know how big Virginia was, but he figured he was going about fifteen miles a night. He was traveling in the woods, which made things difficult, but he figured it was safer. Even if he had to fight briars and poison ivy vines, he thought it was safer than getting on the roads. It was only as light began to dawn each day that he would find a barn to bed down in.

He had spent night after night in the flatlands, but slowly, almost imperceptibly, the land began to change to hills. He thought he must be getting close to the mountains. On the other side of the mountains was freedom! It turned out that there were a lot of hills before he got to the mountains—night after night of hills and day after day of sleeping in barns.

One afternoon, my father woke up and looked out the loft window of the barn where he had spent the night and saw not hills, but mountains! Though he had never seen mountains before, he was sure that he was seeing them now. He could see rock faces and what had to be ranges of mountains. There was more than one. In all the campfire talk of the slaves, they had always said *mountains*, not *mountain*.

My father was so excited that he shouted for joy! That was probably not a good thing for a runaway slave trying to get to freedom to do. It just so happened that someone had heard the shout and wanted to know who was hiding in his barn.

"Come down here!" Oskar Schoenfeldt shouted with an incredibly deep and heavily accented bass voice.

Expecting a man holding a gun, my father was surprised when he climbed down from the loft to see a little man with a smile.

Certainly that deep voice could not have come from such a small man, my father thought.

But when he spoke again, my father's thought was proven wrong as a deep, booming voice asked, "Why are you sleeping in the loft when I've got beds in the bunkhouses?"

He spoke in impeccable English but with a German accent so strong that my father had trouble understanding what he said.

Since my father wasn't really sure what the man was talking about, he didn't say anything at all. It turned out that my father's sense of direction wasn't very good. Instead of traveling north, he had been traveling almost due west and was still in North Carolina. But the good news was that he had woken up that day on the estate of Schoenfeldt, a German-American, a Moravian, and a staunch antislavery zealot.

Schoenfeldt had not always been strongly against slavery. In fact, there was a time when he planned to purchase a large number of slaves to work on his plantation. Schoenfeldt was one of the largest land owners in Surry County. His holdings, nearly fifteen thousand acres in all, stretched from Bethabara all the way to Germantown. He had contracted with plantation owners over in Guilford County to use their slaves for the tedious task of clearing two thousand acres of his land and getting it ready for planting tobacco. He had also built three large bunkhouse complexes on his land for the slaves that would be coming.

Unlike most slave owners who built one-room slave quarters that were as cheaply built as possible, Schoenfeldt insisted that his bunkhouses have separate living and sleeping areas as well as a loft in each house for children that would, inevitably, come. He insisted that the kitchen fireplaces be built of brick, with an oven and the most modern spits for cooking.

Mr. Schoenfeldt built three different "communities" of bunkhouses: one near Bethabara, one on the eastern side of his property near Germantown, and one at the far northwest of his property adjacent to his home. Each "community" was intended to comfortably house about fifty adult slaves and their children. It was his intent to buy intact families, having heard from other planters that this purchase plan was less disruptive. He had hired a foreman and planned to go to the slave auction in Wilmington the first week of September 1756. His foreman had told him that he would need several months to train all of the slaves before planting time, especially if he bought "true Africans," as the foreman put it. True Africans would not even know the language, much less know how to plant acre after acre of tobacco.

Schoenfeldt was a devout Moravian. He went to church on the last Sunday of August and heard a sermon that seemed to be directed just at him. (He later learned that it really was.) The sermon was a simple one based on a profound text: "You shall love the Lord with all your heart, and with all your soul, and with all your mind. And you shall love your neighbor as yourself." His only memory was Pastor Gluck's repeated question, "How can you love the Lord and enslave your neighbor?"

It was a simple sermon with a profound effect. At the end of the sermon, Schoenfeldt did something that most Moravians just didn't do—he went to the altar in a public display of repentance. That very afternoon after church, Oskar Schoenfeldt fired his foreman and cancelled his plans to go to Wilmington.

He did, however, have a problem. What was he going to do with seventy-five empty houses and with nearly two thousand acres of cleared land? Schoenfeldt decided to turn his acres into pastureland and create the largest dairy in North Carolina. He would produce fresh milk, buttermilk, butter, sour cream, and all kinds of cheese. He remembered that back home in Germany, there were many very successful dairies. He knew that distribution would be his biggest challenge, but he would figure it out. He would rent out the bunkhouses to the army of people it would take to run a successful dairy.

Now, ten years later, when my father made his way down the ladder from the hay loft, Schoenfeldt was, indeed, one of the most successful dairymen in North Carolina. Beautiful dairy cows roamed on the two thousand acres (the rest was used to grow hay for the cows and to provide pasturage for a large herd of horses). And Mr. Schoenfeldt had succeeded in renting out most of the bunkhouses.

"My name's Oskar Schoenfeldt," he said as he extended his hand to my father, who wasn't sure what to do. In the Albemarle County, no black man would shake hands with a white man. No white man would extend his hand either. My father decided to ignore the extended hand.

"My name's Thomas. Ain't got no lass name. But I lived on Massa Perkin's plantation afore I run away. So I guess my name is Thomas Perkins."

"Well, if you're going to stay here with me, I suppose you ought to have a name different from that of your former master. Being Thomas Perkins might be a bad idea. You really ought to come up with a new name."

Stay here with him? My father was confused. He hadn't crossed any mountains. He had only gotten to them. How could he be in the land of freedom?

"Am I in Pennsylvania?" he asked.

"Lord, no, son. You are in North Carolina! Surry County, North Carolina."

"North Carolina! But that's impossible. I've been walkin' for more than a month. And those are mountains, ain't they?" my father asked, sure that if they were mountains, then Mr. Schoenfeldt had to be wrong.

"Those are mountains all right," Mr. Schoenfeldt said. "Those are the Sauratown Mountains, and if you go to the west of those, you will find the Blue Ridge Mountains. To the west of those you'll find the Smoky Mountains. Which mountains were you looking for?"

"I don' know. I s'pose I was lookin' for the..." My father struggled to think of a way to say this and finally said, "the Freedom Mountains."

"Freedom Mountains," Mr. Schoenfeldt said, laughing. "I suppose that's as good a name for these mountains as I ever heard." It turned out that Mr. Schoenfeldt's laugh was as deep and booming as his voice.

"Are you goin' to be a turnin' me over to the slave catchers?" my father asked.

"Lord no! Haven't I already said that you would be staying here with me? That is, if you want to."

"Are you going to be my new massa?"

"You aren't going to have any master," Mr. Schoenfeldt said. "As long as you are here, you are a free man. I guess I'll need to get you some papers that say that you are free. That's why you'll need a new name. What kind of work were you trained to do on that plantation down east?"

"I was trained to do mos' everthin', but blacksmithin' is my favorite," my father replied.

"No wonder you've got muscles like that!" Mr. Schoenfeldt said.

The two men could not have been more different. My father towered over Oskar Schoenfeldt. He had the kind of body that any man would have been proud of. Oskar Schoenfeldt was a tiny man—only five feet, one inch tall. He could not have weighed over 110 pounds. My father was a full foot taller. He had the kind of sculptured body that blacksmithing would give a man. His muscles showed clearly through the simple sleeveless shirt he was wearing. Running away with no extra clothes had not been very smart because now his clothes bore the distinct marks of his having made his way through woods in the dark every night for more than a month.

Mr. Schoenfeldt, however, was impeccably dressed in the style of a gentleman. Today he was clothed in dark brown breeches and a burgundy waistcoat. His shirt and stockings were both made of an off-white silk. His buckle shoes had been imported from France and were highly polished. All of the people who worked on the estate were amazed that Schoenfeldt could work all day among the cows and horses and remain completely unsoiled by the place. He took it as a mark of being a gentleman to remain clean.

His only exception to fashion was his refusal to wear a wig. He pulled his hair back into a ponytail, a difficult task for a man with very kinky hair. Making his hair do anything was nearly impossible, but he had discovered that bacon grease would make it lie down. There was a considerable disadvantage to this in the summertime in North Carolina. Flies just loved to zoom around his head. The deer flies and horse flies were the worst because their bites actually hurt. He was determined to find something other than bacon grease to make his hair behave, but so far, his search had been unsuccessful.

The only thing remotely handsome about Schoenfeldt was the glint in his eyes. His eyes were dark blue, and there was something about them that actually glowed. Because the light flickered off them, they appeared lighter than they were. His smile mimicked his eyes. Though not at all handsome, there was a kindness in his face. Despite his deep, gruff voice, there was a gentleness in his manner that made people instantly like him.

My father wasn't sure how to respond to Mr. Schoenfeldt's comment about his body. He remembered that his whole body had been covered with lard to make his muscles shine and that he was forced to flex his muscles when he was sold to Massa Perkins. It wasn't but a moment before Mr. Schoenfeldt's booming voice brought him back to Surry County.

"A blacksmith! Thank God Almighty, a blacksmith!" he roared. "I've always been a man of devout prayer, but I never believed in it much," he said. "Until now, that is. I've been praying for months that God would send me a blacksmith. I just can't run this estate without one. And here you are, an answer to my prayer."

From my father's point of view, one of the only good things about Massa Perkins's plantation was that Massa Perkins had come under the influence of the Methodists. Massa Perkins had been a devout member of the Church of England until tensions developed between the colonies and the home country. The Episcopal priest had been a nice enough fellow, but he was an ardent loyalist. Besides that, his sermons were as dry as dust. He was convinced that the liturgy, especially the communion service, was the most important part of worship. So Massa Perkins and all of his extended "family" started going to the Methodist Church.

When the Methodist circuit rider, a preacher named Joseph Pilmore, came along, things took a dramatic change. Pilmore was a hellfire and damnation preacher who could have you laughing one moment and crying the next. Pilmore even got Massa Perkins to shouting. Of course, if Massa Perkins shouted, the whole "family" joined in. It wasn't long, though, before my father and the rest of the slaves in the gallery were shouting because they too were caught up in the spirit and the power of Pilmore's preaching. And could those Methodists ever sing! There was a Baptist church around the corner that sent one of its deacons to ask the Methodists to sing a little softer because their singing was disturbing the Baptist service.

My father was a Methodist through and through. He hoped that he was a Christian, even though he could never be as good as Preacher Pilmore wanted him to be. But he never thought of himself as an answer to anyone's prayer. He wasn't sure how being a blacksmith could be an answer to any prayer.

But my father thought this might be a good time to observe another good Methodist practice—being quiet during the invitation. It sounded an awful lot like Mr. Schoenfeldt was inviting him to be a part his family and to work the job he liked. So my father just kept quiet and nodded a lot as Schoenfeldt introduced him to "Schoen Oder," his Beautiful Valley.

The first thing that Mr. Schoenfeldt did was to show my father the blacksmith shop. It was in a building just beyond the barn where he had slept. Inside was everything that a blacksmith needed. He looked in awe at all of the equipment. There was both a wood-fired and a coal-fired forge. There were two anvils, one with a rounded end for forming horseshoes and one with a square end for making boxes and hinges and the like. There were hammers and tongs of every description. There were stalls for the horses and mules that were waiting shoeing. There was everything that any blacksmith would need. My father was so overwhelmed at all that he was seeing that he hardly noticed that Mr. Schoenfeldt was speaking.

"The last blacksmith was so bad that I had to fire him. He couldn't make a horseshoe the right size if his life depended on it. Anyway, I'll pay you two pounds a month, plus room and board. I'll get one of the boys who lives on the place to be your assistant. Nobody can shoe a horse, or especially a mule, alone."

My father wasn't quite sure what he had just heard. Was the man offering him a job? And was he offering to pay him the unbelievable sum of two pounds a month? My father had never had a penny to his name.

"Massa. Is you offerin' me a job?"

"I'm not your massa, so don't call me that. You can call me Mr. Oskar. That's what everybody else around here calls me. They can't handle Schoenfeldt very well. And yes, I'm offering you a job. You'll be responsible for all of the blacksmithing needs of the estate. If you're good, the word will spread, and folks from all over the valley will start coming to have their needs met. You can charge whatever you think is fair. I wouldn't be surprised if you made an additional three or four pounds a month. I'll pay your first month's salary today so you can buy some clothes and whatever else you might need. Are you willing to take the job?"

"I suppose so."

"Well, good. Let's shake on it," Mr. Oskar said, extending his hand.

My father had never shaken hands with a white man in his life. He nervously extended his hand. As Mr. Oskar grabbed it, he discovered that although Mr. Oskar was small, he wasn't weak.

Schoenfeldt's handshake was as strong as the bond that would develop between the two men over the years to come.

"Let me take you around to the bunkhouses. Mrs. McAdams is a widow lady who is a seamstress. She lives in one of the houses. She can fix you up with clothes. We'll probably have to go all the way to Salem to get you shoes. I don't know if we have ever had anybody here that has feet as big as you."

As Mr. Oskar talked, my father took in everything. There was the beautiful barn that he had slept in. He hadn't realized how big it was until now. He figured that thirty or forty cows could be in the barn at the same time for milking. Next to the barn was the blacksmith shop, and beside it was a building with four chimneys. Because the most incredible aromas were coming from the building, he figured it was a bakery. He later learned that it was the kitchen for the whole estate. Mr. Oskar had never married and hated to cook, so he built a spectacular kitchen and hired four cooks to run it. They provided enough food for everyone who worked at Schoen Oder.

Beside the kitchen were several smokehouses. My father could see hams and sides of beef hanging in one of them whose door happened to be open. Beside the smokehouses was a large well house, the most impressive my father had ever seen. Four large brick columns held up the roof from which was suspended a pulley system carrying more buckets than he had ever seen. Each rope could be lowered and raised again to bring up multiple buckets of water at once. Each bucket was attached to the rope with a hook and could easily be removed or reattached to the rope. It was clear that the well was set up to fight fires.

My father was amazed at the construction of Schoenfeldt's buildings. In all his journeys across the state of North Carolina, my father had never seen barns and outbuildings made of brick. They also each had solid oak doors and mansard roofs. Clearly, Oskar Schoenfeldt had spared no expense in building his estate.

Just beyond the well was a brick-paved lane that led to a collection of smaller buildings. As my father and Mr. Schoenfeldt made their way down this lane, he saw the beauty of this Beautiful Valley. Just in front of him was a range of mountains. What had Mr. Schoenfeldt called them? The Sauratown Mountains. It seemed like a strange name to him, but they surely were beautiful.

They were just beginning to show their fall colors. Especially up on the tops of the ranges, he could see the brilliant yellows and reds of trees he had never seen before. There weren't scenes like these along the Albemarle. Mr. Schoenfeldt's estate was nestled at the bottom of one of the mountains and stretched out down a huge valley. At the bottom of the hill on which all of the estate buildings were standing was a beautiful lake. It was obviously man-made since my father could see the earthen dam and the spillway at one end. The water was perfectly still and looked almost charcoal gray from the top of the hill, but my father could see the reflection of a mountain with a great rock face. Beyond the lake, as far as he could see, were pasturelands. Dotted across the pastures were a mixture of cows and horses. My father had no idea why a dairy needed so many horses, but if they needed shoeing, he would have plenty of work to do. He was so taken in by the beauty of the place that he was completely embarrassed when he realized that Mr. Oskar had been talking and that they had arrived at the bunkhouses that Mr. Oskar had talked about earlier. They too were made of brick, with a fireplace and chimney at each end and a porch that ran the whole length of the front of each house. The bunkhouses were situated in three community circles of five houses each. At the center of each circle was a well, and behind each of the houses was an outhouse.

Mr. Oskar took my father to the first house on the right in the first of the clusters of houses. He knocked on the door, and a strikingly beautiful middle-aged woman came to the door.

"Mrs. McAdams, this is Thomas. He doesn't have a last name, yet. But he will have one soon. Right?" he asked, looking at

Father. Not waiting for a reply, he continued, "Thomas is going to be needing some clothes. He is our new blacksmith. So you know the kinds of things that he needs. And of course, he needs them right away."

"I will be glad to help him," Mrs. McAdams said to Mr. Oskar. Then turning her attention to my father, she said, "Yer a strappin' young man. How tall ye be?"

Never having heard of measurements, Father was at a loss to answer the question. He figured he was as tall as he was. So once again, he just kept quiet.

"Yer to call me Whispering Wind. That's what everybody else does," she said as she got out her measuring tape and began to take measurements of every part of my father's body. He felt a little bit like he did when he was sold to Mr. Perkins, but Whispering Wind's constant chatter and Mr. Oskar's reassuring presence calmed him. He had never seen a woman like her. Her reddish complexion and straight black hair meant that she had to be an Indian. Father had heard tales of such people, but he had never actually seen one.

In a brief pause in her chatter, Mr. Oskar explained that she was a Sauratown Indian and that most of her tribe had either died out or merged with the Cherokee farther to the west. She had been living at the base of one of the Sauratown Mountains when her husband, Captain Albert McAdams, moved to the area, swept her off her feet, and married her. Not long after they were married, he was called into duty toward the end of the French and Indian War. He never returned from the war, leaving her a widow. But a beautiful child was born some months later, and she named her Elizabeth Ann. At least that's her proper Scottish name. Around the house, she's known as Cooing Dove because that was the first sound Whispering Wind heard after she was delivered.

"I'll have two suits of clothes ready for you the day after tomorrow. They'll cost you 35 pence each. And I take only cash," she said.

My father didn't have any idea whether that was a good deal or a bad one. But Mr. Oskar assured her that he would have cash to pay and assured him that he was getting a great deal. As they turned to go, the most beautiful woman my father had ever seen walked in the door. As their eyes met, he knew that he was in love…and he hoped Cooing Dove was too.

The very next house was empty according to Mr. Oskar. As he pushed open the door, it was clear that it had been a while since anyone had lived there. Leaves and other debris that had blown through an open window littered the floor. And cobwebs were everywhere. But, even dirty, it was the nicest house that my father had ever had. There was a double bed, which was a little too short for him, just like every bed he had ever lain on since he became an adult. There were a couple of chairs and a table.

"I'll make sure that you get the basics. You know, blankets and candles and all the stuff you'll need to set up housekeeping," Mr. Oskar was saying. "You'll need to cut your own firewood. Most of the folk tell me that they need about four cords for the winter. Since it's already the middle of September, you are going to have to get busy. You will have to cut your firewood after you have finished your day's work at the blacksmith shop."

My father didn't care how much wood he needed. All he knew was that he was going to be living next door to Elizabeth Ann McAdams. He started, right then and there, to tell Mr. Oskar that his new last name was going to be McAdams, but he decided against it. He figured he would just think on it for a few days, and then tell Mr. Oskar what his new name would be.

It was almost like what Reverend Pilmore preached about. It was like being born again. He was getting the chance to start over. He had a job doing what he loved to do. He was going to get paid for it. He was going to be living in the finest house he had ever had. He was going to be living next door to the most beautiful woman he had ever seen. And he was going to have a new name. How could all of this have happened so quickly? Just a few minutes ago, he had been hiding in a barn. In fact, he had been hiding in barns for over a month. Barns had been his escape route. That's when it dawned on him: Barnes would be the perfect last name.

"Mr. Oskar," he said. "I've always been Thomas. And I reckon that I wouldna answer to any udder name. So I guess I should keep Thomas. But I'd like my new lass name to be Barnes. Would that be alrite wid you?"

"Mr. Thomas Barnes, blacksmith. Sounds very impressive to me," Mr. Oskar said. "I'll get with my lawyer in Richmond the next time I'm there. He's a good man. He's antislavery too. We'll figure out something about getting you some papers to prove that you are Mr. Thomas Barnes, a Free Man of Color. The letters we produce won't be perfect, but they might help if there is ever a question."

That's how I got my name. My last name, at least. My first two names came from my father's love for the Methodists. I was named for John Wesley, the founder of the Methodists. My father figured that anybody, who could found a movement that would produce Joseph Pilmore, was worthy of having his son named for him, so my father determined that his son, whenever he was born, would be named John Wesley Barnes.

Thirteen years after coming to Beautiful Valley, when I was twelve years old, Father was recognized by a traveler whose horse had thrown a shoe. When the traveler returned home to the Albemarle, he informed Mr. Perkins that his runaway slave was living in Surry County with a crazy German named Schoenfeldt.

About a month later, another traveler showed up at the blacksmith shop. He needed a small repair done on his saddle. My father thought it was such a small job that the man could have done it himself, but nevertheless, he consented to do the job.

"Sure is pretty country," the man said to my father as he began his work.

"I thinks it's bootiful here," my father said.

"Have you ever lived anywhere else?"

"I lived along the Albemarle afore I came here," my father answered.

"Over on the Perkins place?"

"Yep," my father answered. Before the word was out of his mouth, he knew that he had made the mistake of his life. When he looked up from the saddle, he saw a pistol pointing at him and the smiling slave catcher looking down at him.

The slave catcher called for the boy who was father's assistant to come and help him. As he held the gun, he instructed the boy to tie my father's hands behind his back.

"I won't do it!" Johnny yelled. "I ain't gonna tie up Mr. Thomas."

"Mr. Thomas! You got little white boys calling you mister!" The slave catcher sneered in derision. "What kind of crazy place is dis?"

"Do what he says, Johnny," my father said. "And then run along and get Mr. Oskar."

When the slave catcher was sure that my father was well secured with the rope, he took out a pair of leg irons from his saddle bags and began to secure them around my father's right ankle. It was clear that he had done this before because he was able to hold the gun, pointing it at my father, and attach the leg irons at the same time. While this was happening, Johnny was creating a near riot by yelling for Mr. Oskar and telling anyone who would listen what was happening outside the blacksmith shop.

People were pouring out of the milking barn, the kitchen, the stables, and the cheese factory and were surrounding the slave catcher and my father. Angry yells were being exchanged as my father was quietly accepting being shackled. He knew that much worse punishments than leg irons awaited him if he resisted. But my father's restraint didn't keep the rest of the crowd from harassing the slave catcher with every verbal threat imaginable.

Johnny had left the enclosure, the buildings that made up the central part of the estate, and came running up to the bunkhouse where my mother and I were. He crashed in the front door without knocking and yelled, "Some man's come an arrested Mr. Thomas! He keeps saying some'em about Mr. Thomas bein' a slave."

After an initial moment of shock, my mother threw down her sewing and ran from the house. For a moment, she had forgotten me and my best friend, Robert Tyler, who were doing our homework in the corner near the window. We jumped up and ran too, with Johnny right at our heels. We all ran around the central well and down the path which led to the blacksmith shop. As we ran, Johnny was trying to tell us what was happening, but his lack of breath and our determination to get to the shop made it nearly impossible for us to really understand anything.

When we got there, a crowd of twenty or thirty people who were surrounding a man who had a gun pointed at my father seemed to part for my mother, Robert, and me. Each time one of us, or anyone else in the crowd, tried to get close to my father, the man with the gun would threaten to shoot him.

"I get jest as much fer 'im dead as I do alive!" he shouted. "And it's easier fer me to take 'im back dead."

"Thomas!" my mother cried out.

"Lizzie Dove," my father said quietly and incredibly calmly, considering the situation, "don't rile 'im. Just wait for Mr. Oskar to get here. He'll take care of everything." My father was the only person who called my mother Lizzie Dove. Everybody else called her by her proper name, Elizabeth Ann. And usually in public my father did too. Calling her Lizzie Dove now was meant to calm her, but instead, it broke her heart. She burst into tears and grabbed hold of me. Her embrace was not a hug. It was a grasping, a clenching. And I grasped and clenched her back.

"Got yerself a wife, did ya?" The slave catcher said to my father. "And a son by the looks of things."

"Yes," he answered simply.

At that moment, Oskar Schoenfeldt burst into the center of the crowd and took charge.

"Who are you?" he asked the slave catcher calmly. "And why have you shackled this free man of color?" Before he could answer, he asked my father, "You do have your papers with you, don't you, Mr. Barnes?"

It was the slave catcher who spoke first. "It don't matter what my name is. But I shackled this man because he is a runaway nigger slave from the plantation of Mr. Elijah Perkins on the Albemarle Sound in Chowan County."

"I am afraid that you have the wrong man," Mr. Schoenfeldt said. "This is Mr. Thomas Barnes. He is a free man of color as I said to you before. And he has papers to prove it."

"Where are your papers, Thomas?"

"Thar's no use gittin' fake papers. He already admitted to me that he belonged to Mr. Perkins," the slave catcher said to Mr. Schoenfeldt.

Mr. Oskar looked quizzically at my father who said simply, "I'm afraid dat's true. I let it slip."

"It's been thirteen or fourteen years since Thomas ran away," Mr. Schoenfeldt said, turning his attention back to the slave catcher. "Surely Mr. Perkins has already replaced him. There must be some arrangement that we can make so that he can stay on my estate."

"If yer tryin' to bribe me, it won't work," the slave catcher said. "Mr. Perkins already knows that Thomas is here. That's why he sent me to git 'im. Course, him havin' a wife and son complicates matters. The boy has nigger blood, so he'll have to be a slave. I guess I'll have to carry 'im back too." The slave catcher adjusted the hinge that held the leg irons to my father's leg. "Then ag'in," he said, "Mr. Perkins don't know nuttin' bout no boy. I s'pose I could sell 'im to ya. No! No! I'se got to do the right thing and take 'im back."

My mother, who was already crying uncontrollably, burst into an even more violent eruption of tears. She grabbed me even harder as Robert stepped in between me and the slave catcher.

Oskar Schoenfeldt had never failed at anything in his life. But he had already admitted to himself that he was about to fail to keep Thomas Barnes and that Thomas was headed back to slavery. Now he set a new goal—that Elizabeth Ann Barnes would not have a double broken heart. She might lose her husband, but she was not about to lose her son, if there was anything that he could do about it.

But Oskar Schoenfeldt had a problem. He had sworn before every member of Bethabara Moravian Church that he would never own a slave. And, more importantly, he had sworn before God. He would never break either vow.

His pondering on the problem was broken by the particularly loud yells of a boy. When he came to his senses, he realized that it was Robert Tyler who was yelling at the slave catcher.

"You're not going to take my friend away! You have got to be the meanest, foulest, most despicable man I have ever met." *Despicable* was a word in our spelling lesson that week. I'm sure that Robert had never used it before. But it sure sounded good.

Robert and I were both twelve. We were both at that awkward stage between childhood and manhood. Robert was maturing a lot faster than me. He told me he already had hair under his arms and in other places too. He was nearly a foot taller than me. My mother kept assuring me that I would catch up and not to worry. I was pretty irked that he was so far ahead of me. But at the moment when he stepped in between the slave catcher and me, I was thrilled that he was as big as he was. Robert and I had always been best friends, but that moment of sheer bravery cemented the friendship from my side forever.

Robert's yelling at the slave catcher and his stepping forward in a threatening manner was enough for the slave catcher to turn his gun away from my father and toward Robert. Robert didn't back down. In fact, he moved even closer as he yelled, "You'll have to shoot me. I'm not going to let you take my best friend."

"Nobody's going to get shot," said Mr. Oskar as he put his hand on Robert's shoulder and gently moved him back. "We are going to figure something out. Elizabeth Ann, you hold tight to that boy. Don't let go for anything. You hear me?" Oskar Schoenfeldt's deep voice and German accent had never sounded so reassuring. But I don't think there was ever a time when my mother needed those instructions less. She wasn't about to let go of me, unless she could somehow grab hold of my father too.

Deciding to take a more gentle approach and seeking time to work out some solution, Mr. Oskar turned to the slave catcher and said, "You seem to have Mr. Barnes well shackled. Why don't you give him some time with his wife and son so they can say their good-byes? You and I can go down to my office and have a drink and discuss what will happen to the boy. I assume you're a drinking man?"

"I am a drinkin' man. But I ain't leavin' 'im. He already run away once."

"That's true," Mr. Schoenfeldt said. "But he hadn't been shackled by you when he ran away, had he?"

"Well, no," he said, softening for a moment. But just as quickly, he said, "But I ain't takin' my eyes off 'im. This crowd of folks would hide 'im in a heartbeat. Besides, I gotta figger a way to shackle that boy wid out all of you killin' me."

At that pronouncement, at least twenty voices yelled at once. I heard my father yell," You're not a'gonna shackle my son! I'll kill you first."

And I heard my mother cry out "Oh god. No!"

And Robert screamed, "You despicable, despicable, despicable man!" I guess it was the only word he could think of at the time. When I think about it now, it almost seems like a funny line, but it sure wasn't funny at the time. Ironically, the man really was despicable.

All of the other men and women workers who had gathered around also yelled and moved forward to take the slave catcher by force. But he just grinned maliciously and pointed the gun at my father's head. "If any of you get any closer, he will be dead," he said.

It was the only time in my life that I ever saw Oskar Schoenfeldt flustered and unable to control a situation. But, fortunately, there was a man who saw a solution and stepped forward.

"Everybody calm down a minute. I think I have a solution. I know you can't buy the boy, Mr. Oskar, but I can." It was the voice of Joshua Tyler, Robert's father. Joshua Tyler had been the estate manager for Schoen Oder since Mr. Oskar had fired the slave foreman. He had been instrumental in helping to turn the acreage from a plantation to an estate, from a tobacco plantation to a dairy, from a slave-run operation to a community of paid workers. Joshua Tyler was as close to Mr. Oskar as Robert was to me.

"I can't let you do that. I won't have any slaves on my property," Mr. Oskar said.

"He will be a slave in name only. He will still live with his mother. He will still go to school. He'll still help milk the cows in the morning. Nothing will change," Joshua said. "Except that he will be protected. No one else will be able to claim him and take him off if I purchase him."

Turning to the slave catcher, Joshua Tyler asked, "How much do you want for the boy?"

Sensing an opportunity to make a lot of money from a sympathetic man, the slave catcher quoted the outrageous sum of 450 pounds.

"I guess you'll just have to take him then," I heard Mr. Tyler say. I couldn't believe my ears. Mr. Tyler, Robert's daddy, was going to let me be taken!

"But he is sure going to be a lot of trouble for you. He's going to fight you all the way to Chowan County. Aren't you, John?" he asked me.

"I sure am!" I said much more confidently than I thought.

"And his father is going to fight you all the way too. Aren't you, Thomas?"

"Lawd, yes!" Father said.

"And you'll have to feed him all the way," Mr. Tyler continued. "And when you finally get there, the master of the plantation is not going to pay you anything for him. In fact, he might even be mad that you have brought him another mouth to feed. But you go ahead and take him. No slave is worth 450 pounds."

"All right," the slave catcher said. "Make it 300, and you got a deal."

"If he was a fully trained field hand or if he had been trained for housework, he might be worth 200," Mr. Tyler said. "But he's just a child. Heck, he hasn't even produced any man hair yet. I'll give you 25."

I wasn't pleased that Mr. Tyler had pointed out for everybody to hear that I had yet to enter puberty. I started to say that I was certainly worth more than 25 pounds, but fortunately, I kept my mouth shut, which, I was told later, was quite a feat.

"Twenty-five pounds! Are you crazy? I gotta git at least a hunnerd."

"I'll give you 50 pounds cash. And you are going to sign a receipt that I write. And you are never going to mention the sale to anyone else. Because everyone knows that you are not licensed to sell slaves, only to catch runaways, right?"

"Um. Right," the slave catcher said. "Fifty pounds will be fine."

"Come to my office. I'll write out the receipt," Mr. Tyler said to the slave catcher. Turning to us, he said, "Elizabeth Ann, Thomas, and John, you don't have much time. So say the things you need to say."

I don't remember the three of us saying much. Mostly I remember us holding each other and crying a lot. I do remember Father saying in a whisper, "Cooing Dove, do you remember when our eyes met for the first time? Hold on to that moment."

And I remember him looking me in the eye and making me promise that I would look after my mother.

Way too soon, the slave catcher was back. He was pointing his gun at my father. He mounted his horse and ordered my father to walk on ahead. I heard Mr. Oskar say to my father, "I will do everything I can to get your freedom. Don't lose hope." My mother and I wanted to walk along with him, but gentle hands restrained us.

I found myself sitting on a log by the side of the road watching the back of a leg-shackled man until the tears in my eyes made it impossible to see. When my eyes cleared just enough for me to see again, I looked down the road, and he was gone. Beside me, on that same log, was Robert. His eyes were filled with tears too.

We learned later that my father never made it back to the Albemarle. Mr. Schoenfeldt had kept his promise to try and set my father free. He had written to Mr. Perkins, explaining what a valuable servant Thomas was and requesting that he be allowed to negotiate a price to purchase him. Mr. Perkins wrote back and informed Mr. Oskar of my father's death.

Fifteen years of freedom, the love of a wonderful woman, the joy of a son, and having a meaningful profession made the shackles too heavy a burden to bear. One night near Enfield, when he thought that the slave catcher was asleep, he managed to untie the rope that bound him to a tree and started running. Unfortunately, his shackles made enough noise to awaken the slumbering slave catcher.

It wasn't true that Father was worth just as much dead as alive. Mr. Perkins had told the slave catcher that he would pay him only if he brought my father back alive and in good health. But by the time my father had broken free, the slave catcher was tired. Father had decided not to be cooperative. He had fought the slave catcher in small ways all the way across the state of North Carolina.

It only took one shot. The bullet happened to catch him right in the back of the head. The bullet, which exploded in the front of his head, blew off his face. When the slave catcher took the body to Mr. Perkins, hoping to get some money for all his time and effort, it was so unrecognizable that Mr. Perkins refused to pay him anything. It had been a disastrous trip. All he had to show for it was 50 pounds that he couldn't tell anyone about.

The Grand Duke's Invitation

SEVERAL WEEKS AFTER MR. PERKIN'S LETTER ARRIVED, Mr. Oskar knocked on our door. When I opened the door, I was more than a little shocked to see him. To have the owner of the estate visit our home was a bit unusual.

"Good morning, John," he said. "Is your mother here? I'd like to talk to both of you."

"Yes sir. She's here. She's just out back, doing her wash. I'll get her."

"Thank you," Mr. Oskar said.

When we came back into the room, my mom was wiping her hands on her apron. She was, obviously, a bit flustered. *What did Mr. Oskar want with her?* Mr. Oskar greeted her warmly and then began very quietly, almost reverently.

"Elizabeth Ann, I would like to bring Thomas's body back to Shoen Oder. I think he ought to be buried here where he was free and happy. I have written to Mr. Perkins. He has said that it will be fine with him for me to come to his plantation and retrieve the body." He paused, clearly waiting for her to respond.

"I think that would be wonderful, Mr. Oskar," she said.

"I would like to take John with me. I think that we would be gone at least six weeks. I will take along a great deal of material for him to study along the way. I'll see that he doesn't fall behind. I think that his going with me to bring his father home will help him to heal. Do I have your permission to take John with me?"

I could tell that my mother was obviously torn. She had just lost her husband. A six-week trip into the heart of slave territory would be dangerous. It was possible that she would lose her son as well. Finally, after what seemed like hours of silence to me, she asked, "Could you take a gun with you? Just in case."

Mr. Oskar smiled and said, "What if I carry Ben Randolph with me and let him carry both a pistol and a Kentucky Flintlock rifle?"

"That would be great!" my mother said, smiling broadly. "When will you be leaving?"

"I thought that we would leave in the morning," Mr. Oskar said. "You'll need to pack John a bag. Elizabeth Ann, I know that you are going to worry the whole time we are gone. But I am going to take very good care of your son."

"Mr. Oskar," I said. "Would it be alright if Robert came with us?"

"I think it be great to have Robert along. I'll speak to his father this afternoon."

We left early the next morning. Mr. Oskar and Ben Randolph drove up to our house in a flat bed buggy. On the back was a simple wooden coffin, two chests and a couple of bags of luggage. Mr. Oskar told me and Robert to put our bags beside the others. I thought it was strange that Mr. Oskar was taking two chests full of luggage. I made some smart remark about it. He told me that the chests were filled with a library of all of the things Robert and I would be studying for the next six weeks. Even though I was a fairly good student, I was beginning to wonder if going with him was a good idea. When I think back on it now, I can tell you that I have never had a more stimulating six weeks in my life.

Robert and I were both good students. We attended classes in a schoolhouse on the main quad of the estate. Mr. Oskar had built the school, and paid our teacher, Miss Pettyford. Every child at Beautiful Valley was encouraged to attend. Most of the parents were pleased to take advantage of Mr. Oskar's largesse.

Mr. Oskar had brought a special waterproof canvas to cover the chests in case of rain. He had added seats behind the buggy's main seat, so that he, Robert, and I could sit together and study while Mr. Ben did the driving. With the coffin, the chests, and our luggage, it was crowded. But we made do.

Each day, we would study something out of one of the chests for about an hour at a time and then we would take about an hour to enjoy the ride. It wasn't long before I was calling these boxes treasure chests. Mr. Oskar wasn't like any teacher I had ever had. He loved to talk about anything. And he seemed to know everything.

Early in the third morning of our trip east, Mr. Oskar said to Robert and me, "We're going to have a different kind of lesson today. I'm going to tell you a story. It's a true story about me and my father. John," he said, addressing me directly, "I'm going to tell you this story, because I know how much your father meant to you, and I want you to know how much my father meant to me. We'll let Robert and Mr. Ben listen, but this story is just for you.

"The story begins with a secret. It's a secret that all three of you must promise not to reveal to anyone. If you were to reveal this secret, it might cost me my life. Will you promise not to tell anyone?"

We all promised. I couldn't imagine what dark secret Mr. Oskar was carrying that might cost him his life.

"The secret is that my name isn't Oskar Schoenfeldt. My real name is Duke Konrad Heinrich von Schiebmacher."

"Duke!" Robert and I blurted out in unison.

"Yes. Duke," he said. "Let me begin the story when I was a twenty-year-old, trying on my new waistcoat that had just arrived from Paris. It was bright purple with a check pattern in a softer purple. The vest that came with the outfit was a bright pink. The breeches were mauve. The four colors blended perfectly. When I added the off-white silk shirt with the specially made tatted ruffles and matching stockings, my mother said that I would be the handsomest young man at the ball. I was glad that the new buckle shoes had come early so that I could break them in. I couldn't imagine standing in the receiving line in a brand new pair of shoes, let alone dancing in them all night.

"My parents had spared no expense. Two months earlier, we had received a long awaited and highly anticipated invitation for me to attend the Grand Duke and Duchess Ball in Prague. My father was the Duke of Sokolov, a duchy on the eastern border of the Prussian state of German Bohemia. The von Scheibmachers owned an estate of over 40 square miles in the beautiful section of Bohemia which bordered Bavaria.

"The duchy was a fascinating place. Throughout the forty square miles there were German, Czech, and Polish speaking villages. I had been trained to speak all three languages fluently. I was also tutored in French, since it was the new international language. And because the British had, four years earlier, entered into an alliance with the Austrian branch of the German Aristocracy, my father had hired a British tutor to supplement my education. Duke von Scheibmacher was determined to prepare me for a place of high importance at court.

"I especially enjoyed my British tutor, Donald Cooper, an Oxford trained don. Cooper had degrees in divinity, law, and economics. He loved being a student, and would have remained a student for the rest of his life if his banker father had not cut off the funds. He was accepted on the faculty of Eton, but lost the job before he began because of British politics. Since he didn't really want to be a preacher, a lawyer, or a banker, despite his degrees, he decided to make himself available to the royalty of Europe as a tutor. Using his father's banking contacts to receive the names and address of the wealthy elite in Germany, France, and Italy, he wrote to each family offering his services. Though he had never heard of the town of Sokolov, he was glad to have received a letter from the von Scheibmachers, because it was his only reply.

"Cooper had been in Sokolov for only a short time before he was glad my father had hired him for the job. He told me that he thoroughly enjoyed teaching me, because I was a brilliant and enthusiastic student. I don't know if that was true or not, but I took to English quickly, and wanted to know everything about England, especially English politics.

"My father was as thrilled with Cooper as Cooper was with the von Scheibmachers. He was especially delighted that Cooper was able to teach me about economics. He wanted me to be a good businessman. Running an estate of over forty square miles with hundreds of individual businesses was a little bit like running a small country. Furthermore, my father knew if I had good business sense, I would be more attractive to the court.

"Getting me an invitation to the Grand Duke's Ball in Prague was just one step in getting invited to the Royal Court. It was crucial that I prove myself at the ball, and that was one of the reasons that my father had spared no expense in buying my new wardrobe.

"As I stood before the mirror in the drawing room wearing the new purple waistcoat, I was sure I had never seen anything more beautiful. It was true that the colors were much bolder than any clothes that I had ever seen, but they were the height of fashion. The tailor had been brought from Paris to provide me with a complete wardrobe of twenty new outfits. I would be in Prague for a week prior to the ball attending all of the pre-ball activities—parties given by other important members of the court, and parties given by families who wanted to be important members of the court. I would attend the day-long festivities at the Duke's Palace the day of the ball and then the ball that night. Following the ball, there would be another week of events, all of which it would be essential for me to attend.

"As I was taking off the purple waistcoat, my mother was opening the other parcels, each holding an astonishingly beautiful outfit. Bringing in the tailor from Paris had been a great idea. I was sure that I would have the finest wardrobe of all the young men being introduced to society at the ball.

"Not only had my parents spent a near fortune on clothes for me, but they had also spent lavishly in other areas: new wardrobes for both my mom and dad, a new carriage, a new team of pure white horses to pull it, and special uniforms for the carriage drivers, attendants, and footmen. It would be essential that our family arrive at each function in royal style.

"The carriage was the finest German-made Landau, a four-seater with the seats facing each other. It had a special head, and drop-style windows. The head could be folded back and the windows dropped so that the Landau could become an open carriage if the weather was good. There was an outside seat for the coachman and a rear saddle for the footmen. My father had ordered the finest Italian leather for the seats and had our family crest tooled into the leather. The Landau had the finest elliptic springs, a whippentree made of maple where the horse's harness was attached, and steps which folded away for the riders. Buying a four-seater instead of a two-seater was both a political and an economic statement. It was political because the Grand Duke and Duchess always traveled in a four-seater; and it was economic because a four-seater was considerably more expensive. The majority of the ball goers would arrive in the cheaper two seat carriages.

"My parents had arranged for us to stay at the Iron Gate Hotel, the finest Hotel in all of Prague. As the name implied, the hotel was adjacent to the Iron Gate entrance into Old Town, Prague's most beautiful and historic section.

"I understood that my parents would be accompanying me to Prague and to many of the functions. I both understood, and resented, the need for my parents to be present. I was, after all, twenty years old. My future would depend, most of all, upon the way I presented myself, carried myself, and showed the court who I really was. But, it was also essential that I be seen with my parents, the son of Wolfgang and Maria von Scheibmacher, Duke and Duchess of Sokolov. The court needed to be reminded that my mother was the niece of the Grand Duchess of Saxony.

"In spite of the politics involved, I was looking forward to the ball. I had always enjoyed being with people and loved parties. I was especially looking forward to being introduced to all of the young women who were also being presented to society. In spite of what my mother had said, I knew that I would probably not be the most handsome man at the ball."

I agreed with Mr. Oskar about that. There was nothing handsome about him.

"Even though I wasn't very handsome, I was fortunate to have inherited my father's intelligence and my mother's warmth. I knew that I could talk with anyone; that I could carry on an intelligent conversation on almost any topic, and that I had impeccable manners. I also knew that no one at the ball, or any of the other events, would carry themselves with more grace.

"Before the ball, Duke von Scheibmacher wanted to test me by formally introducing me throughout Sokolov as the next duke. Even though I had been with my father on many trips throughout the duchy, I had never been on an official tour. I would have to be able to speak fluent Czech even though there were only two small areas in the duchy where it was spoken. And I had to speak the unique Polish dialect that was part Polish, part German, and part Yiddish that was spoken by the Jews in the northern section of my father's estate.

"My presentation tour would begin in Sokolov, the town where I had grown up. I knew every nook and cranny of the town. I knew every resident by name: who was married to whom, who was engaged, who all the children were, and who their parents were. Every resident also knew me.

"I loved Sokolov. Like most towns built in the Middle Ages, it was dominated by two buildings, the church and the palace. The church was a beautiful gothic structure whose spire dominated the skyline for miles around. Built in a traditional cruciform style, the two arms of the church were used to house the priests and the nuns when the church was Roman Catholic. Ever since Luther, of course, the church had been Lutheran; and nearly everyone in the duchy, except the Jews, was Lutheran. There was a very small group of Moravians of which my parents were leaders. But my father had never tried to convert his Lutheran populace to his "way of thinking."

He opened the palace to the Moravian congregation. One of his political opponents on the Grand Council had expressed his deep concern that one of their numbers was not Lutheran, but my father had assured the entire council that he could be loyal to the king and his council at the same time that he was a Moravian. After all, Lutheran Germany was ruled by a Catholic emperor as part of the Holy Roman Empire.

"The palace was also Gothic. It was built of stone; and, unlike the houses of most dukes, had never been expanded. Three hundred years before the von Scheibmachers had become the residents of the house, its original builders had laid out a structure intended to last forever. On the ground floor, the main doors opened into a grand entrance hall that was round. A great double staircase hugged the curved walls and ended in a balcony that overlooked the hall. To the right of the entrance hall was a banquet hall with a table that was so large that it had to be built in place. Forty people could easily be seated at the table which was lit by three chandeliers that held over a hundred candles each. The builders had been smart enough to attach the chandeliers to cables to raise and lower them so that the candles could be easily changed and lit. A massive triple fireplace was at the far end of the room.

"To the left of the entrance hall was the banquet hall's twin, except that it was furnished as a large parlor. For special occasions, the furniture could be pushed back to transform the area into a ballroom. Like the banquet hall, an identical triple fireplace dominated the far wall. The two fireplace mantles had been carved from marble and depicted scenes from ancient Greece.

"Behind the three front rooms were private spaces. On one end of the house was the drawing room; in the middle, an office, and on the other end, a library. The von Scheibmacher family was proud that we had the largest library in Bohemia. The books covered every subject. Most of the books had come with the house when my great grandfather and great grandmother were named duke and duchess. The library had been the room where I had received my tutoring and where I had come to love learning. Because many of the books were ancient, I had had to learn to read in Latin, Greek, and Middle German."

"How many languages do you know, Mr. Oskar? I asked, interrupting the story.

"Eight, I think," he said, counting them off on his fingers. I was impressed. French was the one subject in school where I struggled, and where Robert outshone me. I just didn't have a knack for foreign languages.

Mr. Oskar went right back to the story.

"On the second floor were six large bedrooms, three on either side of the house, with a large sitting area just off the balcony at the top of the staircase. The circular staircase continued up to the third floor which had numerous smaller bedrooms for the palace staff.

"Attached to the palace with a covered breezeway was a kitchen that was large enough to provide all of the food needed for a full feast in the banquet hall and yet small enough to provide for the daily needs of the palace family and staff.

"There were, behind the palace, all of the buildings that would be necessary to support it. A large carriage house, smokehouses, outhouses, horse barns and wellhouses were placed in the most logical way for their best use.

"The two great buildings of Sokolov were supported by all of the businesses that were necessary to run a great estate. Built around a great quad with the church at one end and the palace at the other were row buildings, also erected in Gothic style, to house a blacksmith, a cooperage, a candlemaker, a baker, a cheesemaker, a winery, a carriage master, a basketmaker, a tailor, and many more tradesmen. One of the buildings was a small jail. There was also an armory which stood by itself. Through the years, the town had expanded beyond the original quad, but the various dukes had never allowed any construction on the quad itself. It was as though the dukes could keep an eye on the church and the church could keep an eye on the dukes. The ever changing politics of the Germans fighting Czechs and Czechs squabbling with Poles and Christians arguing with Jews and Catholics debating Lutherans determined that many different families had lived in the palace. My great grandfather had been raised to the duchy when he had excelled as a general in the Czech army and was honored for his service. My father was doing all he could to ensure our family's continuation as the aristocracy of Sokolov.

"I loved to walk the quad. And just as I enjoyed studying books, I reveled in studying the people of Sokolov. I loved to watch the cooper make barrels. I was fascinated watching the wheelwright construct wooden wheels, and was amazed to discover all of the different kinds of baskets that were needed in a small town. As I studied what the town's people did, I also studied them and learned to love them. They loved me in return. Many of them said they were sure that I was going to be a great duke someday.

"I was already the Earl of Sokolov because I was the only son of the duke and duchess. But with my official presentation, I would acquire the title and the responsibilities that went with it. Being the official earl also meant that I was the duke-in-waiting. I wasn't sure, yet, what the responsibilities would be. My father was waiting until after the ball to make any decisions. He was hoping that I would make such a great impression that I would be asked to serve on the Grand Duke's staff. He even had a dream that my presentation might go so well that I would be recommended to serve on the staff of the King.

"The presentation was also crucial in finding me a wife. My parents had met at their presentation ball and had actually liked each other. It wasn't long before romance budded and a marriage between the two families of the aristocracy was arranged. I was as hopeful as my parents when it came to this part of the parties. I had had crushes on several of the village girls in my early teens, so I had a sense of what love might be. I was eager to turn my fantasy into a reality. Having heard my parents talk about the possibility of an arranged marriage, I much preferred the idea of marrying someone that I loved."

I was enjoying Mr. Oskar's story, so far. I hoped that it didn't turn into a romance. I wasn't ready for a love story. I looked at Robert, and, I could tell by his expression, that he wasn't either! Mr. Oskar must have noticed, because when he went back to the story, he changed the subject.

"I humored my mother by trying on each of the waistcoats that had come from Paris. I was amazed at their beauty and their variety. But the fashion show had taken quite a while; I was ready for a break from the talk of parties, balls, and introductions. I begged my mother's pardon, and made my exit.

"I left the drawing room, exiting the palace through the back door. I was on my way across the back quad to the stable. I loved horses and wanted to see, again, the white Arabians that my father had purchased. As I entered the barn, I was greeted by the head coachman, Johannes.

"Master Konrad," he said. "What a pleasure to see you." He, and the rest of the people of the town, still called me master, even though I was twenty years old. They didn't know exactly what to call me. They couldn't call me just Konrad, because that would be way too informal for the duke's son. But they didn't want to call me Mr. von Scheibmacher either, because that was just too formal for the 'Little Duke,' the name they called me in private. I loved the title of 'Little Duke,' but because I was sure that my father would disapprove, I let them continue to call me Master Konrad.

"Thought I'd take a look at the Arabians," I said. "They are incredibly beautiful horses."

"They are that," Johannes said. "I don't think that I have ever seen a better matched pair."

"But are they matched when it comes to working together?" I asked. "It seems to me that they are pulling apart."

"You have a good eye, Master Konrad," Johannes said. "We have two lead horses here. Both want to be master. When your father picked them out, I warned him that there might be a problem. But they were such a beautiful pair that he couldn't resist. He told me that I was such a good trainer that I could work it out of them without breaking their spirit."

"And he was right!" I assured Johannes. "It's only three weeks until the tour of the Duchy. Will you have them pulling together by then?"

"I don't know, Master Konrad. I want them to be gentle without losing their strength and spirit. Sometimes when you tame a horse, it loses its power. I don't want that to happen to these two," Johannes said, as we made our way across the stable and to the twin stalls that were housing the Arabians.

"Have you named them yet?" I asked, as I reached out to stroke the mane of one of them. I knew that my father always let Johannes name the horses, because as head coachman he was the one who would be working most closely with them."

"Well I've thought about Stubborn and Ornery, but I'm not sure the duke would appreciate that, especially as much as he spent on them. You got any ideas."

"Well, since they are twins, you could name them after the Roman gods, Castor and Pollux. In ancient mythology, they were twin gods of the horsemen. I was surprised that I remembered this piece of trivia. It must have come from one of the books in the library. It was possible that one of my tutors had talked about it, but I didn't remember."

"Castor and Pollux," Johannes said. "That'll be great. I've been thinking of names like "Cloud" and "Snow," and they just didn't seem, well, you know, manly enough."

"Cloud and Snow," I said, laughing. "If you named them that, they would both be so embarrassed; it would break their spirits right away. That's one way to train a horse. Give him a bad name."

"Master Konrad, don't laugh at me," Johannes said. "It'll break my spirit."

"I'm not laughing at you, I'm laughing with you," I said. "And nothing could break your spirit.

"I looked around as he caressed the Arabian. I saw many horses in the stable and I knew that there were many more in the corral and the pasture behind the stable. My father had been collecting and breeding horses since before I was born. He had Budenny horses from Russia, the breed that the Cossacks preferred. They were the fastest horses on the estate, but it took an expert horseman to control one. My favorites were the German Westphalians. They were beautiful horses that were great for pleasure riding, but could also be trained for dressage and even jumping. The estate also had two breeds of work horses, Belgian Drafts and Percherons. The massive Percherons stood up to nineteen hands high and seemed to eat their weight in hay every day. But there had never been a more powerful horse. I had seen just one Percheron pull a stump from the ground without even straining hard. My father had even managed to purchase a pair of Eymera, the ancient breed that went back to Roman times. He wanted to breed them to ensure that the breed would continue.

"No one on the Estate loved the horses more than Johannes, unless it was me. Every day, I made my way to the stables or to the corrals to pamper the horses. I would borrow things from the kitchen for them: carrots, turnips, apples and, occasionally even lumps of sugar. Even my father, who spent lavishly on the horses, chided me for giving them sugar, an extravagance so expensive that it really should be just for people.

"How about getting Josef to saddle Anna for me," I said to Johannes referring to my favorite Westphalian mare. "I think I'll take a ride around the estate." Telling Johannes what I was planning to do was important. It determined the kind of saddle and tack that would be chosen. I especially liked Anna. She was gentle and very responsive to bridle commands. She had been born on the estate, and I had watched as Johannes gently caressed her from wild colt to a fully trained show horse.

"Yes sir, Mr. Konrad," he said. As he turned to go, he realized that he had just found me a new title. It was more grown up than "Master Konrad," but not as formal as "Mr. von Scheibmacher." I noticed the difference and smiled my approval at Johannes.

I stayed with the Arabian that would be named Castor, or Pollux. It truly was a beautiful animal. The horse seemed to love the attention I was giving it, while at the same time it kept prancing and snorting its independence. I wasn't sure that anyone would be able to calm these horses in time for the trip to Prague; but, if anyone could, it would be Johannes.

"They sure are nice horses, aren't they, Mr. Konrad?" Josef said as he came walking up with Anna in tow. Clearly, Johannes had already informed the rest of the servants of my new title.

"They surely are Josef. They're spirited, just like me!" I said, with a smile, as I took the reins. I mounted smoothly and easily, as at home on the horse as I was in the library. As I rode out of the stable, I decided that this would be my first tour of the estate as Mister Konrad and my last as Master Konrad.

"Even though it was only February, the spring thaw had already begun. Everywhere there were sheets of ice that were turning to mud. Anna made her way through it all. She instinctively knew how to "step lightly" until she found her footing. I wish that humans had as much sense as horses.

"I circled around the stable and headed up the quad towards the church. There were some children playing a game of chuck farthing on the quad. I waved at them as I rode by. It didn't look as if any of them had gotten a button in the cup. Normally I would have stopped and chucked a few buttons myself, but today I just wanted to ride.

"I rode up the quad, turning right at the last row shop. A cobblestone lane led out of Sokolov and into the much greater estate that would one day be mine. Anna seemed to know that this was to be a slow-paced, gentle ride. The cobblestones soon gave way to thawing mud, so going slowly was a good idea.

"I wanted, more than anything, to ponder all that was about to happen to me. The arrival of the clothes had brought it all into focus. In just a couple of weeks I would be formally introduced as the Earl of Sokolov. And just a few weeks after that, I would be presented at court. My days of childhood and youth were over. Unlike my father, who wanted a position at court for me, I would be extremely happy living in Sokolov and managing the estate after my father's death. I thought that being here to learn the intricacies of running such a large duchy would be a smart thing.

"It was my father's dream, however, that his only son have a position at the Court. Serving there was the most favorable way to move up to archduke or even grand duke. That was the reason I had been tutored in the arts, why I had been meticulously trained in proper etiquette so that it was second nature to me, and why I had just been outfitted with the finest wardrobe that money could buy. I remember sighing deeply. If I could just be a country duke, I would be happy for the rest of my life. Just then a blast of cold air hit me square in the face. I decided that my tour of the estate would be very abbreviated. I would take Anna along the pasture, turn, and climb the hill that overlooked the valley. I loved the view from the top of the hill and could never understand why the town had not been built there.

"My father made the decision that the tour of the duchy would be made in the old landau. There was just too much mud. It had been years since we had had such a wet winter. It would take weeks for the sun to dry the roads and turn their surface back into hard pack. It just didn't make sense to cover the new Landau with mud. He also decided that the Arabians would be used. The horses needed the work. And it would give Johannes an opportunity to finally figure out which horse would be used as the lead. After watching them work, my father was leaning towards Castor while Johannes preferred Pollux. He decided that mom should stay at home during the tour of the estate; that Johannes should wear his fine new head coachman uniform; and that Josef, also smartly dressed, should come along as the attendant to provide protection. Highwaymen were rare, but not unheard of. Having a man with a loaded pistol made my father feel much safer. Taking the carriage was the symbol of the duke's authority. Every time taxes and profits from the farms and businesses in the duchy were collected, my father was always in his carriage, was impeccably dressed, and had his head coachman and attendant with him. The people would be thrilled to see him in his official role, but without collecting any money.

"My father's plan was to head north first to visit the Jewish towns and then turn east into the predominately German section of the duchy. The final leg of the journey would bring us into the Czech town and farms. My father had told me how ironic it was that he was a German duke who lived in a Polish town and ruled over a Czech duchy in the middle of Prussia. It was an unfortunate testament to the never ending wars which plagued the region and kept redrawing the map.

"As the tour progressed, my father told me that he had never been prouder of me. He was actually astonished to realize just how much of my mother's grace I had received. At each stop along the way, I said just the right thing at just the right time.

"When they entered the Jewish town of Ostrov, I stunned my father by knowing that Passover was approaching. I had asked the Rabbi (who also happened to be the butcher) if there was an appropriate lamb for the Seder. I made a friend for life when I told Rabbi Frieberg that I would scour the duchy to find one, if needed. The rabbi thanked me profusely, in a strange mixture of Yiddish and Polish, and told me that he had set aside a yearling lamb several months earlier which he was sure would suffice.

"The Arabians caused the only problem on the tour. They fought Johannes at every turn. They were so difficult to harness that my father gave Johannes permission to leave the horses harnessed to the carriage all the night the entourage spent in Chodov. It was I who suggested the solution.

"Either horse alone was strong enough to pull the carriage. Pulling the carriage alone, with the brake on, however, would tire the horse quickly. I suggested that each horse be harnessed to pull the wagon alone while the other was tied to the back. As soon as the horse that was pulling the wagon began to tire, he would be switched. Each horse was to be tired out at least four times. Then the horses would be harnessed together to pull the wagon with the brake off. The horses proved to be quite smart. They quickly learned that, if they worked together, they would not grow tired at all. Now Johannes had a team in which neither horse was the lead horse. He had never before had a successful team unless one of the horses took the lead. But Castor and Pollux were truly twins and they were equally in charge.

"The tour was so successful, and the ride home with the Arabians working as a team was so smooth, that my father was sure that the trip to Prague was going to be a great joy. As we were headed back to Sokolov at the end of the tour, my father told me of his own presentation at court. Except for meeting my mother, Maria, it had been a total disaster. He had made every social gaff possible. He had stepped on the grand duke's foot when he had eagerly stepped forward to make a good impression.

He had spilled red wine on the white tablecloth during the grand banquet. He had actually fallen down while he was dancing and had taken his partner with him. Thinking back on it all made him shudder with grief at what a fool he had made of himself. His terrible presentation had doomed him, he told me, to a life of rural servitude at Sokolov. He wanted more for me. I didn't tell him, then, that I would be completely happy living my life at Sokolov."

I didn't have any idea what living and working at a royal court would be like, but I thought that being the Duke of Sokolov would be a lot like being a southern plantation owner. I asked Mr. Oskar about it. He told me that I was absolutely right. Robert, Mr. Ben, and I all agreed that being the Duke of Sokolov sounded like a great life.

"I haven't gotten to the really exciting part of the story yet," Mr. Oskar said. "That didn't happen until we got to Prague. My mother was taking charge of the preparations for the trip. In addition to the new Landau, the old Landau was coming along to carry the enormous amount of luggage. She, my father, and I all had to have a month's worth of clothing. There had to be clothing for the two drivers, the two attendants, and the two footmen. We had to carry all of the equipment that was necessary in case we got stranded. The only time my mother ever camped was when she was on the road. She had never liked it much; but, unlike a lot of the aristocracy, she was willing to make do. She had seen to it that the cooks prepared food which would stay fresh for several days – things like loaves of bread, smoked ham and blocks of cheese.

"She had also made all of the arrangements for the party that she and my father were going to host in Prague. More than a year before the invitation to the Grand Ball came; she had reserved the whole east wing of the Wallenstein Palace. The Duke and Duchess of Mecklenburg, who lived in the palace, were both first cousins of my grandmother and were thrilled to be able to help out with "little Konrad's presentation."

"We are going to charge you only 100 marks for the whole east wing," they had written to my mom. Since the average worker made only about 50 marks per year, the cost seemed high even for my mom; but she was willing to pay any price for me to have a successful presentation. The pre-ball parties were difficult to plan. They could not be better or more elaborate than the actual ball, because the grand duke and duchess might be offended. The pre-ball parties could not be less elaborate either because, if they were, the guests might think that the hosts were cheap. My mom had worried and planned for well over a year and prayed that she had just the right balance.

"Having gotten the official guest list for the ball from the secretary of the grand duchess, My mom had invited every single person on the list as well as their parents. Since the party was being held in the Wallenstein Palace, everyone who had been invited would be present. She was convinced that our party would be the finest of all the pre-ball events.

"When I heard how much money was being spent on this party, I quietly asked my father how much money the duchy made each year. I had never before asked him about the business side of the Duchy of Sokolov. I wasn't sure that I would even get an answer, but my father didn't even hesitate.

"The income is around 20,000 marks annually, "he said. "We are entitled, according to the law, to take a much higher percentage from the farms and businesses than we do. But I have always felt that if I can keep the tenants happy, they will work harder and we will get a higher payout." he said. After a few moments of silence, he added, "Archduke Roeder disagrees, of course. There are always disagreements in politics."

"I had never really considered how truly valuable the title of duke was. I was astonished at the amount of income. I figured in my head, and then said, mostly to myself, "If the annual income is about 20,000 marks, the total value of the whole estate would be around two and a half million marks."

"Yes, that's about right," my father said. "Of course that has a lot to do with politics. If the Lords in favor fall out of favor, the value of their property plummets. Or, if somehow we get blacklisted, no one would buy our products and we would be land poor. Fortunately, ever since my great grandfather was given the title and lands of the duchy, we have been on the side of the aristocracy that is in favor."

"My father had never before spoken to me about the business side of the duchy. And he had certainly never talked with me about politics. But I immediately understood the significance of what he was saying.

"That's why the presentations are so important, isn't it? The better job I do, the more likely we are, as a family, to stay in favor?" I asked my father.

"Well, yes," my father said. "But I didn't want you to know. My father told me, and put so much pressure on me that I failed completely. I just wanted you to go and have fun."

"After a few moments of silent pondering, I said, 'Dad, everything will be all right'."

Robert interrupted Mr. Oskar and asked, "Do you mean that because of politics, you lost Sokolov?"

"Yes, Robert. And much worse. After we have a break for lunch, I'll tell you just how bad politics can be, and how much more we lost than Sokolov."

Mr. Ben pulled the wagon under the shade of a large oak tree. We had a lunch break that was way too long. I wanted to hear the rest of the story.

An Aristocratic Affair

L UNCH WAS FINALLY OVER! THOUGH OUR WAGON was actually headed to Chowan County, I was headed to Prague. We couldn't get there fast enough! I couldn't imagine what could be worse than losing Sokolov.

"Spring had finally arrived," Mr. Oskar began again. "The sunshine and warmth contributed to making Prague a spring time wonderland. Flowers were blooming everywhere when the Landau containing the von Scheibmacher family arrived in Prague. My father, Wolfgang, was thrilled with the weather because the expensive new Landau was not covered with mud. My mother, Maria, was thrilled with the weather because our party at the palace could be held with the windows and doors wide open. The incredibly huge palace would seem even larger. The guests would be even more impressed. I was thrilled with the weather because the warm sunshine brightened my spirits after such a long and wet winter and early spring.

"Leaving absolutely nothing to chance, my mother had gone through my entire new wardrobe and determined when it would be best to wear each outfit. She was sure that the lime green waistcoat and vest would be the best choice for the outdoor party on Monday; the navy blue outfit would be too dark for the night party hosted by the von Richter's. She had worked out a complete schedule of when I should wear each outfit and an alternative plan in case the weather turned wet again.

"Johannes had driven my family to Prague many times before, but he was always confused by the narrow streets that didn't seem to go anywhere. He was constantly annoying Mom by shouting down from the cab at passersby to ask for directions. Mom determined that she would get detailed directions from the concierge at the hotel to every party and function they would be attending over the next two weeks, write them out in detail, and give them to Johannes. She didn't want to be seen in a Landau with a lost driver. It would not give the right impression. What she had forgotten was that Johannes couldn't read!

"As we pulled up to the hotel, the footmen jumped from the back saddle of the Landau and went to work. One of them opened the door to the carriage, lowered the folding step and waited to offer his hand, first to my mom, then to my father, and finally to me. The other footman went ahead to make sure that the door to the hotel was open. They would come back for the luggage later. I remember taking a deep breath of Prague air. Unlike home, there was a stench in the air that went along with a big city. The combination of raw sewage in the gutters, horse manure in the streets, and smoke from thousands of chimneys was an odor that no one would ever get used to. I was glad for all of the flowers that decorated the entrance to the hotel. Their fragrance at least competed with the other smells. As we entered the hotel, we were warmly welcomed by the concierge. As he yelled for bellhops to help with the mountain of luggage, he handed my father a sealed envelope."

"This came this morning, Duke von Scheibmacher," he said as he handed it to him. "I'm told that it is very important."

"My father looked at the wax seal. It contained a family crest that he did not know. He decided to open the letter later and put it in the inside pocket of his traveling jacket.

"In even the finest hotels across Europe, it was customary for multiple clients to sleep in the same room. Often total strangers would end up sleeping in the same bed. The concierge knew that the von Scheibmachers were a very special family, because we had paid extra to have an entire room to ourselves. My mom wanted to have a place where she could lay out all my clothes and make sure that each outfit was perfect. She also wanted to do the same with her own clothes. My father wanted to have a place to be able to bring his friends for private conversation. When the concierge showed us to our suite, we were quite disappointed. It wasn't a suite at all, but just one room that was adequate, but not elegant. There were four double beds, one pushed into each corner. A desk and chair were on the outside wall between the windows. A small table was at the side of each bed. Each table and the desk had a candle stick, holding a fresh beeswax candle.

"My father took one look around and roared in anger to the concierge, 'You call this a proper suite! You are to get some people up here now and get rid of two of those beds. Replace them with a settee, and three wing back chairs.'

He moved to one of the beds and examined the linen. For a second time he roared, 'And I want clean linen. It's clear that this linen has not been changed in weeks! I paid enough money for this room to buy this hotel, and this is the kind of service I get? We will wait downstairs in the parlor until our room is acceptable. Do you understand?'

"The concierge was clearly stunned. He had thought that he was showing the von Scheibmachers a well appointed room. 'Yes Sir! I'll take care of everything!'

"The concierge was not the only one who was shocked. I remember standing there with my mouth slightly open, staring at my father. I had never before heard my father roar. In fact, I couldn't even remember hearing him raise his voice. He noticed my stare and, just as the concierge turned to speak to the servants, he winked at me. As we waited downstairs in the parlor, he explained to me that those who are loud themselves need to be yelled at; having noticed that the concierge had screamed at the bellhops, my father knew that yelling at him would be the most effective way to accomplish what was needed.

"While we waited, my father remembered the letter. He reached into his pocket and pulled it out. The seal looked like the seal of the archduke. But he had never received a personal letter from him. He went over to the window to get a little more light and broke the seal, opened the letter and read the following

Dear Wolfgang,

It is essential that we meet. Come to the narthex of the Church of our Lady of Tyn at noon tomorrow.

—Kurt Roeder

"Kurt Roeder, an archduke, was also the nephew of the grand duchess. My father could not understand such a cryptic note. Why a meeting at the church? It was certainly a public place. The Church of our Lady of Tyn dominated the city of Prague. It was on the main square of Old Town, and its steeples could be seen from nearly any place in the city. He looked again at the seal. He had broken it, or course, to open the letter; but now he was trying to piece it back together to assure himself that it was genuine. As far as he could tell, it was.

"He slipped the note back into his pocket. He would have to go. A note from the archduke could not be ignored. He could walk. It was only seven or eight blocks away from the hotel. He wondered what activity his wife had planned for him the next day at noon. He would make some excuse. As he pondered on how he would manage to escape his wife's grasp, the concierge appeared. He was appropriately contrite and announced that everything was just as the duke has so graciously suggested. Even though all our luggage was in a huge pile in the middle of the room, the situation was much improved.

"We had arrived one week prior to the Grand Ball. There were at least three parties per day for each of the next six days. Our party would be on Friday night before the day-long events surrounding the Grand Ball. It would probably be impossible for me to attend all of the parties, so my mom had prioritized each party by importance of the family who was hosting. I could miss some of the less significant parties, but I couldn't miss them all. If I did, someone would notice and my family could be accused of being prejudiced against the less successful families.

"My mom had also listed which of the parties she and my father would have to attend. She had also worked out a detailed schedule of where Johannes, Josef, and the footmen would be each day. Nothing was left to chance.

"My father asked my mom if he could examine the lists. He 'wanted to make sure that Konrad was going to the most politically advantageous parties' he told her, but he was actually looking at his own schedule. Fortunately, there was nothing listed for noon the next day. He handed the lists back to my mom and said, 'You are remarkable. Everything is perfect.' She simply smiled in reply.

"I was just glad to be in Prague. The months of preparation had heightened my sense of anticipation. Even though my father had feared that our conversation would only add to my tension, the opposite had actually happened. I was determined to put all of my years of education and training into effect. I was, as far as it depended on me, going to have the most successful presentation in the history of the Grand Duke's Ball. My anticipation was not nervousness. I had confidence that I would do well. I just wanted the festivities to begin.

"The first significant party that we would attend would be the one hosted by the Duke and Duchess of Salzburg, the von Richters. Their daughter Elyse was also to be presented at the ball. Women were presented two years earlier than men; Elyse had just turned eighteen. Since she had been eighteen for only a month, her parents had seriously considered making her wait a year, but she had convinced them she was ready.

My mom had assured me that the von Richters' party would be one of the most important that I would attend. Families did everything in their power to schedule parties either on the first day of the first week of the festivities or the day before the ball. If they were unable to acquire one of those dates, they would choose the last day of the second week. Every family had to submit their requests for dates to the grand duchess's social secretary, who would then determine which families received which dates. Bribes to the social secretary were, of course, completely illegal, but every family broke the law—the higher the bribe, the better the date. Clearly the von Richter and the von Scheibmacher families were the two most deserving.

"For the von Richters' party, Mom had picked a sky blue waistcoat, with royal blue vest and navy blue breeches for me to wear. The ruffled shirt was a fourth color of blue that blended perfectly. I remember agreeing with my mother that it was elegant. My mother and father were also dressed elaborately. To complete our preparations, we summoned a footman, specially trained in handling and placing wigs. He placed our wigs exactly straight with all of the natural hair tucked underneath, without getting powder on our clothes.

"I didn't care if my entire waistcoat was covered with powder. I was just eager to go."

I was eager for him to go, too after all this talk of parties and clothes. I wanted him to get to the good stuff. Twelve-year-olds don't have much patience. Later, when the story was finished, I was glad that he had shared every detail.

"Timing was crucial. The party would officially begin at 6:00 p.m. But no one of importance would arrive before 6:15 p.m. Anyone who arrived after 6:30 p.m. was being rude. Sometime earlier that afternoon, My mom had gone over the route with

Johannes. He had assured her that he would get the family to the party at exactly the right time.

"When the three of us got to the door of the hotel, the carriage was waiting for us with Castor and Pollux looking more beautiful than ever. The carriage was shining in the candlelight. Johannes had paid (with my father's money, of course) two of the hotel's livery staff to wash both the Landau and the horses. They had blackened the horse's hooves, shined the silver fittings on the harnesses, and polished every square inch of the Landau. Even though it was dark, the von Scheibmacher family was about to make a great impression!

"When we arrived at the party at exactly 6:22, Johannes maneuvered the Arabians perfectly, so that the Landau's door was exactly in the center of the walkway. Mom was the first to emerge. She went immediately to greet a woman whom I assumed was the duchess. When my father and I exited the Landau, he led me to a very distinguished man who stood to one side of the walkway.

"Duke von Richter, this is my son, Heinrich Konrad von Scheibmacher, the Earl of Sokolov," he said, as he bowed slightly and clicked the heels of his shoes.

"I am extremely glad to meet you, young man," Duke von Richter said as, instead of bowing, he extended his hand. Most people, including my father, would have been thrown by Duke von Richter's familiarity. But I was completely at ease as I both bowed slightly and extended my hand to the Duke of Salzburg.

"It is I who am most honored," I said to the duke as I looked him right in the eye and shook his hand. The duke told me later that night that he was impressed. He had been pulling the handshake ploy all night; I was the only young man to get it right. Just as our handshake ended, my mom appeared at my side with an exquisite young woman by the arm.

"Konrad. This is Elyse von Richter."

"I looked deeply into her eyes and was immediately in love. Like me, she was a petite person, with beautiful blond hair and dark green eyes. She was wearing a gorgeous ivory gown that gracefully flowed over her body. Most of the women at the party wore dresses that were way too tight, revealing too much cleavage. But Elyse was wearing a dress that had exactly the right fit to modestly display her perfectly proportioned body.

"I didn't remember later if I had spoken to her, if I had bowed, or if I had extended my hand. But I did remember that she smiled. I had never seen a more beautiful smile.

"Flanked by my parents, I was led into the grand house where the party was being held. I didn't care about the party, or the Grand Ball, or the presentation, or being a duke some day. Nothing mattered but Elyse von Richter.

"As soon as all the guests had arrived, the von Richter's, including Elyse, made their way into the grand hall. The orchestra was already playing, and couples were dancing. I had only one desire— to dance with Elyse von Richter, to hold her in my arms, to smell her perfume, and to look again deeply into her eyes. I had read somewhere that one could tell when he was in love if that love was reflected in his lover's eyes. I wanted to look deeply. I made my way across the room. It was as though I was Moses and the water was parting. People moved aside. And there she was.

"Later, I couldn't remember if I had actually asked her to dance, but I could remember holding her in my arms and looking into her eyes. And she looked, too. I wondered if she had read the same book that he had.

"I was a perfect gentleman all night, dancing with all the young women at the party and with many of their mothers as well. I had conversations with the other young men who were also being presented that year and with their fathers; but, all night, at every opportunity, I kept coming back to Elyse.

"On the way back to the hotel, as I sat beside my mother in the Landau, and whispered to her, "I think I met my wife tonight."

"She whispered back, 'I think so, too. It was written all over both your faces.'

"As I slept that night, I dreamed of being on a boat with ivory colored silk sails. When I woke the next morning, nothing mattered but Elyse. The only reason for going to any of the other parties was seeing Elyse. The only reason to go to the Grand Ball was to see the presentation of Elyse von Richter. There was to be a party at noon that day at the Bridge Tower. It seemed a strange place to have a party, but I didn't care. I might have a chance to talk with Elyse."

As Mr. Oskar talked about Elyse, there was a glow on his face I had never seen before. I realized that it was the same glow that was on my father's face when he called my mother 'Lizzie Dove.' I may have been only twelve, but I wasn't stupid. I realized that true love changes a person. When I saw that look on Mr. Oskar's face, I didn't mind hearing a love story at all.

"The Bridge Tower was at the entrance to Old Town, just a short walk from the hotel. I asked my father if he would like to come along, and he said he would be glad to walk with me to the Bridge Tower on his way to an appointment.

"My father got to the Church of our Lady of Tyn just as the city's clock tower began to chime twelve. When he entered the massive church and looked around in the narthex, he didn't see the archduke or anyone else who would be considered a gentleman. He stepped through the inner doors into the massive nave in case he had read the note wrong. It was then that he saw the two men dressed in the official green uniforms of the Royal Guard. He knew at that moment his life was over. It was only a matter of time. The letter had been a trap. Knowing they would not arrest him in the church, he made his way towards the altar. The crucified Christ looked down on him from the cross with pity in his eyes.

"At that very moment, I heard Elyse confirm what I already knew. Neither of us had believed in love at first sight until it happened. Now we had less than two weeks to get to know each other. I stepped back to look at her. I simply adored her beauty.

I couldn't understand how anyone as lovely as she could fall in love with anyone as ordinary as me. Was this what love was all about? We spent the rest of the party talking to each other. We each craved to know everything there was to know about the other. When Elyse's carriage came and it was time for her to leave, Duke von Richter smiled warmly from inside the carriage. He was glad that, if his daughter had to fall in love with anyone, at least it was the son of one of his best friends.

"As I made my way back to the hotel, my mom was worrying over the details for the Friday night party. My father was sitting in the Church of Our Lady of Tyn trying to decide if he should tell his wife and son that he would soon be dead. He knew that he would be accused of being a part of a conspiracy against the Archduke. Papers would be produced to prove that the conspirators were meeting at the Church of Our Lady of Tyn to finalize their plot. He decided not to alarm us. He would speak to Hans von Richter first. My father needed Hans to care for his family after he was dead.

"That night at a dinner party at one of Prague's many palaces, I was thrilled that Elyse and I were seated across from one another. My father and Elyse's father were sitting beside each other on one side of the table. Across from him the two mothers were sitting together. Elyse and I were in heaven. We could speak to one another openly and enjoy each other's company because we just happened to be sitting across the table from each other. I happened to notice, during a quiet conversation between Duke von Richter and my father that Duke von Richter shook his head as if to be saying "I'm so sorry," and put his arm around my father's shoulder. But I was so caught up in enjoying Elyse that I let it pass.

"My mom and Elyse's mother spent most of the evening going over the plans for the von Scheibmacher's party. Since her own party was now over, Ann von Richter could relax. She kept assuring my mom 'that her plans were exceptional, and that nothing could go wrong. Besides,' she said, 'Konrad and Elyse are the two best candidates to be presented this season. There was no way that they would not catch the eye of the grand duke and grand duchess. And wasn't it cute how they had caught each other's eye?'

"At the end of the party, during a lot of general confusion, my father slipped Hans an envelope."

"Read what's in it when you get a chance. And thanks for looking after my family," he said.

"Hans von Richter slipped the envelope into his pocket with a nod of his head. When he opened the envelope later, he discovered that it was a letter authorizing him to withdraw funds from bank accounts in Wolfgang von Scheibmacher's name and a list of all the banks where money was held. Beside the name of each bank was listed the name of the right man to see. My father was making it possible for Hans to recover some of the von Scheibmacher's assets before they were seized. He could pass them on, quietly, at a later date.

"The night of our family's party was beautiful. A full moon lit the Wallenstein Palace. A gentle, warm breeze blew through the open doors and windows. The entire banquet hall was decorated to perfection, as all of the guests took their places at the tables for the formal banquet. Fifty waiters were standing by ready to serve the four hundred guests. The cue for the waiters would be Duke von Scheibmacher's "Amen" to his prayer after his official welcome.

"It was during the welcoming speeches that a full troop of men dressed in the royal green of the grand duke's guard walked through the open doors. Wolfgang wondered for a moment if an entire guard was there to arrest more than one man. Had other men also been caught in the trap?

"He stopped his welcoming speech and spoke directly to the captain of the guard."

"May I help you, Sir?' he asked.

"You are Duke Wolfgang von Scheibmacher, are you not?" he asked.

"I am."

"My men and I are here to arrest you. You are being charged with high treason and conspiracy to commit murder against Archduke Roeder."

"No!" I yelled, as I stood in anger.

"My father said, quietly and calmly, 'Sit down, Son.' He was so distraught that the archduke had decided to have him arrested at this party. The archduke knew, of course, that it would have the most horrific effect.

"The troop came forward. Duke Wolfgang von Scheibmacher stooped to kiss his stunned wife on the cheek. He knew that it would be the last time that he would ever see her. Though he was guilty of nothing, he would be executed. He would first be taken, along with other poor souls caught in the archduke's trap, to Prague's Central Prison. A sham trial would be held, but his conviction was assured."

"That can't be!" Robert shouted. "It's so unfair!"

Mr. Oskar took a deep breath, shook his head at Robert, and said, "There is worse to come."

I couldn't imagine what could be worse. Mr. Ben, who had been listening as he drove along, stopped the wagon. He wanted to do more than hear the story. He wanted to see Mr. Oskar's face as he told it. Mr. Oskar took another deep breath and then continued.

"As the guards led him away, the guests sat in numbed silence. Then, as though a balloon had burst, the entire assembly burst into shouting. The party, of course, was over. I wanted to hold Elyse, but I also wanted to comfort my mother. She had slumped to the floor, dissolved into a pool of tears, weeping uncontrollably. She had been around the politics of the aristocracy long enough to know my father's fate. Johannes had somehow appeared. I ordered him to bring the Landau up immediately. I gently took my mother by the arms and picked her up from the floor. I found

Duke von Richter by my side, reaching out to help my mom. She was crying so hard that she could hardly stand. She was nearly blinded by her tears. Duke von Richter and I walked my mom down the length of the banquet hall and out the door. Just as they were approaching the driveway, Johannes was approaching with the Landau.

Josef jumped from the front of the Landau, running to help. As Josef approached her, she reached out to him, as if she needed his support to stand. Josef raised his arms to steady her and exposed the gun that he carried in his belt. She quickly grabbed the gun. Before anyone could stop her, she cocked it, turned it to her heart, and fired!

"The shot threw her backwards into my arms. The wound was not immediately fatal, but it was certainly mortal. I slumped to the ground with my mother in my arms.

"Mom! Why?" I cried out to her with my tears dripping onto her face. Duke von Richter, kneeling beside us, took the gun from her hand and slid it across the driveway.

"O, forgive me, Son. I could not bear to live without your father," she said, as she feebly reached to wipe the tears from my eyes. "O Konrad, they will come after you, too. Run. Run away from them." I didn't know what she was talking about. *Who are they?* I thought.

"Her breathing was becoming difficult. She took a very deep breath and steeled herself to say one more thing to me before she died. 'Konrad, live a life worthy of your father.'

"I was thinking of how wonderful it would be to live a life worthy of my mother, when she took her last breath. Her head rolled slightly to one side. Her body went limp in my arms. I leaned forward, holding my mother even closer, and broke down into uncontrollable sobs."

As Mr. Oskar told the story, he was crying again. It was as though she had died just a moment before. Mr. Oskar wasn't the only one crying.

"I don't remember much of what happened next. Maybe it had something to do with God's Holy Spirit becoming the comforter. Mostly, I was numb. What I do remember is that it was Duke von Richter who took charge.

"The Duke turned to Josef, who was bending down to pick up the gun, and said, 'Get a couple of table cloths from inside and wrap her body securely.'

"Yes sir," Josef said as he ran into the building, tucking the gun back into his belt.

"Turning to Johannes, the duke said, 'Listen carefully. I'm going to give you a lot to accomplish. Put Maria's body into the Landau as soon as it is wrapped and then head back to the hotel. When you get there, send Josef to my house with the new Landau and the Arabians. We will hide them there in my stables.'

"Why do we need to hide them?" Johannes asked.

"Leaning closer to Johannes so that he could speak softly, he said, 'As soon as the archduke's allies find out that the mother is dead, they will go after the son. He must be hidden as soon as possible. A brand new Landau pulled by white Arabian horses will be far too easy to follow. Do you understand?'

"Yes sir," Johannes said sadly, fearing that he would never see the Arabians again.

"After you get to the hotel," the duke continued, "go to the von Scheibmacher's room and pack only Konrad's things. Leave everything else precisely where it is. Put Konrad's luggage in the old landau and then come, with your footmen, to my house. It is essential that you tell no one at the hotel what has happened here tonight, what you are doing, or where you are going."

"Sir," Johannes said. "Josef and I don't know where you live and we don't know the streets of Prague."

"Well that is a problem. You'll just have to remember the directions that I give you and share them with Josef. Can you do that?"

"Yes sir," Johannes said with assurance.

"Duke von Richter told Johannes exactly how to get from the hotel to his home on River Drive in Old Town and made him repeat the directions, word for word. When he was sure that Johannes had it right, he said, 'When you get to my house, we will put Maria's body in the old Landau. I'll have Konrad there, waiting for you. It will be essential that you all leave Prague tonight, under the cover of darkness.'

I won't let you down," Johannes said.

"You're not doing this for me. This is for Konrad," the duke said.

"Elyse had stepped forward to comfort me. She had taken one of her silk handkerchiefs and wiped some of Mom's blood from my face. Then she had put the handkerchief in my waistcoat pocket. There really wasn't anything to say. And so we sat there in silence, holding each other. I had let go of my mother's body so that Josef and a couple of the waiters could wrap it. I was surprised at how beautiful and peaceful she looked. I hoped that she was at peace.

"Elyse and I watched as the men lovingly and tenderly wrapped the body of Maria von Scheibmacher. Duke von Richter leaned forward, quietly telling the men to wrap her tightly, with as many layers as they could, because it would be several days before she could be buried.

"The duke called for his own carriage. It was only then that he noticed his own wife, Ann. She was standing in shock behind one of the massive doors that had been opened to the banquet hall. He realized that she had just lost one of her best friends. He had had a couple of days to adjust to the fact that my father was going to be arrested. He went up to her, and as gently as he could, hugged her. It was only then that they both broke into tears.

"When their driver returned with their carriage, Duke von Richter helped Elyse and me into the front seat and Ann into the back. He left the carriage just long enough to assure himself that Johannes remembered all of the instructions. Johannes assured him that he did and that everything would be done exactly as he had ordered. The duke returned to his carriage, got in beside his wife, and signaled his driver.

"The four of us rode in silence until a bump in the road seemed to jolt me. "Where are we going?" I asked.

"To our home here in Prague," Duke von Richter said. "We are going to smuggle you out of town tonight."

"Am I in danger?" Konrad asked.

"Didn't you hear what your mother said? She said they will come after you, too, so you must run. Your mother was very smart."

"But who are they? Why should I run?"

"Your father's political enemies. Day before yesterday, your father confided in me that he was sure that he had been pulled into a political scheme which would almost certainly cost him his life. He asked that I do all that I could to care for you and your mother. Who could ever have imagined the turn of events tonight? With your mother gone, and your father soon to be, there is absolutely nothing to stop them from killing you."

"But who are they?" I asked again.

"They have to be associated with the archduke. That's all that I know. Konrad, I have to tell you some very important things and give you some crucial instructions. Do you want to hear them now, as we ride, or would you prefer that we wait until we get to the house?"

"Now is fine," I heard myself saying. What I really wanted to do was hold Elyse.

"In a couple of hours, your servants are going to come to my house in the old landau. Your luggage and your servants will be all that is in the carriage. They will get you and your mother out of town tonight and get you as quickly as possible to Sokolov. When you get to Sokolov, if you see even one man in a green uniform, keep riding. That will mean that the Royal Guard will have beaten you there. I really don't think that will happen, but just in case.

"When you get to town, if it is safe, give your mother a Christian burial. I will take care of marking her grave later. Now, I need you to tell me the name of one person whom you absolutely trust in Sokolov. It can't be Johannes or Josef. They are going to be questioned intensely. I am afraid they might even be tortured." Duke von Richter paused to give me a moment to think.

"My English tutor, Mr. Cooper. I trust him completely. And he could even pretend not to understand the language if they question him," I said.

"After your mother's burial, put only what you can carry in a pair of saddle bags on your favorite horse. Go to a secret location that only Mr. Cooper knows. Tell him that he is to tell no one, except me, where you are. This is crucial for keeping you safe. Do you understand?" the duke asked.

"Yes, I do."

"Yesterday, your father gave me a letter that authorizes me to withdraw all of the funds that he has in various banks of Prague. He also gave me a list of the right people to see in each bank so that no questions will be asked. I won't be able to withdraw any funds until next week. As soon as I can withdraw all the funds, I will make my way to Sokolov. I don't know how long you will need to stay in your secret location, so pick wisely.

"When I come to you, I will bring you all the money that I can raise to purchase Sokolov. It will be only between thirty and forty thousand marks. That is not even twenty percent of the value of the duchy, but it will be every mark that I can raise. It will be better for you to get thirty thousand marks and go into hiding than to get nothing and be put to death."

"Are you saying that I have to go into permanent hiding?" I interrupted. "Won't this political thing change?"

"Yes. You have to go into permanent hiding. You have to go to a country where aristocracy has no influence. You have to change your name. You have to give up all contact with everyone in Germany. I really think that you should consider going to the

English colonies in America. Two of them, Pennsylvania and Maryland have large German populations. You would fit right in."

"I didn't realize that Elyse had been listening until she blurted out, 'Give up all contact! Move to America! Change his name! Daddy, how am I going to know where he is?'

"You aren't going to know. If Konrad loves you, and I think he does, he will never contact you again. If he does, he will put your life in danger."

"There was a long silence except for the clip clop of the horses' hooves on the cobblestone streets and the squeaking of the undercarriage. I broke the silence. "How will you explain purchasing Sokolov?"

"I can handle the politicians pretty easily. I'll just pretend that I did what any other smart politician and businessman would have done. I'll just say that I happened to be at the party where Duke von Scheibmacher was arrested and his wife died and I moved as quickly as I could to gobble up the Duchy of Sokolov before it fell into the wrong hands. Whatever side of the political fence I am talking to will think that I am talking about the other side."

"It was then that the carriage rolled into the driveway of the villa on River Drive. The duke said to Elyse and me, 'Why don't you two wait in the parlor until Konrad's Landau comes?'

The two of us needed time together. We were both hurting. Less than an hour before, we had been relishing new love. And now our lives had been torn apart by old politics. We each tried to start a conversation, but there really wasn't anything that either could say to the other. We found it best just to sit in the dimly lit room and hold each other."

I remembered sitting on the log by the side of the road with Robert as my father was led away by the slave catcher. There were no words that day either. Only tears.

"Johannes arrived with the old Landau way too soon. I was, once again, overcome with grief when I climbed in the carriage and saw the wrapped remains of my mother lying on the back seat. It was going to be an incredibly long, and sad, ride back home.

"Ten days later, when the duke presented himself at the palace at Sokolov and asked to speak to Mr. Cooper, he was led to the library by the downstairs maid. Duke von Richter closed the door, introduced himself to Mr. Cooper and asked if he could tell him where I was."

"Of course, I can. But first, you must prove to me that you are who you say you are." Donald Cooper said.

"This was a wrinkle that the Duke of Salzburg had not anticipated. 'How am I supposed to do that?' he asked.

"Donald Cooper said, 'Answer one question for me. What was the last thing that Maria von Schiebmacher said to her son?'

"I don't remember exactly. But it was something like, "Live a life worthy of your father," Duke von Richter said.

"Nice to meet you, Duke." Mr. Cooper said, extending his hand. Duke von Richter gladly grasped it.

"I can't tell you how to get to where Konrad is, but I can take you there," he continued.

"How long will it take to get there?" the duke asked.

"It's at least a full day's ride," Donald answered. "He's staying with a rabbi in some town north of here called Ostrov."

"My horse is spent from the three-day journey to get here. I'll talk with Johannes about loaning me another one and we can start out in the morning. Is that all right with you?" he asked.

"When they arrived in Ostrov, it was not difficult to find the home of the rabbi. He greeted the two new guests with gusto. I had not told him why I was staying there. I had only told him that there would be additional guests later on. I happened to walk in on the three of them when I made my way through the door of the butcher shop and into the rabbi's home. Throughout my time in Ostrov, I had been making myself useful by learning the butcher's trade. Who knew what I would be doing to make a living in the years to come? I had just finished stuffing some sausage casings, and had come to tell Rabbi Freiburg that I was ready for another job.

"Instead, I asked the good rabbi if the gentlemen and I might have a private conversation in his parlor. Rabbi Freiburg agreed, without question, and went into the butcher shop's side of his house.

"Konrad, I'm sorry, but I have some more bad news for you. You father was hanged four days after his arrest," Duke von Richter said.

"I had known, all along, that my father had died. But there had been a small kernel of hope until that moment that he had, somehow, gotten free. I had cried so deeply since the night of my father's arrest and my mother's death that I didn't think there could be any more tears. But I was wrong. Duke von Richter and Donald Cooper held me until my tears were gone."

Mr. Oskar had told me that his story was just for me and that Robert and Mr. Ben could listen in. Now, he looked right at me and said, "I know how hard it is to lose a father. Would it be all right with you for me to be your father for the next several years? At least until you're grown?"

I didn't know what to say. He put his arm around me. Mr. Ben told Robert to get up on the driver's seat with him. The wagon moved along as Mr. Oskar and I held each other in silence. Robert, Mr. Ben, and I were bound to him by the promise that we had made never to reveal his secret. But I was bound to him in an even deeper way. Oskar Schoenfeldt could never actually replace Thomas Barnes, but, in the years to come, he loved me as passionately as if I had been his son.

After we had stopped for the night and were sitting around a camp fire that Mr. Ben had lit, Mr. Oskar said, "I have to finish my story."

"There's more?"

"Oh, yes," he said. "I can't leave us at the rabbi's house. If I had stayed there, I would have been a butcher all my life, and never come to America.

"After Duke von Richter told me about my father, he said, "Konrad, I have a banker's draft for 62,000 marks. This is all of the money that your father had deposited in banks throughout Prague, plus about 40,000 marks that I was able to raise for the purchase of the estate. This draft will be honored by any bank in Europe. But you need to be careful, because the exchange rate might wipe out half the value."

"My father can help you there," said Donald. "He's the president of British Union National Bank in London. I will write you a letter to give to him. He will take the draft and give you one made out in pounds. He will wait until you get the best possible exchange."

"I kept out five hundred marks for you to use as traveling money. It should be more than adequate to get you where you want to go. So you are headed to London?" asked Duke von Richter.

"Just stopping there, I think. I'm thinking of taking your advice and going on to America," I said.

"And by the way," I said, turning to Donald. "You better give your father my new name. It's Oskar. Oskar Schoenfeldt. And I think instead of writing him a letter, you should go with me and introduce me to your father. After all, you are no longer going to have a job in Sokolov.

"Donald Cooper and I traveled across Europe disguised as a gentleman on tour and his servant. I certainly had the clothes for it, and Donald could handle the role of servant quite well.

"Two young men traveling across Europe, and spending liberally, would raise no eyebrows. We would be hiding by being in plain sight. It was not at all uncommon for young men of wealth to tour the capitals of Europe. It was considered to be part of a proper education, especially by those who fit in the new category of the aristocracy of wealth. The true aristocracy did not like this new breed, but there was nothing that they could do about it.

"Donald and I first went back to Sokolov to gather the necessary luggage. We decided that I would ride Anna and Donald would drive a small buggy that was pulled by one horse. This small cart would be adequate to carry our luggage and supplies.

"We decided that the ruse of being on tour would work best if we actually visited a couple of the capitals of Europe on our way to London. We went first to Nuremburg, the capital of Bavaria, then to Stuttgart in Baden where we saw men in green uniforms. We were quite frightened, until we realized that they were Hessians, not the Royal Guard.

"Only when we left Germany and headed to Paris did I begin to breathe a little easier. Paris was astonishing. Being an impeccably dressed gentleman, in the latest French fashion, who spoke fluent French, even with a German accent, I was welcome at Versailles. I was amazed by its gardens and, especially, its fountains. While I was sitting by one of the fountains, I struck up a conversation with another gentleman, and, before I knew it, I had accepted the invitation to spend a few days in the country.

"I would never have believed that I had been invited to the Chateau de Fontainbleau, the Hunting Lodge of the Kings of France, or that the other gentleman that I had been speaking to was the Crown Prince, Louis, heir to the throne of France!

I had to invent wildly throughout the whole weekend that I was at the Chateau to fill in all that I had lost. I had to create a past, a family, a home, a heritage, and hopes and dreams and visions for a future.

"It was after the weekend at the Chateau that I began to come to grips with the magnitude of the destruction of my life. I had lost everything that was dear to me. As Donald and I made our way from Paris to Luxemburg, Brussels to Antwerp, where we were to catch a boat to cross the English Channel, I was depressed, discouraged, and nearly defeated. I deeply grieved my parents. And I grieved the loss of love. All that I had to remind me of Elyse was this blood-stained silk handkerchief."

Mr. Oskar reached into his pocket and pulled out a tattered handkerchief. He opened it, holding it caressingly, almost like he was holding a baby bird. I reached out to touch it, but he pulled his hands back. The handkerchief was too precious for anyone else to touch. But he did let us look at it. We could see the unmistakable blood stains.

"I have carried this with me every day since my mother died. I can't decide if I treasure it more for her memory or Elyse's."

I wished that my father had left me something that I could carry in my pocket to remind me of him. I decided when we got back to Beautiful Valley that I was going to go into the blacksmith shop and take one of my father's hammers. It would be too heavy to carry every day, but I could keep it on the table beside my bed.

"I was sinking deeper and deeper into despair," Mr. Oskar continued. "There was nothing that Donald could say that made any difference. Strangely enough, what happened at Antwerp snapped me out of my gloom. A couple of hours before we were to board the boat for England, Donald said, 'Well, I guess it's time to get rid of the buggy and the horses. I know a man who will buy them from us. Do you want me to take care of it?'

"Sell Anna? I had watched her birth. I had been there the first time that Johannes had put a blanket on her back and watched her throw it off. I had been the first person she had allowed to ride her. I had ridden her as I made my escape from tyranny. I sadly watched as Donald led her away. Although I realized that everything I loved was gone, at that moment I determined to start over. I would build a new Sokolov and a new future. I would take my new name, and, as my mother had requested, I would 'live a life worthy of my father.'

"Everything was gone except a bloodstained handkerchief and hope."

Mr. Oskar went to one of the chests and took out a long sheet of rolled-up paper. He brought it near the light of the fire and unrolled it.

"Do you know what a plat is?" he asked. I shook my head, indicating that I didn't. "It's like a map, but of just one piece of property. This was a map of what I hoped Shoen Oder, my Beautiful Valley, would become. I looked at the map closely and could see some things that looked familiar. There were the three circles of bunkhouses and the two huge barns, one for cows and one for horses. There were many buildings which I couldn't place. I asked Mr. Oskar about them.

"That's the manor house," he said, as I pointed to what would be a large structure. "It's like a large palace. Here in the South, most people would call it the plantation house. I never have built it, because I've never married." he said.

Twelve-year-olds can be very stupid, and, forgetting the story that I was hearing, I asked the question, "Why haven't you gotten married, Mr. Oskar?"

He smiled and said, "There was only one Elyse." After a long pause, he said, "Let's get back to the plat."

He showed me a huge structure that was intended to be a church. He said that he had never built the church because the Moravian officials thought that it would be too great a show of opulence.

"Opulence?" I asked.

"It means an unnecessary show of wealth," he said.

I looked at the plat and saw a lot of structures that had not been built and I asked why.

"Beautiful Valley is a work in progress," he said. "It has taken me a lot longer than I could ever have imagined. When I first came to North Carolina I had fifteen thousand acres of woods. There was no cleared land at all. I had no horses, no cows, no oxen, and no farm animals of any kind. I didn't have any equipment, either. All I had was some money and a dream."

"How did you get to North Carolina?" I asked

"The ship that brought me from England landed in Wilmington, Delaware. That was good for me, because my true destination was Philadelphia, just a short carriage ride from Wilmington. I had a friend in England who had given me letters of introduction to bankers and other important businessmen in Philadelphia.

"One of those important persons was a land agent. When I happened to mention to him that I was a Moravian, he asked me if I had heard of the Wachovia tract. He told me that it was nearly a hundred thousand acres in North Carolina that the Moravians had purchased and on which they were going to build a New Eden. I told him that I had heard of it, but that I didn't know much about it. I contracted with him to be my agent and to seek to purchase some of the Moravian land.

While he was in North Carolina trying to make a deal, I spent some time with a large plantation owner in Tidewater, Virginia. It was there that I was led to believe that the only way to have a large estate in America was to own many slaves. This particular planter treated his slaves much the same way that my father had treated the residents of the estate where we lived, with respect and dignity. Because of that, I obviously had an idealized view of slavery.

"When my land agent informed me that he had been successful in purchasing a large tract of land that actually joined the Moravians, I was delighted. I came to North Carolina, expecting to be a successful tobacco planter and found acre after acre after acre of woods, with no cleared land. It would take me several years to clear enough to be able to plant a crop."

We were camped in a wooded section along the road. Even in the dark, I could see that here were full grown trees. I could also see hundreds of saplings and vines, briars and shrubs of all kinds. It made me think of how hard it would be to clear even one acre, much less thousands.

"The nearest plantations were over near Guilford Court House," Mr. Oskar continued, "so I met with one of the planters near there and entered into an agreement to rent his slaves during the winter months to clear my land. I thought I was actually paying the slaves for the work that they were doing. At the end of the third winter when I was paying the planter, I asked him how he was distributing the funds to the workers."

"You don't ever give a nigger any money," he said, laughing at me. "Niggers are slaves. If you were to give them money, they wouldn't be slaves any longer."

"I was only twenty-four years old at the time. I guess I had an idealized vision of how the world worked. I had this strange notion that one could own other human beings and not really own them. Up until that time, I had never met any slave owners who were actually cruel to their slaves.

"In Europe, there were dukes who were kind, and there were others who were cruel. I just figured that it was the same way with American slavery. But I was wrong. It was just a couple of weeks later that that I heard a sermon at Betharbara Moravian. Pastor Gluck asked, "How can you say that you love God, and own another human being?" I'll never forget that sermon. I've always been a religious man because I was raised that way; however, until that moment, I had never felt that God was speaking to me. I'll never forget how small I felt. I had been planning to be one of the biggest slave owners in North Carolina. I had built the slave quarters. I had hired the overseer. I had withdrawn the money from the bank to go to the slave auction and buy human beings. I felt so sinful. I was sure that I was the worst person who had ever lived.

"Pastor Gluck had not given an altar call, like they do where you go, in the Methodist Church," he said, "but I went to the altar any way. I publically confessed my sin and swore that I would never own a slave."

"Is that why you wouldn't buy me when the slave catcher came?" I asked.

"Yes John. I regret that Mr. Tyler felt the need to buy you. But, I suppose that it was the best way to keep you safe. I have learned, through the years that slavery is a vile, horrible institution. It is true that some of the plantation owners treat their slaves with kindness, but they are still slaves."

The next day, as we rode along, I noticed a big change in the geography. The hills of Surry County were covered mostly in hardwoods and the soil was orange clay. Now that we were in the coastal plain, most of the hardwoods had been replaced with pines. They weren't scrub pines, like back home, but trees that towered sixty or seventy feet or more. The soil was dark black and the land was completely flat. Even though there were large sections of woods, when we came upon cleared land, the fields seemed to go on forever. I had never seen such large fields.

About two and a half weeks into our journey east, we stopped at a small country store to buy supplies. As a nice lady was waiting on us, Mr. Oskar said. "I've had then boys cooped up on the back of that wagon for almost three weeks. Is there a place nearby where they can have an afternoon running, exploring, and just, you know, being boys?"

"Oh, yes sir," the lady said. "There's a place, not far from here called Medoc Mountain. The boys will love it." She gave Mr. Oskar and Ben directions to the place. As we left the store, I looked around, and as far as I could see, in every direction, there was only flat land. How could there be a mountain only a few miles away? As we followed the directions, we didn't see a single hill. She had told us that there would be a sharp curve in the road. When we reached it, we were to stop the wagon and take the path about twenty yards into the woods. She promised us quite an adventure.

She was right! When we got to the end of the path, we saw the most amazing sight! The flat land simply fell away from us. A hundred feet or more beneath us, down a steep hill, was a beautiful creek, dancing over rocks and cascading into a waterfall. "I'll race you to the waterfall!" Robert yelled, and off we went. Down the steep hill we raced. The race to the waterfall was a tie, although each of us claimed to have gotten there first. We spent the next couple of hours splashing in the creek, climbing up and down the rocks over which the waterfall flowed, and just being boys.

It was as we began the steep ascent back to the wagon that we saw all the gold. It was just lying on top of the ground. Nearly every small rock that we picked up had gold on it! Robert and I began to stuff our pockets. We were rich! Mr. Oskar and Mr. Ben were going to be so surprised when we came back from our swim with pockets full of gold.

We both saw the large rock, covered in nuggets, at the same time. We reached, in unison, for it. A wrestling match to rival Jacob's and the angel ensued! Robert may have been a couple of months ahead of me in puberty, but I was just tough enough to win the match and claim the prize! When we reached the top of the hill, we found Mr. Ben and Mr. Oskar stretched out on the back of the wagon, enjoying an afternoon's nap. Robert and I woke them, announced our new found wealth, and began to empty our pockets.

Mr. Ben took one look at our riches and burst out laughing! "Boys," he said, "That's not gold. It's pyrite."

"But it sure looks like gold!"

"Of course it does. That's why they call pyrite 'fool's gold.' It fools people," he said.

Robert and I began to empty our pockets. We threw all our newfound wealth into the woods. I decided to keep the large, nugget-covered stone. After all, I had had to work very hard to win it.

A couple of days later, Mr. Ben pulled the wagon to a stop and I heard him say, "Mr. Oskar, I think we may be there. That's what the man at the inn in Edenton told me Mr. Perkin's plantation house would look like."

Mr. Oskar, Robert, and I got out and looked down a long drive to an impressive, three-story, white house. Large live oaks lined the driveway. There were numerous outbuildings. Behind the house was a huge expanse of water that had to be the Albemarle Sound. I knew because of my father's descriptions. The Sound and the wonderful seafood which came from it were the only things that my father had missed about Massa Perkins' plantation. I wondered if there was any way we might get some shrimp to eat before we headed home. From what my father had said, it was the finest food under heaven.

"I think you are right, Ben, "Mr. Oskar said. "Let's ride up there and see."

Mr. Oskar sat on the driver's seat as Ben turned the wagon into the driveway. Just before we reached the house, the driveway split into a circle drive with a finely manicured lawn in front of the house. As Ben maneuvered the wagon in front of the house, a distinguished looking black man came out of the front door. He was wearing clothes that were every bit as nice as Mr. Oskar's. For a brief moment, I thought that he must be Mr. Perkins, but then I had never heard of black men owning slaves.

"I'm Oskar Schoenfeldt. I'd like to see Mr. Perkins. I wrote to let him know that I would be coming," Mr. Oskar said.

"Yes sir, massa. I'll speak to Massa Perkins for you." The house slave was a bit confused. He had never had a gentleman arrive on a flat bed wagon. He wasn't exactly sure what to do. Normally, a gentleman would be ushered into the parlor to wait. And gentlemen always came with black servants, not white. He decided that the best thing to do was to ask this strange little man with the strange accent to wait by the wagon.

Elijah Perkins came running down the steps and towards the wagon. "Mr. Chernfell," he said, badly mispronouncing the name,

"I am so embarrassed that my man has left you waiting outside like a common servant. Please, please come into the house."

"There is no need to be embarrassed, Mr. Perkins," Mr. Oskar said. "And there really is no need for me to go into your lovely home, either. If you will just show me to the graveyard where Mr. Barnes, or, I guess you knew him as Thomas, is buried. We will retrieve his body and be of no further trouble to you."

"Honestly, I don't know where he was buried. My slaves buried him in the graveyard that is set aside just for slaves." Turning to his house slave he said, "Daniel, do you remember where Thomas was buried?"

"Yes suh, massa, "Daniel said. "Andrew and I took care of burying him and we said a prayer over him. We had to mound up the dirt pretty high because of the shape that the body was in," he said.

I'm sure that Daniel would not have added that last bit of information if he had known I was Thomas' son.

"Could you lead us to the spot?" Mr. Oskar said, addressing Daniel. "We have come to retrieve the body," he added, pointing to the coffin in the back of the wagon.

"I'll not have you do that kind of work, Mr. Skonefell," Mr. Perkins said. "I will see that my men take care of everything."

"That is very kind of you," Mr. Oskar said to Mr. Perkins. Then, turning to Daniel, he said, "There is a very heavy leather bag inside the coffin. Please be as reverent with the body as you can. Ben, please go and assist Daniel and his men." Then, turning to us he said," John, Robert, please stay here with me."

Addressing Mr. Perkins, Mr. Schoenfeldt said, "Sir, it is such a beautiful day. Would it be all right with you if my sons and I enjoyed your beautiful porch while we wait?"

I am sure I was more stunned than Mr. Perkins, but Mr. Oskar's arm across my shoulders clearly told me to keep my tongue. "Of course, sir. I will get the maid to bring you three glasses of tea," Mr. Perkins said.

A Trip to Hanging Rock

TWENTY-TWO YEARS LATER, I WAS JUST ABOUT to turn the key in the lock and close up shop for the day when Willie came running up to me.

"Massa John, I'm so glad I caught you," he said, panting.

"I told you not to call me massa."

"I know, but you are so much older than me," Willie said.

"I'm a colored man and, if people around here hear you calling me massa, we are both going to get in a whole lot of trouble. Just call me John. What in the world are you doing here this time of day anyway?"

It was normal for Willie to come to the office about 10:00 a.m. everyday with the daily instructions from Robert Tyler. But to come at closing time was something that he had never done before.

"Massa Tyler told me to give these to you today. He told me to put 'em in your hands and not to leave 'em on the office doorstep. He told me to put 'em in your hands even if I had to run all the way to your house. In fact, he told me to put 'em in your hands even if I had to run to Mount Ararat and back. And he told me to go back to his office and tell him that I had put 'em in your hands. I don't know what these things are, but they sure sound important."

"They sure do," I said. "You go on back and tell Massa Tyler that you did just what he asked."

As Willie turned to go, a cold wind blew down the main street of Germantown. It blew the oval sign that hung over the door causing it to creak a little. "The Tyler Companies" it said across the top with "Robert Joseph Tyler, Esq." across the middle. Circling the bottom was my name, "John Wesley Barnes, Manager." "I was mighty proud of that sign. I guessed I was the only colored man in all of North Carolina that had his name on the sign of a company.

As I turned to go back into the store, I noticed that Willie had brought me two things. One was a handwritten note in Mr. Tyler's hand with just the name John on the outside. The second item was a specially sealed envelope that was addressed to Mr. John Wesley Barnes, Esq. The envelope was tied with a string and the string was sealed with wax. As I looked more closely, I noticed that the wax seal carried the crest of Mr. Tyler's law firm. I had received many string-tied envelopes, but never one sealed with wax, and especially with the seal of the law firm. I had received hundreds of pieces of correspondence through the years, but I had never received one addressed to Mr. John Wesley Barnes, Esq.

I opened the door and made my way across to my desk. Because it was just before dark, I lit the beeswax candle on the desk and a rich glow of light filled the room. The office was a simple place. I had a desk, a chair for myself and two chairs in front of the desk. I took great pride in having a clean desk. There was one small pile of papers that, for one reason or another didn't seem to fit anywhere. These papers were held down with a paper weight that was very special to me. It was just a rock that was covered with "fool's gold." I had kept that rock for over twenty years. It reminded me, not only of winning a wrestling match, but of a surrogate father who loved me enough to bring my real father's body home.

Behind the desk was a wall of mail slots. In these I would place work orders for each of the company managers, material orders, work orders to be completed, bills of sale, and receipts. Every day the slots would fill and empty as the day went along. Willie would come by with orders from Massa Tyler (he was always Massa Tyler at work, even though he was Robert when we were alone or with family). In front of the desk were two chairs. I rarely needed both of them, but I almost always needed one. The various managers of the Tyler Companies would come to the office each day to pick up their orders and turn in their cash and receipts. I was spending an hour or so a day with each manager reviewing each order and receipt. I worked out a schedule where my day would be full and the managers would not normally have to wait.

To the left of my desk was a large safe. All of the cash receipts of all of the Tyler Companies were kept in the safe until we made the weekly trip to the bank in Salem. Everyone in the county knew that it was the largest and heaviest safe in the county, except for the one in the vault at the bank. Only two people knew the combination, Massa Tyler and me. Robert Tyler had recently hired an armed guard, Matthew Brown, to watch the safe each night and to go with me on the weekly trip to Salem. As I sat down in my chair, I thought that it was strange that Matthew wasn't here yet.

I decided to read the simple note first:

John,

Meet me at Hanging Rock Mountain tomorrow at noon. Make sure that you come alone and are not followed. If you meet anyone along the way; you are not to tell them that you are on business for me.

Robert

I had to admit that I was confused. Robert Tyler, a man who never missed a day of work, was asking me to take a day off, travel half-way across the county, and climb a mountain to meet him when I could just walk down the street to his office. I didn't understand, but I trusted Robert Tyler and would do exactly as he asked.

I instantly began to think out how I would go. I had a couple of options—the level way or the shorter way. The level way would be for me to go north from Germantown to Walnut Cove and then west along the valley of the Dan River to the foot of Hanging Rock Mountain. The other way would be to go through the Beautiful Valley and then along the ridge of hills that paralleled the mountains finally turning west to reach the base of Hanging Rock. The climb to the hanging rock was a difficult one, but the path that the Indians had blazed and used for centuries was still there.

My horse Betsy (I never let my mother know that she was named after her because of the color of her hair) would be best for the trip across the county. But my mule Joe (I never let Robert Joseph Tyler know that he was named after him because of his stubbornness) would be best for climbing the mountain. I decided I would take both animals. I would lead Joe across the county, leave Betsy at the bottom of the mountain, and use Joe to climb the mountain. I would need to leave before dawn. It would take me half a day to get there and half a day to get back no matter which route I took, so I decided to go one way and come back the other.

I was trying to decide how to explain this unplanned trip to my wife, Sally, when it dawned on me that I should open the other envelope—the official looking one.

Robert often chided me about saving the string that tied the envelopes which came from his office with the daily orders and instructions. It was easier and quicker to cut the strings than to untie them. But when they were cut, they were not usable again.

When I looked at the envelope, I couldn't see any way to open it without cutting the string. The wax seal was square atop the knot. And the string was tied in a knot and not a bow. I made a mental note to mention this to Robert the next day at Hanging Rock.

I took my knife and cut the string in two places, so that it fell away from the envelope. I opened the envelope and found three documents and what looked like a leather pouch inside. The first document had a note pinned to the front which read, "John, put this document in the leather pouch and carry it with you at all times." The second document had a note which read, "Put this document in the company safe and never remove it unless it is needed." The third document had a note which said, "Take this document to the Surry County Courthouse in Richmond as soon as possible to be recorded by the Registrar of Deeds. This copy has my official seal attached and will match a copy of this document that has already been recorded."

I went back to the first document and read:

> Be it known to all concerned and to any who read this document that John Wesley Barnes is from this date, Sept. 19, 1806, and, henceforth for all time, a Free Man of Color.
>
> Be it further known that John Wesley Barnes has received this writ of freedom through the Philanthropy and Benevolence of his former owner Robert Joseph Tyler, Esq. as required by the Statutes of the State of North Carolina.
>
> Be it further known that John Wesley Barnes as a Free Man of Color is liberated from servitude and slavery for Meritorious service to his former owner as required by the Statutes of the State of North Carolina.
>
> Be it further known that John Wesley Barnes as a Free Man of Color shall not be subject for sale again or reduced to the state of slavery or subject to any service which would constrain or withhold his freedom.

Be it further known that John Wesley Barnes, as a Free Man of Color, shall be afforded all rights due to any man of honor, including the right to practice his religion, the right to hold property and to obtain sufficiently comfortable sustenance for himself and his family.

This document is signed by Robert Joseph Tyler, former owner of John Wesley Barnes, and his seal is attached.

I sat in stunned silence. I looked again at the document that I had just read. It said it over and over again, a free man of color. I looked at the other two documents and realized they were copies of the first. I took the first document and inserted it into the leather pouch. It was only then that I realized that the pouch was intended to be folded and kept in the inside pocket of a waistcoat. I slipped it into my pocket and felt its warmth next to my heart. Robert wanted me to keep this with me at all times. And I was going to do just that.

He wanted me to keep a copy in the safe and have a second copy recorded in the Surry County Register of Deeds office. He wanted to make absolutely sure that what happened to my father would not happen to me. I took the second copy, folded it carefully, and placed it in the back corner of the safe where the deeds of Mr. Tyler's properties and companies were kept. I couldn't think of a safer place than that. I placed the third copy in the safe as well. I wasn't sure when I would get to Richmond, but it would be safe there until I could make the trip.

For some strange reason, Robert wanted my first day as a free man of color to be spent meeting him at Hanging Rock Mountain. I wasn't sure why. But I trusted Robert Tyler implicitly. I would make the trip in the morning.

I blew out the candle and made my way to the office door. I felt the leather pouch in my pocket. It felt strange and wonderful. I searched in the dark for the key to the door and realized that I should have found it before I blew out the candle. Finally finding it, I stepped into the street and took a breath of the unusually cold September air. Somehow, breathing the air as a free man seemed different. As I locked the door, I noticed the shadows that the candles lit in other windows made along the street. As I turned toward home, I could have sworn that I saw a caped man disappear into the shadows at the end of the block.

I was too exhilarated by freedom to be worried about a man that may not have actually been there.

But I had noticed that Matthew still hadn't gotten to work. He had only been the night watchman for three of four days. I wasn't sure he was going to work out.

As I walked down the street of Germantown, the leather pouch in my pocket, and a cool breeze on the face of a "Free Man of Color," I was trying to decide how I would break the news to Sally and our two children, John Thomas and Anne Marie. I decided that I would let Sally read the Letter of Emancipation aloud to the family at supper. It would be a rich, sweet, wonderful dessert.

I was about to enter my house as a free man for the very first time. I had been a slave for twenty-two years. It's true that neither Mr. Robert, nor his father before him, ever treated me like a slave. But I was one. Most of the people of Lynnmont, the new name that Robert had given the Shoen Oder Estate not long after it came into his possession, had treated me as a free man as well. Robert had insisted on it. But in public, away from the people of the estate and just a few other people in Germantown, it had been essential that we portray ourselves as slave and master.

Even though I had been to school almost as long as Robert and could speak perfect English, it had seemed expedient that I learn the broken English of my black brothers and sisters who were also in bondage. There were times when acting like a slave was the best way to protect myself and my family. It was, after all, illegal in the state of North Carolina to teach a black man to read. It had been deemed appropriate that slaves could be taught simple math, the ability to add and subtract; but, if they could read they could know too much. In my case, of course, I could account for my ability to read and write by explaining that I was educated before I entered servitude.

As I opened the gate to the picket fence that surrounded my house, I thought that I had managed the slavery thing pretty well. My house was a simple one, wood framed with yellow pine siding and cedar shingles. It was a four-room house, with a front room and a kitchen behind it on the first floor and two bedrooms above.

I looked at the porch and noticed that Sally had hung a new wreath on the wall of the house between the two windows. The wreath was, I guessed, a celebration of the coming of autumn. The wreaths were constantly changing. Sally took great pride in the grapevine wreaths that she made. She had sold quite a few. Our front porch was her best means of advertising. I thought it was great that she had her own little stash of money.

The door to the house was to the extreme left of the porch. As I entered the door, the staircase leading upstairs was directly in front of me and I was in what I called the front room and what Sally called the parlor. It didn't seem fancy enough for me to call it a parlor. But it was comfortable. Robert had bought new furniture for the parlor at the manor house at Lynnmont, and some of the perfectly good old furniture came to our house. If furnishings make the difference, then, I guess Sally is right, and our front room really should be called a parlor.

Under the staircase was our only storage, a pantry for the kitchen. At the top of the stairs was a landing and a door that led to the back bedroom where the children slept. It was only a couple of months ago that I had put up a partition in the back bedroom to separate the two sides. Until then, the children had slept in the same bed. It was Sally who reminded me what it was like to be fourteen. The partition went up that very day. John Thomas, who was the fifteen year old, had to sleep on the floor for a few days until I could get a new bed, but it seemed like the right thing to do. Anne Marie was fourteen going on twenty.

They both really liked having their own room. Sally and I had a bedroom at the front of the house.

Robert actually owns the house and the land that it is built on. It was built on a piece of the estate that reached nearly to Germantown. It was near the northernmost community of bunkhouses that Mr. Schoenfeldt had built. Robert had built the new cooperage near there. Sally and I had first met there. It seemed like an appropriate place to build it. Robert let me design the house. When I told him that I wanted two fireplaces, one in each of the downstairs rooms, he gave me the brick from the kiln on the estate. When the land was first being cleared, Mr. Schoenfeldt had found a huge deposit of clay that was perfect for making brick. As a result, one of the first and most successful businesses that he created was brick-making. Even after all these years, they have only quarried about a quarter of that clay.

Sally and I have been married for fifteen years. She came to Lynnmont when her father was hired to be the new cooper. Robert had added a winery to the estate, so having an accomplished barrel maker was essential. There weren't a lot of prospects for a three-race man who happened to be a slave, but was living in a community that hated slavery. Even though I had been bought to protect me from slave catchers who might want to take me to be sold in another location, I was still a slave. Even though I was better educated than almost every white man I came into contact with, I was forced to bow in subservience.

I didn't really look like a slave though. My grandfather, on my mother's side, was a pure bred Scot. He had fair skin that freckled in the summer sun; blue eyes, and flaming red, wavy hair. My grandmother was one of the last of the pure bred Sauratown Indians. She had the beautiful olive, red complexion and jet black hair that nearly every Indian had. Their daughter, Elizabeth Ann McAdams Barnes, was the most beautiful woman my father had ever seen. Her skin was not quite fair and not quite olive with just enough freckles on her nose to be darling. Her hair was not red and not black, but a fascinating combination of the two. As the sun would hit it, you could see each color in the richness of the gentle brunette wave. Even as her son, I would have to say that she had a spectacular figure. That's not something that sons usually talk about, so I will leave it to the imagination.

My father was a black man who did not know anything about his heritage except that he was born on a rice plantation along the coast of South Carolina. He was sold with a gaggle of other children to Massa Perkins. I had learned that some slave owners wanted to get rid of the children and break up families as a show of power and dominance, while other slave owners believed that keeping families intact would lead to harmony and more fruitful work. Massa Perkins was one of those who believed that both sides were right. He would buy up children when he got the chance because he could get them cheaper than full grown, well trained slaves. He would then use the slaves that were already on the plantation to adopt the children and to train them. Though my father was black, he was clearly not pure African. His skin was deep, dark brown, but he was at least one generation removed from being pure African.

When I was born, I got nearly all of my traits from my mother's side. I had skin that was slightly tinged brown or red. My eyes and hair were like my mother, too, except my hair was just a bit curlier. Except for the curly hair, I could have easily passed for an Indian. I did get some of my father's traits though. I was tall, and I had the build of a blacksmith. I was always strong and muscular. I could always outrun and outwrestle all of the other boys on the estate.

I was twenty when Sally came to Lynnmont. She was sixteen and angry with her father for taking her away from her friends, especially the group of boyfriends, from which she was planning to choose her husband. Her father assured her that there would be a new group of boys at Lynnmont. He had not anticipated her seeing a young man who might interest her.

We were good friends long before we fell in love. It was two years before we were married. John Thomas came along right away. I wanted to name him Thomas John and call him Thomas after my father. Sally insisted that John come first. After all, she said, he was my son. After we named him, both names seemed right. We have called him John Thomas ever since. Anne Marie was named after her two grandmothers. Both names seemed to fit for her, too. Sally said that some folks might think that we were an uppity family because we gave our children double names. I told her that I didn't care what people thought because the names were just right.

When I walked in the door, it was clear that Sally had supper going. The smells of late season vegetables stewing, biscuits baking in the oven, and chicken frying greeted me as I called out to Sally and let her know I was home.

"You're late," she said as she poked her head through the door.

"I had some last minute correspondence I had to read," I said as I reached for my pocket to assure myself the correspondence was still there. "Where are the kids? It's mighty quiet around here."

"They have been arguing with each other all day. I've had it up to here," she said as she put her hand up to her forehead. "I sent them out back to restock the firewood and cut some kindling. Both were running low. I'll call them in. I've got supper nearly ready."

Before she moved towards the door, I asked, "Do you have any dessert tonight?"

"I'm sorry, Honey. I got caught up making wreaths and the time got away from me."

"That's all right. I brought something," I said, as I patted the front pocket of my jacket. "It might be the sweetest dessert we have ever had."

"What in the world are you talking about?" Sally asked.

"You'll find out," I said. "You set the table and I'll get the children."

As I stepped out the back door, I saw the children fighting over the ax. Clearly they both thought that cutting kindling was an easier job than stacking firewood. As a result, they had been fighting over the use of the ax, and neither job had been done. When I cleared my throat to get their attention they instantly realized the error of their ways. Both began to apologize at once.

"After supper, I want the kindling box filled and a full cord of wood stacked. Do you understand?"

"Yes sir," they said in unison.

"If you work together, it will go a lot quicker. Now, get inside. Your mother has supper ready."

Supper was our normal family affair. We had great food. Sally and I carried on a normal conversation about the events of the day, and the children sniped at each other. When we had finished eating, I instructed the children to clear the table, put the dishes on the wash stand, then to come back and sit down.

"Don't you want us to do the firewood?" John Thomas asked.

"Yes I do. But, first, there is something else more important."

Sally was looking quizzically at me. She was wondering what kind of sweet dessert I could possibly have in my pocket. When the children sat back down, I took out the leather pouch, carefully opened it, and took out the document inside.

"Sally, I want you to read this out loud," I said as I handed her the document.

"*Be it known to all concerned and to any who read this document*" she read and stopped and said, "What is this, John?"

"Start over and read it all," I said.

She began again, "*Be it known to all concerned and to any who read this document* that John Wesley Barnes is from this date, September 19, 1806, and, henceforth for all time, a Free Man of Color." She stopped again. Instantly realizing its significance, she burst into tears of joy, and through her tears, she kept saying, "O John. O John. O John," as she hugged me tightly around the neck.

John Thomas grabbed the document from her and read it all aloud to Anne Marie. The children also knew the significance. If I was free, they surely were, too.

All thought of firewood disappeared. When Sally finally stopped crying, we all moved to the parlor and sat around the fire, as John Thomas read and reread the whole emancipation document. We talked late into the night about what true freedom might mean for us as a family.

It was nearly midnight when I remembered that I had been instructed to meet Robert at Hanging Rock at noon the next day. I would need to be leaving the house before dawn.

As the children were headed to bed, I said to them, "Even free people need firewood and kindling."

"That's true," John Thomas said, laughing, and he added, "But they can hire somebody to do it for them."

"We may be free, John Thomas. But, we're not rich."

"Sure we are Daddy. There's nothing more valuable than freedom," he said.

Out of the mouth of babes…or even teenagers.

Sally had an inner clock that was amazing. She woke at 4:45 a.m., went downstairs to stir the fires, especially the one in the Franklin stove in the kitchen, and to build a fire in the oven. She was going to bake biscuits for me to take with me.

At 5:15 a.m., she came upstairs and woke me. I got up and dressed quickly. I went down and smelled the biscuits baking. I went to the corral, having decided to take just Betsy. I would go the longer way, up the creek to Window Falls. Betsy could go most of the distance up the creek bed, and I could walk the rest of the way.

When I returned to the house, leading Betsy, I was surprised to see the children stacking firewood. They had, apparently, only been at it for a few minutes but the task was nearly finished. We smiled broadly at each other as I passed.

Sally had prepared a feast. There was chicken left over from last night's supper. More than a dozen biscuits filled a leather pouch, some filled with my favorite cheese from the estate and some with Sally's own homemade apple butter. She had also fried some sausage links and told me to eat them for breakfast because they might not stay fresh all day.

"There's more food here than I can eat."

"Well, if I know Robert as well as I think I do, he will have forgotten all about bringing food," Sally said. "You can share some with him."

I put the two leather pouches of food in the bags behind Betsy's saddle and mounted her. As I sat in the saddle, looking down at Sally, Anne Marie came running up with a large bunch of fall flowers.

"Daddy, will you have time to go by the graveyard and put these on Grandma's grave?" she asked.

"I had planned to go by there, so I'll be glad to put the flowers on her grave for you. Can you tie them to the back of the saddle?" I got down from the horse, just long enough for her to tie the flowers to the back of the saddle, and to give Sally another hug. I waited for Anne Marie to finish tying the flowers, gave her a hug too and said, "Thanks. You are really special."

As I started out, I decided to swing by the office quickly. I wanted to chide Matthew about being late last night. Betsy was in high spirits. It took her only a couple of minutes to get to the office. I was surprised to see that it was dark inside. Not only had Matthew been late, he hadn't even shown up. I would need to tell Robert about this, of course.

As the sun began to rise, I was approaching the hill in Lynnmont where Oskar Schoenfeldt had created a graveyard. Unfortunately, like most graveyards, it was populated with the graves of mostly children and young women who died in childbirth. There were a few older men and women as well. My grandmother McAdams, who had been the community tailor for so long, had died a peaceful death and was one of the first adults buried in the graveyard. Also buried in the graveyard, beside one another, were my mother and father. As I stood beside their graves and put Anne Marie's flowers at the headstone, I remembered a special thing that Mr. Oskar did to honor my father. He had a stone erected over his grave. It read, "Thomas Barnes, died 1778, as a free man." When the prayer service held at the erection of the stone was over, he said something to me that I have never forgotten, "John," he said, "live a life worthy of your father." I remembered, of course, that those were the very words that his dying mother had said to him.

I mounted Betsy and made my way along the hill that would lead me into the main community of Lynnmont. As I rode along, I remembered the day, two years after we buried my father, that Oskar Schoenfeldt gave us our biggest surprise. He had sent a message to every person who lived or worked at Beautiful Valley that the next Monday would be a holiday. We were invited to a great banquet which would be held on the grounds of the community if the weather was good, or inside the stable if the weather was bad. He promised us that the food would be great; and, though he could not command that we be present, it was his sincere desire that everyone be there.

The next Monday, we were all there; over two hundred adults and their children. I remember being stunned as I realized just how many people actually lived or worked at Beautiful Valley. I suppose that the only people for whom it was not a holiday were the cooks. They produced an incredible banquet. Mr. Oskar announced that there were no servants among us. We would have to serve ourselves. After Pastor Gluck offered grace, a double line of folks started down the serving tables. Roasted venison, braised duck, fried chicken, and beef brisket were the first choices. These were followed by a variety of delicious vegetables. There were breads from the bakery and cheeses from the factory.

The cabinetmakers and carpenters had worked together to create simple tables. They were tall sawhorses on which planks of oak from the sawmill were placed. They were just the right height for the adults who stood to eat from their overladen plates. The children were completely happy sitting on the ground and eating. After we had all eaten, Mr. Oskar stood on a workbench that had been brought from the Blacksmith Shop so that he could be seen. His deep voice, still heavily accented in German but now with a strange mixture of Southern drawl, boomed over us. He stunned us with his announcement that he was leaving Shoen Oder. He told us the whole story of being the duke of an estate much larger than Shoen Oder, of his father's arrest, his mother's awful death, and his need to flee.

He told us of a young woman and a silk handkerchief.

"Several months ago," he said, "I sent my love a letter. In case the letter was to fall into the wrong hands, it had to be worded very carefully. I struggled over the letter for several days, before I decided to make it very short and very simple." He paused as if he were seeing the letter.

My Dear Elyse,

I would like to return the handkerchief that you so graciously loaned me. If the time is ever right, please contact me by writing to Oskar Schoenfeldt, Shoen Oder Estate, Surry County, North Carolina.

"I knew that to get a letter from Elyse three things would have to be true. The political opponents who had destroyed my family and caused my flight would have to be gone; Elyse would have to be unmarried, or now be a widow; and most important of all, she would still have to be in love with me.

"Although odds of all those conditions existing were very slim, I sent the letter with a twinge of hope," he said, holding his thumb and forefinger slightly apart. "Two weeks ago today this letter came," he said, as he took it out of his pocket and read, "My Dearest Konrad."

He stopped and looked at all of us."That's my real name! I won't bother you with the last name; you Americans would never get it," he said, laughing.

My Dearest Konrad,

I am very eager for you to return my handkerchief. You have had it way too long. I will wait for you at your manor house at Sokolov. Please come quickly!

Your love,

Elyse

"And so, I am leaving! I have booked passage on a ship leaving from Charleston. I have no family here, but I am leaving the entire estate to a person who has been a brother to me, Joshua Tyler. I ask that you treat Mr. Tyler with the same courtesy and dignity that you have always given me."

It was Joshua Tyler who spoke with shock in his voice that all of us could hear, "Mr. Oskar, I can't accept such a huge gift. Shoen Oder must be worth a half a million dollars."

"It's really worth only about half that much. But, I'm going to give it to you no matter how valuable it is. I am headed back to an estate that is worth five times this much. Besides, I was given the money that made this estate possible, so I am only passing on to you what was given to me."

"But it's just too much," Joshua said again.

"I don't care if you think it's too much. I've already transferred everything to your name. It all already belongs to you. I trust you completely to make the estate prosper."

His speech having ended, he got down from the bench and began to say good-bye. Everyone was stunned, yet they were thrilled for him. He managed to break away from the crowd for a moment and take me aside. He put his arm around me and said,

"Son, it's been an honor to have been your second father. I am very proud of the man that you have become."

He returned to greeting the people, and, as he did so, his carriage appeared, heavily laden with luggage. He managed to pull himself away from those he loved, climbed into the carriage, and left his Beautiful Valley.

Just as Robert and I had sat on a log by the side of the road and watched as the slave catcher took my father away, the two of us now stood by that same road and watched as a carriage took Mr. Oskar back to his love. Everything had dramatically changed. Robert's father had just been given the estate.

Betsy and I were coming up that same road now, but in the opposite direction. We were headed through the community to the mountain range to the west. As I came around the bend, I saw Lynnmont, and wondered again, why Robert had given the estate that new name. The only answer he had ever given was that although Beautiful Valley was a lovely name, there are hundreds of beautiful valleys in North Carolina. There is only one Lynnmont.

Robert's father had died in his sleep, peacefully but very unexpectedly, just a few years after Mr. Oskar left. Robert Joseph Tyler, at the age of nineteen inherited one of the largest estates in North Carolina. Just a few months after his father's death, Robert began one of the major changes that he would make to the estate; construction of the manor house. It was to be a house worthy of the estate.

"Mr. Oskar said that he never built the house because he never married, but I intend to find a wife," Robert told me.

I saw the manor house now as I passed through the community. It was an elegant, colonial style house, patterned after the Governor's Palace in Williamsburg, Virginia. Even though it was a different style from the rest of the buildings, it fit right in because it was made of the same brick that were used throughout the estate.

Not only had Robert used brick from the estate, he had also used lumber cut from Lynnmont's forests and milled at the estate's sawmill. Craftsmen from the cabinet shop had fashioned all of the windows and doors and had even made all of the elaborate moldings which adorned the house. The oak floors, the chestnut fireplace mantles and surrounds, the elm staircase banisters were all from Lynnmont trees and crafted by estate workers.

Robert believed that the more the people of the estate invested themselves in the manor house, the more they would love it. And he was right. This elegant house became the community's home.

I rode past the community and came to one of my favorite spots in Lynnmont. On a crest of the hill there was an entire view of the Sauratown Mountains, from Mount Ararat in the south all the way to Hanging Rock Mountain to the north. The beautiful mountain range was short, probably no more than about thirty miles in length. The walls of the mountains with their sheer granite faces surrounded by hardwood forests were magnificent in every season of the year. I never tired of this view, even though I passed it often. Down at the bottom of this hill was a piece of land that Mr. Oskar had given, along with nearly all of the building material, for a Methodist church.

I came this way so often, not only because I loved the church, but because I had been called to be what the Methodists called a lay preacher. Our Elder was a circuit rider who had about thirty churches. We only saw him four times a year at our quarterly conferences. During those meetings, he would serve the Lord's Supper, baptize the new babies and any new adult converts, perform all the weddings that were necessary, conduct the business of the church, and preach the Word. He was a very good preacher. Our folk looked forward to the conferences. On the Sundays when the Elder was not present, I delivered the sermon.

When I first began to preach, I was tentative. After all, who was I to preach? But my people did an astonishingly Christian thing; they loved me in spite of me. It wasn't long before they loved me into being a preacher. The amen corner was especially helpful. This group of highly dedicated laymen would sit together and comment on the sermon as I preached. The more they commented with shouted "amens," the better my preaching got.

I was proud of the New Salem Methodist Church. Salem is a Hebrew word that means 'place of peace,' and we wanted our little church to be a new place of peace. Most of the time, it was. We had our squabbles; but when it really mattered, we would come together.

I passed by the church and headed on towards Hanging Rock. I figured by the position of the sun that it was getting close to ten o'clock. The road went down the hill until it came to the valley of the Dan River. From there, it followed the river and the valley until it was right at the base of Hanging Rock Mountain. I peeled off the road. Betsy and I began to climb by an old Indian path which continued up after it crossed a little stream. I decided to leave the path and follow the stream itself. Betsy would be able to make it most of the way.

The creek was narrow and, in many places, mountain laurel grew so thick that it was difficult, even for Betsy to make a way through. I finally decided that I had taken Betsy about as far as she could go. I slipped off her back. I unhitched her saddle and slid it off her back. I tied a long rope to her bridle and tied the other end around a tree with a large loop. Now she would not be able to wind herself around the tree. I poured some oats from a bag onto the ground. She could get plenty of water from the creek.

I took all of the food from the saddle bags and continued my climb. Every now and again when the foliage opened slightly, I would get the most incredible view of the beautiful valley and the rest of the land that comprised this part of Surry County. Though most of it was still forested, there were increasingly large sections of farm land. I could see, far in the distance, the pastures of Lynnmont.

Mostly because of mountain laurel, the evergreen plant that seemed to me to be a cousin of the wild azaleas, I found the going more difficult that I had expected. But I was seeing more and more of the huge granite shelf that hung out over the face of the mountain. It truly was an enormous rock. It seemed to be all one piece, though one could see the different layers within the rock itself. I was getting closer, because I could actually hear the waterfall that was located at the base of the rock.

I don't know what the Indians called these falls. But ever since white people came into the area, this cascade had been called the Window Falls. Right at the bottom of the rock shelf was a large, circular hole in the rock that looked like a round window. It was fascinating to stand and peer through that hole up to the falls. I had kind of hoped that Robert might have meant to meet under Hanging Rock instead of at Hanging Rock, because, if he had, I would not have a treacherous climb ahead. Many thousands of people before me had climbed around the falls, up the hill and onto the great rock shelf that jutted out into the valley below. Even though the path was clear, it was extremely steep. I was very winded by the time that I reached the top.

When I got to the rock, Robert was nowhere to be seen. One of the faults that Robert had was that he was chronically late. The sun was directly overhead. I sat on the rock, glad to have a few minutes to catch my breath. Robert could not have picked a more beautiful place for a meeting, but I still could not figure why he wanted to meet here.

If he was coming from above the rock, he would have a fairly steep descent from the crest of the mountain. He probably would not come that way unless he was coming from the other side of the mountain, the western half of Surry County. It was incredible to me that this county was separated by this mountain range that went down the middle of it. Robert often had to pass through the gap to go to the county courthouse in Richmond. He might have left the office last night and made the trip through the gap, and attended to some early morning business in Richmond before heading here.

I laid down on the rock, allowing the sun to warm me and resting from the difficult climb. I knew I would hear Robert long before I saw him, and, sure enough, it wasn't long before I heard a twig break and then the rustle of some leaves. Robert was getting close. He was, indeed, coming from above. Like me, he had had to leave his horse and walk the last half mile or so.

"Good afternoon, Free Man of Color!" he said as he bounded onto the rock.

"That was certainly a surprise! Thanks!" I wanted to say something more about Robert's Letter of Emancipation, but there weren't any words. I decided to change the subject. "Robert, Matthew didn't show up for work last night," I said, as I handed Robert some of Sally's biscuits.

"I know, that's part of the reason that we are meeting here."

"Part of the reason?" I asked.

"I knew no location that could be more secure than this rock. And the other reason is because I love this place. You see, John, it was on this rock that I met my wife." Robert paused to let this statement sink in. I think that he got the exact response from me that he expected.

"Robert, you're not married!"

"Oh, yes I am. Or at least I used to be," he said. "Her name was Lynn, Lynn Johnston."

For the very first time, I understood the name Lynnmont. And I also understood why we needed to meet in secret.

"Judge Johnston's daughter?" I asked.

"Yes. When I was nineteen and she was sixteen we met on this very spot. It was a church outing. The Moravians were trying to have a stronger bond between the churches on either side of the Sauratown's, so they sponsored a picnic. I didn't know who she was at first. She seemed to know who I was, though, and introduced herself to me as just Lynn.

"Even though there were all kinds of activities that the church elders had planned, Lynn and I just sat here on the rock all day and talked. It was the kind of talk that young lovers have. We were both trying to get to know everything we could about the other. We talked so long, that we actually talked right through the picnic. But neither one of us was hungry.

"We decided that we would meet again and Lynn suggested that we meet here. She said that she had a pony that was sturdy and could get her most of the way and we agreed to meet the next Saturday. It was at that meeting that she told me who her father was."

"That must have been an incredibly difficult moment," I said. Judge Johnston had been a mortal enemy of Oskar Schoenfeldt since before Mr. Oskar set foot in Surry County. Apparently, Judge Johnston had been negotiating to purchase the land that became Lynnmont and Mr. Oskar's agent offered a much better deal than the judge could afford.

"Later, in an attempt to heal the breech that had been caused by the land deal, Mr. Oskar had tried to hire Judge Johnston's slaves to help clear the land. That deal had fallen apart when the judge had demanded more than twice the compensation that other plantations owners had asked. Mr. Oskar and the judge were not only business opponents, but they were on totally opposite sides politically. And when Mr. Oskar made the decision that his estate would be slave free, a further wedge was driven between them. Judge Johnston saw each of the conflicts as a personal attack. He developed a hatred for Oskar Schoenfeldt, and Shoen Oder. Since that time, he had used his judgeship, power, and wealth to undermine Oskar Schoenfeldt whenever possible. When Robert's father inherited the estate, Judge Johnston had simply transferred his hatred to the Tyler's.

"It was more than a difficult moment," Robert said. "We knew that Lynn's father would be furious if he knew that we were seeing each other. We decided to keep our romance secret. We did all of our courting right here on Hanging Rock. Then came the day we decided to get married. We were sure that neither of our pastors would marry us, because both knew of the animosity between the two families. We drove into Salem and had the preacher at Home Moravian Church marry us. We spent a couple of wonderful nights at the Salem Tavern and then headed up the Yadkin valley to the judge's plantation.

"When we pulled the carriage in front of the Johnston Plantation House at Yadkin Oaks, one of the servants came running out."

" 'Lawd, Miss Lynn, Ain't you been gibbin' us a terrible scare, bein' gone three nights,' he said."

"I'll never forget when she looked him in the eye and said, 'It's not Miss Lynn, it's Mrs. Tyler. I'd like for you to meet my husband, Mr. Robert Tyler.' The servant was speechless. But the judge sure wasn't. You have never heard such yelling and cursing in all your life," Robert said. "And Lynn yelled back as good as we got. The judge swore that he would never let the marriage stand. Even though we were married, he refused to let us sleep together. He locked Lynn in her bedroom and forced me to sleep in the barn.

"Early the next morning Judge Johnston woke me up by poking me with the cane that he carries but doesn't need. I had snuggled down in some hay in the corner of the barn. Standing with the Judge was the sheriff. He leaned down, and before I knew what was happening, he had put me in handcuffs."

"No!" I said, interrupting Robert's story. But even so, I could tell that he needed to take a breath.

Robert shook his head, affirming that it was true and continued the story.

"'You are under arrest for Statutory Rape and Contributing to the Delinquency of a Minor,' the judge said. 'And you are going to jail. There will be some more charges when I can figure out what they are,' the judge added angrily. The sheriff dragged me out of the barn and threw me in the back of a wagon. He took a chain and ran it through the handcuffs, attached it to a metal ring that was secured to the bottom of the wagon and hauled me off to jail.

"After I had spent four days in jail, I was taken into Judge Johnston's courtroom where he showed up with a piece of paper he wanted me to sign. He said it was an annulment of the marriage. If I didn't sign it, I would spend at least forty years in prison. I told him I just wanted to see Lynn. He said he had sent Lynn out of North Carolina and I would never see her again or even know where he had sent her. Unfortunately, he was right about that. I have never seen her again."

Robert paused. Even after all these years, it was obviously still difficult for him to talk about it. I remembered, many years before, that Judge Johnston had explained his daughter's disappearance by saying that, as a rebellious teenager, she had run away from home, and he had no idea where she was!

"Robert, I'm your best friend. Why haven't you told me about this before ?"

"I was so embarrassed that I had let the judge get his way with me that I just couldn't tell anyone. Besides, I didn't want him to get the satisfaction of being able to lord it over me. If other people had known, it would have made it even more difficult for me to deal with it all these years."

"Robert, I'm sorry. I'm really sorry. But this can't be the reason that we are meeting here today. Something else must have happened."

"The judge has recently learned that I have come to know something so horrendous about him that all of his friends and political allies would defect from him if it were to become public knowledge. Because of this, he has decided that I must be eliminated before I have a chance to expose him. I have learned that he has hired a group of thugs to assassinate me.

"I have also learned that he has bribed the Register of Deeds office to destroy every document that has come from my law firm. Apparently there is going to be an unfortunate fire in the Register of Deeds office. The registrar is going to explain it by saying that as he was trying to catalogue the documents from my firm, an unattended candle burned them up.

"That's why we are meeting here. I know that my will is going to be one of the documents that will be destroyed. That is why I have brought you here to give you another copy of it. In fact, I've got a lot of documents to give to you to keep safe.

"I don't want you to keep them in the office safe in case they might target it. I think that your house is the safest place. The judge's allies are such small-minded people that they would never suspect that I would trust a slave with such important documents."

Robert had laid down a large leather satchel when he had reached Hanging Rock. He now reached for it and began to pull out documents.

"First," he said. "I want to give you these Letters of Emancipation for Sally, John Thomas, and Anne Marie. Most people would never think that they were slaves; but, according to the law, when Sally married a slave, she entered into involuntary servitude herself and your children would be slaves because you were. Second, this is a deed to your house and ten acres of land on which it sits."

Robert saw how stunned I was, and before I could speak, he said, "It is the least I could do for the best friend I ever had. I thought about sending all of this with Willie last night, but I thought I'd let you savor your own freedom first."

"In this packet," he said, pulling out a large bundle of documents, "are the deeds to the business that make up the Tyler Companies, plus copies of all of the current contracts under which we are working. This bundle," he held up documents that were tied together," are deeds to everything at Lynnmont. I think that the judge and his allies are going to try to bankrupt the companies and destroy Lynnmont as an estate. Afterwards, they will want to move in and take control of all of it. That is why they will try to destroy all of the documents that came from my law firm. If there are no records, they will be able to move with impunity.

"You will need to be very careful about when and how you produce the documents. Do not put all of your eggs in one basket. You may need to sacrifice one or two smaller parts of the business before the judge reveals himself as the power behind the scenes. I have quietly moved most of the companies' assets out of the bank in Surry County. I don't know if the Judge has the power to raid the bank or not, but he may. If he does, I wanted there to be as little money in the accounts as possible. There is $2,000 in the safe in your office. I put it there a couple of nights ago. It is to be used to keep our companies afloat until the crisis is past. I have included a list of the new banks and their account numbers so that you can access all of the funds if necessary.

"In this sealed envelope," he said, pulling out the last document in the leather satchel, "is my will and instructions that I want you to follow in case of my death. When I die, I'd like you to preach at my funeral at New Salem and then bury me next to my father at Lynnmont. Then, exactly one month later, I want you to open the seal to this envelope. Inside, you will find a letter giving you some very specific instructions. The letter will announce that you are the Executor of my estate. That fact was one of the reasons that the Letter of Emancipation had to come. The law forbids a slave serving as the Executor of a Will. The letter will instruct you to gather together for the reading of the will the people who are its beneficiaries. I would also like for the reading of the will to be as close to one month after you open the packet as possible.

"Timing is important. I believe that it will take Judge Johnston about two months to fully expose himself. When I die, I want my death to stand for something. The destruction of Judge

Johnston, by his own hand, will do nicely in making my death mean something."

"Robert, do you really think you are in danger?" I asked him.

"Yes, I am afraid that my death is imminent."

"Why don't you flee? or barricade yourself in the manor house? or hire an army to protect you? Have you called the sheriff? Why don't you go public with what you know and expose the judge that way?"

Robert and I seldom argued. But we were arguing now. It sounded like he had made the decision to die, rather than fight. None of the answers that he gave were good enough! But he finally said something that brought the argument to a close.

"The letter in packet will explain everything. I know that you want more answers now, but you will just have to trust me. If I share too much information with you now, you will know too much and the judge will target you! I am willing to sacrifice my own life, but not yours."

He paused for a few seconds and then added, "I let the judge defeat me when he stole my wife from me. Now he is trying to steal my life. And he wants to follow that by stealing everything that I have spent my life building up. He may succeed in stealing my life, but you are going to see to it that he fails in stealing everything else."

I sat in stunned silence for a few moments. Then I remembered.

"What has this got to do with Matthew Brown?"

"Matthew likes to take a drink down at the pub in Walnut Cove. While he was there a few days ago, he heard of the plot to destroy my life. Apparently the judge has not been as careful in selecting his henchmen as he should have been. Because of what he overheard, his life is also in danger. I fired him to give him cover, gave him a couple of month's salary, and I told him to leave North Carolina. I hope that he has successfully gone."

"Robert. Are my wife and children in danger?"

"I've wondered about that. In fact, I've thought about it a lot. I really don't think that they are. But they might be if you move too quickly after my death. Be smart, John. I'm trusting you with everything that is of value to me."

Robert and I sat in silence as we enjoyed the rest of the biscuits and the fried chicken.

"Your Sally sure can cook. I might just get Judge Johnston to kill you instead of me, so I can marry her."

"You wouldn't really like her, Robert. She snores."

How could I have known that we would share our last laugh together on Hanging Rock?

As we sat there talking and laughing together, a dramatic change in the weather occurred. The valley beneath us filled with clouds, even though there was still bright sunshine above us. An extremely cold wind was howling from the bottom of the valley, up the mountain, and over the face of the Hanging Rock.

Even though we were sitting in bright sunshine, it suddenly began to snow. The snow was being blown up from the clouds that were beneath us and into the bright sunshine. Every flake looked like a piece of crystal, as thousands of tiny rainbows burst into sight. I had heard many of the old timers talk about crystal snow, but I had never seen it. I had never, until that moment, realized that each snowflake is actually clear, and that it is the lack of light that makes them appear white.

I sat and thought how wonderful it would be if we could see the whole world through the prism of crystal snow, if we could see everything in the magnified brilliance of true light.

Off to the Races

A S I MADE MY WAY DOWN THE mountain, the brilliance of the crystal snow gave way to the dull gray of clouds. The weather matched my spirit. Robert had left me with more questions than answers. Each step I took down the steep path from Hanging Rock, to the tree where Betsy was tethered, led me to a deeper gloom. I was convinced that Robert had made the decision to die. It didn't make sense to me. Why wasn't he fighting? He had promised me that the letter in the envelope that I was carrying would have all the answers. I was tempted to stop, right there on the trail, and tear open the package. But Robert had made me swear that I wouldn't open the letter until one month after his death.

Why had I made that promise? I hadn't made many promises in my life, but, the ones I had made, I had kept. I had promised my father that I would care for my mom. I had promised Mr. Oskar that I would keep his secret. I had promised God that I would be a faithful pastor and preacher if he would strengthen me in the task. Now, I had promised Robert that I would trust him. As hard as it was going to be, I was going to keep this promise, too.

I got to Betsy, saddled her, tied Robert's packet to the back of the saddle, and eased into the saddle. I had a four or five hour ride ahead of me. There was plenty of time to ponder. Maybe, if I relived some of the history of the tension between Robert Tyler and Alexander Johnston, things would make more sense.

Alexander Johnston is a good businessman, a fine lawyer, and a respected jurist. He is admired in the community, and known to be extremely generous to many charities. Although he has strong political opponents, because of his anti-federalist views, that's just politics. His rivals may disagree with him, but admire him for standing up for what he believes. The judge's one great public flaw has been his feud with Oskar Schoenfeldt and the Tylers. I never understood why disagreements over business had become so personal between Mr. Oskar and the judge. But I certainly understood why the judge had some personal animosity for Robert.

It all sprung from an incident, which happened a couple of months after Robert's father died. Robert was overwhelmed. He was dealing with the inevitable grief of having lost his father unexpectedly. He was trying to cope, at the age of nineteen, with the demands of being owner of a huge estate. He was also dealing with the pain of a nasty breakup with his first girlfriend. All of this combined to drive Robert into seclusion in the small estate foreman's house where he had lived since coming to Beautiful Valley.

I went to see him every day during that time, but nothing that I said seemed to make any difference. Robert was in the doldrums—a deep depression, which robbed him of energy, and which seemed to be getting deeper each day. Immediately following his father's death, and remembering Mr. Oskar's story, Robert had written him, asking his advice on how to cope. He told me that he wasn't going to do anything until he heard from Mr. Oskar. Since it had only been two months since the letter was sent, it probably hadn't even gotten to Germany yet. It might be another five or six months before Robert would receive a reply. I couldn't let Robert hide in his house for six more months. If sadness produces more sadness, Robert would be completely dysfunctional in six more months.

I left Robert's house one morning, after failing to get him to come fishing with me. We had always loved fishing together. If I couldn't even get him to do that, I certainly didn't know how to help him. I went to the horse barn, intentionally to see Ben Randolph. When I told him about Robert, he wasn't surprised. Nearly everyone on the estate had noticed.

"I have an idea that just might help," he said. "Come with me." He led me through the barn to one of the special paddocks . In the paddock was Arrowhead, a beautiful three-year-old chestnut stallion whose only white mark was an arrowhead shaped blaze on his forehead. His name was, of course, obvious. Mr. Ben bridled him, and, leading him from the paddock, said, "We're going to see Robert."

Mr. Ben, Arrowhead, and I walked from the paddock, across the main quad of the estate, and down the path to the house. When we got there, Mr. Ben asked me to hold Arrowhead. Without knocking, he entered the house and a few minutes later he emerged with a reluctant Robert in tow.

"We have won the Surry County Derby every year since I have been at Beautiful Valley," Mr. Ben said. "We are going to win again this year! Arrowhead is the best horse we have ever had. But he is headstrong. Though many people have ridden him, you, Robert, are the only person that can control him."

"So?" Robert asked.

"So, if we are going to win the race this year, you are going to have to train him, and ride him in the race. Mr. Oskar, and your father, took great pride in Beautiful Valley winning this race every year. It helps to increase the value of all of the stock that we put up for sale."

"I don't know," Robert said. "I don't feel much like riding these days."

But while he was talking to Mr. Ben, Robert began to stroke Arrowhead's forehead and to comb through his mane with the fingers of his other hand. Arrowhead, clearly enjoying the attention, gently nuzzled Robert. Without words, Arrowhead had accomplished what I had failed to do.

"What do you mean by training him? Robert asked Mr. Ben.

"We only have two months to get him ready. You will have to run him at least twice every day between now and race day. I'll be there to guide you. We will follow a very strict schedule of alternating short sprints and long runs. It will be very intense, for both you and Arrowhead, and neither of you can miss a single day of training. The two of you will have to bond even more than you already have."

Robert didn't agree until Mr. Ben added. "You can run the race in memory of your father."

The twice daily training was exactly what Robert needed. He was still disappointed about the breakup with his girlfriend, still crushed by the death of his father, and still overwhelmed by his new responsibilities; but he was healing. Mr. Ben worked a miracle. Both horse and rider were trained.

The day before the race, Mr. Ben loaded Arrowhead unto a special, low-slung wagon and transported him to Richmond. Ben didn't want the horse tired out by having to walk all the way there. The afternoon before the race, he walked the horse and Robert the entire length of the course, talking strategy. It was a difficult course, more than a mile and a half long. There were two long curves, one hairpin turn, and a long straightaway to finish. It was a course that required horses that could quickly change direction to avoid other horses, have speed to get out in front, the ability to come to a near halt in the hairpin turn and then get quickly back up to speed, and most of all, because of the length of the race, endurance.

Robert was confident. He had never ridden a horse that had both the strength and speed of Arrowhead. Mr. Ben's training schedule had been successful in increasing both. Arrowhead was ready!

Ben Randolph and Robert Tyler were not the only ones who intended to win. Alexander Johnston was not a horse breeder, but he was proud of the stock that he did have. And he was tired of the losing streak to Oskar Schoenfeldt and Joshua Tyler. This year, he had a special weapon.

The morning of the race, as Robert, Mr. Ben, and I led Arrowhead to the paddock where all of the entrants were to gather, we noticed that a large crowd had gathered around Alexander Johnston and his horse. After Robert secured Arrowhead in the paddock, we made our way over to where the crowd was gathered and saw the most beautiful horse we had ever seen.

"I had him imported all the way from England," the judge was saying. "He's a brand new breed called a thoroughbred. He's the grandson of a horse named Eclipse who won the Epson Derby by more than forty links!"

"What's his name?" someone asked. "Since I bought him from the Duke of Cumberland and brought him all the way from England, I have named him Britannia.

I thought it was a great name. He was regal, stately—taller and more slender than Arrowhead—but with the most exquisite muscles I had ever seen on a horse.

"How much did he cost you, Judge?" someone else in the crowd asked.

"I'm not going to tell you," the judge said, laughing. "But I will tell you that he cost more money than anybody here makes in a year."

Mr. Ben took Robert and gently pulled him away from the gathering. I tagged along behind and heard him say to Robert, "That horse is going to be our only competition. I've never seen a horse with such beautiful lines. But every horse has a weakness, and because of his slender build, he will be jostled at the beginning of the race with so many horses bunched up, and he'll have a hard time at the hairpin turn. It's probably at the turn where you can make your move and then hold him off on the straightaway."

Later, as the horses were being saddled, Judge Johnston came up to Robert and said tauntingly, "You are going to lose! There is no way you can beat Britannia"

"We'll see about that!"

"Beautiful Valley is going down. It's about time, too."

"Judge," Robert said. "Shouldn't you be getting on your horse? You're going to miss the race."

"I'm not riding him," he said, laughing. "One of my niggers, Isaac, is going to ride the beauty."

Robert mounted Arrowhead and turned away from the judge. *He's a coward,* Robert thought. *He won't even ride his own horse.* Robert didn't know Isaac, but when he saw him, seated on Britannia, he realized why the judge was having him ride. He was just a boy, no more than ten or twelve years old, and he couldn't have weighed more than ninety pounds. And he was sitting in the smallest little saddle that Robert had ever seen. In fact, it was hardly a saddle at all. It couldn't have weighed more than a few pounds. Robert realized that Arrowhead was going to have a severe handicap, carrying at least twice the weight as Britannia for more than a mile and a half.

The race was to begin with a running start. All of the nearly fifty horses that were entered were moving up and down the twenty five yards of the main street of Richmond. The challenge was to be as close to the starting line as possible, moving forward, when the countdown ended and the gun sounded the official start. Crossing the line early caused immediate disqualification. It was a delicate balance between moving your own horse into the right position and using your horse to block some other. Getting off to a good start was also crucial because the course narrowed dramatically from the broad street to a country lane after only about a hundred yards. Being out in front before the bottleneck would be a huge advantage.

Robert and Mr. Ben had been practicing the running start every day for two months. Robert knew exactly how long it took for Arrowhead to get to full speed. When he saw the green flag raised, meaning only thirty seconds before the start, he turned Arrowhead away from the starting line, trotted back about twenty yards, turned Arrowhead, saw a small gap right in the middle, and spurred him to a gallop. It was a calculated risk. The gap could close, he could be intentionally blocked by another horse, or cross the line too early.

But the ploy worked. Arrowhead was running at full speed just one yard from the starting line when the gun sounded! Robert glanced back and saw that Mr. Ben had been right. Britannia had been jostled in the start, and Isaac nearly unseated. As Britannia stumbled, Arrowhead rushed to a commanding lead.

Through the first bottleneck and along the long first curve, Arrowhead ran easily. Robert was trying to rein him in. Arrowhead was clearly enjoying being out in front. As they entered the short straight stretch between the two long curves, Robert glanced back. Arrowhead was clear of the pack by more than twenty yards. Britannia had recovered from his poor start and was leading the pack, closing quickly.

It was in the second long curve, just before the hairpin, that Britannia caught and passed Arrowhead. Isaac smiled as his magnificent gray stallion raced by. Robert hoped that Mr. Ben was right about the hairpin curve. Just as he had been practicing the running start, be had practiced the tricky maneuver needed to slow his horse from a full gallop to a near stop, make the turn and then get back up to speed. As they approached the turn, it was clear to Robert that Isaac had entered the turn too fast. Britannia stumbled, losing a step. One step was all Arrowhead needed to take the lead headed down the final straightaway.

Arrowhead was ahead! But the early lead had cost him. He was tiring and Robert could feel his horse giving out. With about a hundred yards to go, Britannia was closing fast. In all their training, Robert had never needed to use his whip. He would simply show it to Arrowhead, and the horse would respond with a new burst of speed. Robert tried that now, but Arrowhead had nothing left!

"I have got to win this race! I have got to win this race!" Robert kept repeating to himself. With eighty yards to go, Britannia's head was right beside Robert. Without thinking, Robert took his whip and slashed. The whip came down right in Britannia's eye.

Searing pain caused Britannia to rear, and when he came down awkwardly on his extended right front leg, the bone snapped. Britannia fell head first, and rolled. Isaac was thrown, landing unconscious on the center of the track. The huge, tightly bunched, pack of horses that followed could not avoid both horse and rider. Isaac was trampled to death.

Robert had seen, out of the corner of his eye, Britannia rear up. He knew that his whip had caused it. But he had not seen the horse stumble. He did not see Isaac being trampled. Though he hadn't seen, he knew something was wrong. The crowd wasn't cheering his victory. The crowd was focused on the horses and riders that were down on the track. Three more horses, which couldn't avoid Britannia, had stumbled and fallen. Two of the horses which trampled Isaac, were so thrown off stride that they unseated their riders.

Robert and Arrowhead crossed the finish line in victory. But it was a hollow victory, at best. Looking back and seeing all the carnage on the track, Robert pulled Arrowhead to a halt, quickly dismounted, handed the reins to Mr. Ben, and made his way back down the track.

Britannia was so badly injured that he couldn't stand. Robert saw a man from the crowd of onlookers take out his pistol and shoot him, putting the stallion out of its misery. Four other horses were so badly injured that they were also put down.

Alexander Johnston rushed from the sidelines to confront Robert. "You, son of a bitch!" He yelled at Robert. "You killed my horse!" He shook his cane in Robert's face and said, "I'll kill you for this."

Many hands reached out to restrain the furious judge and to drag him away from Robert. Robert was sorry about the death of the beautiful horse. Really sorry. But he was more focused on Isaac. Isaac's mother, Rebecca, was holding the trampled body of her son, weeping uncontrollably. Robert knelt beside her. He wanted to say something, anything. Robert knew what no one else knew. He had intentionally hit Britannia. He had, from his point of view, murdered Isaac.

Robert had no words for Rebecca. As other blacks emerged from the crowd to comfort Rebecca and remove her son's body from the track, Robert determined that he would at least try to apologize to Alexander Johnston. He made his way through the crowd and found Alexander Johnston, surrounded by the same group of people who had separated him from Robert just minutes before. Robert extended his hand to the judge and said, "I'm really sorry about Isaac."

Alexander Johnston refused to take Robert's hand. "You killed my horse!"

"I'm sorry about that, too. But aren't you concerned about Isaac?"

"A little nigger boy? I can buy another one tomorrow. But I can never replace Britannia! Get out of my face, you son of a bitch!"

I had been watching the race from a place about half way from the hairpin to the finish. I had seen Britannia fall, knew that Robert had won the race, and seen the carnage that followed. I ran from where I had been standing, finally catching up with Robert, just as the judge threatened him, once again, with his cane. I took Robert by the arm and led him away.

It was the general consensus of the crowd that the deaths of Isaac and the horses were 'just racing.' No one, except the judge, blamed Robert personally. And the people were willing to forgive the judge for promising to kill Robert. They figured it was just talk in the heat of the moment.

But from that moment on, the feud between the Johnstons and the Tylers became personal. Alexander Johnston swore, to himself, that he would hate Robert Tyler for the rest of his life, and that he would do whatever it took to destroy him.

The next day Robert went to Isaac's burial in the slave cemetery at Yadkin Oaks. Except for David Hayworth, the plantation overseer, and his son Horace, Robert was the only white person there. Again, he could think of no words to say, but he did slip his arm around Rebecca and silently held her as she wept.

The Hayworths were furious. "You don't never hug no nigger in public," David Hayworth had said to Robert when he confronted him about it. "You'll make 'em think dey's as good as white folk." Robert had hardly gotten off the plantation before the Hayworths had informed Alexander Johnston of his "consorting with the niggers." The judge was as angry as the Hayworths.

The next Sunday, Robert went to church, thankful that it was communion Sunday. He was looking forward to saying the prayer of confession. He had said it many times before. But today, he really needed to confess. He also needed to hear the words of assurance which always followed, "If we confess our sins, he is faithful and just to forgive us our sins and cleanse us from all unrighteousness."

As he worshipped, Robert realized that confession and forgiveness were not enough. He promised God that he would lead a doubly good life. He was determined to live a life that made up for the life that was lost and would honor Isaac's memory. He was equally determined to live a life that was worthy of his own heritage, the memories that he had of Oskar Schoenfeldt, Thomas Barnes, and his father, Joshua Tyler.

He also resolved to bear the hatred of the judge, and all that the judge may do to him, with dignity. After all, he deserved it.

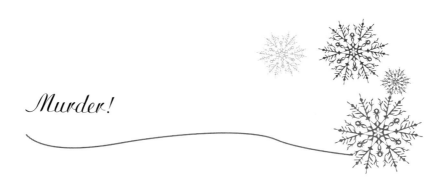

Murder!

IT WAS ONLY TWO DAYS AFTER THE trip to Hanging
Rock, just after dawn, that Ben Randolph came limping out
of the stable and saw the billowing clouds of black smoke coming
from the manor house. Because of rheumatism in his feet, ankles,
knees and every other part of his body, Ben Randolph couldn't
run. In fact, he could hardly walk. He knew that when he got to
the alarm bell, his arthritic hands would not allow him to pull
the rope.

Thinking as fast as he could, Ben Randolph decided that
the closest place he would find help would be the community
kitchen. The cooks always got there early to prepare breakfast for
the few people who would come; but more importantly, to get
started on preparing lunch for the hundred or more people who
would enjoy it. Ben figured that if he saw anybody else along the
way to the kitchen, he would just tell them to go ring the alarm
bell. The community knew that a constant ringing of the kitchen's
huge bell, normally used to summon people to meals, was the
alarm for fire.

People from all over the estate would run to join the fire
brigade. The strongest men would stay near the well to raise the
buckets full of water. The ingenious system that Mr. Oskar had

developed years ago of having numerous buckets on one rope, attached to a large pulley, to make lifting that amount of weight possible, was still in place in the main well.

Ben Randolph did not encounter anyone between the stable and the kitchen. He hurried as fast as his bent and aching legs would allow him, burst through the door of the kitchen, and yelled, "Fire! The manor house is on fire." He collapsed, exhausted, on a stool near the door where the cooks often sat as they waited for their dishes to finish cooking.

At first, the stunned cooks just looked at him. But then one realized that somebody had to ring the bell and that Ben couldn't do it.

She rushed out the door, glancing at the manor house, on her way to the bell. Nancy had never rung the bell so hard, so insistently, or for so long. It took a while to start stirring folk, but Nancy kept ringing that bell. As she did, she kept looking over at the manor house. Now, flames could be seen mixed with the smoke.

Nancy was sure, as she looked at the house, that she saw a man in a hooded cape, silhouetted by the light of the flames, run into the woods beyond the house.

When the ringing of the bell finally, after what seemed like hours, had an effect and the community began to stir, men rushed to the well to begin drawing water. To their horror, they found that the well had been sabotaged. Someone had cut the ropes and all of the buckets were at the bottom of the well.

"We need to lower someone into the well to grab the buckets so we can pull them up," Frederick Lowe, the manager of the Lynnmont Cheese Company, said. "It needs to be a child small enough to go down, but old enough to understand."

After a great deal of discussion, everyone agreed that Joe Culp, the six–year-old son of Jim and Mary Culp, would be the ideal candidate. He was small enough to go down the well easily, but old enough to understand the need and the urgency. The Culps lived in the third house to the right in the bunkhouses, where Elizabeth Ann McAdams used to live. Someone was sent to wake the Culps and get Joe, while someone else was sent to rouse everyone else in the bunkhouses. It was a large fire. Everyone was going to be needed.

Mary Culp was the only person who objected to the plan. "What do you mean that you are going to lower my son into the well? What if he gets stuck? What if the rope breaks? What if he panics and lets go?" Mary Culp had a thousand what if questions.

But Joe was sure that he could do the job. Frederick Lowe seemed to be taking charge. He tied a bowline, a loop knot that won't get any tighter. He slipped the loop around Joe's body so that it was secured under his arm pits. A lit candle was tied to a free rope and lowered into the well. Mary was instructed to pray that the candle stayed lit. Joe would need some light at the bottom of the well. Mary was praying for a lot more than that candle.

"When you get to the bottom of the well, some buckets should be floating," Mr. Lowe was saying to Joe. "Keep moving the buckets around until you find the end of the rope. When you do, tie that rope to the loop that's around you. Then yell for us to pull you up."

Frederick instructed all of the men who were standing by to grab the rope and help lower Joe into the well. "It will be much heavier when we go to pull him up, because many of the buckets will be filled with water," he said.

Mary wasn't the only one worrying as Joe was lowered into the well. Fortunately, the candle stayed lit, and Joe could see quite well. He saw a lot of buckets, but he had a difficult time finding the end of a rope. When he finally did, he realized that he didn't know how to tie a knot. He panicked and yelled up to Mr. Lowe that he didn't know what to do. Mr. Lowe, somehow, calmly talked the little boy through tying a knot. He just prayed that it worked. If it didn't, the house would just have to burn down.

He couldn't believe that they had lowered this little child down a well.

Yelling that he had done the best, Joe asked to be pulled up. At first, the men were stunned by the weight. Water is, after all, very heavy. But slowly they made progress and Joe emerged from the well with the well rope tied securely to his rope. "No sailor could have done better," Frederick said, as he patted Joe on the head. Mary grabbed Joe and held him.

"I told you I could do it," Joe said loudly to his mother, so that everyone could hear. And then he whispered in her ear, "But I don't want to do it again."

Frederick Lowe took charge of threading the rope through the pulley system, the fire brigade was finally in force. Bucket, after bucket, after bucket of water was passed down the line and poured on the fire. The east wing of the house, a one-story section that served as an office for Mr. Tyler, was engulfed. Fortunately, the fire seemed to be contained to that room. The door which separated that section from the main house must be closed.

Everyone thought out loud as they battled to get the flames under control:

"It's a good thing that Mr. Tyler is away."

"The fire has to be arson. Look what the arsonist did to the well."

"Did you see that man in the hooded cape?"

"Mr. Tyler's horse and carriage are in the barn. He must have come home sometime last night."

Men, women and children all joined in the bucket brigade. The children usually passed the empty buckets on the return trip. Joe Culp was given the honor of hooking the empty buckets to the rope. For more than an hour, buckets were passed until finally the fire had been brought under control. The east wing of the house was totally destroyed. The main part of the house certainly had smoke damage, but it could be cleaned and aired out.

Everyone's speculation about the inside door had been correct. The solid oak-paneled door had suffered considerable damage on the fire side, but it had not burned through. That door probably saved the rest of the house. In the east wing some of the ceiling and the roof had collapsed into the room, making it difficult to deal with the "hot spots," embers that could flame up again. The men used heavy iron rakes to break up the embers. Smaller embers could then be doused with water.

As the men were raking and moving pieces of the collapsed roof and ceiling, they discovered the body of Robert Tyler. It was so badly burned that it was unrecognizable and impossible to move. The decision was made to bring a coffin to the spot and place the remains of the body, just as it was, into the coffin. It was the most gruesome task that the men had ever faced.

Death was such an ever-present reality at Lynnmont that the cabinetmaker, who was also the coffinmaker, always had several in stock. One that he was especially proud of had been made of solid cherry. The rich, dark reddish wood would be a fitting memorial to Mr. Tyler. The cabinetmaker and three other men set out to retrieve it from his shop. As they did so, the word spread quickly that Robert Tyler had died in the fire. As they placed the body in the coffin, they discovered a knife stuck between Robert's ribs; it was clear evidence of murder.

Ben Randolph couldn't walk very well, but he could still drive a wagon. He had one of the stable boys harness a gentle mare named Rose to one of the small carriages in the barn. He mounted the seat of the carriage with help from the stable boy and set out for Germantown. Someone had to tell me that Robert Tyler was dead, and Ben Randolph thought that he was the man for the job.

As Ben rode along, he wondered about the man in the cape that so many people had seen. Had he been the arsonist? Was he also a murderer? Ben thought that he must be. He wondered who would hate Robert Tyler so much that he would murder him and then try to cover up the murder with a fire. When he got to the office of the Tyler Companies and told me about Robert's death, Ben got the impression, he told me later, that I didn't seem surprised at all.

But I was saddened. My best friend was dead. Much sooner than I could have imagined, I had a funeral to plan, and a funeral sermon to write. I had preached many funerals as the lay pastor at New Salem, but I had never done the funeral of such a good friend. As Ben and I left my office, I noticed something strange; my fool's gold rock paper weight was missing from my desk.

As Ben and I rode back to Lynnmont, I broke down. Tears began to flow uncontrollably down my face. Ben had seen me cry like this once before when a coffin was placed on the back of a wagon in front of a plantation house beside the Albemarle Sound. I knew that these tears would be tears of healing and that the more I cried now, the more powerful the funeral sermon would be. I sat in the carriage seat, blinded by my tears. Ben wasn't really driving the carriage; he had headed Rose in the right direction. She knew the way back home, and instinctively knew that a slow walk was just the right pace.

At exactly the same time on the other side of the Sauratown Mountains, a fire destroyed many of the files and records in the Register of Deeds office. Unfortunately, the *Richmond Weekly* reported later, Registrar of Deeds Bruce Smithwell had said nearly all of the records from the Tyler Law Firm were destroyed.

Immediately after the discovery of the knife in Robert's side, Franklin Campbell rode to Richmond to inform Sheriff Richard Speight of the murder. Sheriff Speight was on the scene the next day, interviewing everyone at Lynnmont who might shed some light on the crime. There was, of course, the caped man that many people had seen. But that wasn't much to go on. The sheriff announced, after just one day of investigation, that, except for the knife, there was no evidence. "Unless somebody talks, I don't know if this case will ever be solved," he told me. I told him

I thought he was giving up mighty easily, but he assured me he would continue the investigation.

Three days later, on September 25, 1806, the funeral for Robert Joseph Tyler was held, as he requested, at New Salem Methodist Church. I thought that it was appropriate to ask the Reverend Ebert of Bethania Moravian Church to preside. Reverend Ebert would add a note of dignity and decorum that I was sure that I would be unable to provide.

If every seat was taken, the little Methodist Church could seat only about 100 people. Another forty or so could stand up around the inside walls of the building. Fortunately, Indian summer had come streaming up from the south and it was so warm that the windows and doors of the Church could be opened. North Carolina weather is so fickle. Just a few days before, I had watched crystal snow fall at Hanging Rock. Today the temperature was in the seventies. I figured that at least four hundred people had gathered to honor Robert Tyler. I knew that more people came out to a funeral when there was a tragedy, especially if the deceased is young. I also knew that funerals of important business and professional people drew a crowd. For all these reasons, I had expected a big crowd. But this big crowd was different somehow; there was a loving spirit about them. A group of people who actually loved Robert Tyler had gathered at New Salem and were seeking peace. I, John Barnes, a Free Man of Color and Methodist lay preacher, was going to try and give it to them...and find some serenity for myself as well.

I have to admit, however, that I was stunned when Reverend Ebert and I made our way into the sanctuary. I saw seated on the front row Judge Alexander Johnston. One of the ushers had found a seat for the judge, even though he had arrived late. I supposed that one of the members of our church had given up his seat for a man of such importance.

When it came time for me to preach, I rose, dressed in the preaching robe that Robert had made possible with a gift to the church. I began in a loud and confident voice. I knew that I needed to be heard, even by the hundreds that were gathered outside.

While thinking about this service of love and remembrance for Robert Tyler, I found myself wishing that it might follow the pattern set by our Quaker Friends. If it did, we would gather quietly, and have no one person appointed to speak. All would sit in silence, each busy with his own thoughts. It is not hard to imagine what thoughts would fill our minds about our brother, Robert Tyler.

"At least a few among us would think of the great gift of life. We never appreciate life as much as when we linger in the presence of death. When I think of Robert in the days to come, I will think of life. Robert loved life and lived it to the fullest. When we think of life, we think of our capacity to dream, to hope, and to do. We are reminded of our ability to love and to be loved. When we think of life, we give thanks to God, from whom our spirits came and to whom they shall return. When I think of life, I will think of Robert who dared to love his fellow man because he had tasted the fullness of love.

"Others, especially those here who are older, would think about the brevity of life. They would remember when they were children, and the years seemed endlessly long. Those years are but as yesterday now that they have passed, a little more than a "watch in the night" as Psalm 90 tells us. There are many here who have lived beyond the allotted span of life, and their lives will "soon be cut off" and they "will fly away." That is why Psalm 90 admonishes us to "number our days." Only the possibility of a rich fullness offsets the brevity of life. Unfortunately, for Robert, he did not live his allotted time. His life was cut off, apparently by an evil hand. But while he lived, he lived life to the fullest. He loved. He laughed. He dreamed. He sometimes failed. And his life was cut off. Sometimes, life isn't fair.

"Still others, at times like these, think of their own dear and faithful loved ones who have died. They rest in their graves, waiting that wonderful day of resurrection, asleep in the arms of Jesus. I can't think of a more wonderful place to be than in the loving arms of our Lord. Robert has joined so many others that I have loved—my father and Robert's father, and my mother—and he has joined those whom you have loved and lost, the "great cloud of witnesses" as the Book of Hebrews calls them. We cherish the memories of those who have left us, whose faces we can no longer see and whose voices we can no longer hear. But somewhere deep within, we do see and we do hear. And what we see and hear offers us peace.

"If we were at a Quaker service, someone, moved by the spirit, would rise to pray. In the prayer, no matter what was said, we would be reminded of our need to pray, to communicate with our Heavenly Father, to grow so close to him that we can call him "Abba." It is in times like these that we need an Abba, a Father God who will surround us with love and encourage us with hope.

"If we were at a Quaker service, many would speak about Robert whose life on earth has ended, but whose life with God goes on. We would speak of his accomplishments in business, his work as a lawyer to help the disadvantaged, his time in the Legislature, and of his capacity to be a friend. And we would give thanks to God for all of these things.

"But of course, this is not a Quaker service, but a Methodist one. And so, we will speak not just of Robert whom we have loved and lost, but we will also speak of Jesus Christ, who has loved us. He has risen from the grave that we might have life and have it everlastingly. He said to his disciples, 'Peace I leave you. My peace I give unto you. Not as the world gives do I give unto you. Let not your hearts be troubled, and neither let them be afraid.'

"I don't know about you. But I am pretty sure that whether we are Quaker, Baptist, Moravian or Methodist we need that peace. It's a peace that passes all understanding. I can't put it into words. But I am glad that God has given it to me. Otherwise, I could not bear the loss of so dear a friend."

As I finished the sermon and said 'Amen,' nearly every person there said 'Amen' in response. Four hundred people saying 'Amen' will give peace to any preacher.

Unfortunately, my peace didn't last long. As the pallbearers picked up the beautiful cherry casket and turned to leave the church with Reverend Ebert and me in the lead, I heard Alexander Johnston mutter under his breath, "He got just what he deserved." I couldn't imagine such hatred.

Robert's casket was placed on the back of one of the estate's simple flatbed wagons. It was being pulled by a team of the most beautiful Percherons at Lynnmont. Ben Randolph sat proudly on the driver's seat. I knew that there had been a lot of discussion about who would be given the honor of driving the hearse. I was glad that Ben had been chosen.

Every person at the funeral joined the procession from New Salem to the estate cemetery. There were so many wagons and carriages that it took almost an hour for the procession to make its way. The men of the community had gathered together the night before to dig the grave. As they took turns digging in the rock filled, clay soil, they reminisced about Robert, they speculated about his death, and they conjectured about who the man in the cape might be. After the burial service was completed, many of the same men lowered the cherry coffin into the ground and then began to fill the grave with dirt that they have piled up from the digging. There would be dirt left over. But the men had learned to keep the extra soil nearby. It would be needed in the months to come to fill the grave as the coffin deteriorated.

Robert had instructed me to wait one month before I opened the packet that contained the will. In the interim I watched and listened carefully. The first sign that Judge Johnston was at work was so blatant that many residents of Germantown could see it. In the week after the funeral, a group of thugs, armed with Kentucky rifles, wearing masks and capes, raided Robert's law firm. They forced the clerks and young lawyers to leave the building. While some of the men stood outside with their guns at the ready, other men created as much havoc inside the building as possible. They went through the files of the firm, tearing out pages of documents and littering the floor with them. The judge rightly knew that any good law firm would have copies of every document that it had sent to the Register of Deeds office. The thugs' purpose was not only to destroy the firm, but to cause as much mayhem as possible. It would take months for the clerks to sort through all the documents and put them back in their right order. Some of the deeds and other documents had been so badly damaged that they would never be restored. In the meantime, the firm was essentially shut down.

The second attack was much simpler and more subtle. The Carolina Charcoal Company, the business that had been providing charcoal for thirty years to fire the kiln at the Tyler Brick Company suddenly announced that they would no longer sell charcoal to the Tyler Companies. Charcoal was essential for the process because the burning of regular wood would not produce a fire hot enough to season the clay into hard and durable bricks. In the early days of the company, Mr. Schoenfeldt had tried to fire the bricks with oak fires instead of charcoal. The result was soft bricks that crumbled easily. I knew that Tyler Brick was the largest account that the Carolina Charcoal Company had. Five or six wagon loads of charcoal were delivered every day. Only pressure of an extraordinary kind would have caused them to cut off sales.

Fortunately, Cecil Cherry, manager of Tyler Brick, believed that having a large surplus of raw materials on hand was essential to running any large business successfully. As a result, a three month's supply of charcoal was stored in a covered shelter adjacent to the kiln. I hoped that the crisis would be over before our supply ran out and we would be able to negotiate a renewal of sales.

Everyone in Surry County knew of the enmity between the Johnstons and the Tylers. Judge Johnston was Robert Tyler's most antagonistic political opponent. The judge was an anti-constitutional, state's rights advocate. Robert Tyler had worked ceaselessly for the adoption of the US Constitution. He was deeply saddened that Judge Johnston and his allies had delayed North Carolina's acceptance of the Constitution so that it was the twelfth of the colonies to actually become a state. The State was so late in approving the Constitution that it had not even been allowed to participate in the first presidential election. And the Judge was also a business opponent. Lynnmont competed with Yadkin Oaks, the Judge's Plantation, as the two largest and most successful enterprises in the county. Because the judge was a Superior Court Judge for the western District of North Carolina, he and Robert were often in the courtroom at the same time. Even though he was required by law to remain unbiased in cases that were brought before him, the judge always made life in the court as miserable as he could when Robert Tyler was leading the defense.

On and on the rivalry went. So far, the judge had done nothing to expose his involvement in the attacks. But Robert had been right. It had taken the judge less than a month to study the Tyler Companies and see where their weakest points were. It was there that he decided to attack.

As I thought about what the judge was doing, it became obvious to me that the dairy was our next most vulnerable point. The cows could be poisoned. The milk could be contaminated. The milk and butter routes could be interrupted. It seemed to me that the dairy might be the one part of the company that might have to be temporarily sacrificed.

In one more week, I would open Robert's package. The letter would give me instructions. I was looking forward to seeing what Robert had planned for me to do.

Unfortunately, I had been right about the dairy. Five days later, a rumor spread along the milk and butter routes that the cows at Lynnmont had drunk contaminated water. The result was, according to the rumor, that all of the milk and other dairy products were not fit for human consumption. Immediately, sales fell. I moved quickly to shut down the dairy and the cheese production. We would keep the cows and milk them daily. But the milk would just be poured on the ground. We would keep all of the cheese products that we had on hand. After the crisis was over, we would reopen the dairy and the cheese factory under a new name. Robert's $2,000 fund was going to come in handy to pay the workers until production could resume.

Two days later, I went in to my room and closed the door. Sally and the children knew that the only time I ever closed the bedroom door was when I was praying or writing a sermon. They knew not to disturb me; I needed to be alone.

I took the large packet Robert had given me from its hiding place in the bottom of the wardrobe. I broke the seals, dumping the contents on the bed. One unsealed envelope contained at least $100. I found another unsealed envelope addressed to me, a list of names and what appeared to be topics by each, a letter in a sealed envelope addressed to me and a letter entitled "Instructions for the Funeral Banquet." There was a leather pouch, tied with a string and sealed with wax; the note on the pouch instructed me to deliver the pouch to Dr. Richard Allen. Further instructions required Dr. Allen to bring the pouch to the reading of the will. Finally, there was another sealed letter "To Be Opened and Read at the Funeral Banquet of Robert Joseph Tyler" and a large sealed envelope labeled "the Last Will and Testament of Robert Joseph Tyler."

Funeral banquet. Those two words jumped out at me. What in the world was a funeral banquet? I had never heard of such a thing. We had already had a funeral for Robert.

Maybe his letter would explain it. I found the unsealed letter and opened it.

Dear John,

If you are reading this letter, I have been dead for a month. I want to thank you for preaching at my funeral. I cannot imagine a more difficult task than preaching the funeral of a friend. But I am sure that you handled it with grace.

What I am asking you to do now is unique. It is a way for Alexander Johnston to be exposed as the man that he truly is. And, much more importantly, it is an opportunity for me to introduce myself to my son, a young man that I have never met.

I stopped reading. Robert had a son? Robert had shocked me at Hanging Rock when he announced that he had been married. Now he tells me that he has a son. I went back to the letter.

I only recently learned that I had a son. Matthew Brown was more than a night watchman. I had hired him some months before he came to watch the office to see if he could find Lynn. He came back with the story that will be shared at the funeral banquet.

At the same time that he discovered what happened to Lynn, he uncovered the plot to assassinate me. If you are reading this letter, Judge Johnston succeeded in his plot before I could arrange to meet my son.

John, you will have two major tasks. The first is to gather the persons who are listed as beneficiaries in my will. You will find a list of them along with a story that I would like for each of them to tell. When all of the stories are told, it should give my son a good picture of his father. There is a letter enclosed that certifies that you are the Executor of my Will and will have the authority to read the will at the conclusion of the funeral banquet.

The second task you will have is to make all of the arrangements for the funeral banquet: to moderate the banquet, to introduce each speaker, and, if you think that it is necessary, to respond to each speaker. I would like for the funeral banquet to be held at New Salem. The reasons for holding the banquet at a church will become obvious as the will is read. The letter entitled "Instructions for the Funeral Banquet" will guide you.

John, it will be difficult to accomplish this task. There will be persons who will be reluctant to come. There will be persons who will reject you because of your station. This is where a copy of your Letter of Emancipation may avail you to good purpose. It is crucial that this banquet be held in as close to one month from this date as possible. Judge Johnston needs to have moved far enough along in his plot to destroy the Tyler Companies that he might be exposed, but not so far that his damage is irreversible.

You will need to work nearly full time for the next month on this project. I have included money to cover your travel expenses and the expenses for those who will be coming from some distance to the banquet. I have also asked Mordecai Jones from the law firm to be ready to step into your position at the Tyler Companies, temporarily. He will be ready to come when you initiate this move.

I know that I have given you a difficult task. Only a good friend would ask such a thing. And only a good friend would willingly submit. I know that you will handle everything with your usual grace.

Remember that I am with you, even if it is in spirit only.

Robert

I sat, pondering for a moment, why Robert thought that it would be difficult to get people to come to the funeral banquet, when I happened to glance at the list of beneficiaries. One of the names that jumped out at me from the page was Judge Alexander Johnston.

Like I said, I usually prayed when I was upstairs in my room with the door shut. I can't remember ever praying more fervently.

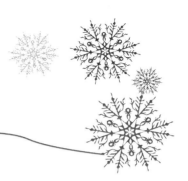

Gathering Storytellers

As I PONDERED ALL THAT NEEDED TO be accomplished to make the funeral banquet happen, nothing seemed as difficult as the gathering of the beneficiaries. I had to convince them that they could receive their portion of the estate only if they agreed to attend the funeral banquet, share their assigned story, and remain throughout the entire event.

Fortunately, most of the people on the list lived in Surry County. There were a couple of people who lived in the Shenandoah Valley of Virginia and one who lived in Chapel Hill. I would take a full day to travel to Chapel Hill and a full day back. It would take me three day's each way to go to the Shenandoah.

I looked at the list and read it again:

Mamie Smith, Cook at Lynnmont Estate, "Stealing Cookies," Lives at Lynnomnt

John Barnes, Manager of the Tyler Companies, "A Day at the Gristmill," Lives in Germantown

Dr. Richard Allen, Professor of Law at UNC, "My Most Difficult Student, Lives on Franklin Street in Chapel Hill

Alexander Johnston, Judge of Superior Court, "Why I Hate Robert Tyler," Lives at Yadkin Oaks Plantation, Surry County

Horace Hayworth, Former Surry County Sheriff, "Arresting Robert Tyler," Lives in Yadkinville in room above Stone's Tavern

Emily Gladstone, Nurse at Apple Blossom Sanatorium, "A Lady Named Lynn," Lives in Harrisonburg, Virginia on the grounds of the Sanatorium

Gilbert Stanley, Captain in the North Carolina Militia, "Standing Before the Cavalry," Lives at Oakmont Plantation, Guilford County, North Carolina

Lawrence Weeks, Lawyer with the Tyler Firm, "Cherokees are People, Too," Lives in Germantown

Franklin Campbell, Estate Foreman at Lynnmont, "Keeping Ben Randolph," Lives at Lynnmont

Abigail Jordan, Maid at Salem Tavern, "Greeting President Washington," Lives in Salem at the Single Sister's House

Adam Robertson, Lives in Harrisonburg, Virginia with John and Emily Gladstone at the Apple Blossom Sanatorium.

As I studied the list, I thought that it would be incredibly difficult to convince Judge Johnston. I also figured that Adam Robertson must be Robert's son since he had no story to tell. I assumed that all the rest knew Robert Tyler, although I wasn't sure about Emily Gladstone. I also wasn't sure what the various stories were about. I knew the one that I was being asked to tell, of course. I thought I might know about Franklin Campbell's, but that was all.

As I sat there, I realized that I was actually looking forward to hearing the stories. I was going to learn some things about Robert that I didn't know, but it was a long time before I would hear them. First, I had to get the people to New Salem Methodist Church on Saturday, November 29, the date I had selected.

I made the decision to go to Harrisonburg first. Emily Gladstone and Adam Robertson would need the greatest amount of notice and travel time. They would have to make numerous travel arrangements. I would then leave the Shenandoah, go down to Yadkinville, then to Salem, and on to Chapel Hill. I could stop in Guilford County either on the way to Chapel Hill or on my return. The people who lived in Germantown and Lynnmont would be my last assignments.

I wondered how I was supposed to do this job and keep an eye on Judge Johnston. Robert's insistence on timing had to come into play. In the month it would take me to gather some of the beneficiaries, compel the others to attend the funeral banquet, and make all of the arrangements for the banquet, Judge Johnston could make one final move to destroy the Tyler Companies or Lynnmont. I would not be there stop him.

I had told Sally about my upcoming adventure and showed her the list and all the instructions about the funeral banquet. *How in the world am I going to convince Judge Johnston?* I wondered aloud.

"Robert gave you the answer. He said it would be difficult, but to use your grace," Sally said as she held out the Letter of Instruction. "You'll find a way. You'll have at least three days on the road to Harrisonburg and three more after you go to Harrisonburg to ponder. Even someone as dumb as you can figure it out in six days," she said, laughing. "After all, the whole world was created in six days."

"I don't know," I said. "I'm mighty dumb. I married you, didn't I?" I asked as I reached out to hug her. The embrace that I received from Sally needed to be a good one. It needed to encourage me and to sustain me on a long and difficult journey. She understood exactly, took my hand, led me up stairs, and reminded me that there was another reason for closing the bedroom door.

The next morning, Betsy and I started out for Harrisonburg. Because traveling alone was always dangerous, I had asked one of the young dairymen, who wasn't needed at Lynnmont these days, to ride along with me. William Pittman was glad for the adventure and I was glad to have the company, except that I soon learned that it was difficult to ponder with a very talkative William alongside. He rode one of the mares from the estate and we brought along a pack horse on which we carried everything that we would need for a two-week adventure. I was using a special saddle for the pack horse that had secret pockets sewn into its underneath sides. Into these pockets, I had spread out the $100 that Robert had given me. I had never seen a saddle like this; it had been specially made in the leather shop at Lynnmont. Even though I knew the pockets were there, they were so well hidden that even I had trouble finding them.

We needed to go north through Fancy Gap and then continue up to Big Lick, a natural salt lick where buffalo, elk, deer, bear and other kinds of animals gathered every day to share the space and to enjoy the salt. Big Lick was right at the southern entrance to the Shenandoah and Harrisonburg was about halfway up the valley.

Even though the roads hugged the valley floor, we were constantly moving upward. The country was absolutely beautiful, even though the leaves were gone because of the early onset of fall. When we finally reached the Shenandoah, William and I were stunned at how wide the valley was. There were places where we could see mountain ranges on each side. I didn't know what the mountains were called, but I knew that we needed to continue to follow the valley until we would come to Harrisonburg.

Because William and I had brought provisions, there was no need for us to find lodging each night. We had an old army tent that one of the men on the estate had brought back from the war. I was quite proficient at using flint and steel for making a fire. William could erect the tent in no time. We could settle down pretty quickly for the night. We had folding camp stools and would use them to sit by the fire and talk.

William was a teenager who had had almost no education. He had come to the estate looking for a job after his father had been imprisoned on a horse stealing charge. William had decided that having one less mouth to feed would be a blessing to his mother. He struck out on his own hoping to make a little money to send back to her. He had been raised in the Blue Ridge Mountains, not far from Roaring Gap where most of the fields were no more than two or three acres. His family had a small farm in the top lands along a ridge. His father constantly talked of buying some bottom land along the valley floor where the soil was richer; but he and his wife were stuck on a ten-acre farm in a small, one-room, log cabin with seven children and another on the way. William's father had run up a bill of over $10.00 at the general store and had a $2.00 payment owing on the land. His crop of corn that year had failed completely. He had hoped to get $4.00, or even as much as $4.25, per acre which would have made it possible for him to pay off his debts and even have enough to make a down payment on a piece of bottom land. Instead, he had a huge debt and no way to pay it.

During the summer months, in between planting and reaping time, William's father had been hunting for deer and had come upon the most beautiful workhorse he had ever seen a couple of valleys away. Several months later, in desperation after his crops had failed, without giving it any thought, he made his way to the farm where he had seen the horse, put a bridle on it and led it straight to his cabin. He tied it to the front porch and went inside to ponder how he would sell it. The owner of the horse and the sheriff's deputy simply followed the oversized tracks of the oversized horse. William's father was arrested and pled guilty. His family was left destitute.

William had learned several things living in the mountains, and one of them was how to shoot. So, I was glad to have William along. I had promised him an extra $2.00 pay if he got me to Virginia and back safely but only if he would promise to send the money to his mother. William may have been a good shot, but it didn't matter how good he was if he wasn't holding the gun. We were sitting by the fire, in front of the tent, with the rifle leaning against the tent pole, when the highwaymen pounced on us.

There were three rough-hewn backwoodsmen. One of them fired his rifle; I think more to shock us than anything else. It worked, because both William and I froze for the couple of seconds they needed to grab control. Before either of us knew it, they had our gun, in addition to theirs. They rifled through everything that we had and were very disappointed that they could find no money. They did find, however, a couple of large bottles of wine from the Lynnmont Winery and they decided to take Betsy and the mare.

"We'll leave ya that ole pack horse," one of them said. "Would'n leave ya here wid nuddin." And they were gone.

William and I sat for a couple of minutes, stunned and shocked. Betsy, the best horse I ever had, was gone. The rifle was gone. William's horse was gone. Most of our provisions were gone. They had even stolen the wine. It was William who thought of it first.

"If you were a robber and you just stole two large bottles of wine, what would you do with them?" he asked me.

"I'd drink them."

"Exactly," William said. "We will follow them, wait for them to get so drunk that they fall asleep, and then take our things back."

Since they had horses of their own and were towing two others, they were not difficult to follow. They were less than a mile away in a holler beside a creek. When we got there, they were arguing over the wine. I wished then that there had been three bottles instead of two. I hoped that there would be enough wine to do the job. William and I sat quietly and waited. It was about an hour before all the wine was gone and another hour or so before they were all sound asleep.

"Do we take just what they stole from us, or do we take everything?" William whispered to me.

"We're not thieves," I whispered back. "Let's make sure that we take back everything that they took from us, including the empty wine bottles. When they wake up, they will have terrible hangovers and be very confused," I said. "What do you think of taking their horses and tying them to a tree a couple of miles from here? That will slow them down some more."

William thought I had a great idea! We stole quietly into the camp, carefully gathering up the things they had stolen from us. We then walked all of the horses down the lane. We probably went further than we needed to before we mounted our horses and rode at a gallop back to our camp. I was so grateful for the saddle with the hidden pockets. If the highwaymen had found that much money, they would have killed us to cover up their theft. As quickly as we could, we packed all of our things and headed up the road in the dark. About a mile from where we had camped, we tied the three extra horses to a large tree in the bend of the road.

"William," I said. "I'm going to give you a $2.00 bonus for that great idea. And I'll give you another $2.00 if you hold tight to your rifle the rest of the trip!" I knew that I was being very generous with Robert's money, but I didn't care.

When we got into Harrisonburg, we found a quaint little town. The Harrison family had built a mansion on the main street which dominated the whole area. Even without their leaves, I could tell that apple trees covered the landscape. The Apple Blossom Sanatorium was obviously named after the beautiful flowers that covered all these trees in the spring. When we got to Harrisonburg, I decided that William and I would spend a night in the town's inn and stable the horses. The horses needed a good cleaning, a hearty meal, and a good rest. The innkeeper told me that the sanatorium was just a half-mile walk down and around the hill.

I had taken the money from the saddle. I knew that I would need to give some to Emily Gladstone to cover the cost of her trip to Lynnmont. Later in the day, when I met Adam, I would need to give him some, as well. As I made my way around a curve in the road, the Apple Blossom Sanatorium loomed large before me. It was a huge, three-story rock structure with iron bars on the windows. A ten- or twelve-foot high rock wall surrounded the building with a massive iron gate, guarded by an armed sentry. Above the gate, in beautiful ironwork were the words "Apple Blossom Sanatorium" and underneath, on a less impressive painted sign were the words "Christian Care for the Insane".

When it was new, the building might have been beautiful, except for the iron bars. But years of use and lack of maintenance had made the once impressive building shabby. The woodwork of the building needed painting and the cedar shake shingles were so old and curled that I was sure the roof must leak terribly.

It was clear to me that the sentry was at the gate, not to keep people from entering, but to keep the wrong people from leaving. When I approached him, he lowered the rifle, smiled and spoke through the locked gate, "Good morning, Sir."

"Good morning. My name is John Barnes. If it is possible, I would like to see Emily Gladstone. I am sorry, but I do not have an appointment with her."

"I am sure that it will not be a problem, Sir," he said as he came forward to unlock the gate. "She usually uses the morning for fulfilling her administrative tasks. If I know Miss Emily like I think I do, she will be glad for the distraction that your arrival will bring."

The gate swung open and I entered, waiting as the sentry closed it behind me. It seemed strange to hear the clanging lock and know that I was locked inside a sanatorium for the insane. I was soon to learn that it was just the first of several locked doors that I would need to pass through to get to see Emily Gladstone. The sentry could not have been nicer as he moved me through the maze of doors. He looked vaguely familiar. But I dismissed that as being impossible. After all, I had never been in Harrisonburg in my life.

He took me to an office door and knocked gently. We both heard a soft voice from inside say, "Come in."

He opened the door and said, "There's a gentleman here to see you." He indicated by the nod of his head that I should enter the room. I did so, and he closed the door behind me.

"Ma'am, I'm John Wesley Barnes, the executor for the estate of Robert Joseph Tyler. I am here because you have been named as a beneficiary of his estate." I paused to let her grasp what I had said.

"Executor?" she questioned. "O how I had hoped to meet Robert in person one day. Though I never met him, I have never known a man who was loved so deeply."

"Did you know Robert through Lynn?" I asked.

"Yes," she said. "Did you know Lynn?"

"Only the little bit that Robert told me, just before his death."

We both sat in silence for a moment. I was remembering Robert. I assumed that Emily was thinking of Lynn. I decided that we both needed a change of subject. I said, "Tell me about the Sanatorium. Have you been here long?"

"My brother, sister, and I founded the sanatorium thirty years ago. It was a project of all of the Churches of the Brethren. My brother, John, is the chief administrator, and my sister, Susan, is the traveling ambassador. She tries to raise the money that we need. And I am the head nurse. All of the patients are really under my care. At first, we had tremendous funding and wonderful support; but, over the years, the churches have 'grown weary with well doing' as the Scripture says we might. Now we struggle daily to meet the needs. We never lose faith that God will supply.

"When we first started, we were so idealistic. We were all three in our twenties. We believed, with the enthusiasm of youth, that we could give these unfortunate people such compassionate care that they could be healed. Unfortunately, we found out that was not usually true. In fact, most people who are sent to us are so mentally ill that they are a danger to us and to themselves. They will never be healed. Our task, now, is to provide compassionate care.

"Can you believe that when we first built this facility there were no iron bars? There was no rock wall either. It didn't take us long to realize that we needed both. This is a very sad place, but, of all the people that have been here through the years, none has brought me more sadness than Lynn," she said as tears welled up in her eyes. She wasn't actually crying, but she did need to take the corner of her apron, which she wore as part of her nurse's uniform, to dry her eyes.

For a woman who was in her fifties, I thought she was beautiful. She was dressed in the plain, simple uniform of a Quaker nurse, but, in spite of that, there was a deep-seated beauty about her. My mother had taught me that 'beauty is only skin deep,' but in this case she would have been wrong. There was a loveliness about her that came from the depths of her being; a beauty that had touched her soul. I could tell that even though these sad people would wring every ounce of energy from her every day, she would come back the next day, renewed and refreshed by some inner strength. I was looking forward to the story that such a beautiful woman would tell.

"Robert would like for you to tell Lynn's story," I said. "He has instructed me, as the Executor of the Will, to ask that you come to a funeral banquet that will be held on November 29 at New Salem Methodist Church on the Lynnmont Estate in Surry County, North Carolina, and tell us what happened to Lynn."

"Lynnmont. Lynn's mountain. I love it," she said. "How long ago did he name his plantation after her?"

"It's been nearly twenty years, I guess. By the way, it's an estate not a plantation. It's a 15,000 acre estate and there is not a slave on the whole place." I was glad to be able to say that. Up until a few weeks ago, I couldn't.

"So he named his estate for her—right after she was taken from him."

"I think so. It might even have been just before she was taken. He looked for her the rest of his life. Her father did a good job of hiding her. Robert was told where she had been taken only a few days before he was murdered."

"Murdered?"

"Yes. I'm afraid so." I started to tell her more, but I didn't want her to know that the man who had ordered the murder would be at the funeral banquet. I was afraid that if she knew that, she might not agree to come. I decided to bring her back to the subject.

"Mr. Tyler's estate has authorized me to pay for your travel expenses. My companion and I were accosted by highwaymen on our journey to see you, so I will insist that you hire a carriage with appropriate guards and stay in secure inns along the way."

"I have never heard of a funeral banquet," she said. "What is that?"

"Well, to tell you the truth ma'am, neither have I. I am a preacher, and have been to a lot of funerals, but I have never been to a funeral banquet. But I think that the main purpose is for Mr. Tyler to introduce himself to his son. That is why every benefactor, except his son, will be asked to tell a story. All of the stories will give his son a picture of the kind of man that Robert Tyler was. Can I rely on you to be present?"

"Yes, I will be glad to come," she said. "And I will be honored to tell Lynn's story. I have never told it to anyone. Not even her son."

I was surprised that she had never told Adam about his mother, but I was sure that she had a good reason.

"Perhaps you can help me with something," I said. "I assume that Adam Robertson is Robert's son. I need to meet him. Obviously, he needs to be at the banquet."

"But you have already met him," she said. "He showed you to this room."

"No wonder he looked familiar! He looks like Robert!"

"I'll call for him," she said. "We can explain together. I promise you that he will be glad you came. He has always wanted to know about his parents. We have always told him that he was left at the Sanatorium and that the three of us were honored to raise him."

William and I had a more boring trip heading back south. With the $2.00 for his monthly salary, the $2.00 for going along with me on the trip, the $2.00 for his great idea, and his $2.00 for holding on to his gun, William announced to me that was close to being rich!

"Remember, you promised to send at least $2.00 of that back to your mom," I said.

"I'm a gonna send all of it back to her," he said. "Eight dollars is half a year's salary for us. I sleep for free in the barn at Lynnmont and I eat for free too. So I don't really need any money. I send everything back to mom. Because I have a paying job, in a couple of months, she will have all the debts paid. I wish some more robbers would come along, so I could come up with another great idea. I might cut that debt back to just one month," he said.

"You better watch out what you wish for," I said. "It just might come true. And you don't have but one bullet in that rifle, do you? How are you going to shoot more than one robber?"

We rode on in silence for a few miles. I was thinking about William's good fortune and it made me think of my own. Robert paid me very well. I made $240.00 a year as the manager of the Tyler Companies. I knew that amount was at least double what any of the managers of the other companies were making. I was now, because of Robert's largesse, living in a house that was paid for and on property that was mine. Most of the managers made fifty cents a day or roughly $150.00 a year. Their employees made anywhere from $2.00 to $8.00 per month depending on tenure and experience.

I was thrilled with my salary; but, because I kept the books, I knew that Robert could certainly afford to pay me. Lynnmont and the Tyler Companies were worth between $250,000 and $300,000. Most people dreamed of one day having a net worth of at least $1,000, but Robert had inherited two hundred times that much. He had worked very hard to increase the value of the estate that he had inherited, but there were people all across the area who resented his affluence. Most of their negativity was a petty jealously, not hatred. Most people, when they got to know him, warmed up to Robert.

Judge Alexander Johnston, on the other hand, was not a likeable man. I knew that many in the county respected and even admired him, but I did not. To me, he was a despicable man. I was biased against him, of course, because of his feud with Robert. Now that I knew how he had also treated his daughter and grandson, I had an even lower opinion of him. I was, reluctantly, headed to see him. William and I had headed west when we got through Fancy Gap so that we could be on the west side of the Sauratown Mountains. I was planning to go to Yadkinville first and convince Horace Hayworth, the former Sheriff, to attend the banquet. I knew that he was a racist and that I might have to deal with that, but I figured that his racism would be less of a test than Alexander Johnston's hatred.

In spite of my wife's assurance that I would be able to solve the riddle in six days of travel, I still wasn't sure how I was going to convince the judge. I was hoping for an epiphany. To tell the truth, a solution would have come sooner if I had not had to contend with William's constant chatter.

When we got into Yadkinville, I went directly to Stone's Tavern and asked if Mr. Hayworth was lodging in a room above the tavern.

"You talkin' bout Horace?" The proprietor asked. "He spends more time asittin in that thar chair," he pointed to a ladder back sitting by the potbelly stove, "spinning his yarns than he does upstairs in that room. If yer here collectin money, all ya gotta do is wait. He'll be 'long directly. Corse, you'll have to git in line 'hind all the udder collectors," he added.

"Actually, I'm not here to collect from Mr. Hayworth," I said. "I am here to see him on a legal matter. Can you direct me to his room?"

"Room rite at the top o the stairs," he said as, with his hand, he directed me up. "Knock loud. He's gittin a bit deaf."

After several loud knocks at the door produced no results, I decided to try the knob to see if the door was locked. It wasn't, and I gently pushed open the door. Horace Hayworth was sitting on his bed with his back to door, looking out the window. The door's swinging caused a shadow to cross the room. There was clearly nothing wrong with Horace Hayworth's eyesight.

He turned to face the door. Expecting the tavern's owner or the barman, he was clearly surprised.

"Who are you?" he asked. He held his hand up behind his good ear.

I shut the bedroom door behind me, moved in front of him, slightly to his right favoring his good ear and said, "Mr. Hayworth, I am the Executor of a Will. You are one of the beneficiaries." It had come to me, as I opened Mr. Hayworth's door that he didn't need to know my name. If he knew who I was, his racism might come spewing forth, but in this dimly lit room, I would look as much like a white man as anyone. My legal status would carry all of the weight I needed. As a former sheriff, he would honor the title of Executor.

Because of his deafness, it was a bit of a challenge to explain to him. But once it became apparent to him what he was being asked to do, he seemed genuinely eager to come share his story. He had a loathing for Judge Johnston that was every bit as deep as the judge had for Robert. He was looking forward to telling a tale which would make Judge Johnston look bad. He promised that I could depend on him being present; I thanked him and took my leave.

As I headed down the stairs, I thanked God for a dimly lit room. I knew that if Horace Hayworth had realized who I was, his prejudice against men of color could have overridden his hatred for the judge. Horace Hayworth was, it seemed to me, a little man who once held a big office.

As I left Stone's Tavern and stepped into the street, it was abundantly apparent that there was not much to this little crossroads community. Besides the tavern, there was Tottenham's General Store, a livery stable, and a collection of ten or twelve houses. The town existed because two roads happened to meet here, one headed along the Yadkin River valley and one running east and west from Guilford Court House to the North Carolina Mountains. I turned towards the livery where William had taken the horses to be groomed.

Having been well groomed and fed, Betsy seemed to have an extra spring in her step as we headed for Yadkin Oaks. She seemed eager for us to complete the journey. I wanted to drag things out longer, because I still had not figured out how I was going to approach Judge Johnston. I was so desperate that I even decided to ask William for his advice.

"He's gonna yell at ya when ya tell him why yer there, rite?" he asked. Before I could answer, he continued, "When he does, jest use yer preacher voice and yell louder than he does."

I was more than a little offended to know that anyone would think that my preaching voice could be considered yelling. I was also pretty sure that screaming at the judge would not seem very professional. It would also not be very graceful.

As we rode on, Yadkin Oaks and my encounter with the judge loomed ever nearer. I found myself hoping that the judge would not be at home. I tried to 'reread Robert's letter in my mind' trying to convince myself that the judge wasn't really on the list, after all. Despite my fantasies, as we came around a curve in the road, the judge's impressive plantation house dominated the hill that was in front of us.

Was Betsy actually speeding up? I pulled in her reins to slow her pace. I had planned, worried, fretted, and puzzled for days. Then it happened. Like a preacher who struggles all week to prepare a sermon, stands up on Sunday morning with no idea what to say, and has to trust completely in God, I finally received the answer from the Book of Jeremiah, "I will deliver thee out of the hand of the wicked, and I will redeem thee out of the hand of the terrible." It was time to trust in God and stop trusting in myself.

So many people, through the years of my ministry, had spoken of my grace. I had always known that it wasn't my grace but God's grace at work in me; but, I had never before had to trust God to deliver me from the hands of the wicked and the terrible.

Now, I found myself standing at the door of the most evil man that I had ever known. I knew he was responsible for the death of my best friend and was plotting, at this very moment, to destroy everything that Robert had ever loved or worked to build up. I knew he would gladly annihilate me as well. Yet, here I was, standing at his door. I was just about to turn and flee when I was ushered into the house's impressive parlor to wait for the judge.

"James, why have you brought this nigger into my house?" Judge Alexander asked his butler when he saw me. "You know niggers are supposed to wait at the servant's entrance; get this nigger out of my house!"

"I'ze sorry Massa. He don't look like no nigger to me." He stepped forward to take me by the arm, but before he could move me towards the door, I said "Judge Johnston, I am the Executor for the estate of Robert Joseph Tyler. You, sir, have been named as a beneficiary in Mr. Tyler's will."

"Impossible!" Judge Johnston shouted.

"Impossible that I am his executor or that you are a beneficiary?"

"Both," the Judge said. "James. Leave us."

As James closed the door to the parlor behind him, Judge Johnston said, "Robert Tyler may have been a scoundrel, but he knew the law. He knew a slave couldn't be named an Executor of a Will in North Carolina."

"You are right, Sir. Robert knew the law." I decided to let the judge lead the conversation. I took out the leather pouch that I had carried every day since September 19 and showed Judge Johnston my Letter of Emancipation. He read it very carefully, checking to see if there was any 'i' that Robert had not dotted or any 't' that he had not crossed.

"I suppose that you are the legal executor. But why would Robert Tyler remember me in his will? There isn't anything that he has that I want," he growled as he handed back the letter.

Before I knew what was coming from my mouth, I heard myself saying in a quiet but forceful voice, "That's strange; I was under the impression that you wanted everything that Robert Tyler had. You have certainly been working hard, before, and after his death, to put yourself in position to take over the Tyler Companies."

"I don't know what you are talking about. I have not set foot on that side of the Sauratown Mountains since that scoundrel's funeral."

"I'm sure that's true," I said. "But some of the people you have hired to do your will have not been entirely trustworthy. Some of your conversations have been overheard. Your entire plot is about to be exposed. The way I see it, you only have two chances to save yourself: the first is to complete your takeover without my being able to stop you; the second is to expose Robert Tyler before I am able to expose you."

I paused briefly, not sure if I was pausing so that I could breathe or that Judge Johnston could. Either way, I was emboldened to continue. "I believe that I have enough resources in place to stop your takeover of the Tyler Companies and Lynnmont."

I knew Judge Johnston would not consider me to be a worthy opponent. But I knew that I had just shaken him, perhaps to the core.

"Judge," I continued in a boldness that wasn't mine, "Robert has requested that you appear at the reading of his will, to tell those gathered for the reading why you hate him so. I believe that that is the best opportunity for you to expose him. By giving the reasons for your deep-seated hatred, if you are eloquent enough, you will have the opportunity to win over all of his supporters."

"If I am eloquent enough?" The judge said, clearly offended by the thought that he might not be. I could tell that he was also challenged by the thought, and intrigued by the opportunity, to expose Robert Tyler.

"I was under the impression that all of Robert Tyler's legal documents had been destroyed in the fire at the Register of Deeds office," Judge Johnston said. It was clear to me that he was fishing for information. Again, I let him lead the conversation.

"And by the band of hooligans that trashed the Tyler Law Firm," I added. "I am sure that copies of Mr. Tyler's will were destroyed in those incidents. He did, however, before his death, trust me with a copy of his will and copies of other important documents. I assure you that they are in my safekeeping." As I said this, I realized that the hidden compartment in my wardrobe at home was not as safe a location for these papers as I had thought. But I knew exactly where to put them.

"Robert's codicil to the will requires that all beneficiaries be present for the entire funeral banquet, tell the story that he has requested, and remain for the reading of the will."

"Funeral banquet?"

"Yes Judge. A luncheon will begin at noon on November 29 at New Salem Methodist Church. During this meal, all beneficiaries will share a story that Mr. Tyler has requested. Following the sharing of the stories, the actual last will and testament will be read. The codicil says that I have the power to compel you to appear, but I would rather not send deputies to your house. Can I rely on you to be present?"

"Yes," he sneered. "I will look forward to being especially eloquent. No one will leave that funeral banquet thinking well of Robert Tyler."

As I turned to leave the room, Judge Johnston asked me a question, "Other important documents?"

"O yes, Judge. Mr. Tyler left me every deed and contract that I would need to save his estate. If you are eloquent enough, you may leave the banquet with all of them."

"As I already said, I will look forward to being especially eloquent." He called for his butler. "See that this gentleman is ushered out of my house and off of my plantation," he told him.

The butler didn't need to do much 'ushering.' I was glad to go. William and I quickly headed off the Yadkin Oaks Plantation. I had planned to go next to Salem, but I knew, now, that I needed to make a detour to New Salem. The altar or communion table at New Salem was actually a three-sided, hollow table that sat against the back wall of the Church under the Cross. It would be the perfect place. No one would think to look inside the altar. I determined to move all of the documents there as soon as I could. Each time I needed a deed or a contract to save one of Robert's companies, I would just make a trip to the church to retrieve it. If Judge Johnston had people following me, they wouldn't think anything of me going into the church where I preach.

"We are going to head home for the night," I told William. "There's nothing like sleeping in your own bed. We'll head for Salem sometime tomorrow morning."

"Sounds good to me," William said. The two of us headed for the gap in the Sauratowns.

As we rode along, I thought, *So the way to defeat evil is to allow evil to defeat itself.* By inviting the judge to the banquet, Robert was giving him, hopefully, the rope with which to hang himself.

Sally was surprised, but pleased, by my unexpected arrival. She had not anticipated my return for several more days. I arrived too late for supper, but she quickly warmed up some leftovers. She knew not to talk in front of the children about the specifics of the trip, but, while I ate, I told the story of the highwaymen and William's brilliant idea.

Later that evening, as we lay beside each other in bed, she asked. "Have you seen the judge?"

"Yes, I felt like I was in the spider's den. Evil literally hangs in the air. But God gave me the words that I needed." I told her all about the conversation and added, "I want you to take the children and stay with your father until after the funeral banquet. I don't think that the judge will attack you, but I think that he might have his men search our house. Hopefully, if no one is here when they come, they will not do too much damage. If you are here when they come, they might feel compelled to hurt you. I would rather sacrifice the whole house than have you or one of the children hurt."

The next morning Sally announced to the children that all of us were going to spend a couple of weeks with Grandpa Myers. It was well passed time for John Thomas to learn coopering. It would take at least two weeks of intensive instruction just for him to get the basics. While Sally and the children were packing to leave, I went into the wardrobe and retrieved all of the documents. By midmorning, they would be safely in the altar.

When we arrived at Grandpa Myers' house, I took him aside and quietly explained the situation. "We thought that our excuse would be that you could apprentice John Thomas for a couple of weeks," I whispered.

He whispered back, "I see."

"I'll be glad to train the boy," he said loudly and added, "At his age, he's about two years behind, but I might be able to make a cooper out of him." Turning to John Thomas he asked, "Son, are you ready for some serious hard work?"

I knew that my family would be safe. David Myers would die to protect them. I mounted Betsy and we made our way past the fire damaged manor house and down the road to New Salem. It didn't take long to slip the altar away from the wall. I placed the deeds, contracts, and the copy of the Will in the hollow space. Down on my knees, I slipped the altar back in place and glanced at the open Bible on the altar. It just happened to be opened to Exodus, 15. I read verse 16, "Fear and dread shall fall upon the people, but by the greatness of my arm, they shall be like stone." Both Robert, in his grave at Lynnmont, and his precious documents were resting in the arms of Christ. As I left the church, I saw a man wearing a hooded cape and riding an unfamiliar horse melt into the woods across from the church. I knew that I was not in danger. The judge would not kill me until he knew where the documents were.

The rest of the trip was a pleasure for William and me. When I got to Chapel Hill and handed Dr. Allen the leather pouch, with instructions that he bring it to the Funeral Banquet, he seemed a bit puzzled.

"Did Mr. Tyler's instructions say anything about whether this should remain sealed until the banquet?" he asked.

"No sir. He just instructed me to give it to you for you to bring to the reading of the will."

"Well, in that case, I am curious." He broke the seal, untied the string, opened the flap of the pouch, and peered inside. "Aha," he said. "I assume that Captain Gilbert Stanley is one of the beneficiaries, too. Is that right?"

"Yes sir."

"I'll be more than happy to bring this pouch and to reveal its contents when the time is right."

The other people on Robert's list were thrilled to have been named beneficiaries. All were eager to tell the story that had been requested of them. Nearly all of them were both confused and intrigued by the thought of a funeral banquet, but they willingly accepted their summons.

When I returned to Germantown after my last stop, I decided to check on the house before I went to see Sally and the children. The house had been trashed! They had done more than a thorough search, they had sent a message: just as we destroyed this house, we can destroy you. But I had sent an even more powerful message. They had found no documents. As long as I had the deeds, the contracts, and the will, the judge could not complete his takeover.

My first thought was that I didn't want Sally and the children seeing this destruction. The hooligans had slashed all of the furniture and mattresses, broken the wardrobes, torn the curtains, and made such a sticky mess of the kitchen that I wasn't sure that it would ever be set right. Every jar and sack that Sally had in the kitchen had been emptied. Salt and corn meal, flour and molasses, and even our precious supply of cane sugar were strewn about the kitchen.

I thought about enlisting the help of the clerks and lawyers at the firm to help put things right. But then I realized that the only people who could put things right were Sally and the children. I knew that we were safe now, and that the house would not be searched again.

I decided that it was time to show the children just what evil can do. Their house had been invaded. Darkness had entered their lives. I was going to enlist Sally, John Thomas, and Anne Marie as soldiers. We were a small squad, only feeble candles against the darkness, but I had never seen darkness defeat a candle.

I mounted Betsy. As I rode towards Grandpa Myers' house, I thought of the mess that Robert Tyler had left me. At least I was alive. Robert was dead.

Getting Ready

ALEXANDER JOHNSTON WAS SITTING IN HIS FAVORITE wingback chair in the drawing room of his spectacular plantation house at Yadkin Oaks. A roaring fire in the fireplace was helping to force some of the cold out of the room. Just as fall had come too soon, so had winter. There was such a heavy frost outside that it looked, at first glance, like there had been a light snow fall. The plantation house was a great place in the fall and spring, but it held the heat in the sometimes oppressive North Carolina summers and it could not seem to fight the cold of the winters. Alexander wrapped the warming shawl more tightly around his shoulders, leaned toward the fire, and stirred it with the poker.

As he leaned back into the chair, he looked around the room. It was an incredibly beautiful space. Hand-painted Belgian wallpaper with a hunting scene adorned the walls. A handwoven damask rug covered the center of the floor. The floor itself was made of imported mahogany with an inlay of cherry which banded the room. The area was so large that two chandeliers were needed to adequately light it. All of the chandeliers in the house had been made at an iron works in Boston and then sent to a silversmith in Philadelphia who silver plated them. When the chandeliers were lit at night, the light from their candles reflected off the beautiful dental molding which crowned the walls. The elegant Windsor furniture was imported from England.

Alexander Johnston used to love this drawing room. In fact, there was a time when he enjoyed the whole house. The house had been designed, built, and decorated for entertaining. This room flowed into a large dining area with a dining table which could easily seat twenty people. Here, too, the furniture was Windsor so that the pieces could be easily interchanged with those in the drawing room.

At the far end of the dining room, bifold paneled doors could be opened into the study. The mahogany of the floors continued up the walls with beautiful, paneled wainscoting and built-in bookshelves, filled with an impressive collection of law books. The room was dominated by a massive desk, also made of mahogany. The top of the desk was completely free of clutter, just the way Martha had liked it.

Alexander had allowed Martha to design the house, select the furnishings, and decorate the entire place to her liking. And when it was all done, she was happy. He could not have been more pleased, because nothing was more important to him than making Martha happy.

He had always been pleased with Martha and everything that she did. His father had not been so pleased with her. Alexander was the son of one of the wealthiest shipbuilders in New England. Martha was the daughter of a common sailor and an even more common wife. Alexander was a Harvard educated lawyer. Martha was, according to his father, an uneducated trollop.

Alexander had met her when he had come home to Nantucket during a break in his last year at Harvard. There weren't a lot of prospects for a young woman whose father was a sailor and whose mother was a prostitute. Martha was making a living as a waitress at one of the seaside bars, which was supported mostly by sailors. It wasn't often that a young gentleman would come to the establishment. Alexander had gone there that night to escape his parents. They wanted to plan his future. He just wanted to have some fun. When he walked in the door, Martha was intrigued by this handsome, well-dressed young man. He was even wearing a wig. Only the wealthy wore wigs.

Martha was a young woman with extremely large breasts. She was wearing a dress that had been picked out by the owner of the bar that showed every bit of cleavage that she had. If the truth were told, that dress left almost nothing to the imagination. Martha liked the dress about as much as she liked the job, but she had to make a living.

Fortunately, she had a smile that was nearly as large as her breasts. Young Alexander was impressed. He noticed her breasts, of course. They were a little hard to miss. He liked what he saw. But it was the smile that captured him. Above the smile were two beautiful blue eyes that sparkled in the candlelight. She had long, flowing brown hair tied in a pony tail. When she left his table after taking his order, he noticed that the rest of her figure was very nice, too.

It was a slow night at the bar. When she came back with his drink, he had asked her to sit with him and talk. They were immediately attracted to each other. Their conversation quickly became very intimate. Alexander had liked everything that he saw and heard. His parents had wanted to plan his future, but he had just discovered it for himself.

The very next night that he had gone back to the bar and impulsively asked Martha to marry him. He would be done with law school in just three months. They could be married in May or June. Was she interested?

She was very interested. He promised to write her every day while he was finishing at Harvard. They could plan the wedding by correspondence. "Alexander," she had said, "it will be great for you to write, but I can't read. Why don't we just go to the minister in the morning and get married?"

Alexander had agreed. He picked her up in his father's best carriage the next morning. She was wearing the best dress that she had, made of a simple light blue homespun cloth that accented the blue in her eyes. It was considerably more modest than her bar dress. Her hair was braided and coiled in an elegant bun on top of her head. She seldom wore her hair this way because it was just too much trouble. But for her wedding, she figured that the two hours she spent putting it up were well spent. After all, she wanted to look her very best.

They had gone to the Church of Good Hope, one of the many congregational churches in Nantucket. Martha had asked to go there because it was her home congregation. It was a church that was dominated by the sea. Almost the entire congregation was made up of people who went to sea, or who supported those who did. Reverend Albright knew Martha and her mother well. The congregation had accepted them in spite of Martha's mother's occupation...That was mostly because Martha's mom had started bringing the child when she was just a precious three-year-old. Martha's wonderful smile had been with her even then, and she had won the entire congregation with her warmth. Reverend Albright was pleased that she and the young gentleman were marrying. He knew that this marriage would be her only chance to escape from the wharf. The wedding ceremony had been a very simple one. It wasn't until the ceremony was nearly over that Alexander thought of a ring. When it came to that part of the ceremony, Alexander promised to give her one in the future and his promise was good enough for Martha.

After the ceremony he took her home to meet his parents. When he had left the house early that morning, well dressed and in the family's best carriage, his parents knew that something was up. So his father had stayed home from work that day. He and his wife waited for Alexander's return. When he pulled the carriage to the front of the house, his parents, who had been peering out the window, went to greet their son and the young woman who was with him.

"Mom, Dad," he said, "I'd like for you to meet my wife, Martha."

Both Mr. and Mrs. Johnston's greetings were cordial. And cold.

Martha couldn't tell whether Alexander had noticed or not, but she had. She had not really expected any other response. She knew where she came from. Though she was dressed in her best, she knew that the servants who worked in this house were probably wearing better. In spite of their coldness, she put on one of her warmest smiles. She had not known Alexander Johnston long enough to love him, but she had known him long enough to know that he was her ticket to a better life. She had just promised to love, honor and obey him. She figured that if she did the honoring and obeying, the love would come.

Allen and Diane Johnston were part of the new money aristocracy of Massachusetts. Allen's father started the shipbuilding business. It was Allen who had reaped the benefits of his father's business acumen. He had built the massive house they were standing in front of as a sign, a symbol to the whole community that he was as powerful in Massachusetts as his house was large. And now his son was bringing home this lower class woman. It would never, never do.

Alexander took Martha by the arm and gently guided her up the steps, across the slate covered porch, through the ornately carved door (which had not fared well in the salt air) and into the entrance hall of the home. A massive staircase greeted them. "Let me show you our room," he said as he started to the stairs, but before they got to the stairs Betty, the downstairs maid, appeared and Alexander turned to her and said, "Betty, this is my wife, Martha."

"It is a pleasure to meet you, ma'am," Betty said with genuine warmth.

"I want you and Thomas to go with Martha to her old home and gather her things. Can you do that this afternoon?" he asked, looking at both Betty and Martha. Before they could answer he asked Martha, "How long do you think it will take to pack all of your belongings?"

It was an incredibly awkward moment. His father, who had followed them into the house, was not about to let this young woman move in. Betty, who had really raised Alexander and loved him like a son, wanted him to be happy. Diane Johnston, who had also been a woman who was below Allen's station, had decided to give Martha a chance. Alexander didn't care what any of them thought as long as he could make Martha happy. Martha realized that she was caught in the middle of what would inevitably become a massive struggle.

"I don't think it will take me more than an hour or so to gather my things," she said to both Alexander and Betty.

"I'm sure that Thomas and I can go this afternoon," Betty said. "But I will go and ask him to make sure." She turned, intending to leave.

"Betty! Stay right here!" Allen Johnston's voice boomed. Turning to his son he asked, "What do you mean by bringing *this woman* into my house? And how dare you imply that you are going to move her in?"

"Betty," Alexander said in a quiet, but commanding voice, "it's all right for you to go talk with Thomas," He was both giving her permission to leave and dismissing her. She was happy to go.

Turning to Diane, he said, "Mother, would you please escort my wife to our room while I speak with Father?" His mother was also glad to get away. She quickly took Martha's arm and headed up the stairs.

Alexander Johnston, who was at least a head taller than his father, looked down at him and said, "The conversation that we are about to have would best take place behind the closed doors of your study."

The entrance hall was empty as Thomas, the coachman, came through. He was headed to the front drive to take the carriage to the coach house and the horse to the stable. Betty had not yet found Thomas, but she would. She knew that Thomas, Martha and she would be taking a carriage later that day. Allen Johnston was loud, but Alexander would get his way. He always had, and she figured that he always would.

When Alexander and his father emerged from the study, a peace accord had been struck. Martha would live in the home while Alexander finished his work at Harvard. While he was finishing his degree, his father would explore possibilities for his son's future. His mother would train Martha in the art of being a lady. This would involve her spending lavishly on her so that she would look the part.

Betty had been right. Alexander had gotten his way so far, by winning the first battle.

Martha's warmth and gentility won over the staff immediately and, Diane was also a soft touch. Over the next several months, Diane did, indeed, spend lavishly on her new daughter-in-law. A complete new wardrobe for each season of the year was purchased. She had also been instructed by her husband to buy Martha a set of traveling trunks. Though she wasn't sure why, she had secured the best set that she could find.

Allen Johnston was the one person that Martha's smile had not melted. Though he was cordial, he was cool. He simply refused to accept that Martha, the daughter of a common woman (whom he knew more intimately than he wanted any one to know) would someday be the mistress of this house. He determined that his son and daughter-in-law would both be banished. He took the money that he was planning to give Alexander to help establish him after college and purchased a large plantation in North Carolina. Alexander and his common wife would fit in perfectly in the backwoods of a southern state. In the Yadkin Valley, in Surry County, the plantation was already established, with thirty adult slaves and their children. There were no cities nearby. Allen Johnston was sure that Alexander's new wife would fit in perfectly. But he wasn't completely heartless; he would send Alexander south with a five thousand pound note in his pocket and with letters of introduction to all of the important businessmen and politicians in North Carolina.

When Alexander first got home from Harvard, he was stunned and furious at what his father had done. He could not believe that he had built up such hatred for Martha. But after thinking about it for a few days, he decided that his father might actually have done a good thing. He and Martha could move to North Carolina where she could live like a queen. He, as a Harvard-educated lawyer, should rise quickly to the top of North Carolina business and politics. Even though he knew that he had been bought off, he just hoped that he was not settling for too low a price. To him, Martha was priceless.

The journey south from Nantucket started with a weeklong sea voyage to the Cape Fear and into Wilmington. Once there, two carriages and teams of horses had to be purchased, one for their belongings and one for themselves. The young couple also purchased two slaves at the auction in downtown Wilmington to drive the carriages and to take care of the Johnston's needs. The trip was much more difficult than any of them, slaves or masters, could have anticipated. They had been told that rivers were much better highways than the roads and so they hired a boat in Wilmington to take them as far up the Cape Fear as they could.

It was as they were approaching the first falls in the river that it became evident that their river travel was coming to an end. The rest of the trip would be by carriage. They made their way west from the Cape Fear River valley to the Pee Dee River. They had been told that the Pee Dee would lead to the Yadkin. The people who had told them that river travel would be far easier than wagon travel had been right. Existing roads were usually nothing more than paths. Great ruts filled low spots that turned to mud when it rained. Even though it was early summer, the mosquitoes were already out in force. Because they were following the river, they were staying right in the mosquitoes' beds. The mosquitoes were not a good welcome to North Carolina!

In spite of the hardship of the travel, Alexander was thoroughly enjoying being with Martha. The more time he spent with her, the more he came to love her. He was teaching her to read and discovered that she was as bright as she was beautiful. She was learning quickly, and so was he. They would close the carriage doors and windows "to keep the mosquitoes out" and then enjoy exploring each other. Their silent lovemaking was extremely difficult. They both wanted to shout with joy as they grew to know each other intimately. As they did, they also grew to love each other, not just passionately, but deeply.

When they first came to Yadkin Oaks, Alexander and Martha found it to be just as his father had said it would be. It was well established, but it suffered from neglect. His father had purchased the plantation through an agent from the estate of a childless widow who, after her husband's death, had allowed nearly everything to fall into disrepair. The original owners of the plantation had done what most folk do who are trying to establish one; they had focused on the buildings that are necessary to run a large plantation. As a result, the plantation house had never been built. There was a small, but comfortable, four-room dwelling that was serving as the owner's home.

Alexander promised Martha that they would build a magnificent house. She could design it. Together they would supervise its construction. When it was completed, he would furnish the house with the finest furniture that money could buy.

"How long will it take to build the house?" she asked Alexander. Before he could answer she added, "I'd like to have a room for the baby."

"The baby?!"

"Yes." She said. "Sometime around Christmas, I think."

He reached out to hold her and gently touched her stomach. "I don't think the house will be ready by then, but we will get the carpenter to build the finest crib this world has ever seen."

Martha went into labor on Christmas Eve. One of the slaves, trained as a midwife, was called to help with the delivery. The baby, a beautiful little girl, was born with the umbilical cord wound tightly around its neck. There was nothing that could be done. The child had not survived the birth.

Alexander was called in to comfort his wife. Even though he was Harvard educated, he could think of no words to say.

"Do you think we should give her a name?" Martha asked, as she held her lifeless child and stroked her hair. Tears streamed down her face as Alexander heard himself say, "What name did you have in mind?"

"We could name her Emily Diane, after my grandmother and your mother," she said.

"That would be fine," Alexander said. All he could think about was that he was going to have to take this dead child from Martha, dig a grave on Christmas Eve, and bury her. There was a cemetery on the property where former owners and their children were buried. There were a couple of other graves, too, but Alexander had no idea who the people were or why they were buried there. He decided he would start a new graveyard just for his family, and he hoped it would not be used very much.

Unfortunately, over the next three years, Martha gave birth to three more, perfectly formed, stillbirth children, two more girls and a boy. Each was buried in the Johnston family graveyard in miniature graves, each marked with a stone that was carved with a cherub. After the last birth, the midwife told Alexander and Martha that she should not get pregnant again. The next time both she and the baby would die.

Each time that Alexander had passed the graveyard, his anger towards God had increased. Unlike the Deists, who believed that God was absent from the world, Alexander believed that God was very present. If God were an absent God, he could have had no part in the death of his children; but if God were present, then Alexander could legitimately rage at him for killing his family.

Martha wasn't angry so much as she was numb. She hid her frustrations in the planning and building the great plantation house where Alexander was sitting now. She had ordered drawings of many of the great houses of the world, using them to design Yadkin Oaks. With the death of each child, the scope and cost of the house increased. Alexander didn't mind. He knew that it was her way of coping with the grief.

Because he was the only Harvard-educated lawyer in western North Carolina, he was appointed to be a judge when the legislature established a Superior Court for the area in the small town of Richmond. Yadkin Oaks was centered between the towns of Yadkinville and Richmond, so it was certainly convenient. Alexander actually enjoyed being away from the Plantation. Working as a judge took his mind off the Johnston family graveyard.

Martha's numbness seemed to work on her system. In her mid-twenties, after four still births, she went into an apparent menopause. Her cycle stopped completely. She assumed she would never have a child.

It was a complete shock when she was thirty-four and Alexander was thirty-six, that she found herself pregnant. Like all of her previous pregnancies, everything seemed to go really well. When she gave birth to Deborah Lynn Johnston and actually heard her cry, it was the most glorious sound she had ever heard.

As she held the child, the midwife worked furiously to stop Martha's serious flow of blood. She knew that most deliveries included some bleeding, but this was too much. As Lynn exuberantly suckled her mother's breast, life was slipping from Martha Johnston.

Alexander held her hand, as God robbed her of her life. He was thrilled to have a child, but crushed to lose his wife. She had died in the room just above where he sat now. It had been their room. It had not been used since the night she died.

After Martha had learned to read, the Bible had been her favorite book. She read from it each day. She decided to name each of the slaves on the plantation after Biblical characters. Even the older slaves who had gone by the same given name for years were renamed. Alexander called now for Joshua, the plantation's carpenter, and Jude, the chief coachman.

To Joshua he asked, "Do you have any special wood? I want her casket to be as beautiful as she," he paused for a second and finally added, "is."

"We have some clear maple and just a little bit of tiger maple that I could mix together to make the casket with. We also have some quarter sawn oak, and the mahogany that was left over from building the bookcases in your study. Any of them would be beautiful." Joshua waited for a reply. He would need to work through the night to have a specially-made casket ready.

"I think the mahogany," Alexander said. "I want you to make it as beautiful as you can. I know that your time is limited, but I trust you to give it your best." With his instructions completed, Joshua departed for the carpentry shop.

Alexander turned to Jude and said, "I want you to go to Bethania and tell Pastor Kornfeldt what has happened. Ask him if he would be willing to do a funeral here on the 26th in the morning." Alexander was not a churchgoer, but Martha had been. Pastor Kornfeldt was new to the congregation, but Martha had marveled at his sermons. Before Jude left, Alexander added, "Tell the pastor everything you know about Martha. I want him to say some nice things at her funeral."

Jude left. All this time, Alexander had been holding Martha's hand. And little Lynn was still firmly attached to her breast. He picked up one of Lynn's tiny hands. Her fingers wrapped tightly around his thumb. For the first time in his life, Alexander began to weep. Through his tears, he heard the midwife say something about a wet nurse. Her name was Anna. She had just had a baby, so she would be able to nurse both children.

"She is to come to this house. She can bring her child with her. I don't want Lynn to leave this house," Alexander had said through his tears. He took little Lynn from her mother. Since she had not yet been cleaned from the birthing process, he gently and tenderly washed her, wrapped her securely in a blanket to swaddle her, and laid her in a beautiful cradle at the foot of Martha's bed. Alexander and Martha had built the cradle in the first year of their marriage. After all these years, it was finally being put to use.

Later that evening, Alexander was going through Martha's dresses looking for just the right one to bury her in. He had nearly given up when he found a simple, homespun light blue dress that had been carefully folded and placed in a box in the bottom of her best traveling chest. Alexander asked Mary, the house maid, to braid Martha's hair and arrange it in a bun on top of her head. When she was placed in the newly-made mahogany casket the next day, Alexander gently folded her arms across her chest and made sure that her braided gold wedding ring was on top. It had been specially made to match her hair.

The graveside service that Pastor Kornfeldt performed was simple. He had certainly listened to the kind things that Jude had said about Martha. Hoping to bring comfort to Alexander, he had quoted from Romans Chapter 8, "All things work together for good for those who love the Lord." After hearing that verse, Alexander Johnston was absolutely sure that he hated God. There could be nothing good about Martha's death. Nothing.

Even after all this time, Alexander Johnston was bitter. He had not been able to find a way to get revenge on God, so he had taken out his rage on his political and business opponents. He had drawn a kind of sick pleasure from seeing his opponents suffer. Each time he caused someone else to suffer, he was making all things work for bad for those who loved the Lord.

Anna had proven to be more than just a wet nurse. Alexander had taken advantage of his ownership position to bring himself the comfort that he needed. Anna never liked comforting very much, but she loved Lynn as much as she loved her own child. From the very first day that she came into the house, she was a true mother to Lynn. She had seen to Lynn's training as a little child and, when she was entering her teenage years, Anna had taken her aside and explained to her what it meant to be a woman.

In spite of the hatred Judge Johnston had for God and the world, he had an overpowering love for Lynn. Somehow, he was able to hide from her all of his animus. To Lynn, he was a kind, compassionate, overly generous father. He did have a very possessive nature when it came to her, but she didn't mind. She saw only the love of a doting older father.

Alexander had insisted that his daughter be taken to Bethania Moravian Church every Sunday from the time that she was three. Anna would get her up early each Sunday morning and see that Lynn was properly dressed for church. Jude would arrive with a coach. The Plantation had eight different styles of coaches, and he would pick the one that was best for the day. It was at least a two hour trip by carriage from Yadkin Oaks to Bethania. Even though Alexander hated God, he wanted Lynn to have the same simple faith her mother had had. Whenever Lynn asked him why he didn't go to Bethania with her, he would always tell her that he wasn't worthy to go.

As he sat in his chair in the drawing room, Alexander Johnston remembered noticing that his daughter was becoming more like her mother every day. He had known, logically, that she would grow to become a woman. But in his heart, she was always the baby that wrapped her hand around his thumb.

When Lynn had told him that the church was sponsoring a day of fun at Hanging Rock, he consented to her going. How could he have known that that awful man, that despicable man, that hateful man would tempt her into his evil lair?

And then, just weeks later, she had disappeared for three nights only to show up with Robert Tyler! Certainly, Robert had bewitched her. There could be no other explanation. Judge Johnston had taken care of everything. He had had the Tyler boy thrown into jail and he had sent Lynn away. He was going to protect his daughter's honor from that man. Robert Tyler would never see her again!

As he sat in his chair, he was deeply proud of how successfully he had hidden Lynn from Robert Tyler. Now, twenty years later, Robert Tyler was finally dead. He would be able to bring Lynn home soon. First, he had to write the most eloquent speech that he had ever written. He had to write a speech that would prove, once and for all, that Robert Tyler was the devil incarnate. He had only one week to get his speech perfected. Next Saturday, he would leave Yadkin Oaks as a victim of Robert Tyler, follow the road to Lynnmont, and return on the same road as a victor. He poked the fire one more time as he pondered his speech.

———————

Many miles away in Harrisonburg, Virginia, Adam Robertson was trying on the gentleman's clothes that he had purchased, second hand, from Edward Harrison. Since he had been raised by Quakers, all of his clothes were plain and they simply weren't appropriate for attending the reading of a will that might turn him into a gentleman.

Edward Harrison was the third son of the Harrison family for whom the town of Harrisonburg had been named. He and Adam had always been good friends. They had grown up together, exploring the hills around Harrisonburg; playing in the creeks; building kites to fly in the spring winds; chasing butterflies; and, as they grew older, dreaming together about what their lives would be like as adults.

When a man from North Carolina had shown up at the Sanatorium and announced that Adam was the heir of a great fortune, and within a month's time would be a gentleman, the first person that he had gone to tell was Edward. That had been three weeks ago. From what the man, a Mr. Barnes, had told him, his father was the owner of an estate and multiple businesses that were worth around $300,000.00. Because he had not actually seen the contents of the will, he did not know what portion of the estate would be given to Adam, but he had assumed that the largest portion would, indeed, come to him.

Instantly, Edward and Adam had changed positions. As a member of a family of substance, Edward had had the privilege of attending the College of William and Mary. Even though he was not the primary heir to the Harrison fortune because he was the third son, his father had assured him that he would be well established in the community. Adam had been tutored at home by Miss Emily, Miss Susan, and Mr. John. They had done a more than credible job of educating him. He could carry on an intelligent conversation with Edward on almost any subject. Edward had been prepared for a life of privilege. Adam had been prepared to live out his life serving the unfortunate people at Apple Blossom Sanatorium.

But now, it seemed, Adam was going to be one of the wealthiest men in North Carolina and had the potential to also be one of the most powerful. How was he going to run an estate and manage numerous companies when he knew nothing about leadership and even less about business?

Edward had assured him that he would do fine. He was smart. He had a warm and friendly nature. He was taller than most people and, Edward assured him, tall people were more powerful than short people. Edward even tried to convince Adam that his good looks would be an asset to his future. Miss Emily and Miss Susan had always said this, too, but Adam had just dismissed it as parent talk.

"There are only two things that you are lacking," Edward had said to Adam when he had told him about Lynnmont. "You need experience, which I can't give you, and a gentleman's clothing, which I can give you. If you don't know how to be a gentleman, at least you can look like one."

Edward and Adam were almost exactly the same size. Adam was only slightly taller, and, when he had tried on one of Edward's waistcoats, he discovered that he was also slightly broader. But the differences were truly slight; Adam could wear Edward's clothes. Edward had offered to give the clothes to his best friend, but Adam had insisted on purchasing them.

Mr. Barnes had left him and Miss Emily a considerable sum of money to finance their way to North Carolina. Adam considered preparing himself by having the appropriate clothing to be as essential as hiring the right coach. He left the details of the trip to Miss Emily. He knew they would be leaving on Monday. They had been told the trip would take three days, but they were giving themselves two days extra in case they ran into any trouble along the way.

Adam had picked out four of Edward's outfits and had paid him $4.00 for the lot. His favorite was a forest green jacket and waistcoat with a contrasting pair of tan breeches. He was planning to wear this outfit to the funeral banquet. He and Edward had talked about the banquet. Edward had never heard of a funeral banquet either, but his father had assured him that Adam should be proper and quiet throughout the entire affair. It would be inappropriate, apparently, to show too much emotion. Adam was concerned about that because Mr. Barnes had told him and Miss Emily the funeral banquet had two purposes—the reading of the will and the introduction of Adam to his father. He understood that he could and should be proper and quiet during the reading of the will, but he didn't know how he should react to the various stories that he would hear. Miss Emily had staunchly refused to tell him anything about the story that she had been asked to tell. "You will hear it at the banquet," was all that she would say.

Adam and Edward had spent nearly three weeks speculating about what Adam's new life would be. The only thing that they both knew for sure, was that Adam was about to have a new life, a life he was not prepared for—that was the gift of a stranger.

"I hope my father's not a stranger after the banquet," Adam had said. But he wondered how a few stories could really introduce him to his father. Mr. Barnes had told him that his father had only learned of his existence a few days before his death. It was all so strange.

"I like the green outfit, too," Edward said. "It has enough color to be bold, but it is sedate enough for a funeral. Are you going to stay at Lynnmont after the reading of the will?" he asked.

"I don't think so. Miss Emily wants me to come back here afterwards. She says that the will might offer me nothing. My father might have decided that the whole estate should go to someone else. She told me not to count my chickens before they are hatched.

"Besides, she has hired a carriage that couldn't possibly carry all my possessions," he continued. "I suppose that if I do inherit Lynnmont and the rest of the businesses, I will need to come back here to say all the appropriate things to everyone who has loved me." Adam placed the clothes carefully in a large box that Edward had found. As he was tying the box, a thought came to him.

"I know. I can have a funeral banquet here, in Harrisonburg. It can be a death to my past banquet," he said.

"Or a death to your youth banquet," Edward said, laughing.

"Or a death to all my former friendships banquet." Adam's statement was intended to be funny, but even before he had finished it, the enormity of all that faced him, the challenge of a whole new life overwhelmed him. He would have to leave behind Edward, Miss Emily, Mr. John and some of the sweet, wonderful people at the sanatorium who loved him unconditionally just because they saw him every day. He would be starting a whole new life with people he had never met, in a place he had never seen.

"Maybe I can bring you to Lynnmont to manage my estate," Adam said.

"That would be great! But I'm not sure mother would let me go to North Carolina."

They both sat on the bed for a while in silence. It was difficult for twenty-year-old young men to say that they loved each other. When Adam wasn't looking, Edward slipped the $4.00 into the box of clothing. He couldn't think of any better way to say what he wanted to say.

After a brief time, their banter continued. As they left Edward's room and headed for the door, they joked of Adam being a Lord Proprietor. They kidded about Adam having so much money that he would not know how to spend it all. And they laughed about Adam being way too ugly to have a wife to take with him.

But deep down inside, Adam Robertson knew that having found his father would change his whole life. He was not the man that he was three weeks ago, or the man that he would be a week from today. He was also discovering that having a new life was painful.

———

Abigail Jordan could not believe she had been named as an heir to Mr. Tyler. She was looking forward to telling the story of President Washington's visit. It was a story that she had told many times before. All of her relatives and friends had heard it over and over again. She was sure that she could tell the story to the distinguished men who would be at the church next week.

The only question was what Mr. Tyler left her. Maybe there was some memento of the event that he wanted to share with her. Whatever it was, she would be glad to get it. She had always liked Mr. Tyler. She had cared for the needs of many people in her twenty years as the head maid at the Salem Tavern. She had discovered that everyone, whether President or peasant, had all filled the chamber pots with the same stuff. Most of the gentlemen either didn't see her or treated her with contempt. Mr. Tyler was one of the few gentlemen who gave her respect. She had always appreciated that.

She had been stunned a few days ago when the owner of the tavern had announced that he had sold the business and would be leaving Salem. He said that the business had been bought by an anonymous businessman through an agent. He suspected that the new owner would make an appearance in the next several weeks. He hoped that all of the employees would manage the tavern until the new owner came. The new owner could, of course, fire all of them if he wished and start over with a new staff. But he believed that the new owner had bought the tavern because it was a well-run business that made money. So, he didn't expect many changes.

Abigail had seen many staff changes in the years that she had been there. Cooks and waiters had come and gone, most of the maids were temporary at best. She had constantly been training new staff. If she owned the tavern, she would pay the staff just a little bit more. If they made just a little bit more money, they would be more likely to stay. Stability and continuity would improve the service the inn could offer.

She had had to ask for special permission to get a whole day off to go to the funeral banquet. The owner was, at first, reluctant. But when she told him that the deputies would come for her if she didn't attend, he relented. The last thing he needed was for the new owner to hear that deputies had been called to the tavern. The new owner might back out of the deal and he didn't want that to happen. He could not believe how much money he had received. He wondered, even now, what this new owner was thinking.

As Abigail cleaned the chamber pots, collected from the upstairs rooms, she wondered how many times she had done this disgusting task. At least next Saturday, for one day, she would be free of it.

———wwooo꙰ooo꙰ooowww———

Captain Gilbert Stanley had not worn his full dress uniform for many months, but he was pleased that Robert Tyler had requested that he wear it to the funeral banquet. He had carefully laid out the entire uniform on the bed. It was quite an ensemble. Before him were his white breeches and vest, both made of pure linen. There was a blue waistcoat, made of wool. The tails on the coat were each tapered to a sharp point. The six silver buttons on the waistcoat would need to be polished.

Two sashes, one red, one white were beside the waistcoat. Gilbert was not sure that he liked this new part of the formal wear. Each sash wrapped around his neck, across his chest, and then around his waist. The two sashes crossed in the middle of his chest and were held in place with a silver gorget. Gilbert thought it was strange that a gorget, originally a piece of armor that was worn to protect the neck, was now just an ornament in the middle of the chest worn to tie two sashes together. He had to admit that the silver shield was beautiful, though. He had heard that some of the counties in the state were adopting a copy of the gorget as shields for their sheriff's to wear. He would not need to polish his new black boots. He had had to purchase them because the regulations had changed and called for the boots to have tassels now. He had kept his tassel-free boots. He was sure that the regulations would change back.

The black-cocked hat was certainly beautiful, but it was difficult to keep cleaned and shaped; it was so easy to crush. Fortunately, the white-feathered plume could be removed and stored within the hat to protect it. Gilbert had always liked the small silver eagle and the silver cord and tassels which completed the hat. He was glad that in one of his many quiet times in the militia, he had been able to create a wood form for his white buckskin gloves.

The form kept the gloves perfectly shaped. He would rub them with oil before next Saturday to soften and shine them.

He was glad that it was winter and he could wear his surtout: the long, heavy, woolen coat. Like the waistcoat, it was also dark blue; but, unlike any other piece of his uniform, it was gilded. Real gold plated the forty buttons that adorned the front, and gold thread was used to sew all of the seams. There were even gold epaulets on the shoulders. Unlike the silver that adorned all of the rest of his uniform, the gold kept its shine, never needing to be polished.

Gilbert would take his sword, of course. But he wasn't sure about the Espontoon. The seven foot long lance was an official part of the full dress uniform for a captain. Mr. Barns had told him that the codicil to the will requested full dress. He would make the decision next Saturday morning before he headed for Lynnmont.

Gilbert knew that another very important part of his uniform was his horse and saddle. He would wash and curry his horse on Friday afternoon and put her in the stable for the night. He knew that if he left her in the corral, she might decide to wallow in the dirt and he would have to start all over again. He would also detail every inch of the saddle. It would be perfect.

As Gilbert looked over the whole ensemble, he knew that some care would need to be given to the silver in the numerous buttons, his awards for service in the War for Independence, and his captain's bars.

He shook his head in disgust as he had so often before. *Thirty years a captain*, he thought. *That's got to be a record.*

Regardless of his anger at the politics of the militia, Gilbert Stanley would do whatever Robert Tyler asked. He would wear his uniform with distinction and, he would proudly tell the story of Robert facing the British cavalry.

I had already written my sermon for the next day. Most Methodist preachers that I knew did not spend any time in preparation. They believed that the Holy Spirit would give them all the words that they needed when they stood to preach. I believe that the Holy Spirit can lead me to actually prepare a sermon. I didn't know if my preaching is any better than the other preachers or not, but I felt better about it. It seems to me that those preachers who rely on the Holy Spirit to give them words ended up with too many words and not enough Word.

Since my sermon about Ezekiel and the valley of the dry bones was ready, I decided to give some time preparing for the funeral banquet. I had glanced over the letter of instructions that Robert had given me, but I had not really studied it. We were all still staying with Grandpa Myers until the new furniture and mattresses came, so I didn't have a private place for things like this. But I figured that the letter of instructions couldn't be that private, or Robert would have handled it differently. I spread it out on the table before me and read:

Instructions for the Funeral Banquet

John, I would like an elegant meal served to begin the funeral banquet. You can get with the cooks at the estate to work out the details of what will be served. I will also leave up to your judgment how New Salem will be arranged and how the meal will actually be served. As people are eating, I would like you to facilitate as much fellowship as possible. I know that this may be difficult since many of the people will not know each other, but do the best you can. People should have assigned seats at the table. I will leave it up to you to determine who sits where.

Following the meal, I would like for you to begin the funeral portion with whatever comments you think are appropriate and then call on persons to tell their stories. I would like for the stories to be told in the following order:

Mamie Smith, "Stealing Cookies"
John Barnes, "A Day at the Gristmill"
Alexander Johnston, "Why I Hate Robert Tyler"
Horace Hayworth, "Arresting Robert Tyler"
Emily Gladstone, "A Lady Named Lynn"
Gilbert Stanley, "Standing Before the Cavalry"
Richard Allen, "The Most Difficult Student"
Lawrence Weeks, "Cherokees Are People, Too"
Franklin Campbell, Keeping Ben Randolph
Abigail Jordan, "Greeting President Washington"

John, it will be very important for you to be prepared to give an appropriate response after each story, if you believe that one is necessary. I am not going to tell you what the stories are about, even though you can get a pretty good idea from some of the titles. I want your responses to be authentic and unprepared. John, you are a man of tremendous grace; I have always admired your wonderful ability to express yourself simply, but powerfully.

After all of the stories have been told, I would like for you to unseal the will and read it. The Last Will and Testament will call for a response from some of the beneficiaries. Allow time for that to happen and facilitate the responses as necessary.

I would like for the funeral banquet to conclude with a worship experience. John, I trust you to use your grace to plan a service that will honor God, bring comfort to my son, and bring the event to a meaningful conclusion.

Thanks for all you are doing.
Robert

As I sat and held the letter, my first response was that Robert was very presumptuous. All he wanted me to do was to turn a Church into a banquet hall, serve a meal where there was no kitchen, find a place to seat Alexander Johnston, respond to the stories even though I didn't know what they were about, facilitate the responses to the will, and plan a meaningful worship experience to conclude the event!

For the first time in a long time, I was angry with Robert Tyler. I know that one is not supposed to speak evil of the dead, but what he was asking me to do was impossible. In all of his letters, he kept referring to my grace. But I don't have any grace!

I am not saying that I don't have some gifts. I am reasonably intelligent. I am kind and compassionate. I obviously have a strong belief in God if I am willing to be a preacher. I love my wife and family and I try to be honest in my work.

But most of what Robert is asking me to do is impossible. Next Saturday will come, and I will have to try to do what I am unable to do. Just as I was about to curse the memory of Robert Tyler, I remembered these words from Proverbs, "Lean not unto thine own understanding, but in all your ways acknowledge him, and he will direct thy paths." I remembered a few days before when a conversation with Judge Alexander Johnston had gone far better than I could have imagined.

But it was all still impossible. If I hadn't loved Robert Tyler so much, I would throw my hands up in frustration and walk away. In many ways, the whole thing seems ridiculous—having a banquet in a church in front of the altar; honoring a man who has been dead for two months; introducing him to a son that he has never met and who may not even be worthy to know his father; inviting his worst enemy and giving him a seat of honor just like everyone else; giving gifts from his estate to all of these people; and even promising a gift to Alexander Johnston!

Oh! There I go again, trusting my own understanding.

Final Preparations

I SWUNG BY THE OFFICE ON MONDAY MORNING to tell Mordecai I would probably be out of the office for at least another week. I had to make all of the final preparations for the funeral banquet.

"I'm not exactly sure how long that will take," I told him. "I might be in the office some days, but I'm not sure,"

"Well, I can't exactly do your job," he said, "but I'm holding down the fort as best I can."

"I'm sure that you are doing fine," I said. "By the way, did you see a rock covered in fool's gold anywhere in the office? I use it as a paper weight and it has just disappeared."

"No sir. I haven't seen it. But I'll keep a lookout for it. If I find it, I'll put it on the desk for you," he said, with a quizzical look on his face.

"Thanks. It's just strange that it has disappeared. It was a prize that Mr. Tyler and I wrestled for when we were kids," I explained. I shook my head, wondering, as I closed the door. Betsy was patiently waiting. I mounted her, and we headed to the estate.

I wanted to stop at the manor house. I had ordered that the burned out east wing be torn down to the foundations. The men who were doing the work were asked to divide all of the various pieces of wood into piles, usable and unusable. All the unusable would then be cut for firewood in the kitchen. Almost nothing was to go to waste. The job was going slowly because we were saving every nail. It took considerable time to drive all of the nails back out of the wood. I was using men from the cheese factory to do the job. They were glad to have something meaningful to do. The women from the cheese factory were busy cleaning every square inch of the rest of the house. Smoke damage is hard to recover from; but I knew that, if the men and women did a thorough job, the house could be restored. I wanted to check on the progress of this work. After all, in just one week, depending upon what Robert's will said, there might be a new master of the house.

I also wanted to go to the house because I thought that I had remembered some tables that were there. Like most men, I saw things without really seeing them. Sally noticed all the details of every place we went. She could recall the kind of furniture, the color of the curtains, the pile of the carpet, what all of the various accessories were that were used on the tables. I usually just got the bigger picture. I either liked a room or I didn't. I either thought that a whole house was nice, or I didn't.

The front of the house had six large, floor-to-ceiling windows, three on either side of the door. I thought that I had remembered that there were specially made tables which hugged the wall between the windows and held all kinds of nice accessories. When I got to the house, I found out that my memory was pretty good after all. The tables were there and would be perfect for the funeral banquet. Made of walnut, they were finished with clear shellac which brought out the beautiful soft grain of the wood. I knew that the dark walnut would be a great counterpoint to all of the lighter oakwood in the church.

The tables were just the right height and length. I could take out the first two rows of pews along the front of the church and line the tables up end to end. I would need to borrow chairs from the dining room too. There were no chairs at the church, and I didn't think that pulling pews up to the tables would be a good idea. I was glad that the pews had not been secured to the floor; it would make moving them a lot simpler. We didn't have any storage place at the church, so the pews would have to be stored outside. I would have to bring some waterproof canvas tarps to wrap the pews in. I did not want them to get damaged. The men of the church had worked too hard to build them.

I called to Matthew Griffin, the man from the cheese factory that I had named foreman of the teardown crew, "Matthew, I'm going to need for you and the men to give me a little help moving some tables and chairs."

"I'll call them right now. Where do you want them moved?" he asked.

"Before you call anybody, you're going to need to get a flatbed wagon from the coach house and a team from the stable. We're going to be moving the tables and chairs to New Salem."

"Do you want me to do this now or maybe right after lunch?" he asked.

"After lunch will be fine. Oh, by the way, you'll need to gather all the quilts that you can find. We will need to wrap all of these pieces so they don't get damaged. I also need for you to go to the barn and get the largest waterproof tarp that you can find. If it's dirty, it will need to be cleaned. We are going to wrap some of the pews from the church in it."

"I'll take care of everything, Mr. Barnes."

Matthew turned and headed back to the east wing of the house. I was sure he was going to tell the others what he would be doing for the next hour or so and that they would have a different job right after lunch. I decided to take the time to go to the kitchen and talk with the cooks. A banquet had to have a meal and I didn't have a clue what should be served or how the meal could be prepared at a place that didn't have a kitchen.

I walked out of the back door of the house and headed across the compound to the community kitchen. About half way there, I stopped to look around. This part of the estate was truly beautiful. On each end of the compound were two massive barns, one for the dairy and one for horses. In between were a collection of buildings tied together with brick paved lanes. The lawn was still lush, even though the frosts had begun to turn the grass brown. The caretakers had done a great job of introducing English boxwood hedges to the landscape. Robert had asked that they be added to finish the look of the estate. Although each of the buildings had a brick façade and cedar shingles, they were each unique. The blacksmith shop, the kitchen, and the cheese factory were still the largest of the buildings, except for the barns, of course. Tucked in between these three were about fifteen smaller buildings which housed many craftsmen, from a basketmaker to a tailor.

The one room school house, where I had spent so many hours in my childhood, was nestled between the kitchen and the lane which led to the compound of bunkhouses. In the other two bunkhouse communities there were similar buildings, like the cooperage where my father-in-law worked. Other larger businesses were spread around the estate, like Tyler Brick and the gristmill which were not connected to one of the communities. I remembered the plat that Oskar Schoenfeldt had shown me so many years ago. I think that he would have been very proud to see the progress Robert Tyler had made in completing his vision. The only major building that Mr. Oskar had planned that was not built was the large church.

When I entered the kitchen, I asked if Miss Mamie was available. Even though there was not an official chief cook, Miss Mamie had earned the title. She had been living and cooking at Lynnmont longer than I had been alive. One of the younger cooks found her in the little office at the back corner of the kitchen and brought her to me.

"Are you looking forward to Saturday?" I asked.

"Well," she said, "I am curious. I have just racked my brain trying to figure out what Mr. Tyler would have left me in his will. I can't think of a thing. So, yes, I'm looking forward to Saturday."

"Is this a good time to talk? I know that you all are getting ready for lunch."

"It's never a good time to talk around here. When we get finished with lunch, we are already getting ready for supper. But we cover for each other," she said. "How can I help you?"

"Mr. Tyler wants us to have a meal at the funeral banquet," I said.

"Well, of course he does. You can't have a banquet without a meal," Mamie said, looking at me as if I were stupid.

Realizing that this question might seem just as dumb to her as my previous one, but needing to know, I asked, "How can you serve a meal at a place that doesn't have a kitchen?"

"Son," she said. (I loved it when she called me 'Son.' It made me feel a little younger). "Have you ever heard of a picnic?"

"Sure," I said, "but I thought that a banquet ought to have a hot meal."

"We can do that, too, John. It all depends on what you want to eat."

"Well, I don't know. I've thought about it a lot. And I just can't decide what the right meal would be. What do you think?"

"How many people are we talking about feeding?" she asked.

"There will be eleven at the banquet. Plus, I guess we should feed the people who are there to actually serve the meal."

"So, twenty people at the most," she said, mostly to herself. "There are lots of things we could do," she said, speaking now to me. "We could have the boys go out behind the church and dig a pit to roast a whole pig. We would start cooking the pig the afternoon before and slow cook it all night. There is nothing better than roasted pork with all the fixings."

The roasted pork sounded mighty good to me, but I could tell that she was about to offer another suggestion.

"Or we could fry up a passel of chicken. We could give each person a half a chicken so that they get both dark and white meat. Again, we would add all the fixings. If we did that we would do the cooking here and then take everything over to the church."

"But if you do that," I interrupted her," how will you keep everything hot?"

"We have special baskets," she said, taking me over to a shelf in the kitchen which held large baskets. When I went to take one off the shelf, I found that it was extremely heavy. She smiled at me and said, "They are lined with pewter. We put the food in them right out of the pan and it stays hot for a right good while. If we were going to cook the food here, we would put a large bunch of hay in the back of a wagon, put the food in the baskets, and nestle the baskets in the hay. The food would still be so hot when we got to the church, we would have to use spoons or forks to get it out of the baskets."

I was amazed. I had no idea that any such thing as pewter-lined baskets existed, and I told her so.

"We use these baskets almost every day. When you cook for as many people as we do, you can't have all of the food coming off the stove, or out of the oven, at the same time."

"I love the idea of having fried chicken," I said. "I know that the fried chicken from this kitchen is the best in the world." I didn't want to tell her that I wasn't too excited about a pit being dug out behind the church. "And I'll trust you and the other cooks to come up with the best side dishes. But, I want you to remember something, Mamie. You are one of the beneficiaries. You are one of the honored guests. I don't want you cooking that day. It's time for somebody else to cook for you."

"Yes sir, Mr. Barnes. I'll plan everything. I'll organize the help and train the ones who will serve. Mr. Tyler had special uniforms made for the servers when we had a banquet in the manor house.

I'll make sure that they are cleaned and pressed and that the servers are all appropriately dressed for the banquet. I'll also make sure that we have some of Lynnmont's finest dinnerware to serve the meal on. Is there anything else? Oh, yes, I promise you that I will enjoy being served that day."

"Thanks Mamie. By the way," I asked, "why did you call me Mr. Barnes?"

"I don't know," she said. "It just seemed like the right thing to do."

"Well don't do it anymore. You are old enough to be my grandmother. And besides," I added as I gave her a hug, "I love you like a grandmother."

"O John," she said. "Get out of here. I've got work to do."

As I left the kitchen, I noticed that people were streaming into the new dining hall. It was a large building adjacent to the kitchen. People used to eat out in the yard in good weather or in one of the barns in bad weather. They would often forget to bring back their plates and flat wear and the stuff was getting spread all over the community. Robert decided that the best solution was a dedicated space where people could eat. The building had been completed about a year ago. Though it was a large space, it was dwarfed by the dairy barn which was its closest neighbor on the compound. I decided to join the crowd and eat before I helped to move the tables and chairs. I seldom ate with the community because I was usually in Germantown. But every time I did eat here, I was amazed at the quality of the cooking. To cook for around a hundred people for lunch and supper every day was an amazing feat. Throw in cooking breakfast for a smaller crowd and providing all the specialty baking items that any dedicated bakery would prepare, and it was simply astonishing what these ladies did every day.

While I ate a large bowl of piping hot bacon, potato, and onion soup with a wedge of hot fresh baked cornbread, various persons from the community came up to me with questions. After one inquiry, it became obvious to me why Miss Mamie had called me Mr. Barnes. Since the death of Robert, I had become the presumptive 'owner' of Lynnmont and the Tyler Companies. No one would have said that I had actually inherited anything. But I had been Robert's closest friend, as well as the manager of the companies; and they were all assuming that I was about to inherit everything. None of them knew that Robert had a son.

In just a few more days all of Surry County would know. It would be the talk of every hearth. Robert Tyler had had a wife! Robert Tyler had a son! Robert Tyler was married to the judge's daughter! I could just see it happening. Before the next week was out, hundreds of people would step forward to proclaim that they had known all along. Many people from Home Moravian Church would suddenly remember that they had attended the wedding. One of the former maids of the Salem Tavern would claim that she had personally provided new linen for the happy couple. A wheelwright at the Salem Livery would remember that he repaired a wheel on their carriage as Robert and Lynn sat in the back of a horse stall "Just acooing and adawdling over one another." All of these memories would be harmless enough. But as I sat here wondering about them, I began to wonder what all of this talk would do to Alexander Johnston.

The old man had been devastated to learn, twenty years ago, that his daughter had been married. Now he was to learn, if he didn't know already, that he had a grandson who had been forced to live a life of servitude in an insane asylum, instead of a life of privilege at Yadkin Oaks. Adam Robertson was the living proof that Judge Alexander Johnston was a man who had given his life over completely to hatred.

When I finished my bowl of soup, I made my way over to the manor house. Matthew Griffin was waiting in front with the flatbed wagon. It looked like he had gotten every quilt on the estate. A huge pile of them were on the back of the wagon. Underneath the quilts, I could see the corner of a canvas tarp.

Not knowing exactly how much weight we would be hauling, he had picked a team of Percherons, the huge working horses that weighed about 1,600 pounds each, to pull the wagon. Everyone on the estate knew that this breeding pair, George and Georgia, were the two favorite horses of our estate foreman, Franklin Campbell. Robert had made the decision, several years before, to invest in three breeding pairs of Percherons. Because they were so valuable, a special barn had been built behind the paddock just for the six of them. Franklin made his way out to this barn nearly every day just to talk with George and Georgia, stroke their manes, and give them special treats. Some of the skeptics on the estate said that the only reason that he did this was because he was protecting the estate's investment, but I knew better. He had simply fallen in love with these gentle giants. One thing was sure; these two horses would have no trouble hauling our tables and chairs.

I took Matthew and his crew into the house and showed them four of the tables that I wanted to be transported to the church. Four or five knick-knacks adorned each of the tables. I asked one of the men to move them carefully to one of the tables we would not be taking with us. "You'll need to remember where each item goes, so everything can be put back like it was."

"We will need to take eleven of the dining room chairs, too," I said, "Each piece will need to be carefully wrapped in quilts. I don't want to find even one scratch."

It didn't take long for the men to carry the pieces out to the wagon. The tables were long enough that three quilts were needed for each. Two of the tables were laid upside down in the wagon and the other two were nestled on top of them. Each chair received its wrapping. They were wedged against each other. Matthew ran a rope around the lot to hold them in place, the men jumped on the back, and George and Georgia easily moved the wagon down the road.

Matthew took the wagon at a deliberately slow pace. Each time there was even the slightest dip or hole in the road, he slowed the team down to a crawl. He was taking seriously my insistence that there not be even one scratch. When we got to the church the men jumped down and started untying and unwrapping the chairs.

"Before we start taking things into the church, we are going to have to take some pews out," I said. "Let's go inside. You all can help me decide just how many pews we will need to move."

We entered through the main doors directly into the sanctuary. It was a simple, rectangular shaped building. There was a center aisle with ten pews on either side and two side aisles. At the end of the center aisle was the "u" shaped altar rail. On each side of the church, outside the rail, were three shorter pews which held the members of the choir. Inside the rail to the left side was the lectern, a small speaking stand which held a Bible. It was traditional in the Methodist Church that the Bible always be open; it was a symbol that the people were always open to the Word of God.

On the right hand side was the pulpit which was much larger than the lectern. It was enclosed on three sides to protect the preacher from an attack of the devil. The pulpit was also three steps higher than the chancel floor, one step for each person of the Trinity. Every sermon was supposed to be preached in the name of the Father, Son and Holy Ghost. On the wall behind the rail, at the very center, was the altar. New Salem was unusual because it had another open Bible on the altar, from which I had read the words of the Book of Exodus when I had hidden Robert's important documents. We had two Bibles instead of one, because two different families had given them in memory of loved ones. I was determined that both Bibles would be used so that neither family would be upset. I regularly switched the Bibles from altar to lectern so that neither family could say that the other got some kind of preferential treatment. Also on the altar were two candles as symbols of the light of God and a bowl of water representing baptism. Just above the altar, a large wooden cross dominated the back wall of the church.

The men of the carpentry shop at Lynnmont had built the chancel furniture and the prayer rail, all built with exquisite precision from oak boards harvested from Lynnmont forests, milled at Lynnmont's water driven mill, and dried in the carpentry shop. I had given the craftsman a general idea of what I thought the pieces should look like, but I could never have envisioned how beautiful they would be. The men of the church had gotten together and built the pews. Because they were built by amateurs instead of professional woodworkers, they were rough hewn. But we all took great pride in them, because they were the work of our hands and an offering to God.

Everyone at Lynnmont knew that a funeral banquet was going to be held the next Saturday. But nobody had a good idea of what that actually meant. Matthew and his crew knew that they were helping to prepare, but they didn't understand what they were preparing.

"At the funeral banquet," I began to explain, "four important things are going to happen. First, there will be an actual banquet with the guests being served a special meal. That's why we need tables and chairs. Second, each of the honored guests will be asked to speak. I think that this will take place from the pulpit. The third thing will be the reading of Mr. Robert's will. I'm not sure, but I think that I will use the lectern for that. The final thing will be a closing worship service."

"I'll be glad to have your advice," I indicated that I was talking to all the men, "but I thought that we could arrange the tables in one long row across the front of the church. We would need to take out the first two rows of pews on either side."

It was Max Dunn who said, "Preacher Barnes, how about if we arrange the tables around the rail? It will make it easier for everyone to see each other."

Max's idea would mean that we would have to remove the choir loft pews, as well as those along the front, but it was a great idea. Instead of gathering in front of the altar, the 'Throne of Grace,' we would be gathered around it.

It was Matthew who said, "We need to be as careful with these pews as we were with the tables and chairs. Each one will need to be carefully wrapped. Then we will need to cover them all with the tarp to protect them." Turning to me, he asked, "Do you want them to be stacked outside at the back of the church?"

"Yes," I said. "That would be great. Then I need all of you to come back Saturday night, after the funeral banquet and put everything back the way it is now."

As the men were moving the pews, I thought of all of the crucial documents that were hidden in the altar. I wondered when I should retrieve them. I was sure that they were safe where they were. I made the decision that the documents would be retrieved as a part of the banquet. I didn't know how or why I came to that conclusion. I just knew it would be the right thing to do.

It didn't take the men long to arrange the furniture. There were three chairs to the left of the altar, six in front, and two to the right. Because the tables were of some length, there was ample room for each beneficiary. Now my only concern was determining the seating plan. Was there a seat of honor? And if there was, who should sit there? Who was I going to seat beside the judge? Would Alexander Johnston be willing to sit beside a cook or a chamber maid? Should Adam be given the seat of greatest honor, even though I didn't know for sure if he was going to be given the greatest benefits?

I wasn't sure where I was going to seat people, but I was sure that I was going to ask Sally to write out the place cards, because she had beautiful script handwriting. It was not quite as fancy as calligraphy, but it was eloquent. I knew that her writing would add a note of sophistication without being too fancy. I would need to drop by the law firm to get some card stock cut in the appropriate size. Having limp place cards would be far worse than having none at all.

As we were headed back to the manor house with Matthew and I on the seat of the wagon, he asked, "How long will it be before we can begin making cheese again?"

"I don't think it will be long after Mr. Robert's will is read. I think that the people who have been attacking the Tyler Companies will be publically exposed soon," I said. "Of course, we are going to have to repackage everything, and we've got to come up with a new name for all the dairy products. The Lynnmont name will be tainted by the rumors which shut us down."

"I've been thinking about that," Matthew said. "Why don't we go back to the original name, the Beautiful Valley Dairy?"

"That's a good idea Matthew. But we are going to have to wait and see what the new owner wants to do."

"Wait! Aren't you the new owner?" Matthew asked with a note of incredulity.

"Not that I know of," I said. "Mr. Tyler's will hasn't been read yet. I don't know what's in it. I don't know if anyone knows what's in it. He might have written it out in his own hand instead of having a clerk do it, so that no one would know before it's read."

Matthew looked at me with a stare which clearly said that he didn't believe me. He was sure that I had read the will and knew who would be living in the manor house soon. I decided that the best response was silence. Besides, we were nearly back to the manor house. Matthew dropped the men off with instructions to get back to work on the east wing.

He dropped me off at the barn on the way to the carriage house. I had asked one of the stable boys to feed and curry Betsy while we were gone. I knew that she would be inside in a stall. The massive double, sliding doors were standing open. As I walked in, I was confronted with more than fifty stalls, each containing a water trough, a bin for oats, and a large hay box. Above the stalls were massive hay lofts, completely full of hay from the summer's harvest. Five vented cupolas kept the lofts cool and cut down on the danger of a dust fire. Because many a farmer had learned that hay dust is as explosive as gunpowder, the cupolas were more than a pretty architectural feature; they were an essential safety device.

When the barn was built, Mr. Schoenfeldt had used all of the latest technology. He had invested in a built-in sewer system which made it possible to flush out of the liquid waste. The solid waste still had to be hand shoveled each day, but because each stall was cleaned daily, the dominant odor in the barn was that of fresh hay.

Mr. Oskar had brought from Europe a love of horses and a desire to have the best breeding stocks in America. He had not only several breeds of draft horses, but horses which were specially bred to pull wagons, and others that were intended as riding horses and racers. There were also ponies and asses for breeding mules.

The breeding, raising, training and selling of horses and mules was one of the most successful of the Lynnmont enterprises. Every spring, Lynnmont would host an auction in which four hundred or more animals would be offered for sale. At any given time, at least eight hundred horses were either roaming the Lynnmont pastures, in the paddock, or one of the stalls.

"Hi John," I heard a voice off to my side say. Turning, I saw Ben Randolph hobbling towards me. I wasn't sure how he was even able to walk. He was bent nearly double with rheumatism and his hands were so gnarled that he had difficulty holding his cane.

"Hello, Mr. Randolph," I said. I still called him Mr. Randolph. He was, after all, more than twenty years my senior. Like Miss Mamie, he had been on the estate longer than I had been alive. "I don't think that I ever thanked you for coming to tell me about Robert's death."

"It was the least that I could do," he said. "I couldn't help much with anything else," he said indicating his hands. "Betsy's about half way down on the left. I made sure she got extra oats."

"You're going to spoil her and she won't want to leave."

"I spoil all the horses," he said. "I don't think you can love a horse too much. Some trainers try to beat their horses into submission. But I was always afraid that, if I tried, I might beat the spirit out of them. If Betsy acts like she wants to hang around here, just whisper in her ear how wonderful she is and she'll do whatever you ask."

"Does that work with the studs as well as the mares?" I asked him.

"Sure," he said. "Horses are smarter than people."

I thanked him for seeing that Betsy was well cared for, saddled and bridled her, and headed for Germantown. I had enough time to get to the law office and pick up the card stock that I would need. While I was there, I would pick up a new nib for our pen. Sally would want to have an especially sharp point to do the pretty scroll work on each of the capital letters.

As I rode along, I worked out a seating plan. I would be on the right hand side near the pulpit. Because I would be doing the most speaking, it made sense for me to be there. I would have Emily Gladstone sit with me since I was the only person, other than Adam, that she would know. I thought that she would be more comfortable.

On the opposite side, I would put Abigail Jordan, Adam Robertson and Lawrence Weeks. I put Adam on that side so that he would be directly across from his mom. It seemed to me that if he and Emily Gladstone had eye contact, they could communicate silently with each other and support each other in that way. I also wanted Adam to be next to Abigail because I knew that she could converse easily with anyone.

At the long table, facing the altar, the people would be arranged in the following order: Judge Johnston, Professor Allen, Frank Campbell, Captain Stanley, Mamie Smith and Horace Hayworth. There was such enmity between the judge and the former sheriff that I thought that they needed to be at opposite ends of the table.

Since the judge was at the far left, he was between two lawyers, Lawrence Weeks and Richard Allen. At least the three of them could carry on a conversation with each other. Because Frank Campbell was a war veteran, he and Captain Stanley would get along fine. I felt a little sorry for Mamie since she had to sit next to Horace. As he was mostly deaf, conversation would be difficult for them. I thought of shifting Mamie and Adam, but the more I thought about it, the surer I was that I had it right.

There was no perfect seating arrangement. St. Peter had not been happy when Jesus had given Judas the seat of honor at the Last Supper. If the people weren't happy, they would just have to bear it. We would only be there for three or four hours. When I thought of Peter, I knew, for the first time, what I was going to do as a closing worship experience.

The next morning, I set out from Germantown to Richmond. I wanted to talk with Sheriff Curry. It had occurred to me that the reading of Robert Tyler's will might be such an event that a large crowd might show up. I was personally going to ask the sheriff to send several deputies to the funeral banquet to act as security. He would not need to know of my concern that Judge Johnston might try to sabotage the entire event.

The Banquet Begins

T HE MORNING OF NOVEMBER 29, 1806, DAWNED crystal clear. There was usually a haze that hung over the area, especially the mountains. But not on this day; I could see every rock on the distant hills through the bedroom window of my father-in-law's house. With the clear skies came a crisp coldness. I knew that fires would have to be built in the potbellied stoves at the church to knock the chill out of the building. Even though it was nearly six hours until the funeral banquet would be held, I was ready to go! Lighting the fires would be a good excuse to go early.

I wasn't usually up at this time of the day, but, today, I was wide awake. I had not really slept well. As I sat on the side of the bed, Sally stirred and said, "You sure had a restless night. Did you get any sleep?"

"I guess I slept some," I said, "but every time I rolled over it would wake me up. I guess I'm just anxious for this day to be over."

"I'll be glad when it's over, too. You've been out of sorts lately. It's not much fun living with a grumpy husband." She made this statement with both a slight smile and slight sternness. I realized that I must have been truly out of sorts for Sally to mention it.

She almost never complained. I must have been impossible for the last few weeks.

"Let me give you a treat," I said. "You can roll over and go back to sleep. There is no need for you to get up."

"I'm not going to trust you to make tea," she said as she was getting out of bed. "You'll probably burn this house down as distracted as you have been lately."

She was probably right. The funeral banquet had consumed me for a month. One of the reasons that I was so anxious was the task that Robert had given me to respond appropriately to the stories. I still didn't have any idea what that meant. And I had no way to prepare. It was like being asked to ride a spirited stallion when I had never before ridden a horse. I might be able to hold on, but that didn't mean that I would be graceful in the saddle. I was just hoping that, as the day went along, that I didn't get thrown completely.

After two cups of piping hot tea and some biscuits left over from last night's supper, I put on my coat and reached over to give Sally a parting hug. One of my hands moved to caress her more intimately than a hug. She blocked me and said, sternly, "Not here."

Sally's father had been more than gracious to let us stay with him. But I was especially ready for the arrangement to come to an end. It would be at least another three weeks before the new furniture would arrive. We had ordered all of the pieces we needed from a furniture maker in Charlottesville. An entire household of new furniture would be shipped to us on one wagon, arriving the third week of December. At least we would have a nice Christmas. In the mean time, Sally would not permit me to have more than just a peck on the cheek as long as we were under her father's roof. No wonder I was out of sorts and distracted.

I was even more out of sorts as I left the house. In fact, I was downright irked. I had let Sally know it, too. Then I took my anger out on Betsy. As I saddled her, I threw the saddle on her back, instead of easing it into place. I pulled the cinch more tightly than I needed to. Betsy turned her head towards me, snorted loudly and stamped her foot. Then to make sure that I got the message, she swatted me with her tail.

I don't know if it was the combination of the three or just the swatting with her tail but I got the message.

"I'm sorry, girl," I said, as I loosened the cinch and rubbed her mane. What had Ben Randolph said to do? Whisper in her ear how wonderful she is. I took his advice and Betsy quickly forgave me. I decided to give it a shot with Sally, too. Leaving Betsy in the stall, I said, "I'll be right back girl," and headed for the barn door. As I reached the door, I nearly ran into Sally. There was a gentle caress and all kinds of wonderful whispered words. I don't know if she believed my words or not, but I certainly believed hers. As I rode Betsy to New Salem, I thought that maybe all of my responses to the speeches at the funeral banquet ought to be whispered.

When I opened the door to the church, I was stunned by what I saw. Miss Mamie and her crew had been there the day before. She had truly thought of everything. If we had been hosting the king and queen of England, the tables would not have been more eloquently prepared. She had set the tables with the finest Wedgewood china and sterling silver. Beautiful cut glass goblets and pitchers, ornate candelabras with new beeswax candles, pure linen napkins in silver rings, and a centerpiece of cut-dried flowers adorned each table. Behind each table was a large round tray on a stand, draped in table cloths which matched the napkins. To each of the chairs, Mamie had added a needlepoint cushion brought down from the manor house. I was glad that they were there. We were going to be sitting for at least four hours. The only thing that I needed to do to complete the tables was to put Sally's place cards in place.

Not only were the tables perfectly decorated, but fires were already burning in the stoves. The church was comfortably warm even though it was still quite cold outside. I was wondering how Mamie had managed to do this when her grandson, Jimmy, opened the door and walked in with an armful of firewood.

"Hello Mr. Barnes," he said. He walked over to put the wood in a box beside one of the stoves.

"How long have you been here, Jimmy?"

"I spent the night. Grandma figured it would be cold this morning. So she asked me to stay up and keep the fires going. She didn't think the church would get warm enough if we waited till this morning to light the fires."

"She was probably right, Jimmy. Your grandma usually is. Would you mind keeping the fires going until just before the banquet begins?" I asked.

"I'll be glad to do that, Sir."

"If you'll leave the wood boxes full, I'll be able to keep the fires going once the banquet starts."

It was only about 7:30 a.m. We had more than four hours until the banquet would begin. "Jimmy, I'm going to take a walk. If anybody needs me, I'll be back in about an hour."

Just behind the church was an old logging road that led to the top of a rise. I knew that I would have a great view of the Sauratown's from the top of the hill. That would be a good place for me to quietly go over my story. I knew the story of the gristmill, but I needed just a little bit of time to perfect it. I remembered that Judge Johnston had said that his speech would be the most eloquent at the banquet, but I wanted to give him a run for his money.

As I headed up the old road, it dawned on me that I was wearing my finest black satin waistcoat, new white knee stockings, and highly polished buckled shoes. If Sally could see me right now, she would forget about all the sweet things she had whispered in my ear and tell me how stupid I was for stomping in the woods in my finest clothes. I thought about Mr. Oskar and how he was always perfectly dressed and spotlessly clean. I decided that if he could pull it off, so could I. I would just need to be careful not to catch my stockings on any of the briars that had invaded the road and to watch where I stepped so that I didn't scuff my shoes.

Because I was watching where I was stepping instead of where I was heading, I didn't see the animal that went crashing through the woods ahead of me. I thought that I had stirred up a deer until, just over the next rise, I came upon a crude lean-to. Hanging from one of the support poles was a hooded cape. So the assassin and arsonist must be camping here.

Had the judge instructed him to be here? Was he planning to strike again at the banquet? I wondered why he had run when he heard me coming. Certainly, I had surprised him. But was he now lying in wait, ready to pounce? I never carried a weapon with me. At that moment, I wished that William was alongside me again. I was glad that I had asked the sheriff to send deputies to the banquet. Certainly the assassin would not strike again while the officers were present. But in the mean time, I might be in danger.

I decided that the best thing for me to do was to get down the hill as quickly as possible. I didn't care if I did snag my new stockings along the way, at least I would be alive.

⸺◦◦◦◦◦◦⸺

I'm not sure what I did for the next few hours, but the time passed. By 11:30 a.m. all the beneficiaries had arrived at New Salem. In addition, as I had feared, nearly a hundred other people had come to watch and listen. I was glad to have the deputies present and instructed them to make sure that the observers stayed a reasonable distance away from the church. I also let the deputies know what I had discovered in the woods. I had asked one of them to investigate. He came back to report that the camp had now been deserted. As each of the beneficiaries arrived, I ushered them into the church and introduced them to each other.

Emily Gladstone and Adam Robertson had been the first to arrive. They had spent the night before at an inn in Walnut

Cove. Adam was eloquently, if somewhat stiffly, dressed. He kept tugging and pulling at his wig. It was clear that he was not used to wearing one. Or, it may have been that tugging at his wig was just an outward expression of nervousness.

When Captain Stanley arrived, he displayed perfect military bearing in his full dress uniform. Every piece of silver and gold sparkled; his tassels had been combed, and his white plume was fluffed. His horse was as stately as he; a beautiful roan gelding, the horse walked with as much military precision as Captain Stanley. When the captain entered the church, he placed his Espontoon, the long lance with a number of regimental banners, in the corner of the church nearest his seat.

Judge Johnston was driven to the church in one of his finest carriages accompanied by three of his slaves. When he got out of his carriage, he was carrying a large leather satchel which he took into the church. When he found his place at the table, he placed the satchel on the floor next to his chair.

When Abigail Jordan arrived, I noticed that she and Mamie Smith seemed to gravitate to each other. It may have been because they were dressed similarly, or because they were persons of a relative station in society. Horace Hayworth seemed totally out of place. It may have had to do with his deafness, so I was pleased to see that he had brought an ear trumpet.

At 11:50 a.m., I saw the kitchen wagon arrive. I had the guests sit down and gave a brief summary of what would take place during the day, followed by an invocation. As if they were waiting at the door to hear the Amen, the waiters promptly entered the church. That was when I got a nice surprise. Mamie had asked if it would be all right to hire some of the teenagers from Lynnmont to be waiters for the banquet. She had assured me that she would personally train them. I had given her $2.00 to hire the waiters; she had told me that she needed four, so they would each receive fifty cents, enough money to keep any teenager happy for weeks.

So when John Thomas and Anne Marie entered the church with their two best friends I was surprised, and pleased! The four of them were wearing identical uniforms of navy blue breeches, a lighter blue waistcoat, a white shirt and matching stockings. Each had been assigned one table to serve. Mamie had done a wonderful job; the kids served with grace and precision.

The first course was a specialty at the Lynnmont kitchens— cheddar cheese and onion soup. The onions were cooked in a sugar and water solution which made them both tart and sweet. When the sharpness of the cheddar cheese was added, it made a soup that was simply delicious and truly warming.

After the soup was finished, large platters of food were brought in and placed on the trays. Each waiter served the individual plates from the platters. Deep fried chicken, roasted potatoes, succotash (a mixture of sweet corn and butter beans), sautéed mushrooms and yeast rolls made up the main course. Our waiters also served each of us three pats of butter and a small vial of honey for our rolls. Copious amounts of hot, sweet tea were served throughout the meal.

Dessert was one of Miss Mamie's specialties: pumpkin pies with whipped cream. Along with the pie, each of us was also given a small glass of sweet scuppernong wine from the Lynnmont Winery. It was a very special meal. I could not have been more proud of our waiters. They had served with distinction and had certainly earned the fifty cents that had been promised to each of them.

When the tables had been cleared, I offered everyone a brief break. With as much tea as was drunk, I was sure that most of us would need one. I asked everyone to return as quickly as possible. I had no trouble getting a positive response for this request. All of the participants were as eager to begin the real part of the funeral banquet as I was.

When everyone had returned to their seats, I said, "When Charles Wesley, the brother of the founder of the Methodists, John Wesley, lost a very good friend to death, he penned this hymn:

> If death my friend and me divide, Thou dost not, Lord, my sorrow chide,
>
> Or frown my tears to see; Restrained from passionate excess,
>
> Thou bidst me mourn in calm distress for them that rest in Thee.
>
> I feel a strong immortal hope, which bears my mournful spirit up
>
> Beneath its mountain load; Redeemed from death, and grief, and pain,
>
> I soon shall find my friend again within the arms of God.
>
> Pass a few fleeting moments more and death the blessing shall restore
>
> Which death has snatched away; for me thou wilt thy summons send,
>
> And give me back my parted friend to that eternal day.

Robert Tyler was the best friend that I have ever had. We grew up together at Lynnmont, or Beautiful Valley as it was called then. When he died two months ago, a part of me died with him. Like Wesley, I have grieved the loss.

I know that most of you here today share my feelings of loss. You, too, have lost a friend. There are a couple of people who are here today who didn't know Robert Tyler, and at least one who has hated Robert as much as I have loved him.

It is my hope that when our time together today has ended, that all of us will see that we have lost a good man. It was Mr. Tyler's hope that those of you who do not know him will be introduced to him through the stories that will be shared.

One of you will be given the opportunity to try to convince all of us who knew and loved Robert Tyler that we have been completely wrong about him. That person is Judge Alexander Johnston. I nodded towards the Judge and he returned the nod.

Before the judge speaks, however, we are going to hear two stories about Robert's childhood. I would like to introduce Mamie Smith to you, who is going to share our first story. Mrs. Smith has been a cook, and the chief baker, in the Lynnmont kitchens since before I was born. Three generations of her family live on the estate. You had a sampling of her artistry with the pumpkin pie that you had for dessert. Miss Mamie, why don't you come and stand here in the pulpit and tell us about some stolen cookies?

Miss Mamie got up from her seat, made her way around the altar rail and stepped into the pulpit with such an air of confidence that anyone would have thought that she made her living doing public speaking. Her voice was strong and full of enthusiasm.

"As Preacher Barnes has already told you, I'm as old as the hills around here. I started working in the kitchen as an apprentice baker when I was fifteen years old. That was fifty-five years ago. Lord how time does fly. When I came to work here, Mr. Oskar Schoenfeldt was the owner of Beautiful Valley. He hired a young man named Joshua Tyler to be the estate manager, and Mr. Tyler moved to the estate with his five-year-old son, Robert Joseph.

"Robert's mom had died when he was only two. When Mr. Joshua came to the estate, he asked all of us ladies to adopt Robert. The boy had more mothers than you could shake a stick at. Mr. Joshua had told us all, that if Robert ever needed correcting, we should go ahead and correct him and then tell him about it later. He figured that Robert would then get corrected again, and that two corrections would be better than one.

"It was about this time of the year, when Robert was six years old, that we received a very special treat in the kitchen. We were able to get our hands on a whole gallon of genuine maple syrup all the way from the Green Mountains in Vermont. We would only get maple syrup about once every two or three years, so when this came in, I decided to make twenty dozen sticky maple cookies. Now, my sticky maple cookies are the stickiest, gooiest, sweetest, best cookies ever made. The cookies are so rich that nobody would ever be able to eat more than two at a time. I've discovered, through the years, that if they are taken right out of the oven and taken outside in the cold air they set better.

"So the morning that I baked all those cookies, I put them on cooling racks that I had moved outside. I covered them with cheese cloth just in case there were any bugs still around from the summer and went back into the kitchen. About a half hour later, I went to check on the cookies. I thought that as cold as it was, the cookies had probably cooled enough and were a good sticky mess.

"When I got to the racks, I noticed right away that the cheese cloth had been disturbed. At first I thought that I might have a squirrel problem, but when I looked more closely, I saw that one of the baking sheets with two dozen cookies on it was missing. I wondered where the thief would be and, I decided to look in the closest hiding place that there was, the lean-to shed where all the firewood for the kitchens were kept dry.

"I took one look inside and saw Robert sitting on the ground with the tray of cookies in his lap. Almost a dozen of those special cookies were already gone. I stepped into the shed and said, "Robert, did you take those cookies off the rack?"

"No ma'am," he said. "I just found them right here."

"Is that right?" I asked. "Did you eat any of them?"

"No ma'am. I was just looking after them for you."

"Now, Robert. If you didn't eat any of the cookies, how come your fingers and your lips are all sticky?

"I'd been a mother long enough to know the difference between when a child is sorry and when he is just sorry that he got caught. And I gotta tell you, that child was sorry. He burst into tears. And they were genuine tears, too.

"You know I've got to punish you, don't you? I asked him. "I've got to punish you for stealing the cookies. And I've got to punish you even more for lying to me about it. And I've got to tell your father, too.

"The poor child was crying so hard that I felt right awful having to spank him. I knew that he was in for even more punishment when his father got off work that night. And I knew that he was going to be sick as a dog for eating so many sticky, sweet cookies.

"The next morning, Mr. Tyler and Robert came into the kitchen. 'Do you have something to say to Miss Mamie?' he asked Robert.

"I'm really sorry, Miss Mamie," he said and burst into tears again.

"I didn't know one little boy could have so many tears. It took Mr. Tyler and me a right good while to calm him down. It was through his tears that we finally discovered why he was so full of remorse. The preacher at Bethania Moravian had said that if you got caught stealing and lying that you would go straight to hell. He had certainly gotten caught, and he was scared to death!

"He figured that he would be going to hell most any minute. Joshua Tyler and I took turns holding the boy and teaching him the lesson of forgiveness. Though he wasn't old enough to understand about grace and redemption, he certainly knew that he was loved, and that he wouldn't be going to hell—at least not that day.

"After an hour or so of caressing and loving him, he was finally ready to go out and play. I sent him out by saying to him, 'Robert, if you ever want a cookie, all you have to do is ask.' When he had left, I turned to his father and said, 'He must have had a long night. Being scared of dying and going to hell and being sick from eating all those cookies.'

"'It's a strange thing,' Mr. Tyler said. 'But he never did get sick. He must have a stomach made of iron.'

"It was nearly a year later that one of the older boys let it slip that a couple of them had convinced Robert to steal the cookies, and that they had eaten most of them. They had run when they saw me coming out of the kitchen door and had left Robert holding the evidence of his crime.

"I learned several things from Robert and the sticky cookies. One is that you can tell true repentance. There is a difference between feeling sorry about something and turning away from it. Another thing I learned is that even six-year-olds know the meaning of loyalty. Robert Tyler never told on the older boys. He took the punishment for them all. The last thing I learned is that six-year-olds can have a life changing experience. Robert's tears were so deep, his remorse so heartfelt, that he never wanted to feel that pain again."

Mamie Smith left the pulpit and returned to her seat. We all sat in silence. I know that I was thinking about some of the whippings I had received as a child, and I was wondering if I had had as profound an experience as Robert. I don't know how long we sat there pondering before it dawned on me that I was supposed to give an appropriate response.

I rose from my chair and stood beside the pulpit. "There is a prayer in the communion service which says, 'We are not worthy even to gather up the crumbs from under thy table, O Lord. But it is thy desire always to have mercy.' Let's all just take a few more minutes to reflect silently on our need for mercy and on our need to be merciful."

When there is a crowd of people, silence can be uncomfortable. Even when we are alone, we tend to talk to ourselves. It wasn't long before people began to get restless and I knew that our time of introspection was over. I got up, replenished the wood in the stoves, and then moved to the pulpit.

Mr. Tyler has asked that I share the next story. It is also a story from our childhood, but by the time of this story, Robert and I were both eleven. Those of you who live at Lynnmont know that there are several mill ponds on the property. Back when Oskar Schoenfeldt first laid out the estate, he planned four water-powered mills, a gristmill for grinding corn, a flour mill, a sawmill and a weaving mill. Each of these mills required a strong flow of water which was best achieved by damming up a creek and forcing water through a spillway.

There are numerous creeks which crisscross the estate. Mr. Oskar had surveyors pick out the best locations for his mills and then began the process of building dams. He first diverted the creeks and built large earthen dams. The workers put layer after layer of soil, hand tamped, into place. When these earthen structures were complete, a coating of concrete mixed with cobblestones was applied to each of the structures. It was only after the cement had been given weeks to cure that the creeks were rediverted and the water began to back up.

Mr. Oskar had four mill ponds created but only three mills. The weaving mill was never built even though the dam and pond were both in place. It was this particular pond that became a favorite haunt for all of the boys of the estate. It was the deepest of the ponds and had the highest dam. The water, which rushed through the spillway, could only have been described as a torrent.

Nearly every day during the summer months, the boys would gather there to swim or fish or just hang around with each other. Fishing was usually best right up against the dam while swimming was best on the other side of the pond away from the spillway. All of us knew that swimming too close to the spillway would be deadly. Not even the strongest swimmer would be able to swim against that current.

At eleven years old, Robert and I were right on the cusp of having to work all day long every day. We were both employed in the dairy, milking the cows each morning and evening, and we both had school each morning. The rest of the day we had pretty much to ourselves. He and I sat in adjacent stalls in the dairy barn as we milked; and we often worked out intricate plans of how we would spend our day. We had decided that morning that we were going to go fishing. Robert was going to get the poles and other equipment that we needed, while I was digging a pail full of worms.

We met up at his house and began the half-mile walk along Buffalo Creek to the pond. It was a beautiful early summer day. It was hot, but not the oppressive hot that comes in late summer. We knew that if we did get too hot, we could just slip off our clothes and go naked into the pond to cool ourselves off.

Robert and I were both avid fishermen. We had taken some of the money that we made milking and paid my dad, who was the blacksmith, to create us a whole collection of different-sized hooks. We had taken long strands of string and coated every inch of them with beeswax to make them strong. We created bobbers out of birch bark and poles from the reeds that grew along the creek beds.

When we got to the pond that morning, we made our way around the right side and headed for the dam. We wanted to fish off the top of the dam. There were basically three kinds of fish in the pond: crappie, bream, and bass. Occasionally we would catch a gar; once in a while a trout would make its way down the mountain streams and into our pond. Today, we were going to fish for crappie which seemed to like the deeper water near the dam. If we were going for bream, we could fish along any of the banks of the pond and do fine. We had headed to the right because it was the shortest way, but it meant that we had to cross the spillway. The spillway was too wide to jump across, but even if it hadn't been it would have been too dangerous to try. To fall on the pond side of the dam meant risking getting caught in the spillway current, and to fall on the other side mean a drop of about forty feet straight down.

Usually crossing the spillway was not a problem because the boys had bridged the gap with numerous pieces of wood; but when we got to the spillway that morning, everything had changed. All of the pieces of wood except one were gone. One plank about an inch thick and six inches wide was laid across the ten foot opening at the top of the dam. The board was only about six or seven inches above the torrent of water.

All of my life, up to that point, I had been brave enough to dare new things but scared enough not to be stupid. I freely admit to you that I was scared about crossing that board. It didn't seem strong enough, and it sure didn't seem wide enough. Robert and I actually discussed our options. We took a quick look around to see if there were other boards which could be added to supplement the bridge, but we couldn't find any. We talked about walking all the way around the pond and coming up the dam from the other side, but we decided that it was too far to walk and too much trouble.

We finally decided to cross on the plank. Robert reasoned that the fishing poles in one hand and a pail of worms in the other would give me balance. He did tell me to move across quickly because if I lingered on the board, I might lose my balance. I was about halfway across when I heard a crack, but the board held and I found myself on the other side. Robert had not waited for me to get completely across before he stepped out on the board. When he got to the middle, the board broke in two with a load crack.

I heard the crack and Robert's yell of "Oh no!" I spun around and, at first, didn't see Robert at all. But when I glanced down, I saw Robert clinging to the top of the dam, with his body caught in the spillway. His fishing poles and tackle box were gone and the board was nowhere to be seen. I knelt quickly and grabbed hold of Robert's arms. Robert was in real trouble. He had enough strength to hold on to the dam, but the current was so strong that he could not pull himself out of it. No matter how hard I pulled, I couldn't budge him either.

Both of us were panicked. I couldn't go for help because Robert wouldn't be able to hold on very long without me. I kept looking over the side. At the bottom of the spillway jagged, broken logs and other debris, including the broken board, stuck up from the water. I knew that a fall into that would kill Robert. We were both crying, mostly out of frustration that there seemed to be nothing that either of us could do.

Suddenly, Robert's expression changed. It was like he had seen the face of God! At that very moment, the largest, strongest black man that I have even seen stepped over me, reached one arm under Robert's armpit, picked him right up out of the water, and stood him on the top of the dam.

I heard him say," You boys need to be more careful."

Then Robert and I did something that eleven-year-old boys just don't do. We hugged each other! While we were celebrating this miracle, both of us, at the same time, realized that we needed to thank the man. But when we looked up from our hug, he was not there. How could he have disappeared so quickly? To this day, I have no explanation.

I don't know if angels can look like black giants or not. But I have always believed that he was an angel. There was no other explanation. Like Moses being drawn forth from the Nile so that God could use him to free the Israelites, Robert was drawn forth from the spillway so that he could do great things. Robert and I spoke often of our sense of utter helplessness and frustration, and of how neither of us wanted to ever feel that way again. We also spoke often of the incredible joy of the miracle. We both decided that we shouldn't try to explain away the miracle but simply to bask in its glory.

As I made my way from the pulpit, I was surprised that tears were running down my cheeks. I wasn't sure why, after all these years, the story would still be that emotional. As I looked at each of the beneficiaries, I realized that I wasn't the only person crying. Apparently the story of the redemption of a child was a very emotional one, especially for those who were parents.

I made my way to the altar and held up the bowl of water. "Water is all through the Bible," I said. "It is a symbol of our birth and of our rebirth. As we remember Robert Tyler's life today, also remember your own. Remember you own mill ponds."

When I saw the judge's face, I was reminded that not everyone shared in the celebration of the miracle. Because Alexander Johnston was about to speak the whole atmosphere of the funeral banquet was about to change dramatically.

An Eloquent Speech

"I WAS RAISED IN A FAMILY OF PRIVILEGE in Massachusetts," Judge Alexander Johnston began. "My father had inherited a very successful shipbuilding company from his father. As is often the case with businesses, the second generation makes far more money than the first. My father had done quite well, and he wanted me to share in his good fortune. One of the great benefits of wealth is the privilege of getting an education and as a young man of great wealth and position I was given the privilege of studying at Harvard.

"Harvard was founded by a Congregational preacher in 1636. From its very beginnings, every student was required to study the Bible. It was believed that the Bible informed and elucidated every subject and even though I was attending the college to study law, I was drilled in Bible every day for four years. Our professors believed that recitation and rote were the only acceptable means of learning, therefore I was taught to recite long sections. Even to this day, more than fifty years later, I can still quote whole chapters."

The judge moved from the pulpit where he had begun his speech to the altar. He tucked his ever present cane under his arm and picked up the Bible from its place. He held it gently for a second, then slammed it shut and threw it on the floor.

"No!" I yelled as every other person in the room gasped in horror. I abruptly stood and started towards the Holy Book to pick it up.

"Sit down!" roared the Judge as he brandished his cane at me. "Robert Tyler demanded that I speak to all of you" he gestured with his cane around the tables. "I assume that he was hoping that I might teach you something."

From the very first time that I had seen the list of beneficiaries, I had wondered what Robert was up to. Now, I was more certain than ever that he had made a horrible mistake. I had always trusted Robert, but at this moment I was having a hard time doing that. From the very first day we had moved into New Salem, there had always been an open Bible on the altar. I was just glad there was still one open on the lectern. I hoped that Alexander Johnston would leave it alone because I didn't ever want there to be even one moment when God's Word was shut in His sanctuary. I reluctantly sat back down, fearing what would come next.

As instantly as the snap of his fingers, the judge's demeanor changed. He smiled broadly and tapped his cane on the floor as if to signal a new beginning.

"I hope that my acted out parable will be memorable to you. I am reminded that the prophets Jeremiah and Ezekiel, were asked to act out their prophecies. Jeremiah wore a yoke made of iron to symbolize the awful task that God had given him. Ezekiel was asked to lie on his left side for 390 days and on his right side for 40 days to symbolize Israel's punishment. Hosea was even asked to marry a prostitute to show how God had remained faithful to Israel, even as she had prostituted herself with foreign Gods. I have a difficult task, because I am being asked to introduce you to a new way of thinking, one in which we are asked not to worship the God of the Bible, but to be obedient to the God of the Bible.

"The best I can tell from all my years of study is that the God of the Bible is a harsh and strident master. If you believe the New Testament, He even executed his own son to pay for the sins of the world. One of the greatest problems in believing that God is a god of love is the problem of pain. If God loves the world, why is there so much sin, trouble, and death?

"It seems to me that there is only one answer to the problem of pain. And that is to come to the conclusion that God is the author of suffering, that God is the bringer of death, and that God is the creator of evil. He does these things because God is a God of hate.

"I know that most of you will object and say that God is a God of love. But there are many more verses in the Bible that speak of God hating than there are those that speak of a loving God. The Bible speaks over and over again of God bringing curses, woes, destruction, mourning, exile and judgment. How could a god who is the God of love be the author of such devastation?

"Most of us would agree that there are things that God does hate. Time and again we are told that God hates evil and idolatry. We read that he hates false worship and that he sets his face against injustice. We are glad that he does hate these things, because we have all seen the negative effect they have on our world.

"O how I have longed to believe that God is good. My wife was a person of simple faith. She loved God and was sure that God loved her. Every day of her adult life, after I taught her to read, she read His Word and offered heartfelt prayers. She trusted God even when, it seemed to me, that God dashed her trust. When our first four children were all stillborn, she had faith that something good would come out of each tragedy. 'It's all part of God's plan,' she would say. 'I'll see my babies in heaven.' But each time I buried a child, I was more convinced than before that if it was God's plan that babies die, then he was simply cruel.

"Then came an even more horrible and heart wrenching day. I watched my dear Martha finally give birth to a living child. As she cradled Lynn in her arms, the moment of the greatest joy in her life, Martha died. At her funeral, Martha's preacher quoted from Romans, 'All things work together for good for those who love God and are called according to His purpose.' I'm sure that the preacher meant well and that he was trying to bring me comfort, but all he brought me was agony. Martha, my dear, sweet Martha, was dead. God had either murdered her or he had been a God who was too weak to do anything to save her. How could I possibly follow such a God?

"At least I had Lynn. She was such a sweet child. She had been given Martha's capacity to love. She was innocent and kind, compassionate and caring. Even though I had come to distrust and doubt God, I was determined that she should have the same simple faith that her mother had had. I saw to it that she was raised in church, and I never shared with her my anger and doubt. I simply could not follow such a cruel and mean spirited God.

"But God wasn't through with me yet. If I would not be obedient to him, he would destroy the only thing I had left in the world. The day came when Lynn came home and announced that she was married to Robert Tyler! She had gone mad! Insanity was the only explanation. If my Lynn had been in her right mind, there was no way that she could have fallen in love with Robert Tyler. To this day, twenty years later, she remains a patient at an asylum for the insane in Virginia."

Judge Johnston paused. He sighed deeply. Emily Gladstone and I looked at each. She leaned towards me and whispered in my ear, "He really believes she's still alive? We sent word to him of her death and of Adam's birth." Before I could answer her, the judge continued.

"The day that I sent her to the asylum was the darkest day of my life. I remember finding myself at the Johnston family graveyard. I'm not sure how I got there, but I was standing at the foot of Martha's grave. The four headstones of my babies were lined up beside hers. A large limb had fallen from the oak tree under which they were buried and lay across the graves. In a blind rage, I picked it up and swung it with all my might as I cursed God. When I swung the limb, I accidentally hit Martha's gravestone. The headstone shattered and the only words left were the words that she had asked to be there, 'At Peace.' When her headstone shattered, my life was shattered with it. I fell, prostrate on her grave, and wept.

"They were not tears of grief, or mourning, or sadness. They were tears of anger and bitterness. Like Jacob, who spent an entire night struggling with God, I spent an entire night lying on Martha's grave, weeping, under the words 'At Peace.' It was in that dark and awful night that I finally came face to face with God and understood that the only way that I could know this God was to hate. My whole life, God had been calling me to join him in hating."

Judge Johnston walked forward to where the altar Bible lay on the floor of the chancel just inside the prayer rail. He leaned down, picked it up "I have come to admire and respect this book. My acted out parable was meant to teach us that, if we are unwilling to follow all of its teachings, we should throw it away." He turned to the Book of Malachi and read, "Jacob I have loved, but Esau I have hated; I have laid waste his hill country and left his territory to jackals of the desert says the Lord of Hosts." He closed the Book and laid it on the rail.

"'Esau I have hated.' Those are God's words. We find it hard to believe that God hates individuals, but that is exactly what he does. He hated the Egyptians and destroyed their nation. He hated the Assyrians, the Babylonians, the Hittites, and the Jebusites. He hated the Philistines. He hated the people of Jericho and saw to their utter destruction. God hates people, and those whom he hates he sets out to destroy. Now if God hates, shouldn't we, as his creation, also hate. Aren't we being most like God when we hate the very people that he hates?

"The night that I spent lying on Martha's grave, God enlisted me in his army. I might not be capable of bringing justice to the world by loving, but I could by being an agent of God's destruction by hating all that he hates. And that is why I hated Robert Tyler.

"God damn Robert Tyler! And God damn all the other Robert Tylers in this world! The New Testament states, in Jesus' own words, that the people God hates the most are hypocrites— people who say one thing and do another.

"Robert Tyler hated me. He came by that hate honestly enough. He was raised at Beautiful Valley by another hypocrite named Oskar Schoenfeldt. He was taught, from a very early age, that I was an evil man; that my way of life, my business practices, and my judicial decisions were all abhorrent. He was so blinded by prejudice that he was unable to see any redeeming quality in me, and that is why I hated Robert Tyler.

"When he was a young man, right after he had inherited Beautiful Valley, he was so driven by his hatred for me that he purposefully caused the destruction of the most valuable race horse I have ever owned. One of my most trusted young servants was killed in the incident. Most of the public believed that the incident was just a racing accident, but I knew differently. He was so driven by desire to destroy me that he murdered my horse and caused the death of my slave, and that is why I hated Robert Tyler.

As an attorney, Robert undermined my judicial authority. He ignored my summons, sought to overturn nearly every ruling that I have ever made, disrupted my courtroom over and over again, and turned the judicial process into a carnival sideshow. He did all these because his hatred of me twisted his view of justice and destroyed his ability to reason. And that is why I hated Robert Tyler.

Robert Tyler also undermined my plantation. Even though he was a slave owner himself, he sought to convince my slaves that they were of equal value to whites. He caused a near rebellion when he actually hugged one of my niggers in public! To treat our blacks with such familiarity convinced many of them that they were on the same social standing as whites. Only the strong discipline of my overseer was able to correct the situation, and that is why I hated Robert Tyler.

Robert Tyler also destroyed my relationship with one of my most trusted associates, Horace Hayworth. I handpicked Horace to be the sheriff of Surry County. I trained him in the job. But, somehow, Robert Tyler convinced him to rebel against my authority and abandon my friendship; and that is why I hated Robert Tyler.

"I never knew a more evil man than Robert Tyler. Robert Tyler was a modern-day Pharisee. He claimed to be a man of love and yet his hatred for me led to Lynn's destruction. Robert Tyler was so manipulative, so conniving, and so mean-spirited that he gladly and joyfully annihilated her. Like the devil luring Eve to eat from the tree, Robert Tyler lured Lynn into believing that he loved her. He pretended to be kind; he was actually cruel. He pretended to be loving; he was actually hateful. He pretended to be compassionate; he was actually mean spirited. When he found me too strong to destroy, he destroyed her! I have hated Robert Tyler because that is exactly what God would have done.

"God enlisted me to do all that I could to help send Robert Tyler to his well-earned damnation. Like the Pharisees, Robert Tyler wore a mask of elaborate godliness. But he was actually a missionary of evil. God has great compassion for honest sinners, persons who know they have fallen short and are repentant. But he roars with righteous anger at those who think that they are above reproach. God sets out to destroy those who, like Robert Tyler, claim one way of life and live another.

"My great challenge has been to expose Robert Tyler's hypocrisy without falling into his trap of evil. Even though God has enlisted me in his army of hate, He still expects me to rise above pettiness. For more than twenty years, I have sought Robert Tyler's destruction. I knew that the only way that I could succeed in the task that God had given me was to help Robert Tyler expose himself. I have to admit to you that I never succeeded. Robert Tyler was always too clever to let the public see what was so obvious to me."

Judge Johnston walked out of the chancel towards his seat at the table. I wondered if he was through with his speech. I was just getting ready to stand and respond to him when he picked up the leather satchel that he had put under his seat earlier, pulled from it a sheath of papers, and returned to the chancel area. Holding the papers, he continued his speech.

"Sir Isaac Newton, the great British scientist, has a good friend whose name is William Cowper. It was Cowper, in trying to describe some of Newton's great scientific discoveries, who penned the words, "God works in a mysterious way, his wonders to perform." Those words encapsulate better than any others what happened just a few days before Robert Tyler died.

"He came, unexpectedly and unannounced, to my house one night. He told me that an associate of his, named Matthew Brown, had discovered a plot to assassinate him. He confessed to me that he instantly assumed that I was behind the plot; and only later learned that his true enemy was someone else. It was in discovering how wrong he had been, that he came to realize that his hatred of me had destroyed his very soul. He confessed to all of the things that I have shared with you, all of the reasons that I had hated him in return. He begged my forgiveness, claiming that he could not die until his soul was restored!

"I have to admit to you that I was strongly tempted to let his soul burn it hell. It seemed to be the only just and fair thing to do.

But then, to prove that his confession was genuine, he offered me this." The judge held up the bundle of papers that he was holding.

"This is a copy of Robert Tyler's Last Will and Testament. In it, he leaves the bulk of his estate to me, even though there are some small gifts that will come to each of you, Robert told me that leaving the estate to me was the only way that he would be able to atone for his multiple offenses. I assure you that this will is quite genuine, but that we might all be assured of that, I would like for Dr. Allen, who is the professor of law at the University of North Carolina to examine it, and attest to its authenticity."

Judge Johnston handed the will to Richard Allen. I couldn't believe his audacity, or his cleverness. He was audacious, because I had told him that Robert had given me a copy of his will. He knew that I would produce it when the time was right. He was clever, because, if Dr. Allen announced his document to be genuine, there would be competing wills. The fight over the estate could be dragged out in the courts for years. The fight, itself, could destroy the estate. Alexander Johnston would either win the entire estate, or tear it to pieces. Either way, he would win.

Dr. Allen had finished his examination. He found no reason to suspect that the document wasn't genuine. Judge Johnston returned to his seat with a look of triumph on his face. It had certainly been an eloquent speech. If I hadn't known Robert so well, or known that the real will was safely hidden in the altar, I would have believed Judge Johnston. I wondered how many other beneficiaries believed him.

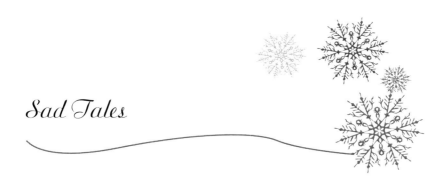

Sad Tales

THE JUDGE'S LOOK OF TRIUMPH WORRIED ME. Was now the time to pull the altar away from the wall and introduce the other will? Something inside me said, "Wait!" I hoped that none of the other speakers would soften their stories for fear of contradicting the judge. The next two speakers would tell stories which would give a completely different view of Alexander Johnston. Horace Hayworth was going to remind him of all of the events surrounding the arrest of Robert Tyler, and Emily Gladstone was going to tell of Lynn's captivity and death. The only thing to do at this point was to remain faithful to the schedule that Robert had given me. I introduced Horace Hayworth.

"I was raised at Yadkin Oaks," he began. "My father was de slave master there long before Alexander Johnston became the owner. We lived in a small house right beside de nigger quarters so that my father could keep an eye on them. I never much liked livin' that close to all de niggers, but my father said that it was a necessary evil that went along wid de job. He was trainin' me to take over the slave master's job. I didn't want to be a slave master because I just didn't like hangin' around de niggers. I wasn't trained to do nothin' else and, even though I was already in my twenties, I was stuck at the plantation. Managin' the niggers wasn't that hard; giving one a good whipping every month or so pretty much kept all the rest o' them in line.

"It was a couple of years after Alexander Johnston came to Yadkin Oaks that he was named Judge. Back in those days, de sheriff of the county was appointed by de judge. When Judge Johnston came to me and asked if I wanted to be de sheriff, I was right pleased to get de job. One o' the reasons that I was glad was because I could move away from de plantation and into Richmond. De jail house had a room I could move into rent free; de job came with a couple of horses and saddles; and I was getting a monthly salary of $4.00.

"Thar warnt much to the town of Richmond in those days. Jest a courthouse, a couple of lawyer's offices, a tavern, ten or twelve houses, and de jail. De jail was the only building in town that was made o' brick; and, when you walked in de front door, there was a big lobby. De doors to the only two cells were directly in front o' you. Off to the right was a bedroom where I slept and off to the left was another room dat de judge could sleep in when court was in session. The cells were small, only six feet wide and eight feet deep. De only things dat a prisoner had inside the cell were a cornhusk mattress on de floor and a chamber pot. Thar warnt no windows, so when the door to de cell was shut, the prisoner would be left in near total darkness even during the day. The only light would come from a little slot in de door that was used to pass food through.

"Court was in session only on the first week of the month, so a lot o' the prisoners that I had were people who were waitin' trial or petty criminals who were serving a three or four day sentence. In fact, most of de time, de jail was empty. We had only one regular, a drunk named Albert Schmidt. Albert was the kinda drunk who got mean when he drank, and de drunker he got the meaner he got. It seemed like every time he got drunk, he got into a fight with somebody, and I would have to throw him into jail for a couple o' days till he sobered up.

"I was really surprised when I got woken up after midnight, one night, with a poundin' on the jail house door. When I got to de door, Judge Johnston's house nigger, James, was there. 'James, why you wakin me up this time o night?'

"'All hell dun broke loose at the plantation. Miss Lynn dun gone crazy or somethun."

"Nigger," I said. "What in the world are you talkin' about?"

'I don't know Massa Horace. All I knows is dat Massa Johnston wants you to come to the Plantation afor dawn. He wants you to bring the pris'ner wagon. An he wants you to tote along Albert Schmidt.'

"Before I could git another word outta him, he had turned and jumped on his horse. I didn't have no idea what was going on, but I knew dat I had to do just what the judge had asked. I could certainly understand bein' asked to go to the plantation to arrest someone, but I couldn't figure why the judge wanted me to bring Albert Schmidt along. I went to the livery, got the team of horses dat pulled the prisoner wagon, harnessed them to de wagon, and then went and woke up Albert."

"Whadda ya reckon the judge wants with me?"

"I don't have no idea. But as long as you are a prisoner, he can ask you to do anything he wants."

"When we got to Yadkin Oaks, the judge met us out on the driveway. He jumped up on the prison wagon and told me to drive to de barn. When we got there, he showed me a young man who was sleep in the corner o' the barn and, he told me to stay right thar and watch him. 'If he wakes up don't let him go anywhere,' he told me. From where I was a standin' in the barn, I could see through de open front doors as Judge Johnston took Albert with him into the plantation house. Through the open back doors o' the barn I could see dat James was hitchin' a team o' horses to one o' the plantation carriages. When everything was ready, James drove the carriage round to the front o' de house, jumped down and ran into de house. It wasn't long afor I saw the judge, James, and Albert come outta de house in the pre-dawn light.

They were dragging along a screaming and kicking Lynn, the judge's daughter, and even though I was a long way from them, I could see dat they had her hands tied behind her back. I warn't close enough to hear exactly what she was yelling, but I could see that she was putting up quite a fight as they were putting her into de carriage. I stood thar, completely stunned, as I watched John and Albert tie her to de seat o' the carriage and then take extra pieces of rope and tie de doors o' de carriage shut. After they seemed satisfied dat she couldn't get out o' the carriage, Judge Johnston took Albert aside for a moment to tell him something. Then Albert got up on the carriage seat, clicked the reins, and set off down the driveway. Almost immediately, the judge turned away from the carriage and started towards de barn. The young man that I was awatchin' was still sound asleep.

"When the Judge got to the barn, I said, 'Judge, what in de world is goin' on? Who is this young man, and what's he done?'

"That's Robert Tyler and he raped my little Lynn. When I wake him up, I want you to place him under arrest and take him to the jail. You keep him there and don't let him speak to anyone. Do you understand?"

"As we were walkin' towards Robert, I asked, 'Judge, where is Albert taking Lynn?"

"That's none of your business! I have sentenced Albert Schmidt to lifetime banishment from North Carolina. If you ever see him again, arrest him immediately. All you have to know is that he is leaving Surry County and North Carolina, hopefully forever. Have you got your handcuffs ready? He's likely to put up a fight," he said pointing his cane at Robert. He jabbed him in the stomach with his cane, much harder dan he needed to, to wake him up, and said to him when he was clearly awake,

"You are under arrest for Statutory Rape and Contributing to the Delinquency of a Minor," he said as I slapped the handcuffs on him.

"What?" he yelled. "I haven't raped anybody! I married your daughter! "

"There will be some other charges as soon as I can think of them!" the Judge yelled as we dragged Robert to the prisoner wagon.

"Where is Lynn? I want to talk to Lynn!"

"Lynn didn't want to see you," the judge lied. "She left early this morning to go to a place where she could get as far away from you as she could. Besides, you are going to spend the next twenty years in prison if I have anything to say about it! So you don't need to know where she is."

"De Judge and I threw Robert on to de back o' the wagon and I run a chain through his handcuffs and secured it through an iron eyebolt dat was attached to de bottom o' the wagon. 'Keep him in the cell with the door shut, and remember, don't let him speak to anyone,' the Judge told me as I drove off. All the way to de jail, Robert kept asking me about Lynn and whar she was. I didn't know whar she was, but I knew dat the judge had lied to him. I also knew dat if I wanted to keep my job, I couldn't tell him dat. When we got to the jail, I did as I had been told and shut Robert in the dark cell. For four days he kept beatin' on the cell door and yelling, 'Where is Lynn? I want to see Lynn!' He would yell himself to sleep each night and begin again as soon as he woke. On the morning o' the fifth day, Judge Johnston came to the jail and told me to take Robert to de courthouse at noon.

"But Judge," I said. "The court's not in session dis week."

"We know that, but he doesn't."

"When we got to de court room, the judge was robed and wearing his judge's wig. He was seated behind de bench as I led Robert into de room.

"Where is Lynn? I want to see Lynn!" Robert yelled at him.

"Silence!" Judge Johnston roared back. "Don't you know that you are in a court of law? Don't you have enough sense not to yell at the judge? I have the power to destroy you completely. It would be smart for you to show a little respect." For the first time in five days, except when he was asleep, Robert was silent. "You have already been charged with Statutory Rape and with Contributing to the Delinquency of a Minor. Since you held Lynn against her will for three days, I am also adding a charge of Kidnapping. I have Lynn's sworn statement that you are guilty of these charges," the judge said as he held up a sheet of paper. "If you come to trial and are found guilty, I will sentence you to twenty years each on the rape and kidnapping charges and to another five years on the Delinquency charge. You will probably die in prison."

"May I see Lynn's sworn statement?" Robert asked as he looked the judge square in the eye. He obviously did not believe that Lynn had written anything.

"No," the Judge answered. "It's evidence for the trial." He took de piece of paper and slipped it into his leather satchel. He flipped through de other papers dat were before him on de bench as if he were looking for a particular thing and den held up another document. "But I am willing to offer you mercy. If you will sign this Annulment of the Marriage and promise not to look for Lynn or ever to speak to her again, I will set you free. It's up to you. You can go to prison, or you can go home."

"I'll never sign anything," Robert said. "And I'll never stop looking for Lynn. You can bring me to trial if you want, but I'm not guilty of anything. I'll be found innocent."

"Do you really think that you would be found innocent at a trial in my court? Maybe you just need some time to think about this. Sheriff, take the prisoner back to the jail and keep him there until he signs this document."

"I took Robert back to de jail, locked him in his cell, and den went back to de courthouse to speak to de judge. 'Why are you lying to de boy?' I asked him. 'You know dat he hasn't done nothing wrong, except fall in love with your daughter'."

"Not done anything wrong? He bedeviled my daughter, convinced her that he loved her, kidnapped her from her home, and robbed her of her innocence and her sanity. I may not have enough evidence to convict him in a legal sense, but I certainly have enough evidence to know that he is both evil and corrupt. I'm willing to set him free if he signs the annulment, but I am going to do everything that I can to make his life miserable. And I will see to it that he never sees Lynn again."

"Judge, I just think dat what you are doing is wrong. Lynn's an adult. You know dat sixteen-year-old women get married all de time. You oughta jest let the boy go."

"How dare you tell me how to do my job! And you better remember how to do yours. If you don't do exactly as I say, I'll fire you."

"I stood dere and thought for a couple of seconds and den said to him, 'Judge, I'll do everything dat I can to get him to sign de paper. When he does, I'll release him and see to it that he gets back home. But after dat, you'll need to get a new sheriff. I can't work for a judge dat would destroy a man's life just because he fell in love.

"It took me a couple o' hours to convince Robert to sign de annulment. I told him dat he couldn't find Lynn while he was in jail, and I told him dat when he did find her, he could just get married a second time. After he signed, I took him back to Yadkin Oaks whar his horse and carriage were and den escorted him back to his home. It was on the way back to his house dat he broke down and tears flowed freely down his face. He kept saying over and over again, 'Lynn, Lynn, my dear, sweet Lynn.'

"When I got back to de jail, I found all of my personal belongings out in de street. De judge determined from dat day on to make my life as miserable as he did Robert's. Because of his power and influence, de only job that I have ever been able to get is night watchman at de livery.

"I'm sorry dat Mr. Tyler never was able to find Lynn. Once or twice a month, for twenty years, he would come by de livery and ask me if I had heard anything or if I remembered anything from those days dat might help him. The only thing dat I was ever able to tell him was dat Albert Schmidt had left Yadkin Oaks with Miss Lynn in a carriage and headed north. Jest a couple o' months before he died, Mr. Tyler brought a man named Matthew Brown wid him and told me to tell de whole story to him. He said dat he had hired Matthew to try and find Lynn. I don't know if Matthew ever succeeded in finding her, or not, but I hope he did. I'm not a soft man, or a romantic one, but it seemed to me dat de only jest and fair thing that could have happened would have been for those two young people to get back together."

Horace Hayworth returned to his seat. I had been wrong about Horace. He wasn't a small man in a big job as I had thought. He was a big man who had lost an important job. He was still a racist, but I thought better of him now than I ever had before. The judge had snarled at Horace when he had called him a liar. I didn't know if anyone else had heard it or not, but it really didn't matter. What mattered was whether there was even the slightest scrap of goodness in Alexander Johnston that could be moved. Could a man who was so completely consumed by hatred feel any remorse? He was one of those people who believed that any act committed in the name of justice was acceptable, that there was no sin in doing evil if the evil act that was done was intended to stamp out an even greater evil. The judge's speech had made it clear—he was convinced that all that he had done to Robert was acceptable because it was being done to bring Robert to justice. I remembered that he had muttered under his breath at Robert's funeral, 'He got just what he deserved.' But, Lynn and Adam had also been casualties of his crusade. Maybe Emily Gladstone's story would make him finally see what he had actually done.

"When we were first gathering this afternoon and while we enjoyed our meal together, many of you were able to meet Emily Gladstone," I said as I put my hand on her shoulder. "I had the privilege of meeting her for the first time just a month ago when I informed her that she was a beneficiary of Mr. Tyler's estate. Miss Gladstone is the head nurse at the Apple Blossom Sanatorium in Harrisonburg, Virginia. The sanatorium is a ministry of the Quakers where persons who are insane are given compassionate care. Miss Gladstone, will come now and share her story with us."

Emily Gladstone rose from her seat and gracefully made her way to the front of the chancel. "I don't think I should stand in the pulpit," She said. "Would it be all right with everyone if I speak from here?"

We all nodded our agreement and she began. "I will never forget the day that Lynn Johnston was brought to be a patient at Apple Blossom. When she arrived, she was tied to the seat of a carriage, and she had obviously been tied there for the duration of her trip. She was completely covered in her own excrement. The man who delivered her, whom I have just found out from Mr. Hayworth was Albert Schmidt, had not let her out of the carriage, even to relieve herself for three days. I was appalled at how she had been treated, but, I have come to learn that many people treat persons suffering from insanity as though they were less than human. I instructed Mr. Schmidt to release her from the carriage and to untie her hands. He told me that he had strict instructions not to untie her hands until she was in her cell. Then he handed me a letter, a letter that I have kept in Lynn's file all these years."

She held up the letter, turned slightly so that she could have better light from the window, and read

> Dear Miss Gladstone,
>
> This patient, who is to be under your care, is my dear, sweet daughter Lynn. She has recently lapsed into a state

of insanity and has been led to believe, through coercion and deception, that she is in love with a man who took advantage of her innocence, kidnapped her, raped her, and forced her into a sham marriage.

I am hopeful that her insanity is temporary, but it is clearly, at this point, quite severe. I am convinced that the only possible means of a cure is for her to be kept in complete isolation until she returns to her right mind. I am instructing that you keep her in isolation until she goes at least one full week without mentioning the man or her supposed love for him. You are not, however, to let her know that this is the condition of her release. It is my hope that, in her isolation, she will be able to think clearly and come to understand that she has been treated with nothing but cruelty and spitefulness.

I will be in Harrisonburg in a few weeks to see her and to assure myself that my wishes are being fulfilled. I would remind you that I am one of the largest annual contributors to your facility. (If you doubt this, check with your brother John). You do not want to run the risk of losing this support by failing do to as I am asking.

I love my daughter and want what is best for her. Please keep her well fed, clean and as comfortable as she can be in spite of her isolation.

Respectfully,
Judge Alexander Johnston

"I couldn't believe what I was reading. Having worked with the insane for over a decade, I knew that someone who had suffered the trauma of rape needed to talk about it. If this evil man had also deluded her into believing that he loved her, only conversations with someone she loved and trusted would help her.

"As I was reading the letter, Lynn stood beside the carriage and looked around. She saw the massive stone building, the twelve foot tall wall, and the iron bars on the doors and windows. She came to the realization of where she was and what was about to be done to her. Two emotions, rage and embarrassment, came pouring from her. She began to weep uncontrollably, and, at the same time, to cry out in rage at where her father had sent her.

"I once again instructed Mr. Schmidt to untie her, but he refused to do so. 'Not until she is in her cell,' he said. When I stepped forward to untie her myself, he blocked me, pushed me back, and said again, very loudly this time, 'Not until she is in her cell.'

"Follow me," I said, reluctantly and led them into the sanatorium. The isolation cells were in the basement and were reserved for those patients who were a danger to themselves or to others. A locked door was at the top of the staircase that led to the basement. A second locked door was at the bottom. The stairs landed at a center hallway that extended the length of the building. Five cell doors were on either side of the hall, nine of them shut and locked. Only one of these isolation cells was opened. I remember wishing that all of the cells had been in use. Then I could take Lynn to one of the wards where she could have interaction with other people. I led her into the open cell. Mr. Schmidt finally untied her. As I locked her in the cell, I told her that I would be back quickly, but that I had to escort this man out of the building. As we were leaving the building, I asked Mr. Schmidt about her clothes and was told that she didn't have anything except what she was wearing. I thought it was strange that her father professed to love her, but had sent her to Apple Blossom with no clothes and with a man who had clearly been cruel to her. 'Did you even feed her?' I asked, and he told me that she had not had anything to eat in three days. I was glad to get rid of the man and hoped that I would never see him again.

"As I was on the way back to Lynn's cell, I stopped and showed the judge's letter to my brother, John, the administrator of Apple Blossom. He told me that Judge Johnston was, indeed, one of the Sanatorium's largest contributors. We would have to do as he had requested. I then stopped in the storage area and picked through the clothes that we kept there, to find a dress that I thought would fit Lynn. I went to the kitchen to get a pitcher of hot water for her to bathe with and some food for her to eat.

"Even before I had returned to the cell, she had ripped off her soiled clothes and thrown them into a pile in the corner of the cell. She was clearly more embarrassed to be soiled than to be naked. As she was cleaning herself and putting on her new clothes, I really looked at her for the first time and realized how incredibly beautiful she was. She had the natural beauty of any sixteen year old; her skin was silky smooth, with just enough natural color not to be pale. She had long, straight blond hair and piercing blue eyes. Her nose, ears, chin, and lips were all small with gentle curves that matched the natural curves of the rest of her body. The dress and underclothes that I had picked out were not nearly as nice as the ones that she had discarded, but they were clean and she was glad to put them on.

"After she was dressed, I had her sit on the only chair in the cell and, as I brushed her hair and she ate, she told me the story of falling in love with her Robert, of their elopement, of everything that had happened when she had returned to her father's house, and of the terrible journey from Yadkin Oaks. It was towards the end of her story that she asked the most incredibly profound question, 'If my father has sent me here, to a place like this, what in the world has he done to do to my dear Robert?' She spoke of him with such tenderness that I was finding it hard to believe that he had actually raped her. If her father was right, Robert had succeeded in completely twisting her mind, and destroying her ability to think clearly.

"The cells were small and bare, made of stone that was cold and wet in the summer and even colder and wetter the rest of the year. We had learned that many patients who are in isolation destroy nearly everything in their cells. The only furniture in each cell was a bed and a chair that also served as a latrine. In the ceiling of each cell a series of portholes had been cut to allow some light into the cells. The patients could then be observed from the floor above. My office was on the first floor, just above these cells. I could step out of my office, walk down the hall, and inspect each patient safely. Not only could I see the patients, but because the potholes were open except for the iron bars that crisscrossed them, I could hear everything the patients might say. The only time that patients in isolation had any actual contact with a member of the staff was when meals were delivered, or when the chamber pots in the latrine chairs were emptied. I usually did this duty myself. Each time that I would open the door to Lynn's cell, she would ask me something about her Robert. Did I know where he was? Had I heard anything from him? In our conversations, she rarely spoke of herself or of the injustice being done to her, even though she was certainly angry with her father. Her most profound emotions were not anger, but sadness, loss, and confusion.

"The judge did just as his letter said he would. About two weeks after Lynn had arrived, he appeared one day. He seemed deeply and genuinely concerned about her; but, much to my surprise, he did not want to speak to her.

"I know that she is angry with me," he said. "She believes that I have betrayed her and stolen from her the love of her life. If I let her see me now, she will get even angrier and it will take her longer to heal." I told him about the portholes through which he could at least see her. He stood in the hallway outside my office in such a way that he could see her, but that she could not see him. He watched her in silence for nearly an hour as she alternately sat on her latrine chair, paced the cell and lay down on the bed. When he returned to my office, he was wiping tears from his eyes.

"I thought that he might have softened a bit and that his heart might be as broken as hers. I tried to convince him that she needed interaction with others, but he absolutely refused and insisted that she be kept in isolation. 'She is to have no contact with anyone outside her cell except when she is given her food. Only after she goes one full week without speaking of him,' he said to me,' can you move her from isolation to a regular ward. When that happens, send word to me and I will come and get her.'

"It was about six weeks later that I saw her getting sick one morning. I thought, at first, that she had the stomach flu, but, when the morning sickness continued for several more days, I knew that she was pregnant. I think that she must have come to that conclusion about the same time that I did. Pregnancy only deepened her sadness; her Robert was not with her. She slipped into a deep melancholy. Hour after hour, day after day, she cried out for her Robert. I longed to tell her that if she would only be silent for one week, she could be set free, but I had been forbidden by the judge to tell her the conditions of her release.

My brother, John, and I had a long and heated argument about the judge's conditions. I wanted to move Lynn to one of the wards upstairs. John was fearful that Judge Johnston would visit unannounced, find out that we had disobeyed his instructions, and cut off his support. I finally won the argument by convincing John that we were in a locked building where people had to wait to be admitted."

Emily moved in front of the judge and addressed him directly. "I defied your orders, Judge. They were just too cruel. I reluctantly agreed not to tell Lynn the conditions of her release, and I regret that decision to this day. Unfortunately, moving her out of isolation did not have as positive an effect as I had hoped." Even though Emily was speaking directly to the judge, he did not respond. She stepped back to the center of the chancel and continued.

"When she had been with us for about two months, she asked if she might have paper, pen, and ink. She wanted to write letters to her father and to Robert. Her father had given strict instructions that she was not to have any contact with anyone outside her cell, so I knew that he would not allow a letter to be sent, especially one to Robert. We also didn't normally let patients have a pen because they could use it as a weapon, but she had never shown any sign of hostility to me or any of the other nurses, so I gave her a diary, pen, and ink. I told her that she could keep a record of her feelings to share with Robert when she was finally released and they were reunited. I hoped that writing down her feelings would help her heal, but, the more she wrote, the more deeply depressed she became. It seemed terribly ironic to me that the longer she spent in isolation, the more mentally ill she became. I watched her spiral down as she became more and more depressed each day. I am sure that being pregnant added to her depression. The only thing that sustained her was her undying belief that her Robert would come and set her free.

"This poem in her diary, which she wrote just a month before her baby was born, tells something of the battle that raged within her between her undying love for Robert and her deep sadness at their separation." Emily turned to the appropriate page of the diary and read:

My Robert's love sustains me through dark and dreary days.
   Though rock and mortar walls contain me
   And oaken doors and iron bars restrain me
   My Robert's love is all I need to feed my broken heart.
   To fight the pain and hurt of loss, though dark and dreary are my days,
   I have my Robert's love for me.
   And that is all if need to feed my broken heart
   And set my spirit free.
   My Robert's love sustains me and breaks the darkness in my cell of grief.
   Though I cannot touch my Robert's hand, I remember his caress and know that I can
   Make it through another day. Belief
   That he will come is all I need to feed my broken heart.
   My Robert's love sustains me, but I am growing weak.
   If only I could speak to him and hear his voice, I could obtain

A new resolve to make it through another dark and dreary day.

"In the nine months that Lynn was with us, she never once questioned Robert's love or doubted that he was looking for her. Every day, she confessed her passionate love for him. And every day she expressed her total belief that nothing could stop his love for her. In the first few months, she took great care, every day, to be as clean and beautiful as she could be in case 'her Robert' came that day to set her free. At first, she seemed genuinely excited about being pregnant. The child would be a daily reminder of the love that had produced it.

"But every day she also had to deal with her anger at her father and with the depression that separation from Robert was causing. I have often heard it said that love can conquer anything, but in Lynn's case, bitterness at her father and hatred at what he had done to her were winning. As she spiraled downward into deeper and deeper depression, she began to eat less and less. She began to lose weight, even though she was pregnant. And she began to lose her beauty; not just because she didn't brush her hair as often, but because grief, pain, anger, and bitterness began to show on her face. Nine months in Apple Blossom robbed her of life.

"By the time that she was ready to deliver her child, I was deeply concerned for her. I was worried that she had not eaten sufficiently to sustain the baby or that she was going to be too weak to deliver it. Her labor was extremely long, difficult, and draining. For three days, she labored with little progress. Each labor pain sent a shockwave through her body that sapped more and more of her strength. When her son was finally born, I was surprised, but pleased, that he was healthy. But Lynn was not. The final effort to deliver him had taken away her life. Before she could even hold him, or before she ever heard him cry, she slipped away. Because he was the first child ever born at Apple Blossom, we named him Adam, and because he was Robert's son and we didn't know Robert's last name, we made up the last name "Robertson."

"My sister, Susan, my brother, John, and I decided to care for the child until his grandfather, Judge Johnston, came to get him. We sent a letter to the judge, informing him of the child's birth and the unfortunate death of his daughter, Lynn. In the letter, we informed him that the child would be well cared for until he came and that we would bury his daughter with dignity and a full Christian service. To be sure that the letter was delivered, we hired a courier to make the trip from Harrisonburg to North Carolina and deliver the letter personally."

Emily walked over to where the judge was sitting. She looked him straight in the eye and asked in a very quiet and gentle way, "You did get the letter, didn't you Judge?" She stepped back and waited for him to respond. After what seemed like hours, he nodded yes.

"I thought the letter was a hoax, a cruel joke to make me come and see Lynn. I couldn't come and see her again, because it was too painful. Plus, I thought that Robert Tyler was having me followed. If I went to Harrisonburg, he would know where she was."

He closed his eyes and lowered his head. His look of triumph was gone. Everyone in the room stared at him. I looked around and saw a mixture of pity and anger in their eyes. This was what Robert had meant when he told me at our meeting at Hanging Rock that he had discovered that the judge had done something so horrible that even his friends would desert him. He had not only sentenced his daughter to death in an insane asylum, he had also denied that his grandson even existed, sentenced him to be raised in an asylum, and denied him both a father and a grandfather. Emily stepped back to the center of the chancel and began again.

"There have been many deaths and funerals at the Sanatorium over the years," she said. "When most of our patients die, it is both a release and a relief. They are set free from a life that none of us would want to live. They are released from this world into heaven. Most of our funerals are not sad events, but joyous ones. But that was not the case with Lynn's funeral. I have never been to a more tragic funeral than hers. Her death was so unnecessary. She was sentenced to die for only one reason. She had fallen in love, and refused to deny it.

"It wasn't until earlier today, when Judge Johnston gave his speech that I realized that he had been in denial all these years. When he said that she was still a patient at Apple Blossom, I came to understand the great irony that the only person who is truly mentally ill in the Johnston family is Alexander Johnston."

She walked back to the judge. In a compassionate and caring voice, she said, "I hope, Judge Johnston, that someday you will be able to find the healing that you denied your daughter."

She returned to her seat and placed Lynn's diary under her chair. As she was doing this, I looked at Adam Robertson. Tears were running down his cheeks. I wondered if they were tears of anger or tears of grief.

Robert's instructions for the funeral banquet called for the opening and reading of a letter to Adam next. I didn't know what was in the letter, but I knew that it would be emotional. I decided that Adam needed a little time. I announced that we were taking a fifteen minute break.

A Love Letter

WHEN EVERYONE HAD RETURNED FROM THE BREAK, I began by speaking directly to Adam. When I met you for the first time at Apple Blossom and invited you to come to this funeral banquet, I told you that there were two reasons that your father wanted you to be here. The first, and most important reason, was for you to hear the stories that would introduce you to your father, giving you insight into the kind of man he was and the values that shaped the foundation of his life. The second, and less important, reason was that you might receive your inheritance with the reading of his Last Will and Testament.

In the instructions that he left me, he asked that, following Miss Emily's story, I read a letter to you. I don't know what's in it, but I hope that it might ease some of the pain you are feeling right now. I walked over to the altar and picked up the envelope with the words 'To be Opened and Read at the Funeral Banquet' on the outside. I used my pen knife to break the seal. Inside the envelope was a tri-folded letter tied with a white silk ribbon. I untied the ribbon, laid it on the altar, opened the letter and read to Adam.

September 17, 1806

Dear Adam,

I have just learned, a couple of days ago, that I have a son. I have a son! I am simply astonished at the news. I have spent my entire adult life looking for your mother, but I never dreamed that in finding her I would also find you.

Several months ago, I hired a man named Matthew Brown to see if he could find your mother. He has returned and told me the story of your birth and her unfortunate death. In discovering the true story of her death, he also uncovered a plot to assassinate me and to rob you of your inheritance. If you are hearing this letter, it means, unfortunately, that the plot has succeeded and that I died before I was able to meet you.

My very first thought upon hearing of you was to drop everything and rush to Harrisonburg to meet you. But Matthew Brown convinced me that I needed to spend at least a couple of days putting together all of the necessary documents to secure your inheritance should the plot to assassinate me succeed. It was while I was writing a new will to make you the chief beneficiary that I happened upon the idea of a funeral banquet. I put together the list of persons whose stories you are hearing today. I hope that, in hearing the stories, you will be able to get a picture of the kind of man that I was. There are some things, however, that the stories will not be able to reveal and that is why I am writing this letter.

The first thing that you need to know about me is that nothing in the world meant more to me than your mother's love. I first met her at a church picnic at the Hanging Rock, an incredibly beautiful mountain from which there is a panoramic view of the whole valley beneath the Sauratowns. I was sitting on the Rock, enjoying the view, and marveling at the beauty of God's creation when she came and sat down beside me. "Hi, I'm Lynn," she said, introducing herself to me." The other girls tell me your name is Robert." Her bright blue eyes glistened like crystal and her beaming smile was so warm that I actually felt it. Her long, blond hair was so soft that any lamb would have been jealous. Just one second before, I had been thinking that the valley was beautiful!

But now, sitting beside me, was beauty like I had never seen before. We spent the entire day talking with one another. It wasn't long before I realized that her beauty came from deep within. It may take a lifetime for love to fully develop, but it can begin as a bud in just one second with a warm and genuine smile. It can blossom into a full grown flower with a day's conversation. Before our first day together was over, your mother and I had agreed to meet again at Hanging Rock. It became our special place.

During our second meeting, she told me that she was Judge Johnston's daughter. I was, of course, stunned. But, I marveled at the courage it took to risk her father's anger to introduce herself to me and continue to see me. More than the Sauratown Mountains separated us; there was a great mountain of animosity and hatred between the two families. It was a hatred that neither she nor I completely understand, but one that had been carefully taught and nurtured through the years. We joked with each other about being a modern day Romeo and Juliet. As we laughed together, we swore an oath to each other that neither of us would ever drink a secret potion.

We had only five Saturdays together before we made the decision to marry. Lynn had told me the story of her parent's elopement, after knowing each other for only two days. We believed that her father would understand our love and accept our marriage. We were celebrating only the fourth day of our marriage when we made our way to Yadkin Oaks to tell your grandfather. Neither of us could ever have envisioned your grandfather's response. His hatred for me was so pervasive that it blinded him to the possibility that your mother and I could actually love each other. From his perspective, I had not joined his family; I had destroyed it. I did not love his daughter; I had acted out of hatred for him to rob her of her innocence and destroy her future. Adam, your grandfather had obviously loved your grandmother and passionately loved your mother.

It has been possible for me to be in his presence all these years only because of my belief that he acted out of love for Lynn and not out of hatred for me. I believe that there is a kernel of goodness in him, but, unfortunately, it is buried so deeply in hatred that it may never be retrieved. Son, you will have to make an unbelievably difficult choice in the days to come. You will need to decide whether to try to love him as your grandfather, even though he destroyed your parent's lives, or hate him as a man who is so evil that he is beyond redemption. I cannot tell you which road to take. I ask only that you make a decision that will bring you peace.

Your mother and I only had nine full days together before we were separated, but in those nine days there grew within us such a passionate love that it sustained us until our deaths. Though I had many interests in my life, my driving passion was to find your mother and rekindle our life together. It is my sincere hope that you, too, will find such a passionate love and be blessed to know the joy of being faithful to one who has earned your trust.

Since you never knew me, it might seem strange to you that I would give you fatherly advice on how to live your life, but I do want to share some insights with you that I would have taught you if I had had the privilege of raising you. I hope that you will take this advice to heart. My advice might sound a bit preachy, but that's what parents do.

Always remember that you have a future. Too many people make the mistake of living totally in the past. All of us make mistakes, many more than we would ever want to admit. We need to learn from our mistakes and put them behind us, living our lives forward and not backward. All of us will stand before the throne of judgment; we need to live our lives looking toward that day. If we prepare for our future we will, one day, hear God say, "Well done, good and faithful servant, enter into the joy of your Lord."

Always remember that even though life is full of pain we have a choice as to what pain will do to us. We can choose to allow pain and suffering to forge, strengthen, and empower us, or we can choose to let pain weaken and destroy us. Rise above the pain that will inevitably come into your life so that it can make you a better person, not a bitter one.

Always remember that your soul has eternal worth. You were created in the image of God and your soul bears His fingerprints. You are so valuable to him that he left his place of honor and glory in Heaven to become one of us and to die that we might have eternal life. A life lived without faith in the one who created you is a life lived in darkness. Live in the light!

Always remember that memories are a treasure chest. Though you will have no personal memories of your parents, trust in the memories of others who knew us to come to understand who we were. Build your own memories and return to them often in your thoughts. Allow them to be a foundation upon which your life is built.

Always remember to live your love. There have been many men through the years that have professed love, but have not lived it. Everything you do and say actually means something. Your actions and words work together as the building blocks of your life. You have a choice to lead a meaningless life, devoid of love, or a purposeful life, driven by love.

If you move to Lynnmont in the days to come, you will have the privilege of getting to know the wonderful people who live and work on the estate. One of the joys that you will have is hearing all of the stories of the estate's history, especially the stories about its founder, Oskar Schoenfeldt. I want to share just one of those stories with you. Mr. Oskar had been raised as the son of the Duke and Duchess of Sokolov in Bohemia and was forced to flee to America immediately after the death of his parents. His parents had been the victims of a political struggle within the aristocracy which not only cost him his inheritance, but also forced him to leave behind in Bohemia the love of his life, a beautiful young woman named Elyse.

Because of the terrible infighting of the aristocracy, Elyse's life would have been in just as much danger as his, so he reluctantly agreed to separate himself from her. Her father had insisted that he have no contact with her; not even the writing of letters, because any contact could be deadly. The only thing that Mr. Oskar had to remind him of his love for Elyse was a silk handkerchief that had been hers.

After being in America for nearly twenty years, Mr. Oskar wrote to Elyse and offered to return her handkerchief. He knew that three nearly impossible things would have to be true for him to be reunited with his love—the political situation would have to have changed, Elyse would have to have remained unmarried or now be a widow, and third (and most improbable of all), she would still have to be in love with him.

He was so thrilled when he received Elyse's letter in which she said that he had "had her handkerchief for far too long." He returned to Bohemia and later wrote to us at the estate about what a joy it was to renew his love. "It was as though not a single day had passed since we had seen each other," he said.

I was reminded of Elyse's handkerchief the day that I returned to Lynnmont after my days in jail. As I was putting up the carriage that your mother and I had used on our honeymoon, I discovered a beautiful white ribbon, the ribbon that she had worn in her hair during our wedding ceremony. I remembered how she had untied her hair after the ceremony as we had ridden from the church and laid the ribbon on the seat of the carriage. I remembered her broad smile as she tossed her hair, set free from the ribbon. I held that ribbon in my hand and wept. It was all that I had. I have kept it in my pocket every day since then. Every time that I put my hand in my pocket and felt the ribbon, I was reminded of my love for Lynn, of her wonderfully happy smile, and of my determination to see her again.

I used that same ribbon to tie this letter. I hope that you will cherish it and that it will remind you that you are tied to a love that transcends the grave. Though your mother and I did not have the privilege of knowing you and loving you in person, I am sure that we are loving you from heaven and that we will continue to love you for all eternity.

One more Mr. Oskar story will bring my thoughts to you to a close. As his mother lay dying in his arms, she asked Oskar to 'live a life worthy of your father.' I am not going to ask you to do that. Instead, I ask you to live a life worthy of your mother. Her passionate love and her undying faithfulness should be the perfect model from which to pattern your own life.

Your loving Father,
Robert J. Tyler

I folded the letter, turned, and went to the altar to retrieve the ribbon. I walked over to where Adam was sitting and handed him the letter and the ribbon. He put the letter into the inside pocket of his waistcoat. But he simply held the ribbon, fingering it, and looking deeply into it as if trying to see his mother's beauty in the simple elegance of the silk. After a moment or two, he looked up at me and asked, "Would you mind tying it around my wrist?"

As I was tying the ribbon, Judge Johnston looked at us. He leaned forward in his seat, and speaking directly to Adam, said, "I remember that ribbon. It was her favorite. She was wearing it in the portrait that was painted to celebrate her sixteenth birthday. I'll see that you get the painting."

Maybe Robert had been right. Maybe there was a kernel of goodness in Judge Johnston after all. Nothing else needed to be said. Adam Robertson may not have living parents, but at least he would know what they looked like. The portrait of his mother could be hung in the drawing room at Lynnmont beside the portrait of Robert already hanging there.

Facing the Cavalry

AFTER SPEAKING TO ADAM, THE JUDGE LOOKED at me for only a moment. He cocked his head with what could only be described as a wry smile on his face. It was as though his expression was saying, "It was the least that I could do." He then sat back straight in his chair and said, "Let's hear the rest of these stories."

I introduced Captain Stanley. He rose from his seat and marched with perfect military precision to the center of the chancel, stood at parade rest with his feet shoulder width apart, both hands behind his back, and began his speech.

"Before I tell you about the battle of Guilford Courthouse and Mr. Tyler's part in it, it might be good to remind you of some history. Before and even during the Revolution all of the colonies were split between patriots and loyalists and North Carolina was no exception. After the Boston Tea Party, the North Carolina Legislature met in open opposition to the Royal Governor, Josiah Martin, and made the decision to establish a North Carolina militia. The Legislature decided that the militia would have only eight full time officers who would recruit and train the volunteer force. Four colonels and four captains, who had been trained in the British military but who were now all zealous patriots, were recruited. I was one of the four captains. We divided the colony into four zones, one centered in Charlotte, one in New Bern, one in Tarboro and one in Hillsboro with a colonel and captain assigned to each zone and empowered to build a militia in that area. Col. John Harvey and I were assigned to the Hillsboro area which covered the entire north central and northwest sections of the colony.

"One of the unique challenges that Col. Harvey and I faced was that the Wachovia Tract, settled by the Moravians, was right in the center of our area of operations. Most of the Moravians were of German descent, and even though King George of England was actually German, they had no real loyalty to him and certainly none to England. The Moravians were also staunch, anti-war pacifists. Col. Harvey and I met with leaders of the Moravian communities and we entered into an agreement with the churches that their members would remain neutral. But the Church also agreed that its members would provide stores to the militia and would provide comfort and medical care to any wounded soldier, from either side, if the need ever arose.

"In each of the four zones, recruitment of volunteers went smoothly. In less than a year, over two thousand men had joined and their training had begun. So, on the first three days of each month, unless the first landed on a Sunday, the Hillsboro regiment gathered for training. Because our geographical area was so large, from Hillsboro to the mountains, we varied the place of our encampments. I was surprised when we were gathered in Surry County in the spring of 1780 that Robert Tyler volunteered. I knew that the Tylers were loyal members of the Moravian community; and the Moravians were, as I've already said, devout pacifists.

"I've discovered that there are some things that are worth fighting for," he said to me when I asked him why he had volunteered.

"But are they worth breaking the law of your church?"

"One of the reasons that I am willing to fight is so that my church can keep the freedom that it has to practice pacifism. I still believe in pacifism and that war should always be the absolute last resort," he told me. And then he said one of the most powerful things that I have ever heard to explain the necessity of war. "I believe that evil should be given every opportunity to be redeemed, but there are times when evil is so entrenched, that it refuses to be changed. Evil which refuses redemption must be destroyed."

"Isn't that astonishing? 'Evil that refuses redemption must be destroyed.'"

Captain Stanley paused for a moment. I wasn't sure if he was trying to grasp the significance of the statement more deeply for himself, or allowing all the rest of us to ponder. I was glad to have the time to think. It really was a powerful statement; but, after only a few seconds, he continued.

"Robert was a natural when it came to being in the militia. He loved the regimentation and the discipline. He was clearly a leader and after just a couple of months of training, he was made a second lieutenant, and by the time of our engagement at Guilford Courthouse, he had joined me in the rank of Captain.

"There was one serious flaw in our militia. All of the senior officers, except the original four colonels, were political appointees. Some of the political appointees, like Alexander Lillington and Richard Caswell and General Richard Allen, who is here today, proved to be excellent officers, but most, were appointed only because they happened to be related to some member of the legislature. Most of our officers had no military training, and many had no leadership skills. This proved to be a very serious problem for us when we engaged Cornwallis at Guilford Courthouse.

The War in the south from 1777 through 1780 proved to be one disaster after another for the Patriots. One general after another, appointed by the Continental Congress, led their forces into battles in which they were thoroughly defeated. In desperation, the Congress finally authorized General Washington to appoint a new southern commander, and he chose Nathaneal Greene who took command of a decimated army of only about 1,500 troops in the fall of 1780.

General Greene knew that the only way to defeat Cornwallis was to draw him away from his base of supplies and support and win a long struggle of attrition. He moved his army into South Carolina, close enough that Cornwallis had to respond and then began a long, tactical retreat. From December 1780 through March of 1781, he led his army on a six hundred mile trek through South and North Carolina, staying just far enough ahead of Cornwallis to keep his army safe, but close enough that Cornwallis kept up the pursuit.

At the same time that he was drawing Cornwallis away from Charleston, General Greene made a decision that every military expert would tell you was a huge mistake—he divided his army. He put Col. Dan Morgan in charge of a small, but very mobile force. Col. Morgan's forces circled behind Cornwallis, cut off his supply lines, harassed him at every point, and made it impossible for him to return to Charleston.

"In February, General Greene called for the senior officers of the North Carolina and Virginia militias and his own officer corps to meet at Guilford Courthouse to discuss tactics. Nearly everyone present believed that the time was right to face Lord Cornwallis and the British head on, but General Greene made the decision that at least one more month was needed before the British would be weakened enough for us to face them and to have a chance at victory. He made the decision to cross the Dan River into Virginia. He knew that there were no bridges over the Dan, and if he could commandeer all of the boats along the river, he would have a couple of weeks to rest and resupply his army. He ordered Colonel Morgan and his cavalry to continue to block any supplies from reaching Cornwallis and he ordered the militias and the Continentals to gather at Guilford Courthouse on March 13. He wanted to meet Cornwallis on a field that he had chosen, where he could command the high ground. While the Patriots were camped across the Dan, Cornwallis camped at a place that he called Pudding Creek.

"On March 13, a force of 1500 Continentals, 2000 North Carolina militia and 900 Virginia militia came together at Guilford Courthouse. General Greene established three lines for battle. The North Carolina militia formed the first line. Three hundred yards behind us were the Virginia Militia and three hundred and fifty yards behind the Virginians were the regular army and the artillery commanding the high ground along New Garden Road. Colonel Morgan's cavalry was spread out in a semi-circle around the field and was used to funnel Cornwallis' troops to the center of the field so that they could not attack one of our flanks. Once Cornwallis's troops were where General Greene wanted them to be, Colonel Morgan was to join the forces along the ridge at New Garden Road.

"Colonel Harvey and I were deeply concerned when the North Carolina militia was placed in the front line of the battle, with our regiment in the very center. It was not because we doubted our men's courage, but because we doubted our leadership. The Hillsboro regiment was under the command of Brigadier General Joshua Eaton, a political appointee, who had absolutely no military experience. In addition to his lack of experience, most of our regiment had never fought in a 'front line' battle. Our men had been involved in skirmishes with the loyalists and even some British regulars, but we had never before stood in formation and faced an opposing army head-on. Colonel Harvey and I feared that General Eaton would be a poor leader once the battle began, and the two of us went quietly to General Greene to express our concern.

"Rather than single out General Eaton, General Greene ordered the entire North Carolina Militia to stand their ground for at least two volleys and, if they failed to do so, he ordered that the Virginia Militia was to fire into the North Carolina line. Fortunately, the North Carolina Militia did have two strong leaders on our flanks, Colonel Alexander Lillington and Colonel Richard Caswell who had both distinguished themselves at the Battle of Moore's Creek Bridge. General Greene also ordered Colonel Harvey (in a private conversation rather than a public pronouncement) to stay beside General Eaton and keep him on the field.

"On the morning of the battle, Robert Tyler and I were stationed on the left side of our regiment's line and Colonel Harvey and General Eaton were stationed on the right. Robert and I went up and down our end of the line encouraging our men and reminding them of our plan to fire two volleys and then to fall back in an orderly fashion and reform with the Virginia line. At the same time that we were doing this, I saw Colonel Harvey doing the same on his end of the line. General Eaton was sitting on his horse, just behind our line, staring across the field as the British advanced.

"Because most of our men were using guns rather than rifles, we knew that the accuracy of our fire would be negligible at best, so we planned to wait until the British were no further than fifty yards away before we took our first shots. I will never forget the bravery of the British soldiers as they marched with perfect precision straight into our line of fire. Our first volley did not slow the British down at all. They knelt and returned our fire. As our line took the fire, I happened to look to my right and saw, to my horror that Colonel Harvey took a bullet straight through his throat. I was sure that he had died instantly. In the same volley, Gen. Eaton's horse was shot out from under him. When his horse stumbled, General Eaton was thrown over its neck and landed on the ground just beside Colonel Harvey's body. He stood up, took one look at Colonel Harvey, and started running as fast as he could away from the British, shouting as he ran, "Retreat!

Retreat!" The portion of the regiment under his command broke, leaving a huge gap in our line.

"Robert and I were able to keep our men in formation for our second volley, which had a better effect than our first because the British were now closer and slowed their advance just long enough for our men to begin to fall back to where the Virginia Militia were stationed along Reedy Fork Road. Falling back in an orderly fashion is an incredibly difficult task, especially when more than two thirds of your troops have already broken and started running.

"Hold the line! Hold the line!" Robert and I kept shouting as our brigade began the retreat. We quickly discovered how difficult it is to walk backwards, while trying to reload our guns and keep an eye on the advancing British. But because our second volley had been effective enough to slow the British down and there was a gap of about a hundred yards between our forces and the British, General Greene took advantage of this gap, using his artillery, stationed on the high ground at New Garden Road to slow the British advance even more than our volley had done. This gave us a chance to reform our lines as those of us who stayed on the field formed up with the Virginians.

"Despite our artillery, General Cornwallis' men continued to advance and it wasn't long before they engaged our second line. The orders for the second line were the same that ours had been. Two volleys were to be fired and then the men were to fall back to where the Continentals were stationed on the high ground at New Garden. Our hope was that our retreat would draw the British regulars quickly away from the support of their artillery and that when they engaged our third line, Colonel Morgan and his cavalry could sweep behind them.

"Cornwallis was the best field officer that the British had for good reason. As we were preparing our second volley, I looked up and saw that he had ordered the British artillery to advance. Our hope of drawing the infantry away from their artillery's support had not worked.

"One of the greatest challenges that any army faces in today's modern warfare is how to deal with smoke. When thousands of guns and cannon are all firing at the same time, great clouds of smoke engulf the battlefield. The smoke is both a blessing and a curse. It's a blessing because it can hide your position from the enemy, but it's also a curse, because it also hides the enemy's position and movements. After our second line of the Virginians and the remainder of the North Carolinians engaged the British Infantry, the smoke hung so heavy over the field that none of us could see.

"Colonel Banaster Tarlton, commander of the British Cavalry, decided to use the cover of the smoke to charge into the fray. We could hear the charging horses before we saw them; and, when they finally broke through the smoke, they were less than thirty yards from our line and headed straight for us.

"That was when Robert Tyler did something unbelievable. He threw down his rifle and began to run! But he wasn't running away from the enemy, he was running directly towards them! Colonel Tarlton, one of the bravest and, at the same time, most evil of the British Commanders was leading the charge and Robert was running directly towards him without a weapon. Although everything was happening so fast, I did have time to think, "What in the world is Robert doing?"

"Colonel Tarlton had his sword raised above his head, ready to strike at the lone soldier who was charging him on foot. Robert was obviously running as fast as he could directly at Tarlton's horse; and, just as they were about to meet, Robert jumped, grabbed the horse around its head, and literally tackled it. Robert, the horse, and Colonel Tarlton went tumbling in a heap. Fortunately for Robert, when Tarlton was thrown from his horse, he lost his sword, and so now both men were unarmed as they struggled to their feet. Robert was just a half a second quicker than Tarlton, and while he was still trying to get to his feet, Robert swung his right fist with all his might and caught the colonel right on the chin, briefly knocking him out. Robert looked up and realized that all of the British Cavalry was coming to their commander's aid, and he started to run again, but this time towards us.

"When Tarlton's horse went down and his men stopped to help him, the British charge was effectively halted. Our men had time to aim and fire into the cavalry troop. The largest loss of life that the British suffered that day may have come in that one volley. One of Tarlton's men had jumped from his horse and run to Tartlon's aid. He grabbed the now semi-conscious colonel by the arm and lifted him on to a horse whose rider had been shot. He mounted the same horse, behind the colonel to help keep him on, and what remained of the cavalry quickly retreated.

"It was amazing. The British Cavalry had charged our line; but, because of Robert's action, they were stopped short and had not been able to engage us. If they had been able to break into our line, the battle may have been lost at that moment.

"'I've never tackled a horse before,' Robert said as he threw himself down beside me. 'I didn't know it would hurt that much. My shoulder is killing me,' he said as he grabbed his left shoulder with his right hand. I took one look at Robert and realized that when he had collided with the horse, his shoulder had become separated. I had never set a separated shoulder before, but I had seen it done.

"This is going to hurt like hell," I yelled at Robert over all of the noise of the battle that was continuing around us. I put my left arm under Robert's arm pit and with my right hand I pushed down as hard as I could on Robert's shoulder. I heard and felt the joint pop back into place, followed by Robert's scream of pain. I laid him on the ground and said, "Most of the pain should go away in a few minutes, unless you've torn something loose in the joint. Just lie here!"

"I looked up and realized that the British infantry, which had stopped its advance when Tarlton charged, was now moving forward and would be upon us in just a matter of moments. I left Robert lying there and began to run down the line, ordering everyone to fix their bayonets. The British were too close to our position for us to withdraw. In any second, hand-to-hand combat would begin.

"General Greene also realized that we would not be able to withdraw to his position, and ordered the Continentals to advance. The Continentals did not advance as the British do, deliberately marching in a straight line. They ran, as fast as they could, across the open field and thrust themselves into the battle. Everywhere I looked, small groups of men were engaged in hand to hand combat. When bayonets broke, men used their guns as clubs. And when their guns broke, they used their bare fists.

"Within just a couple of minutes, the lines of both armies had broken and a huge melee engulfed the field. The lines were so broken that there was no way to command. All of the soldiers, on both sides of the battle were simply fighting their own personal battles to save their own lives.

"Watching from his position in the rear, General Cornwallis came to the conclusion that there was only one way for the battle to be brought to a conclusion. He had to break up what had become nothing more than a riot. He then made the decision that would become the most controversial one of his entire military career. He decided to have his artillery fire grapeshot directly into the fracas. He knew that he might kill as many of his own men as he did the enemy, but he also knew that such a devastating barrage would bring an end to the battle. I don't know how many rounds of grapeshot were fired, but I do know that all around me men and horses fell. There were so many wounded and dead men and horses lying on the ground that it became almost impossible to move without tripping over one. In effect, the battle was over, and General Greene gave the order that we should leave the field.

The British did not interfere as we set about removing our dead and wounded. They were also caring for their own. I had lost Robert when the two armies came together, and I wasn't sure where to look for him. It wasn't until we had completely left the field that I found him. Someone had taken a piece of rope and tied his left arm tight to his body to keep it from moving.

"As long as it doesn't move, the pain is nearly gone," he told me. "Every time that I tried to get up during the battle, I would move it and the pain was so intense that it would throw me back down on the ground. I guess that's a good thing, because when the grapeshot was fired, I was lying on the ground and it just went right over me."

"When the battle was over, we had lost the field, and technically, the battle. But in reality, the British had suffered far worse than we. We Americans had 79 killed and 185 wounded while the British had 93 killed and 413 wounded. In addition to the men that we lost, every single horse on the Patriot side was killed by the volleys of grapeshot, so there was no way for us to move our artillery after the battle and it was surrendered to the British. The most discouraging statistic of the battle however, was the number of Americans missing. One thousand and forty six, more than half of the members of the North Carolina Militia, had run from the field with General Eaton and, probably in disgrace from their cowardice, simply gone home.

"After the battle, General Greene ordered all of the senior officers to meet in his quarters. The first thing he said when we were all gathered was, 'Who was that man who charged the British Cavalry on foot? That was the most foolhardy and bravest thing that I have ever seen a man do?'

"I looked at Robert and he shook his head at me as if to say, don't say anything. But I agreed with General Greene that it was an incredibly brave act that deserved recognition. "General Greene, here is your man, Captain Robert Tyler," I said as I placed my hand on his good shoulder.

"Captain Tyler, you single handedly won the day for us. If Tarlton had broken our line, there would have been no way that we could have moved up the Continentals fast enough. Thanks for your bravery."

"I wasn't being brave sir," Robert replied. "Like you said, Sir, it was mighty foolhardy. I didn't think; I just acted. Fortunately, it turned out all right."

"Maybe our army needs to have less thinking and more action, then," General Greene said. "I am going to award you the Badge of Merit for Bravery. It's the highest honor that I can give you."

"It was the consensus of all the officers that if General Eaton and his portion of the militia had not broken and run we would have had more than enough force to win the day. General Greene asked me, as the officer who was closest to General Eaton when he left the field, to write a report to be sent to North Carolina's Governor Nash to be included with a report that he would send. In my report to Governor Nash, I referred to Eaton's "cowardice under fire," a phrase that all of the general officers agreed should be included. At the time that the report was sent, none of us knew that General Eaton was the nephew of Governor Nash. Unfortunately, for me, even though we all agreed, my name was the only name on the report, and the consequence is that I have been doomed, by the power of politics, to be a captain for the entirety of my military career.

"General Greene also sent a report to Governor Nash. I'd like to read it to you.

'Time will not permit me to be very particular and therefore I shall only confirm the account of their having been an action on the 15th. The battle was fought near Guilford Courthouse. It was long and severe. We gave up the ground and were obliged to leave our artillery, all the horses being killed. The enemy loss is very great. We ought to have had the victory, and had your militia stood by my officers, it would have been certain. However, the enemy has gained no advantage except the ground and the field pieces. Their operating force is greatly diminished in such a manner, that I am not without hope of turning their victory into defeat, if your Militia don't leave me.'

"General Greene did succeed in turning the defeat into a victory. Cornwallis's army was so decimated from its six hundred mile march and the Battle of Guilford Courthouse that he was forced to abandon North Carolina and return to his base in Charleston. As you remember, after being resupplied, he made the decision to move his army to Yorktown, Virginia, where he hoped to join forces with a large army under the command of General Clinton. General Clinton, however, never arrived, and Cornwallis was forced to surrender his entire force to General Washington, effectively ending the war.

"As I have thought about and relived the Battle of Guilford Courthouse many times over the years, I have often pondered General Greene's words to Robert, "You, sir, single-handedly won the day for us." There is no question that Robert Tyler's action was a pivotal moment in the battle and that he greatly deserved his Badge of Merit, but he was not the only brave person who was on the field that day. The 770 men on both sides who were either killed or wounded all laid aside their fears and fought for what they believed was right.

"Robert Tyler was a hero that day, but so was Colonel John Harvey, my dear friend, who died in the very first volley of the day. Robert Tyler was a hero that day, but so were all of the rest of the North Carolina Militia who did not break and run with General Eaton. Robert Tyler was a hero that day, but so was our flag bearer, a young boy, whose name I don't know, that had the courage to face the British head on, without a weapon, and never let our regimental banner hit the ground."

Captain Stanley moved from parade rest, and walked to the corner of the church and retrieved his Espontoon. He returned to the chancel area and stood directly in front of Adam. "Young man," he said, speaking directly to him, "you should be very proud of your father. He was the only man that day to receive a commendation for bravery. But you need to know one more thing about that day. Your father took the Badge of Merit that General Greene had given him and pinned it on our regimental banner. To this day, the Hillsboro Regiment remains the only militia regiment to receive the honor."

He leaned the Espontoon forward and showed Adam the banner on to which the Badge of Merit had been sewn. "This badge belongs to you now, but I hope that you will leave it with the regiment. It means a lot to us."

Captain Stanley took a step back, came to full attention, with the Espontoon held firmly in his left hand and saluted Adam Robertson. "If your father was here, it would be my privilege to salute him. It's just as great an honor for me to salute his son."

Adam stood. He had never been in the military and wasn't exactly sure what to do. He simply extended his hand and Captain Stanley stepped forward to shake it. "Keep the Badge of Merit," Adam said. "If you ever need to tackle a horse, it will remind you that it can be done." Their handshake lasted much longer than a normal one. It was as if Captain Stanley was trying to grasp something of Robert from Adam.

Robert had asked me to have appropriate responses to the speeches. So far, I had only responded to two. Captain Stanley's speech had been so profound. As far as I knew, Robert had never told the story of the battle to anyone. I certainly didn't know he had received the Badge of Merit. Adam's offer to let the brigade keep his father's award was so genuine that there was no need for any other response.

As I stood to introduce Richard Allen, I glanced out the window of the church and I happened to notice a flash of light, reflecting off something on the hill more than a hundred yards away. I was glad the deputies were here. If the assassin, whose camp I had disturbed earlier, was hiding in the trees, he would stay right there.

Law or Justice?

RICHARD ALLEN HAD BEEN A PROFESSOR AT the University of North Carolina since its founding. He had joined the faculty at the request of the Legislature after his service as a general in the militia during the war. Since he had already had a role in the day's proceedings when he had examined the judge's will, there was no need to introduce him. I simply told him that he was up next. He stepped forward and began.

"The University of North Carolina is still a very small school. We don't yet have enough students or faculty to have specialized departments in our university. Our students can have a major course of study, but there is no law school or divinity school, or any other special schools that some universities have. Because our faculty is small, each professor must teach a wide range of subjects. I was hired to teach English grammar and composition, literature, world history, and basic law.

"In 1784, when Robert Tyler came to the university to study, he quickly fit in to the university and Chapel Hill communities. He was a little bit older and more mature than most of the other students. He was already the owner of a huge estate. He had had the experience of fighting in the War of Independence. We at the University knew that Robert had played a role in the battle and that he had been honored in some way, but we didn't know the particulars. It was nice to hear the story and to see the Badge of Merit," he said, speaking directly to Captain Stanley as an aside. He quickly regained his train of thought and said, "As I was saying, Robert quickly made friends with the professors and many of the townspeople. He just had a natural ability to connect with people. From the parish priest to the university president, from the owner of his boarding house to the other students, he built genuine friendships, many of which lasted until his death.

"The same year that he came as a student, the university hired a young man named Tommy to be the campus caretaker, janitor, and general handyman. Tommy didn't have a last name because he was a bastard child and his mother has never revealed who Tommy's father was. Robert struck up a friendship with Tommy. I am sure he was the only student who ever spoke to Tommy, unless one of the other students wanted to tell Tommy to do something.

One day Father Frederick, the Episcopal priest, asked if I would go with him to talk with Robert. He was deeply concerned that Robert's relationship with Tommy might be inappropriate. I understood why the Father was worried, because all of us were taught by our mothers that we are "known by the company that we keep." Robert had told Fr. Frederick that I was his favorite professor. He hoped that my presence would add weight to what he had to say.

"I made an appointment to meet Robert at his boarding house on Franklin Street and Fr. Frederick and I were right on time. I was surprised when Fr. Frederick, ignoring the proprieties, jumped right to the point.

"Robert, you just can't be friends that that boy, Tommy! Maybe you don't know who he is."

"Tommy is the bastard son of a woman of ill repute and a father who is a coward for not taking responsibility for his actions," Robert said. "Everyone in town has told me about him.

You are not the first one to warn me about hurting my reputation by being seen with him."

"Why haven't you listened to what other people are telling you?" I asked Robert, hopefully with a little more tact in my voice than Fr. Frederick had used to begin the conversation.

"Because I think that Tommy is a good person, in spite of his parentage," he replied. "He is kind and gentle, nice to everyone. Whoever raised him certainly did a good job."

"All of that is true," I said. "But don't you realize that Tommy is, according to the law, a non-person? Because he has no father, he legally doesn't exist. Because of that, he has no prospects. We at the university have been very liberal in our dealings with Tommy, having given him employment. He may now save enough money to, some day in the future, move away from Chapel Hill and establish himself where no one knows his past."

"That's very kind of you,' Robert said. "But I would think that liberal professors would completely ignore the bastard laws. Don't you see how incredibly unfair they are? They punish a child for being born!"

"We're not here to talk about the laws of bastardy," Fr. Frederick interrupted. "We're here to talk about your reputation."

"I think that you, of all people, would be deeply concerned about the laws on bastards, since, from a strictly legal sense, the Lord you worship was a bastard," Robert said quietly, but pointedly to Fr. Frederick.

"How dare you call Jesus a bastard! Have you no shame?"

"I would never call him that. But the law would. And, of course, if it's legal, it's got to be just. Right?" Robert replied.

"Fr. Frederick was obviously completely flustered, so I stepped in to try to move the conversation back to the point that Fr. Frederick and I were trying to make.

"Robert, we are here because we love you and are concerned about you. If you have the wrong associates; and make friends with the wrong people, it could affect the whole rest of your life."

"'I appreciate what you are trying to do,' Robert said. "I just completely disagree with you. It was Jesus himself who said, 'When you do it unto the least of these my brethren, you do it unto me.' I think that he was referring to loving the unlovable people, the Samaritans of the world, the bastards who really are people even though the law doesn't think so."

"Nothing will shut a preacher's mouth quicker than quoting Scripture to him. Nothing will quiet a lawyer more quickly than asking a legal question for which there is no answer. I don't remember the rest of the conversation, but I do remember that Fr. Frederick and I got nowhere with Robert Tyler. The fact is, both of us were embarrassed that a young man, who was not yet fully educated, was smarter and wiser than either of us.

"It was in the weeks and months to come in our law classes that Robert proved to be the most difficult student that I ever had. He was difficult because he wanted to know the 'why' of the law, not just the 'what.'

'The study of the law necessarily focuses on the minutia of the law, the details that every lawyer must know if he is going to be successful. Every law that is passed by a legislature must relate to a law or a series of laws that are already in existence. For instance, if a law was passed imposing a tax on property, there would have to be laws which defined what property is, who can own property, and how that property can be transferred from one legal owner to another. There also have to be laws which define what taxes are, how they will be imposed and collected, and how the money that is raised will be used. Laws would also have to be written that would explain any exceptions to the property laws or tax laws that might be allowed. Churches are not taxed, for instance, on the property that they own. That means that another set of laws must be passed which define what a church is. And on it goes.

"Robert was not a bad student when it came to knowing the details. In fact, he passed every test easily. But he was interested in far more than the details. He was interested in justice. It was ironic that just a couple of weeks after Fr. Frederick and I had confronted Robert, the laws about bastard children were on our schedule. Let me tell you a few of these laws that were on the books in our State so that you can understand more fully.

"A bastard child cannot take legal residence in the county of his father, if the father is known. Because of his illegitimacy, a bastard child has no right to a last name, no right of property, no right of an inheritance. Bastard children may be supported by the church, but no public money shall be expended for their support. Giving birth to a bastard child carries a sentence of a public whipping and one year in jail for the mother of the child. A bastard child whose father is known has no right to any of his father's property, but may petition the county courts to require the father to give annual support until the child reaches the age of eighteen. In such cases, if the man denies, under oath, being the father the man's oath shall supersede that of the mother.

"When these laws came before our class, Robert Tyler wanted to know why the state was so hard on the child. After all, it's not the child's fault that it is born out of wedlock, that the mother sometimes doesn't know who the father is, and that there may be a dishonest man who will deny, even under oath, that he is the father of the child. Robert was especially incensed by the law which provided for a public whipping and a year in jail for the mother. 'What is to become of the baby if the mother is thrown in jail?' he wanted to know.

"Even though I assured Robert that the law providing for a year in jail for the mother was almost never enforced, he was still furious.

"These laws punish the child. Why should an illegitimate child be any less valuable to our society than a legitimate one?" he asked.

"We had a long discussion in class about bastard children. Most of the discussion was in a general sense. We weren't talking about any specific person, but about the problem bastard children cause society. Most of the students understood that the laws were made to protect men from unscrupulous women, or children who would make false claims about the identity of their fathers. One of the students pointed out that it was the most prosperous men who might become victims of these mothers and children, because they had the most to offer. It was Robert who brought the discussion back to the children themselves.

"But how should society deal with people like Tommy?" he asked. "All of you know Tommy. You see him on campus every day and you all know that he is a good man. Why should the laws preclude him from rising to the top of our society when he has done nothing wrong? And why do the laws on bastard children offer no opportunity for recompense for the child? Wouldn't it be fairer to have laws that protect both the rights of the father and the rights of the child?"

"It was those kinds of questions that made Robert Tyler the most difficult student that I ever had. Robert understood the need for laws. He understood that utter chaos would erupt if a society had no laws and he knew that law was necessary to promote the general welfare of the whole society. Robert's problem was that many of the laws that we studied seemed unfair and even unethical. He asked over and over again, how a law could bring justice if it took away liberty.

"It was when we moved on to the laws about marriage that Robert was the most passionate. It wasn't until today, when I heard the story about his marriage, his arrest, and the false charges that were brought against him, and the underhanded way the law was used to manipulate him, that I fully understood Robert's passion. It's clear to me now that Robert's whole adult life was a search for justice.

"In one of our class sessions, Robert made an impromptu speech about the need to justice, fairness, and laws that create good order, not just order. Robert reminded the class that the people of America realized that we had a very orderly society under the rule of the British and King George. The people of America wanted a society that was not just orderly, but one that was also good. We wanted a society where justice, ethics, and fairness were built into the very fabric of the laws which make us a people. We wanted a society where the people 'are created equal and endowed by their creator with certain inalienable rights—life, liberty, and the pursuit of happiness.' We wanted to create a society where people could know that the laws that the government passed were all intended to make these rights available to everyone.

"When Robert finished his speech that day, the class rose in a spontaneous ovation. I'll never forget how embarrassed he was by the applause. He quickly retreated to the back of the classroom. When the class was dismissed, all the other students quickly left, as they usually do, but Robert stayed in his seat, his head bowed. I made my way to the back of the room and sat in the seat beside Robert. It wasn't until I sat down that I realized that Robert was silently crying.

"Robert, what's wrong?" I asked him.

"I am such a hypocrite," he said. "I really believe everything that I said in class. I really believe it, but I don't live it."

"What do you mean?"

"How can I say that I want good order for everyone at the same time that I am a slave owner? Not only am I a slave owner, but the man that I own is the very best friend that I have ever had, or ever hope to have."

"Robert told me the story of his father's purchase of a young boy named John Barnes. Mr. Tyler had wanted to protect John from being taken from Beautiful Valley estate by a slave catcher. This man had come to capture Thomas, John's father, a runaway slave from a plantation in eastern North Carolina. Thomas had found sanctuary at Beautiful Valley where Robert's father was the estate manager.

"When my father died, I inherited John Barnes," he said. "I didn't want to own him, but I was afraid to set him free. I have seen how people treat free black men. In many ways they are treated with even more contempt and outright hatred than slaves. I just don't know what to do. If I keep him in servitude, I will be going against everything that I believe. If I set him free, I may be sentencing him to a life that is full of nothing but vile hatred from whites and petty jealousy from other blacks."

"Robert, you have just settled on the great conundrum of the law. We seek to do that which is right, just, fair, and good; but way too often, we have to settle for that which is expedient. Hopefully, when the time is right, you will be able to move from expedience to justice," I said.

"Some years later when Robert was elected to the North Carolina Senate, the first bills he proposed were a set of laws to do away with all of the State's statutes on bastardy. Almost all of the laws which he proposed were eventually passed and signed by the Governor. 'I don't know what I can ever to do to help John'" he told me. 'I don't think that I will ever see an end of slavery. But at least I could do something for Tommy.'

"After the bills were passed which did away with all the bastard laws, Tommy was allowed to take a last name. Tommy Tyler (that's right, he chose the name Tyler) still lives in Chapel Hill, but he no longer works as the janitor and care-taker at the university. He is a well respected and prosperous businessman. He is the owner of a mercantile, something that would have been illegal prior to the new laws.

"Robert didn't give up on his dream of helping John Barnes, and the other slaves that would have been freed, if the existing laws had not made the emancipation of slaves so difficult. When Robert first came to the Senate, he introduced a bill to change the emancipation laws that was so sweeping that not a single senator would support him. Robert realized that he would have to take small steps over many sessions of the legislature before the laws which prevented a Free Man of Color to own property, to have meaningful employment, be legally married, or worship in the church of his choice could be overturned. But from his first session until the last, just before he died, Robert Tyler slowly, methodically, introduced legislation which changed those laws.

"We have in our presence today a Free Man of Color, John Wesley Barnes. When Mr. Barnes came to Chapel Hill to inform me that I was a beneficiary to Robert Tyler's estate, he showed me the Letter of Emancipation that he received, just before Robert was murdered. He carries it with him at all times, because, unfortunately in our society, most persons (both black and white) would not believe that any man of color could actually be free. So he needs to have the letter with him to prove that he is indeed free. Mr. Barnes would be glad to show the letter to any of you. If you were to see it, you would find that John Barnes has nearly every right any other free man in our state has.

"Unfortunately, John Barnes is not completely free. There are states in our union which do not recognize the right of a slave owner to emancipate any slave, and there are other states which do not recognize any Letters of Emancipation which were issued in any other state. There are states in our union where John Barnes would be arrested as a runaway slave, and sold at the nearest slave market, if he even showed his Letter of Emancipation.

"The Robert Tyler's of this world have brought us a long way, but we are still a long way from the New Eden. Unjust and unfair laws still abound.

"Robert Tyler was the most difficult student that I ever had because he was seeking justice, not just law. He believed that the legislature, just like individuals, should turn from their hypocrisies, and do everything in its power to make the state a better place for the Tommy's of this world. I asked Robert Tyler, just before he died, what his most important legislative accomplishment was, and he said to me, 'The next one.'

Oh how I long for more students like Robert Tyler. Many of the students who are so good at quoting all of the facts of the law make excellent lawyers. But the students who want to know more than the 'what' of the law;' the ones who want to know the 'why' of the law, they are the special ones. And once in a while I even get a difficult student who also wants to know the 'why nots' and the 'why can't we's' of the law. Those are the ones who are most likely to hear, as Robert did a couple of months ago, "Well done good and faithful servant."

Dr. Allen returned to his seat to a chorus of "Amens!"

I couldn't think of a more appropriate response than that. I was about to introduce Lawrence Weeks when Captain Stanley said, "John, I'd like to hear you read your Letter of Emancipation. I bet it sounds mighty good coming out of the mouth of a Free Man of Color."

I was surprised when everyone, even Horace Hayworth and Alexander Johnston, applauded the suggestion. I took the leather pouch from my pocket, carefully opened the Letter and read it. I had never read it out loud before. I was stunned at how much more powerful it seemed as I heard each line than when I had just read them silently.

The Tale of Kahnungdatlegeh

LAWRENCE WEEKS WAS THE NEXT SCHEDULED SPEAKER. I wanted to give a simple introduction, but I also wanted to convey to everyone how much I appreciated him. Since Robert's death, Lawrence and I had drawn strength from one another as we dealt with the tragic loss, but I was sure I had received far more comfort from Lawrence than he had from me. I pondered for a moment what I might say to convey my thanks, without getting maudlin. Then I just plunged ahead.

Lawrence Weeks came to Germantown fifteen years ago to serve a one-year apprenticeship with Robert Tyler. He had just finished studying law at the College of William and Mary and wanted to have the experience of serving in an established firm before he began his own. Because the Tyler Law Firm and the Tyler Companies have a lot of interaction, I got to see a lot of young Lawrence, and I was impressed. He was clearly a bright and ambitious young man. He also intended to stay only one year. He told me that he was determined to go back to Virginia, establish his own firm, and get involved in politics. He told me that he had every intention of being the governor of Virginia one day.

But one of the first things that happened to Lawrence when he came here is that he fell in love with Germantown. At first glance, there doesn't seem to be much to fall in love with. Germantown is just a quaint little village. There really isn't anything outstanding about it, except for the people, who as the name implies, were mostly of German descent. Surprisingly, most were not Moravians, but German Baptists, who had suffered greatly at the hands of the mostly Lutheran population in their homeland. Because there was already a large German-speaking population living in the Wachovia Tract, this smaller group of immigrants decided that settling in an area adjacent to the Moravians would at least give them a group of like-minded people with whom they could communicate and do business. With the success of Lynnmont and the Tyler Companies, the town was soon attracting craftsmen and businessmen, of all nationalities and backgrounds, who were seeking to work in one of the Tyler companies. They were also establishing other companies that would support one of Robert's enterprises. So, Germantown grew quickly, populated by hard-working, good people who just wanted to make a good life for themselves. As I said earlier, Lawrence Weeks quickly fell in love with these wonderful people. And then something really wonderful happened to Lawrence Weeks. He fell in love with just one of these wonderful people.

Betsy Hobbton is the daughter of Jim Hobbton, owner of Germantown's best general store. Except for my wife, Sally, she is the most beautiful woman in Germantown. Betsy's father, mother, and the children work diligently to run the store. Jim swears that he has one of everything in his store. If he doesn't have it, you don't need it.

Lawrence had been in town only a few days when he stopped at Hobbton's General Store. Betsy waited on him. They were immediately attracted to each other. It wasn't long before Lawrence Weeks decided that becoming the husband of Betsy Hobbton was more important to him than being the governor of Virginia. It's amazing how love changed Lawrence's life, especially when his future wife announced to him that she had no plans to ever leave Germantown!

"It also wasn't long before Lawrence also fell in love with the Tyler Law Firm. Robert Tyler always referred to himself as 'just a country lawyer,' but everyone who worked with him knew that he was far more. Robert Tyler could draw up a deed or a contract as well as any other lawyer, but it was his commitment to the weightier matters of the law that attracted young men like Lawrence. He was willing to come to a little out-of-the-way town in the back woods of North Carolina to work with Robert.

Robert asked that Lawrence come today and tell a story about one of the cases that the Tyler Law Firm has been handling. Lawrence, before you speak, I want to say just one more thing. I want to thank you for your friendship. Though you are much younger than I am, you have a wisdom that far exceeds mine, and insight far surpassing your age. You always have the knack of saying just what I need to hear at just the right time.

Lawrence made his way into the chancel. He had a presence about him that would have made him a great politician. He was tall, handsome, and regal. As he walked around the altar rail, I thought that, if looks had anything to do with it, he could easily have been elected governor. He strode up to me, shook my hand, and said, "You are far too kind."

"Reverend Barnes is right. I did, indeed, fall in love with Germantown, especially with Betsy! I can't imagine living or working anywhere else. The Tyler Law Firm is a completely different place these days without Robert, but those of us who remain are determined to carry on the work that Mr. Tyler saw as crucial to our firm—seeing that the law is fairly applied to all.

"I want to tell you a true story today about a man, a visionary leader of his people. At the end of the story you will hear about a case that Mr. Tyler and the other lawyers in our firm tried before the courts of North Carolina, including the Supreme

Court, in support of this man, a White Chief of the Cherokee, named Kahnungdatlegeh, or in English, 'the man who walks the mountain top.' I'm going to read to you the story that that he shared with our firm as we were preparing his case. The story is a bit lengthy, but I am sure that you will be glad that you heard it."

Lawrence slipped on a pair of spectacles. He took a sheath of folded papers from his coat jacket and began to read.

> I wasn't always known as 'the man who walks the mountain top.' I was given that name by the Tribal Council when I was elected as one of the seven White Chiefs of the Cherokee Nation. The Cherokee have White Chiefs during times of peace and Red Chiefs during war. The White Chiefs are both the judges, who settle disputes, and the spiritual leaders. But I'm getting way ahead of myself. Let me go back to when I was a child and my name was Goochankah, or Little Beaver.
>
> When I was fifteen years old, my father, Black Fox, came home from a meeting of the council and announced that he, and two other White Chiefs, Little Turkey and Pathkiller, had been selected to travel to London, England, as representatives of the Cherokee people to sign a treaty of cooperation and mutual protection. He also announced that the council had decided that each of the chiefs was to carry their eldest son with them. Sons of White Chiefs were often trained to eventually take their father's place, and the council couldn't think of a greater training experience than having us go to the home of the Great White Father.
>
> I was going to sail across the great sea and go to a great city. I had heard of boats that were large enough to carry hundreds of men, and horses and cattle; but I had never seen such a thing. And I had heard of great cities where thousands of people lived, but I could not begin to imagine what a city would look like.
>
> We were going to be leaving in four days. We could not leave before the White Chiefs presided over the most

important ritual of the year, the Green Corn Festival, a three day event which would begin the next day. I had this day free and decided to spend it at my favorite place, the top of Attakulla, or Black Dome Mountain. Black Dome is the highest mountain in Cherokee land. From its peak I could see for hundreds of miles in each direction. I knew that it would take me nearly half a day just to climb to the peak, but I didn't care. There was something spiritual about sitting on top of the Black Dome.

Most of the other teenage boys in Kituwa, our village, clung to the valleys as they made their way around the mountains. Climbing over the mountains took too much time and too much energy. It was so much easier to go around the mountains than to go over them. But I loved to go over them, because when I stayed on the valley floors, I seldom saw the real beauty of the land. I made my way to the top of the mountain that day to see as much of my homeland as I could. I would be gone for nearly half a year and I wanted to fix in my mind all that I would be missing. I also wanted to fulfill the Cherokee practice of facing all four directions when I was in deep thought or prayer. I could be blessed by the four powers that held the ends of the earth apart.

I first sat looking east for a long time. I was trying to imagine a sea voyage. I had never actually seen the sea, but the elders who had, spoke of it with such awe. The British had told the chiefs that the voyage to England would take anywhere from eight to twelve weeks depending on the winds. I was trying to imagine a body of water so large that it would take that long to cross.

After a long while I turned and looked south. It was from the south that our fiercest enemies, the Shawnee and Catawba always came. As far back as the elders could remember, the three tribes had been raiding each other's villages. For at least a generation, the Cherokee had become quite wealthy, capturing Shawnee women and children and selling them to the British as slaves. The Shawnee had tried to retaliate by raiding our villages, but our system of defending our villages was so well coordinated that the Shawnee seldom succeeded. Their most successful raids were not against our villages, but against our hunting parties, when our men were most vulnerable.

When I looked west, I remembered the stories of our ancestors coming into contact for the first time with white men, and the massive animals which they rode. Our people were intrigued by the pale skinned people, but greatly frightened by their horses. These men were Spanish who had made their way up the great river, the Mississippi, and then traveled east to the borders of our land in Tennessee. In my father's house hung a Spanish shield, which was won in battle by my great, great, great grandfather. Unlike the shields which our warriors sometimes carried that were made of deerskin stretched tightly over a wooden frame, this shield was made of iron and adorned with silver. Every time that my father went to a council meeting, in which war with the whites was being considered, he always took that shield with him. It was not to remind the chiefs that we could win an occasional battle against the white men, but to remind them that ultimately deerskin shields and rock-tipped arrows could not defeat iron.

As I looked to the north, I thought of the Iroquois tribes, who like the Cherokee lived in settled villages and were a more agricultural people than the Mississippians to our south. We had banded with the Iroquois tribes in fighting with the British and against the French. We had been promised that all of the Kentucky land that we claimed as ours would be protected by treaty; but that treaty, like so many others, had been broken. The delegation that was going to London was to sign a new treaty. I didn't know what the new treaty said; but, like most Cherokee, I had a healthy mistrust for the British. The word "Cherokee" means "principled people." Most of us wished that the British and the French would adopt the principled ways of the Cherokee.

My day on top of the Black Dome had been a good one. I had been empowered by the One Above and by the four powers. I had spent time, as the elders always told us to do, remembering my heritage and dreaming of my future. I was proud of my people and our land. As I made my way down the mountain and towards Kituwa, my village, I was thinking of the Green Corn Festival which would begin the next day. It, too, was a celebration of the past and a preparation for the future.

The Cherokee Nation was divided into seven clans, each containing ten settled villages. Each of the clans had a White Chief who, along with his assistants, cared for the spiritual needs of the people in each of the villages in his clan. The White Chief moved throughout the year from village to village. In each clan there was also one village that was the gathering village for the clan and the true home of the White Chief. Kituwa was the gathering village for our clan and like all of the others, included a large Council House in the center of which was the sacred fire.

The Green Corn Festival always began at dawn on the first day with the extinguishing of the sacred fire and all the other fires in the village. There would be no cooking for two days as the people fasted to prepare themselves for the purification rites happening on the third day. After the fires were extinguished the people would make their way to the river. The men and boys bathed on one side of the bend, and the women and girls around the bend and down the river. It was crucial that every person in the village be as clean as possible before the purification rites and the rebirth of the fire.

After the ceremonial baths, the men, dressed in new deerskins, would gather in the Council House. The men would divide into four groups. Each group would spend one fourth of the day sitting in each of the four corners. Only the White Chief stayed in the center, praying to the One Above. The men prayed prayers to the Ancestors for guidance for the year to come; to the Corn Mother, Selu, for a bountiful harvest; and to the four powers to give everyone in the clan the strength they needed to ward off evil and disease in the years to come.

On the second day of the festival, all offenses in the past year would be heard and all would be forgiven, except for the sins of rape and murder. Those two offenses were unforgiveable and required banishment, not just from the village, but from the tribe itself. Not only were offenses forgiven, but those who had been harmed were expected to forgive those who had harmed them. The purification of the clan could not take place if anyone harbored animosity to another. Because the corn, squash and bean crops (which we called the three sisters) could not flourish if there was impurity in the village, any woman was in her cycle of discharge during the festival was banned from the village until three days after the festival came to an end.

As daylight of the second day was beginning to fade, the White Chief would build a fire in the very center of the dance ground. The fire had to be made with wood from a tree that had been struck by lightning. From this Thunder Fire, every woman in the village would gather coals to start the fires in their log cabins. These fires would be used to cook the feast that would end the festival on the third day. After every cabin in the village had fire, the women would return to the dance ground. It was the women who initiated the dancing; and, unlike dancing during the rest of the year, only sacred dances were allowed during the Corn Festival. During the rest of the year, very sexually explicit dances were commonplace, but during the Corn Festival, especially after our fasting and purification, such dances were strictly banned. This night would be a night of sacred dances, to the animals which were so crucial to our survival, the bear, buffalo, beaver, deer, elk, and rabbit, and to the sacred hawk and eagle who brought messages from the One Above. There was also a dance to the Three Sisters. Each of the dances was led by a woman, the Mother of the Dance, who wore a rattle on each leg. The sound of her rattles determined not only which dance was to be performed, but also the cadence and rhythm of the steps. About an hour before dawn, just as the pre-glow of the sun was being seen in the east, the Mother of the Dance would begin the most important of the festival's dances, The Running Dance, in which all of us walked slowly from our past and ran quickly into our future. The dance began as the mother began with a slow deliberate pace and the women joined in, pacing from west to east to take us back to our beginnings.

Four songs, sung by the women as they danced, and handed down to us by the Stone Coat monster, told the history of the Cherokee and reminded us that we, alone, among all peoples, were the principled people. After the fourth song ended with a great shout, the men joined the women. Just as the sun dawned, the direction of the circle changed; we began to go from east to west. At first, the same deliberate pace continued, but with each rotation of the circle, the Mother of the Dance, now joined by the White Chief with a drum, quickened the pace. After many rotations of the circle, the people could not dance without running. Then each family would run once more around the sacred thunder fire. As quickly as they could, they would run to their own cabins to carry the blessings of the One Above into their home for the year to come.

The festival concluded with a great shared banquet. Every family gathered around the sacred fire and every family contributed food for the feast. The entire clan had been purified, prayers had been offered for the sick, and peace had replaced any turmoil that might have been among us. The greater the peace that pervaded us, the greater the harvest would be in the months to come.

I have told you all of this because I want you to understand how vitally important my Cherokee heritage is to me. But two great events in my life would rattle the very foundations of my soul. The first was the trip to London. On the morning after the festival, my father and the other two White Chiefs and their sons met with the two British emissaries and began our trip. One of the British was a Colonel named James Hill. He spoke a little Cherokee and my father and I spoke some English. We had learned English from a trader who had been adopted into our clan when he had risked his own life to save three Cherokee from a Shawnee raiding party. Colonel Hill let us know that we would be boarding a ship at Charleston, South Carolina and that it might take us several weeks to get there. Even though I had been to every village of the Cherokee nation with my father, I had never before left Cherokee land.

When we came into the city of Charlotte, I saw for the first time the difference between the British settlers and the Cherokee. Here I saw buildings made of brick and stone with glass in the windows, paved streets with gutters to channel rain water and large city squares covered in mown grass. Our hard packed clay dance grounds turned into a sea of mud with the spring and fall rains. In Charlotte, our delegation was joined by a troop of British soldiers. We were going to leave Charlotte and go through the land of the Cheraw, a tribe that would love to kidnap three Cherokee White Chiefs and their sons and hold us for ransom. The Cheraw would not do us any harm, because they would not want to go to war with the much more powerful Cherokee, but they would gladly cause us mischief if they could. The British soldiers were there to prevent that.

The farther east we went, the more impressive the farms of the whites were. When we reached the flat lands of the coastal plain, I saw for the first time great plantations where individual fields were larger than our entire village.

We made our way into Charleston. Charlotte was impressive, but it couldn't compare with this beautiful port city. The public buildings, the schools, the churches, the government buildings and courthouse were nothing short of amazing. When I saw the houses of the wealthy merchants and shippers, I asked Colonel Hill how many families lived in each one of these buildings. I'll never forget when he told me that usually only one family lived in each house. In our village families of six or more all lived in just one room. Each person who lived in a Charleston house could have two or three rooms to themselves!

When we got to the port I was completely amazed by two things, the ocean and the ships. When I had sat atop Black Dome trying to imagine the size of the ships and the vastness of the ocean, my imagination had failed me completely. We were welcomed aboard the HMS Allegiance by Captain Tom Riley and his crew of three hundred sailors and marines. The ship was over 400 feet long, so large that it carried 150 cannons. Even after all these years, as I think back on it, I still wonder how something so large could float. I was fascinated with the effort that it took to get the ship out of port. Six long boats were lowered over the side and tied to the front of the ship. Sixty sailors lowered themselves over the side of the ship on rope ladders, climbed into the long boats and began to row. This massive ship was being pulled by the longboats out of the shelter of the port and into the ocean beyond.

Getting the ship through the breaking waves at the mouth of the port took incredible effort from the sailors. When the ship hit the breakers, I realized for the first time the power of the ocean. The ship was tossed around like a leaf floating down a mountain stream. Once we were through the breakers, the water became calmer, though great swells still bobbed us up and down and side to side. But the men in the long boats had pulled us into the wind. The men and the longboats could be retrieved and the sails unfurled. All of this was fascinating to me, until we lost sight of the land.

Almost the minute that we left the land behind us, I became sick. The sailors called it sea sickness. They promised me that I would get over it eventually. I'll never forget how faithfully I prayed to die. I was sure that only death would make me feel better. For three weeks I hung over the side of the boat, miserable. Because I was constantly on deck, I developed the worst sunburn that I had ever had. One of the sailors, feeling sorry for me, placed a large wide-brimmed hat on my head to shield my face and neck from the sun. As soon as the hat was placed on my head, the sea sickness left me. I don't know what it was about that hat, but I refused to take it off until we had reached England and my feet were planted once again on solid ground.

After eleven weeks at sea, we docked in Bristol. The port was crammed with hundreds of ships, each one a beehive of activity. As our delegation walked the docks, Colonel Hill pointed out the wares being unloaded—bales of raw cotton, bags of rice, casks of tar and pitch, pallets of tobacco, kegs of rum. Sugar, spices, salt, pine and mahogany logs, and hundreds of other goods lined the docks. Colonel Hill explained that these goods were being shipped to England from British colonies around the world. Many of the items arrived in a raw state, like the bales of cotton, and would later be shipped back to the colonies as manufactured goods.

In Bristol, I was introduced to English beer and, I ate, for the first time in my life, at an establishment called a restaurant. I was amazed that people would spend their entire lives cooking for others and that people were willing to pay for their meals. In Cherokee society, if anyone was hungry, he could go to any cabin in any town and would be fed. We had a two-day carriage ride from Bristol to London. Along the way I saw English manor houses that were, until we got to London, the largest buildings that I had ever seen.

I know I have used the words 'stunned' and 'amazed' frequently in describing the things that I saw, but I can think of no better words to describe my reaction to London. Colonel Hill told us that over 750,000 people lived in the city which was both amazingly beautiful and stunningly squalid. Human excrement dumped on the streets, mixed with the manure of thousands of horses, gave the city a stench that made me nearly as sick as the sea voyage. But the beauty far exceeded the stench. The buildings were magnificent! If I had seen only two of them, Westminster Abby and Whitehall Palace, I would have known that the whites had a culture far more advanced than ours. We, Cherokee, would be foolish not to learn from them. As I stood in the great cathedral of Westminster, I realized just how far behind we were. Our Council House, the largest structure in all of the Cherokee Nation, would fit within the cathedral at least two hundred times. Not only was the building huge, it was also beautiful beyond words. The stained glass windows were intricate art; the stone carvings and statues which adorned the walls were so magnificent that I was ashamed of our people's poor imitations of art. Then the organ played. I had never heard such music. Our only instruments were rattles, drums and simple wooden flutes.

As we boarded the ship on our way back to America, I put on the wide-brimmed hat, the miracle hat. I wore it the entire voyage home, never once getting seasick. Because of weak winds, the voyage home took longer than the one to England. For fifteen weeks my father, the other White Chiefs, their sons and I talked of all that we had seen and all that we had learned. Little Turkey and Pathkiller were as amazed as I had been. But their reaction was that we had the far superior culture. We cherished the land and kept it clean. There was no stench in a Cherokee village. No one had to walk through human waste to cross our dancing grounds. Though the English had built great cathedrals, we had the cathedral of the mountains and the sky.

Our discussions and debates were intense. My father seemed to lean towards the opinions of the other White Chiefs. I disagreed, but I was only fifteen. Who was I, in the end, to disagree with three of the most important spiritual leaders of our people? I spent many hours on the ship pondering. Out on the ocean, it was impossible to know where the four corners of the world were. I wasn't sure if the One Above was above us here or only at home. I couldn't wait to get back to climb Black Dome. Maybe there it would all make sense. For the next twenty-five years, I climbed to the top of a mountain at least once a week to ponder and pray. I knew what the One Above was calling me to do for my people, but it took me a long time to get the courage to do it.

The second big event which changed my life was the outbreak of small pox which occurred fifteen years after our return from London. One half of the Cherokee died. By that time, I was a thirty-year-old assistant to my father. For three months, we prayed the prayers of our ancestors, performed the rituals that had been handed down to us for the healing of the sick, and watched our people die. For three months, we performed multiple funerals every day. When at last the crucible was ended, the Principled People who remained had lost faith in the White Chiefs and our heritage. Our entire priesthood had been discredited because of our inability to heal the sick. The same thing would have happened in the Christian community if someone had been able to convince Christians that the resurrection was a farce and the dead body of Jesus was rotting in a tomb somewhere.

The people did not remove the White Chiefs, even though their importance waned tremendously. My father did everything in his power to restore the people's faith, but when he died ten years after the epidemic, the people were going through the festivals and rituals only because of tradition. No longer was there power in the dances or the thunder fire.

It was after my father's death that the council elected me to be the new White Chief for our clan, the Eutowa, and gave me the name 'Kahnungdatlegeh.' On the day after my selection, I climbed Black Dome. I needed a day to confirm what I already knew.

When I came down from the mountain the next day, I requested a meeting of the entire clan. I asked that both the men and women be present. Never before had women been invited to a meeting of the clan, but, because I was the new White Chief, the men reluctantly agreed. When all had gathered, I rose to address them and began by saying, "You have given me a new name, 'the one who walks the mountain tops,' but the One Above has given me a different name that I would like for you to call me from now on, John Ross."

Instantly, a near riot erupted. "How dare you take an English name!" they yelled at me. "You are forsaking your entire heritage. You are leaving the Principled Way."

Even before I had spoken, I knew that the abuse would come. I had spent twenty-five years trying to build up enough courage to speak to my people. When the people finally finished shouting their hurt, pain, and anger, I was able to speak once again.

"I know that what I am about to say will seem like a betrayal to most of you, but I ask that you listen. I know that most of you will not agree with what I have to say, and that it will cause a great division among you, the people I love so dearly. You are right when you say that I am about to leave the Principled Way. I believe that if we are to thrive as a people, we must accept a new way while we hold on to all that is best of the old way."

I explained what I had learned in London. I told them that we must accept the English culture and religion while, at the same time, holding on to the things about our way that had stood the test of time. At the end of our meeting that night, about one in ten people were willing to try the new way. For the next several months, discussions were held nearly every night. Finally, the decision was made that my followers and I would be asked to leave Kituwa. Because we were brothers and sisters of the Principled Way, we would not be banished, but we were asked to withdraw to another part of the Cherokee land and establish a new village.

It seemed to me to be an immensely fair compromise. My followers and I established a new town that we called Qualla, the Rock. The One Above blessed us so that we prospered in ways that I could never have imagined. At the end of our twentieth year, I made a survey or our community and found that we had amassed 1,560 black slaves, 22,000 cattle, 7,600 horses, 46,000 pigs, 2,500 sheep, 762 looms, 2,488 spinning wheels, 172 wagons, 2,942 plows,10 sawmills, 31 grist mills, and 62 blacksmith shops. We invited Moravian missionaries to come and live among us. As a result, nearly every one of the 5,000 residents of the Qualla was converted to the new faith. We built schools in which our children were educated, churches in which we worshipped, a court system exactly like that of the State of North Carolina, and businesses in which we prospered. I had personally become so prosperous that I hired an architect from Philadelphia to design a house which I built at a cost of over $10,000. When it was built, it was the most expensive house in North Carolina.

Then, in 1800, a crisis arose that I could never have imagined. The State of North Carolina informed me that it was illegal for Cherokee people to own property. I and my people would have to forfeit everything. Their reasoning was that Indians were not citizens. Like the black slaves we owned, we were considered nothing more than partial human beings. By their reasoning, only white people were really people.

Even though we had completely adopted the culture of Americans, converted to their faith, and adopted a constitution patterned after the Constitution of the United States, we were being told that we were not even real people. It was then, more than ever, that I wished that I had the power to turn all of the whites to the best of the Principled Way.

When we were told that we were not really people, had no rights, and were about to lose everything that we had built, I hired the Tyler Law Firm to help us fight our battle in the courts. For six years, now, we have been in court after court. Each time, Robert Tyler and his team have convinced the court that the state is wrong. And each time, the state has appealed to a higher court. Mr. Tyler's main argument in each case was the need for justice to be done. He has continually asked, "How can we look these men in the face and declare that they are not human? We must always remember that Cherokees are people, too."

Lawrence Weeks paused. The story of John Ross had come to an end.

"We have won every step along the way," Lawrence said. "But the state refuses to accept defeat. The state has now appealed to the Federal Courts, with the intention of taking the matter all the way to the US Supreme Court. Robert Tyler and I were in the process of preparing the briefs to appear before the US Fourth Circuit Court of Appeals when he died. Chief Ross and I have been in discussion many times since Robert's death, and he has asked that the Tyler Firm continue to represent him and the people of Qualla.

"It is my firm intention to win the case, even before the Supreme Court of the United States. To do less than win would be to sully the reputation of Robert Tyler. And that is something that I will never do."

Lawrence turned and addressed Adam. "There has never been a man who was more committed to justice than your father. You can be very proud. Very proud, indeed."

Two Short Tales

L AWRENCE WEEKS HAD GIVEN SUCH A POWERFUL speech that I felt sorry for Franklin Campbell, the foreman of the Lynnmont Estate, who was scheduled to go next. Franklin, a shy man, is certainly no public speaker. I felt the same way about asking him to speak next as I would if someone had asked me to preach a sermon immediately after Bishop Francis Asbury, the most powerful preacher in American Methodism. But Franklin had to speak sometime, and this was the order that Robert had chosen, I introduced him and returned to my seat.

"I have a very short story," he said. "In fact it is hardly a story at all. It might even be referred to as nothing more than a statement. Robert Tyler hired me to be the foreman of Lynnmont five years ago. As foreman, I am responsible for growing the crops, purchasing the supplies, maintaining the buildings and fences, managing the timber, caring for the livestock, cooperating with the managers of the Tyler Companies that have any connection to the estate, and supervising the employees who are needed to fulfill these tasks. As part of my role of supervisor, Mr. Tyler empowered me to hire and fire employees, but he did ask that before I actually fired any employee, that I run the decision by him.

"When he hired me, Mr. Tyler said that, like any other businessman, he wanted his estate to be profitable and that part of my job was to see to it that every employee gave his very best. He told me something that I already knew. 'The harder you work, the harder the people who work with you and for you will work. You need to lead by example.'

"I can tell you that I have never worked harder in my life than I have in the last five years. And I can also tell you that I have been very fortunate to work with more than two hundred people who are dedicated to making Lynnmont the most successful estate in North Carolina. Only a handful of people have had to be fired, and with an operation this large, that is truly remarkable.

"There was one employee, however that I wanted to let go, not because he was unwilling to work, but because he was physically unable to do his job. His name is Ben Randolph. He has been at Lynnmont for more than forty years as the estate's horse trainer. It is his responsibility to train every foal before it has reached its first birthday. Since our horse operation is so large, Ben Randolph is responsible for taming and training at least four hundred horses per year.

"Those of you who know Ben are aware that there has never been a better horse trainer than Ben Randolph. He has a remarkable knack with horses, and even mules, and donkeys. It is as though he can speak their language. He is what the Indians call a horse whisperer. But those of you who know Ben also know that he is a man who is racked with rheumatism. He is so afflicted by the disease that he can no longer mount a horse, much less ride one. His rheumatism is so bad that he can hardly walk, and his hands have become so misshapen and weakened that he is no longer able to hold the reins of a spirited horse.

"Remembering that Mr. Tyler had told me he wanted the estate run as a profitable business, I told him that it was time to let Ben Randolph go. Mr. Tyler looked at me and said, 'I have agreed with every other personnel decision that you have made, but I can't agree with this one. I will never fire a person because he is too old or too sick to do the work. We have asked our employees to give the very best of themselves to us. In return, they deserve our loyalty. Besides,' he added, 'Ben Randolph has been at Lynnmont longer than I have.'

"Mr. Tyler," I said. "I appreciate your loyalty, but from a strictly business sense, Ben Randolph is costing you money. He simply can't do the job any more. When it comes time this spring for our annual sale, we may have only half as many horses ready for sale as we should."

"From a strictly business sense," Mr. Tyler said, "we cannot afford to fire Ben Randolph. No one knows more about training horses than he does. And we have never had a more loyal employee. We are simply not using him in the right way. What we need to do," he said, "is to hire as many assistants as Ben needs and have him train them. I want you to promote Ben Randolph and give him a dollar a week raise. Give him the title Senior Horse Trainer, and then have him hire his assistants. Tell him that his most important task will be to train his assistants so that the job will get done."

"Well, I reluctantly did exactly what Mr. Tyler asked me to do. It seemed to me that it was going to be mighty expensive. Not only was Mr. Ben getting a raise, but we were going to have to pay these new assistants, too. And there didn't seem to be any guarantee that the job would get done.

"Mr. Ben was right pleased with the promotion and with his new title. He hired three of the teenaged boys whose fathers worked at Lynnmont. He told me that he picked teenagers because, like young horses, they were the most easily trained. Besides, we wouldn't have to pay them as much as we would adults. It turned out that Ben Randolph had a way with boys, just like he did with horses. He never raised his voice to any of them.

"In a matter of a few months, we had three new master horse trainers on the estate. Not only did he train them, but he gave each one a specialty. One trains horses and mules to the plow, one is an expert in preparing horses for pulling wagons and carriages, and the other is one of the best trainers of riding horses that I have ever seen. The result has been that in one year we have been able to more than double our capacity to prepare horses for our annual spring sale. Next year, we may have as many as eight hundred horses ready for market.

"I believe that Mr. Tyler would have insisted that we keep Ben Randolph even if the experiment had failed. It seems that loyalty to employees really is good business. Not long before he died, Mr. Tyler told me that Ben Randolph would have a job at Lynnmont for as long as he wanted it. And he told me to tell Ben that even if he decided that he could no longer work, he would always have a home at Lynnmont and be welcome to eat at the estate kitchen.

"Even though Ben's rheumatism gets worse every day, and it gets harder and harder for him to do his job, or even to walk to the barn, he is always there every morning before I get there. It must take him close to an hour to walk the two hundred yards from his bunkhouse to the barn. Most days now, he needs the support of two canes, not just one, to be able to make that painful walk. He makes that painful walk every day. He comes out of loyalty to those who have been loyal to him.

"I hope that the new owner of Lynnmont, whoever he may be, will take the time to watch Ben Randolph walk to work one day. It will inspire the new owner to work as hard for the estate's employees as they do, inspiring everyone who works at Lynnmont to work even harder."

Franklin Campbell's simple statement was simply profound and I told him so as he returned to his seat.

Abigail Jordan is our last speaker, I said. She lives in Salem and has been a long time employee of the Salem Tavern. Mr. Tyler has asked that she tell the story of President Washington's visit to Salem in 1791 as a part of his Southern Tour. Miss Abigail, we are pleased to have you with us."

Abigail Jordan's smile was as broad as her face, as she made her way from her seat to the chancel area. She walked with a lilt in her step that belied the dull, yet demanding, work that she did every day.

"I have been the head maid at the Salem Tavern for more than twenty years," she began. "I started working there at age thirteen when my father moved the family to Salem so that he could take a job as a wheelwright at the Salem Carriage Works. Unfortunately, my dad died very unexpectedly, not long after we had moved here. My mother was left with a household of children and no means of support. She made the decision to move back to Virginia to be near her family, but, since I actually had a job, she encouraged me to stay in Salem. I moved into a room in the Single Sister's House on south Church Street and continued to work at the tavern.

"My daily tasks have always been the same. Every morning, I begin the day by gathering the chamber pots from the guest's rooms, taking them to the outhouse to be emptied and then to the wash house where I thoroughly clean each one. This usually happens before most of the guests have even awakened. So when they do wake, clean chamber pots are ready for their use. Of course, after they are used, the whole process has to be repeated.

"After the guests have risen and made their way to the dining room, I thoroughly clean each of the rooms, sweeping and mopping the floors, dusting the furniture and, when they need it, washing the windows. Every day I change all of the linens and take the dirty linens out back, and hand wash them. I hang the linens to dry and after they have dried, I iron and fold them so that they will be ready for the next day. Salem Tavern is the only inn I know that provides fresh linen every day. Most of the inns that I have seen have linens and mattresses that are infested with bed bugs and lice. There won't be any bugs as long as I am the head maid at Salem Tavern!

"My job is to do all my work without really being seen. That isn't usually a problem, because most of our guests are men of importance who never really see people like me. I can tell you one thing, for sure, that I have learned about men of importance—they have exactly the same stuff in their chamber pots as everybody else," Abigail said, laughing.

I noticed that Emily Gladstone, who did exactly the same task for her patients every day, nodded laughing as loudly as Abigail.

"One of the important men who stayed at the tavern was different from almost all the others. He was a man who introduced himself to me the very first time he stayed there and actually asked me my name. I'll never forget how stunned I was when, several months later, when he was spending the night again, that he actually remembered my name. "Miss Jordan," he said, "I hate to ask this of you, but my boots need scraping. I have failed to bring my scraper with me. Would you mind bringing me a scraper?"

"Oh, Mr. Tyler," I said, "just give me your boots and I will be glad to clean them."

"I wouldn't dream of asking you to do such a disgusting task," he said. "I must have stepped in a pile of horse manure last night as I walked to the tavern in the dark."

"Mr. Tyler," I said. "Scrapping boots is one of my most important jobs. But I have to admit, that unlike you, most men are actually wearing their boots when they ask me to scrape them. They expect me to kneel at their feet with a chamber pot and a scraper and clean their boots. They don't really see me, and none of them has ever asked me my name. Now give me your boots. It will be a great privilege to clean them!

"Robert Tyler did give me his boots that day. I not only scraped them, I washed them and polished them. I don't reckon I have ever seen a cleaner pair of boots than the pair that I returned to Robert Tyler. Any man who would care to know the name of a maid who waits on him deserves to have clean and polished boots.

"I soon learned that Robert Tyler would spend the night at the tavern if he had an early morning meeting in Salem. So once or twice a month, for all the years that I have worked there, Mr. Tyler has been a guest. And every single time that he has come, he has greeted me warmly, treating me with a kindness and respect that maids seldom receive.

"Salem folk were thrilled when word came that President Washington was planning an overnight stay. In fact, everyone in northwestern North Carolina was excited. But I can tell you that there was no group of people who were more filled with anticipation than the owner and staff of the Salem Tavern, because we had received word that the President would be spending the night in our establishment.

"As word of the impending visit spread throughout this part of the state, dignitaries from all over the region gathered in Salem and drew up elaborate plans for greeting and entertaining the President. Important men, and those who wanted to be important, met for two days at Salem College to work out all of the details. One of the longest discussions concerned who would be invited to be in the receiving line to officially welcome President Washington. Not only did this group of distinguished men have to decide who would be included, but they had the arduous task of deciding the order in which the men would stand. The most important person in the community would be the last person to greet the President before he spoke to the common folk in the town square. I don't remember everybody in the line, but I do recall the president of Salem College and the pastor of Home Moravian church being there. Also in line was Alexander Johnston, the area's highest ranking judge. I definitely remember the most honored greeter, Senator Robert Tyler!

"Another decision this group of distinguished men made was that all of the thirty men who had been selected to be in the receiving line would gather on the porch of the tavern. A maid at the tavern would be present to scrape and clean everyone's shoes before they left the porch and formed the line.

"I don't remember how I got the message that I had been given the high honor of scraping horse manure off the shoes of the important people. Maybe it was the owner of the tavern who informed me. All I know for sure is that on the day that the President was to appear, all of the men were right there on the porch of the tavern, just as they were supposed to be. It was the Pastor of Home Church who took charge of putting the men in the right order.

"As the men got in line, I began crawling on my hands and knees, dragging my chamber pot and shoe scraper, with a wet towel draped over my shoulder to wipe away anything that may have gotten on the top of anyone's shoes. I made my way down the line, cleaning each man's shoes. As I approached each man, he would raise one foot at a time to allow me to do my job. Except for raising their feet, not a single man acknowledged my presence. But I really didn't expect them to.

"When I got to the end of the line, Mr. Tyler allowed me to clean his shoes and then leaned down, took me by the arm and had me stand directly in front of him.

"Miss Jordan," he said, "I want you to take your scraper, pot and towel to the wash room. Put on a fresh apron, and come back here as quickly as you can. I have something very important that I need for you to do."

"Yes, Sir, Mr. Tyler," I said. I quickly made my way down the front steps of the porch, ran around the tavern to the laundry room in the back yard and threw the scraper and the pot into the basin that was there. I slipped off my apron, which Mr. Tyler must have noticed was stained, slipped on a newly laundered, and freshly starched one, and made my way back to the front of the tavern. As I was hurrying along, I wondered what Mr. Tyler needed me for. Whatever it was, I would be glad to do it.

"When I got back to the front of the tavern, the men were already leaving the porch and walking across the street to the Salem Square. I stood by the steps, looked up, and caught Mr. Tyler's eye. He made a motion with his hand that clearly said to me, 'Stay right there.' When he came down the steps, he took a firm grasp of my arm and said, 'I want you to come with me.'

"I looked out at the sea of people who were parting to let the line of dignitaries through and said, "Oh, no." But Mr. Tyler tightened his grip on my arm and said again, 'I want you to come with me.' As we made our way towards the speaker's platform where the receiving line was to stand, he said, 'When we get into position, I want you to stand directly behind me. I want you to have the honor of being as close to President Washington as you can be.'

"As we walked through the crowd, I could hear people saying 'What is that woman doing with Mr. Tyler? And 'Who does she think she is?' Hearing these comments, I wanted to leave. But when I tried to pull away, Mr. Tyler's firm, yet somehow gentle, grip on my arm kept me in line. When Mr. Tyler reached his position right next to the steps leading up to the platform from which the President would speak, he positioned me directly behind him, right up against the platform where I couldn't move, even if I wanted to.

"There was a great stirring in the crowd as President Washington suddenly appeared and began to make his way down the receiving line. He seemed to be in no hurry, taking time to speak with each person. I was amazed at how tall he was. Even though I had seen pictures of him, none of them had done him justice. Finally, President Washington was speaking to the man just beside Mr. Tyler. I knew that he would speak to Mr. Tyler next and then be up the steps and on the platform.

"Just as the President stepped toward him, Mr. Tyler turned, took me by the arm again, and pulled me into the receiving line.

"Mr. President,' he said. "I want to introduce you to the most gracious hostess in all of North Carolina, Miss Abigail Jordan."

"The President extended his hand, but rather than take it, I curtsied. Then the President of the United States of America returned my curtsy with a bow. The President was bowing to me!

"My dear Miss Jordan," he said. "It is a great honor to meet you."

"For the only time in my life, I could not think of a single word to say. The President of the United States of America was speaking to me! It was Mr. Tyler who spoke on my behalf.

"Miss Jordan will be taking care of your needs tonight and tomorrow morning during your stay at the tavern. I assure you that you will never receive better care than that which you will receive from her. If you have any requests, simply let her know, and she will graciously see to it."

"Miss Jordan, I will look forward to seeing you later this evening," Mr. Washington said.

"I nodded and smiled. I still couldn't think of a word to say to him. But there were many things that I wanted to say to Robert Tyler! I had never been so embarrassed, or so honored, in all my life!

"Later that night, after all the speeches and all of the festivities, President Washington was settling into his room at the top of the stairs. I was sitting in a chair in the small hallway which connected the upstairs rooms in case I was needed. The President and all of his aids had gone to their various rooms. It seemed that everyone was tired and just wanted to go to bed. I was a bit surprised when President Washington opened the door to his room and said, 'Miss Jordan, would you mind getting me a fresh pitcher of water. I'd like to wash up a little before I go to sleep.'

"He remembered my name! He must have met a thousand people today, but he remembered my name!

"'I'll be glad to Mr. President. Would you like a fresh towel as well?"

"'That would be very nice.'

"When I returned with the pitcher of water and the towel, the President's door was shut. I knocked softly and heard him say, 'Come in.'

"I walked in the room, put the pitcher of water on the wash stand, and laid the towel on the end of the bed. As I turned to leave, President Washington said, 'Thank you. You are very kind.'

"'I'll be in the hall if there is anything else that you need, Mr. President.'

"I turned and left the room, closing the door behind me. As the latch on the door clicked, I leaned against the door for a moment, weakened by my encounter. As I stood there, I realized that, in my years of service, only Robert Tyler and George Washington ever said, "Thank you." It was then that I knew that these two men were cut from the same bolt of cloth. I could hardly wait until the next time I saw Robert Tyler. I simply wanted to say two words to him, 'Thank you.' I thought that those words would say enough. They certainly had been enough for me.

"Through the years, many people have asked me why I never married. I always answered them with a laugh, "I'm waiting for Robert Tyler to ask me." People would always laugh with me. We all knew that a woman of my station and a man of Mr. Tyler's importance could never be married. But, I will confess to you that there was some truth to my statement. I was waiting for Robert Tyler. I suppose that I really did love him. And I guess that I always will."

As Abigail was returning to her seat, Adam Robertson rose from his seat, blocked her path, took her hand, looked directly into her eyes, and said, "Thank you." Abigail smiled broadly and returned to her seat. Adam had spoken for all of us. Absolutely nothing else needed to be said.

The speeches had come to an end. All that remained now was the actual reading of Robert's will and the closing worship service.

A Military Ceremony

AFTER ABIGAIL JORDAN HAD TAKEN HER SEAT, I stood and said, "Folks, we have completed the first two of the four parts of the funeral banquet. Mr. Tyler told me in his instructions that he considered the telling of the stories to be the most important thing that we would do today. I'm sure that Adam would agree and will ponder the things that he has heard today for the rest of his life."

I turned to faced Adam and said, "Adam, I want you know that you are not the only one to learn things about your father today. I had never heard the story of Robert's role in the Battle of Guilford Courthouse. I knew that he had come home with a hurt shoulder, but, when I asked him about it, he told me that he had tripped over a wounded soldier and fallen. I suppose that, even a good man like your father told little white lies now and then. Adam, your father wasn't perfect, but he was the finest man I have ever known."

I turned again so that I could address everyone. "We have two more very important tasks to accomplish. The first is the actual reading of Mr. Tyler's Last Will and Testament, and the second is a closing worship service. We have been here for a long time. Is anyone in need of a break before we proceed with the reading of the will? Although we were all eager to hear the will, a few took a brief break and returned.

The time had finally come to retrieve the real documents. I asked Adam to help me move the altar, and took from inside the large packet which contained the will.

"Which will are you going to read?" Judge Johnston asked, 'the fake one you have, or the real one that Robert gave to me?"

"Maybe they are identical Judge." I didn't think so, but, I guess it was possible. "I think that, as the executor of the will, I should read the one that Mr. Tyler gave to me. Dr. Allen, do you agree that my decision is the best legal choice for me to make?"

"Yes. I think that the document that Mr. Tyler gave you would carry precedence over the one that the judge has."

I took my pen knife out of my pocket and used the blade to break the wax seal and cut the string which bound the envelope. I opened the flap of the envelope and reached inside. I pulled out a large collection of documents which were also bound with string. On the very top was a note addressed to me.

John,

Before the reading of the will, you will be honored to be a part of a special military ceremony. Please read the letter to Captain Stanley and then call on Retired General Allen to proceed.

Robert.

I removed the note from the top of the papers. Directly underneath was a letter addressed to Captain Stanley.

"Captain Stanley, there is a letter here, addressed to you, that Mr. Tyler has asked that I read."

Gilbert Stanley looked both surprised and confused, but nodded that I should continue.

I opened the letter and read:

September 18, 1806
Captain William Gilbert Stanley,
Guilford County, North Carolina

Dear Gilbert,

Just as I sent a special letter to my son, Adam, that was to be read to him only if I had died, so I address a special letter to you. I regret with every fiber of my being that I am not present to participate in the ceremony that is about to take place.

Every year since I was elected to the Senate, I have sought to undo a terrible miscarriage of justice. Every year, until this year, I have failed. The miscarriage of justice has been the result of the worst kind of politics; evil politics have caused the destruction of your good name and your military career. I regret that it has taken my colleagues and me so long to right the wrong that has been done to you.

Please know that I have always held you in highest regard. I have never known a man who has been more faithful to his oath of office. For you to have remained loyal all of these years, in spite of the unfair disputations brought against you by your political enemies, is a testimony of your character. I send to you, even from the grave, a most heartfelt salute.

Though I have no right to give you an order, I ask that you come now and stand before this gathering in full dress uniform and at attention so that your Ceremony of Promotion may proceed.

Sincerely,
Robert J. Tyler

Captain Stanley sat in his chair, clearly stunned.

"General Allen, Mr. Tyler has asked that I call on you to lead a special ceremony. Maybe you can get Captain Stanley to move."

"I'll be happy to do that," General Allen said. Addressing Captain Stanley, he said in a very commanding voice that he had not used earlier, "On your feet soldier!"

Captain Stanley rose so quickly that his chair toppled over behind him. He came to attention and saluted General Allen. The general returned the salute and said, "I would be grateful if you would come and stand before the altar."

While Captain Stanley made his way inside the chancel rail, General Allen removed the leather pouch Robert had sent to him from the inside pocket of his waistcoat. He opened the pouch and looked inside, making sure that all that he needed for the promotion ceremony was there. He closed the pouch and held it in one hand behind his back.

"Captain Stanley," he said, "promotions are reserved for those soldiers who have exhibited extraordinary hard work, dedication to the service, discipline in the face of difficulty, obedience to orders, and sacrifice of themselves. Promotions into the officer corps are reserved for those who have exhibited a unique ability to lead and those who their superiors believe have the ability to faithfully execute the oath of their office.

"Though it's not required that you repeat the oath each time you're promoted, I would like for you to do so now. I want to remind you of the oath's significance. If you don't remember it all, I'll be glad to prompt you."

"I think I remember," Captain Gilbert said. *I have repeated it to myself every day for thirty years,* he thought.

He came to attention and said in a clear and unwavering voice,

"I William Gilbert Stanley do solemnly swear that I will support the Constitution of the United States of America and the Constitution of the State of North Carolina against all enemies, foreign and domestic, that I will bear true faith and allegiance to them, that I take this obligation freely, without mental reservation or purpose of evasion and that I will faithfully discharge the duties of the office on which I am about to enter. So help me God."

"I am quite impressed that you remember it so well," General Allen said. "Loyalty depends, not so much on the words of the oath that is taken, but on the character and integrity of the individual who is taking the oath. As you know, the oath has changed some over the years. When you first became an officer, there was no constitution for either the federal government or the state. Even though the words have been adapted to reflect the changing times, the essential truth of the oath has never changed. Those who take the oath to be an officer are agreeing to defend the militia's core value—faithfulness to duty.

"You, Sir, have been completely faithful to your office. You have been faithful even though the militia has failed to be faithful to you. Following the Battle of Guilford Courthouse, you made the horrible mistake of telling the governor of North Carolina the truth. You rightfully referred to General Eaton's cowardice under fire, not knowing that General Eaton was the nephew of the governor. I have always believed that you would have used the same words even if you had known, because you were telling the truth. Unfortunately, as you know, telling the truth, especially to a politician, can often bring out the very worst side of politics, the dirty side, by which politicians use their power and position to destroy rather than build up. You, sir, have been the victim of the very worst that politics with unchecked power can do.

"That is why the oath of office concludes with the words, 'So help me God.' We ask our officers to ask for God's help, not for religious reasons, but because we know that every officer will fail to fulfill the high calling of their rank unless they rely on a power greater than themselves. I don't know if you are a man of faith, or not, but I do think it is incredibly ironic that you are about to receive a promotion that is thirty years overdue here in a church, standing before the altar and underneath the cross.

"I would like to read to you now the Orders for your promotion."

General Allen opened the leather pouch and took from it a folded document. He slipped the pouch back into his pocket, carefully opened the document and read

A Resolution of the Legislature
of the State of North Carolina

Passed, September 1, 1806 and attested by the signatures of the Honorable John Moore, Speaker of the House of Representatives, Senator Robert J. Tyler, Senate President Pro-tem, and Governor Nathaniel Alexander.

Whereas Captain William Gilbert Stanley has been a faithful and loyal officer in the North Carolina Militia for more than thirty years, and

Whereas Captain Stanley has been denied promotion only because of the most egregious abominations of political disputations, and

Whereas the Governor and Legislature have agreed that these abominations can only be rectified by the prompt promotion of Captain Stanley to the rank of Brigadier General

"Brigadier General!" Captain Stanley interrupted.

General Allen smiled broadly and said, "Sir, it is not appropriate that you would interrupt the reading of the official orders."

"I'm sorry, Sir. I had hoped for Major, but General?"

"I understand, Gilbert," General Allen said softly. "I know it's a shock, but let me finish reading the resolution. There is even more to come. Now, where was I?" He looked again at the resolution and said, "Oh yes, here we are."

...rectified by the prompt promotion of Captain Stanley to the rank of Brigadier General...

Therefore be it resolved by the joint agreement of the Legislature and the Governor of the State of North Carolina that this Resolution shall serve as the official

Order for Promotion of William Gilbert Stanley to the Rank of Brigadier General, and

Be it further resolved that the Legislature authorize that the sum of $3,000 shall be paid to General Stanley as back pay, and

Be if further resolved that Senator Robert J. Tyler be authorized to devise an appropriate Ceremony of Promotion, and

Be it finally resolved that following the Ceremony of Promotion, that this Proclamation be published in all of the newspapers of the State of North Carolina as a fitting tribute to General Stanley.

General Allen folded the resolution and placed it on the altar. "Sir," he said, addressing Gilbert, "I would appreciate it if you would kindly remove your captain's bars."

Gilbert had not realized how much he was shaking until he tried to unpin the captain's insignia. After several minutes, it was clear that he was making no progress. General Allen said, "Miss Jordan, would you mind coming and helping the general?"

Abigail Jordan smiled broadly as she rose from her seat and came to Gilbert's aid. At first, Gilbert was still trying to help until she said, "It might be easier for me to do this if you just stood at attention." Gilbert smiled at her and said, "My lady. I will be glad to obey your command."

He came to attention and Abigail was able to quickly unpin the captain's bars. She handed them to Gilbert, who slipped them into his pocket. Abigail stepped back and General Allen said, "Please remain at attention." He stepped forward and pinned a star on each side of General Stanley's collar.

General Allen took one step back, came to attention himself, and said, "General Stanley, it would be my honor to be the first person to offer you a salute, the highest form of military courtesy." He saluted the new general and when the salute was returned, the two men stepped forward and embraced one another.

General Allen, with one arm still around General Stanley, turned and said to all of us, "It is appropriate at a Military Ceremony of Promotion for there to be applause and then for each person present to offer personal greetings and congratulations. Even though none of you are military, I am sure that General Stanley would be pleased to receive your greetings."

Everyone rose from their seats clapping. The ovation was long and heartfelt. The altar rail was separating us from General Stanley, but, surprisingly to me, it was Judge Johnston who was the first to make it around the rail to greet him. It was, after all, Judge Johnston's political party which had denied Gilbert justice all these years. I stood in stunned amazement as Judge Johnston warmly congratulated him. It was amazing to me how a man who could be so ruthless as to order Robert's murder could also be a kind and compassionate gentleman.

With that, conversation broke out around the room as we each waited our turn to greet the new general, talk with each other about the astonishing miscarriage of justice, and discuss the equally astonishing righting of the wrong. It was while these conversations were taking place that I saw the door open and the deputy enter the church. He caught my eye, and motioned for me to come and speak with him.

"There is a man at the door, demanding that I let him in. He is wearing a cape with a hood so large that I can't see his face. I told him that no one was allowed to enter. Then he gave me this" he extended his hand, "and told me to give it to you. He said that it would explain everything."

The deputy opened up his hand and I saw a rock, covered in fool's gold. It was my paper weight from the office. Only two people knew the significance of the rock: Mordecai Jones, who certainly didn't need to be hiding his face, and Robert Tyler.

It just couldn't be. Robert Tyler was dead! I had performed his funeral. I had buried his casket. It just couldn't be! But...maybe...

I rushed to the door and opened it. The man standing before me threw off his hooded cape. I, and everyone else standing near the porch and watching, yelled in unison, "Robert Tyler!"

Robert turned to the crowd and said, "I will explain everything to all of you later." Then he turned to me, with a grin, and said, "Is it alright if I come in?"

Still too stunned to speak, I nodded. Robert took me by the arm and we walked through the door of New Salem Methodist Church together.

Making Things Crystal Clear

AS WE WALKED INTO THE CHURCH, ALMOST everyone was still focused on General Stanley. It was Richard Allen who was the first to see Robert.

"What the hell?" he shouted. Everyone stopped where they were and looked to where he was pointing.

"You really shouldn't talk like that in church, Richard," Robert said, smiling.

Just like outside, there was a moment of stunned silence followed by "Robert Tyler!" being shouted by nearly everyone present. The ones who knew him rushed forward with everyone speaking at once.

I heard questions like "How can this be?" and "Aren't you supposed to be dead?" and "Who did we bury two months ago?"

I noticed that Emily Gladstone and Adam Robertson were standing back. Neither of them had ever met Robert Tyler, of course; and, of all the people in the church, they had to be the two that were the most confused. After all, Adam had come here to be introduced through the stories to his dead father, not to a living person.

Robert finally managed to get everyone quiet. "I'll explain everything to all of you, but first, I would like to meet my son."

Robert quickly walked down the aisle of the church and went to Adam and Emily. Standing before Adam, he extended his hand, and said, "Son, I'm your father."

Adam hesitated, still too much in shock to know what to do or say. He did not shake Robert's hand, but simply stared at him, with an incredulous look on his face. I was amazed as they stood facing each other at how much alike they looked. The only real difference, other than age of course, was that Adam's ears, nose and chin, were slightly softer than Robert's. I figured that he must have gotten these softer features from Lynn.

"I know you are shocked, Son. But before this afternoon is over, I will explain everything."

As Robert was speaking to Adam, Alexander Johnston moved slowly and quietly along the side aisle towards the door of the church. No one noticed as he slipped through the door and made a beeline to his carriage. We were all too focused on Robert Tyler to care about Alexander Johnston.

Robert turned and spoke to Emily Gladstone. "You must be Emily Gladstone. Matthew Brown told me how you cared for Lynn and showered love and affection on Adam all these years. I want to thank you for being a friend to my wife and a mother to my son."

He stepped forward and embraced Emily. She returned the embrace and then the two of them each stepped back slightly while their arms slid down each other until their hands were clasped together. They stood, less than a foot apart, and simply looked at each other. Each was trying to think of what the next words should be. It was Emily who spoke first.

"When Mr. Barnes came to the Sanatorium and told me of your death, I told him how sorry I was because I had always wanted to meet you. I had never known a man who was loved as passionately as you. You need to know that Lynn loved you with such passion that I am sure her love has even transcended the grave."

"I have always had a strength that wasn't mine," Robert said. "Just the memory of her love…"His voice trailed off to nothing and a single tear rolled down his cheek. Emily Gladstone reached up and wiped the tear away with the back of her hand and then embraced Robert a second time. Adam, standing beside them, was silently crying with tears running down both cheeks and dropping to the floor. Were they tears of happiness? Or sadness? Or grief? Maybe they were tears of confusion or even anger. The tears seemed to sap him of all his strength and he slumped down into the chair that was nearest to him.

When Emily's and Robert's embrace came to an end, she glanced to her side and saw Adam, sitting in the chair, leaning over with his head in his hands, looking through his tears at the two of them. She stepped up to him and cradled his head against her breasts as any mother would her child.

"Adam," she said tenderly. "Just let your tears come. Tears are always a blessing." Robert stepped beside Adam and put his hand on Adam's shoulder. He had been a father for twenty years, but he had never been a dad. He didn't know what to say, but he hoped that his hand on Adam's shoulder was speaking for him.

Everyone else in the church stood in silence and watched as Adam cried, as Emily caressed him, and Robert stood beside him. It wasn't but a moment before all three of them were crying. Tears seemed to be the only language any of them could manage.

The rest of us made our way to the back of the church. We all sensed that the three of them needed time alone, without us gawking at them. We gathered near the door and quietly whispered to each other. We all had the same questions. We all had the same need for answers. The answers could wait until Adam was ready.

It was the loud commotion in the church yard that broke the solemnity of the moment. The judge had reached his carriage and was just about to step into it when he was grabbed from behind by the strong arms of a man he had never seen before. His cane fell to the ground, as he struggled with the man.

"You aren't going anywhere, Judge," the man said, as he tightly held him.

"Who the hell are you?"

"A friend of Robert Tyler."

"Get this man off of me!" Judge Johnston yelled to the crowd of onlookers.

People in the crowd rushed to his defense. After all, who was this stranger who was accosting the judge? The shouting match that ensued was what got our attention. Inside the church, Robert was the first to understand. He took Adam by the arm, stood him up, and said," Quick, come with me!" As they rushed down the aisle of the church, Robert yelled to me and the other men, "All of you men come with me!" We ran out the door of the church, across the porch, and down the steps. Under a large oak tree, forty feet from the front door, the judge was wrestling with a man. Other men were trying to help the judge, but the man, whose back was to me, was holding on to the judge for dear life.

Robert, Adam, Horace, Lawrence, Gilbert, Franklin, Richard and I rushed down the steps and toward the crowd. The crowd surrounding the judge and the man was growing larger by the second as people rushed to the scene, either to help the judge or simply to watch the fight. The deputies, who were at the church to maintain order, were trying, but failing miserably. There were so many people yelling that I was amazed when Robert's voice, yelling, "Let us through! Let us through!" could be heard.

The crowd began to part. It was only then that I saw that the man holding Alexander Johnston was Matthew Brown!

As we broke through the crowd, Robert yelled to us. "Surround the judge and move these people back!"

As we circled the judge and Matthew, Matthew loosed his grip. Robert leaned down, picked up the cane and handed it to Judge Johnston. As he shook hands with Matthew, he said, "Thanks

Matthew. I didn't see him slip out." Then turning to the judge, he said, "I didn't think you'd be very happy to see me, but I didn't think you'd run away. I've never thought of you as a coward."

"I'm not a coward! It just wasn't necessary for me to be here any longer!" Johnston said.

"Alexander. You couldn't be more wrong! It's essential that you be here. The codicil to my will said that every beneficiary must attend the funeral banquet, tell a story, and remain throughout the entire event. As a judge, you know that codicils are legally binding. You wouldn't want to break the law, would you?"

Without waiting for him to answer, he instructed us to "help Alexander find his seat." Speaking directly to Lawrence and Gilbert he added, "and make sure he stays there." I had never heard Robert call Judge Johnston 'Alexander.' Robert had always just called him 'Judge."

Turning to the now silent crowd, Robert said, "All the excitement's over now. If all of you would just back up and let us through, we'll just go back into the church." Lawrence and Gilbert each took one of the judge's arms and ushered him forward. The judge tried to throw them off, saying, "I can walk by myself!" Each man loosened his grip slightly, but did not let go.

"Matthew," Robert said. "I'd like for you to come inside with us."

As we approached the church, I looked up and saw all that the ladies had followed us, standing on the porch, watching all that had happened.

"Let's all go in," Robert said. "We have a funeral banquet to complete." When we were all back in the church, Robert introduced Matthew Brown as the man who had saved his life. We were all standing around, not sure what should come next. It was Adam who took charge.

"We have heard a lot of stories today. But I am sure that we want to hear one more." He turned and looked at Robert and said, "What should I call you? Mr. Tyler? Robert?" He paused and then added softly, "Father?"

"Whatever you feel most comfortable with, Son."

Adam hesitated for a moment. Finally he said, "Mr. Tyler, why don't you tell us how a dead man can speak." Then he added, "Why don't we all sit down. I'm sure it's going to be quite a tale."

No one needed a second invitation. Everyone went quickly back to their assigned seats as Robert made his way inside the altar rail. "Matthew, come join me. We ought to tell this story together." Matthew made his way from the back of the church, where he had been standing, to the chancel.

"About a year ago," Robert began, " I had a conversation with a fellow lawyer who happened to mention that he had hired a man named Matthew Brown to track down lost persons who were due an inheritance. 'He is the best we have ever found,' he told me. 'He can find anybody.' I had spent my entire adult life looking for Lynn but every trail I followed ended in a dead end. So, when I heard about Matthew Brown, I quickly engaged him. Maybe, I thought, he could do what I had failed to do so often.

"The first thing I did when Matthew came to Germantown to meet me was to warn him that Judge Johnston must not know what he was doing. He had to be extremely careful to whom he spoke. If the Judge found out, he would use his power and influence to block him at every turn. The second thing was to take him to meet Horace Hayworth." Robert nodded his head at Horace, acknowledging him. "I had Horace tell him everything that he remembered about the day that Lynn disappeared. Matthew, why don't you take up the story from here?"

"After the conversation with Horace, I knew the key to finding Lynn," Matthew said, "was finding the last person who was with her, Albert Schmidt. Albert had been banished from North Carolina. He had no visible means of support. He would have done the only thing that he could have done, seek out some family for help. With a name like Schmidt, I knew he had to be

German. I knew of small settlements of German speaking people in the mountains of Virginia and western Maryland. There was also a large population in central Pennsylvania, especially the Bethlehem area. I simply headed north. I went from town to town until I found Albert Schmidt.

"I found him in a jail cell in a little town called Nazareth just outside of Bethlehem, Pennsylvania. Albert was still a mean drunk. He was in jail because he couldn't afford to pay a fine for public drunkenness and assault. I offered to pay the fine and get him out of jail if he would tell me where he had taken Lynn. Albert agreed to tell me, but only when he was out of jail and only if I also agreed to buy him a bottle of whiskey. For a five dollar fine and a fifteen cent bottle of whiskey, the mystery of Lynn's whereabouts was finally solved.

"I made my way from Nazareth to Harrisonburg. There I met with Emily Gladstone who told me the whole story. She told me about the horrible man who had delivered Lynn to Apple Blossom, about Lynn's isolation, her pregnancy, the birth of Adam, and about her death. I left Harrisonburg and came quickly to Germantown to tell Mr. Tyler everything that I had discovered.

"When I got to Mr. Tyler's office, I decided to begin with the sad new first. I said to him, 'I'm sorry to tell you that your wife is dead. She died at the Apple Blossom Sanatorium in Harrisonburg, Virginia, twenty years ago.'

"My whole life," Robert said, "I had known, deep down inside, that she was dead. If she were alive, she would have found some way of contacting me. I never believed you, Alexander," Robert said, pointing directly at the judge, "when you told me that Lynn never wanted to see me again. I knew that you had lied to me. I had always held on to a small kernel of hope that maybe, just maybe, she was alive and being held in some place where she could not contact me. Hearing the words, 'I'm sorry to tell you that your wife is dead,' was devastating. Then I heard even more devastating news."

"I told him that Albert Schmidt was incredibly cruel to Lynn," Matthew said. "I told him how horribly Schmidt had treated Lynn on the journey from Yadkin Oaks to Harrisonburg."

I'll never forget how angry I was," Robert interrupted. "I remember rising from my chair and telling Matthew that I was going to kill Albert Schmidt."

"I made Mr. Tyler sit down," Matthew said. "I understand why he wanted to kill Albert Schmidt. He is the vilest, most corrupt, man I have ever met. I am sure that he would gladly sell his soul for a bottle of whiskey. I told Mr. Tyler that before he killed Albert Schmidt, there was a lot more of the story that he needed to hear. I remember telling you," Matthew said, looking directly at Robert, "when you do, there will probably be one other person that you will want to murder as well."

"I didn't think that I could hear anything worse than what Matthew had told me about Albert Schmidt. But then he told me that Lynn's father sent her to the Sanatorium with instructions that she be kept in solitary confinement, that she have no interaction with anyone, until she went one full week without mentioning my name or her love for me."

"That's right. I told Mr. Tyler that Lynn's father condemned his daughter to death, because she refused to deny her love. I looked you right in the eye and said, 'If I were you, Mr. Tyler, I'd want to put Judge Johnston on my list of persons to murder, too.'

"I remember sitting in my chair, filled with rage at you, Alexander," Robert said, pointing directly at the judge, "and, at the same time being overcome with grief at all that Lynn had suffered. There was a war going on in my soul. Rage and grief were battling for supremacy within me, and neither could get the upper hand. I was emotionally paralyzed. But Matthew Brown wasn't through. There was more of the story that I needed to hear." Robert nodded to Matthew, cueing him to continue.

"I told Mr. Tyler that even though the judge condemned his daughter to be confined in the Sanatorium, that didn't mean she was treated badly. I told him that Emily Gladstone, the nurse who cared for her every day, truly came to care for Lynn and gave her the most compassionate care that she could. And then I told Mr. Tyler, 'Before you set out murdering people, you need to go to Harrisonburg and thank her.'

"So, then, I had another emotion to deal with," Robert said. "I didn't want to feel thankful or grateful to anyone. I wanted to lash out in hate. I didn't want to think about how someone had been kind to Lynn. I am glad that Matthew told me how much you cared," he said as he walked up to Emily and took her hand, "because I would not have wanted to hear what he said to me next, if I had been filled only with anger, hate, and rage.

"I told Mr. Tyler that there was another reason he needed to thank Emily Gladstone," Matthew said. "I remember exactly how I told you. I said, 'I haven't told you yet how Lynn died. Lynn died giving birth to your son. Miss Emily was with her the whole time, and has cared for your son ever since. She has been the only mother that Adam has ever known.'

"I'll never forget how stunned I was. I have a son! Just a couple of minutes earlier, I had been ready to rush out and murder Alexander Johnston and Albert Schmidt. Now all I wanted to do was rush to see you, Adam. I remember asking Matthew, 'Where is he?' and Matthew telling me, 'He is in Harrisonburg. He's really a fine young man. Emily and her brother John have done a great job raising him.'

"I jumped from my chair and said, 'I've got to go. I've got to go to Harrisonburg right now!' Matthew took me by the arm, and forced me to sit down again. 'I have something else to tell you. It's something that you have to hear before you rush off and do anything or go anywhere.'

"I couldn't imagine what was more important than knowing that I had a son, a son that I had never met. And I told Matthew so! But he held me in the chair and said that what he had to say was more important. When he was sure that I had calmed down enough to listen, he told me the rest of the story." Robert looked at Matthew and said, "I'll be quiet a while and let you speak."

"I told Mr. Tyler that, while I was making my way from Harrisonburg to Germantown, I spent the night in the tavern at Walnut Cove. After I got settled in my room, I went downstairs to get something to eat and was stunned to see Albert Schmidt sitting at the bar. He had already had a couple of drinks and was already drunk enough that he didn't remember me. But I had learned in Nazareth that the drunker he was, the more easily he talked, so I offered to buy him a drink and kept buying him more until he didn't care who I was and was talking freely.

"After I had found him in Nazareth, he decided that he would come to North Carolina and warn Judge Johnston that I had found him. He said he was going to tell the judge that I forced him to tell me where Lynn was. He was sure that the judge would reward him handsomely. He had also decided that if the judge didn't offer him money, he would extort funds from him by threatening to go public with what the judge had done to his own daughter. If the public found out, the judge would lose every friend he ever had.

"When Schmidt got to Judge Johnston's house early in the evening, he was surprised that the house slave, who opened the door, took him right to the judge's study. "Massa Johnston, this gentleman wishes to see you," the slave said, then ushered Schmidt into the room, and shut the door. Judge Johnston was sitting in the chair, behind his massive mahogany desk. He took one look at Schmidt, rose from his chair, and roared, "What the hell are you doing in here? Don't you know that I can have you arrested?"

"Schmidt told me that he said to the judge, 'I don't think you want to do that judge. I have come to warn you about something. The information that I have is so valuable that I'm sure you will be more than willing to give me $100.00 to share it with you. If you're not willing to pay me, I'll just go and sell the story to the local paper.' Schmidt was stunned when the judge replied, 'How dare you try to extort money from me? You are going to tell me what you think I need to know,' Johnston roared, 'and if you don't, then I'll just throw you into jail and keep you there till you rot. Since you have so much alcohol in your system, preserving you, it will take an extraordinary long time for you to rot.'

"Schmidt had not anticipated that turn of events. He's clearly not very bright. Even if he had some intelligence in the past, he has so polluted his brain with alcohol, that there are times, even when he is sober, that he has difficulty putting words together to form a sentence. But he was smart enough that night to go ahead and tell the judge what he knew.

"Schmidt told me that when he finished telling the judge about me and that I knew the whole story, he heard the judge mutter, 'If they find out about Lynn, they will find out about the boy, too.'" There was a sudden look of panic on his face. The judge quickly walked around his desk, digging into his pocket as he approached Schmidt. He pulled a wad of bills out of his pocket, handed them to Schmidt, and said, 'This is all the money that I have. Take it and get out of my house!'

"As Schmidt made his way from the office to the front door, he quickly counted the money. There were three fives and three ones. Only $18.00! He had ridden all the way from Pennsylvania for $18.00. He was furious, but he was at least smart enough to get out of there. The last time he had been in the judge's house, he had helped the house slave tied up the judge's daughter, get her out of the house, and into a carriage. He was sure that if the judge treated his daughter that badly, he would certainly fulfill his promise to throw Schmidt into jail and keep him there.

"Schmidt had been riding for ten straight days, and he was frankly more than a little saddle sore. Instead of mounting his horse, he decided to walk while leading his horse. He untied the bridle from the hitching post and headed up the long, tree lined driveway of the Yadkin Oaks Plantation. He had only gone only about forty of fifty yards when he heard the door to the plantation house slam open. He turned around and saw the judge rushing towards the barn, waving his cane like a baton, and yelling, "Get my carriage! Get my carriage!"

"Without thinking, Schmidt impulsively decided to follow the judge's carriage. He walked his horse into a small thicket of trees near the driveway and waited. It wasn't long before Judge Johnston came by. The judge, himself, was driving and had already urged the horse into a fast trot.

"Schmidt followed the judge to a small house on the edge of Richmond. The carriage pulled right up to the door and the judge went in without knocking. It was a warm night and the windows were open, so Schmidt made his way right to the side of the house and stood directly beside one of the open windows. It just happened to be the window in the room where the judge was speaking to another man.

"I could hear the judge, clear as day," Schmidt told me. "And what I heard him say, well, I can hardly believe it myself, so I know that you are going to have a hard time believing it." But then he told me that 'all this talking was making his throat mighty dry and unless he got another drink, he wasn't sure he could remember any more of the story.' It was a couple of drinks later, before I could get him to go on," Matthew said.

"'What did you hear the judge say?' I asked.

"He answered, 'Well, he was talking to a man he called Bruce, and said that Robert Tyler was about to learn the truth about Lynn, and that if that truth became public knowledge, he, the judge, and all of his allies, especially the other man in the room, would be destroyed.'

"What are we going to do?" the other man asked.

"The only thing that we can do,' I heard the Judge say. "We have to get rid of Robert Tyler before he can destroy us. And we will have to take care of two other people, a man named Matthew Brown, who Tyler hired to find Lynn, and Albert Schmidt, a no-account drunk who couldn't keep his mouth shut if his life depended on it. I don't care how you go about it, but make Robert Tyler disappear as quickly as you can. If you can make it look like an accident, that's fine."

"It was the other man in the room who said, 'I'll take care of it, judge. But it will have to wait until my men and I can find Robert Tyler alone. We probably won't be able to do it at Lynnmont or in Germantown. There are too many people around. Of course, we might be able to sneak into his house late one night. I don't know; it's really complicated. Why don't we call a special meeting of the society tomorrow night to work out all the details?'

"Then I heard the judge say, 'With Tyler out of the way, it will be much easier for us to move in and take over all his businesses. We will have to find a way to get rid of all of his legal documents, his deeds, and contracts.' It was the other man in the room who said, 'I suppose that an accidental fire at the Register of Deeds Office could be arranged.'

" 'We can't destroy all the records for the whole county,' I heard the judge say, 'and then he said something about the records that Tyler would have in his law office, and the other man said, 'We'll figure all that out, too. Trust me, Judge; we can work out everything at the meeting tomorrow night.'

"The last thing that Schmidt heard the judge say was, 'We have to get this right. If I get destroyed, you and all the men of the cause will go down with me.'

"I remember summing up the story for Mr. Tyler. I told him that he and I and Albert Schmidt were all about to be killed. Then the judge was going to use our deaths as another way to keep covering up what he had done to his daughter and grandson. He would also use Mr. Tyler's death as the catalyst to take over Lynnmont and all of the Tyler Companies."

"I remember sitting there, overwhelmed at all that I had heard," Robert said, taking up the story. "I was a widower and the love of my life had been dead for twenty years. I was a father, but I had never met my son. I was the target of an assassination attempt. The people who wanted me dead also wanted to take over everything that I had spent a lifetime building up.

"I remember that Matthew said, 'Mr. Tyler, before you rush off to Harrisonburg, you have got to figure out a way to defeat Judge Johnston. You must devise a plan to protect all that you have. Even if you die, your son must still get the inheritance that he deserves.'

"Matthew was right. I asked him if he would watch my back for several days while I put together a new will and gathered the documents needed to protect the estate. He agreed, suggesting that the safest place for us was in Germantown. I was glad to hear that, because I would need to have access to all the documents at the firm. We would be fairly safe during the day, but it was at night that the attempt on our lives would probably be made. I agreed to hire him as the new night watchman for the Tyler Companies office. We then decided that I would go into the office the next morning, as usual. Once there, I would stay until I had finished building a wall of protection that the judge could not destroy.

"After he left me in my study at the manor house that night, I struggled about my next move. I still wanted to get in my carriage and go to Harrisonburg. Adam, more than anything else, I wanted to meet you. But, I first had to take the time to write a new will, to make you the chief beneficiary. As I thought about the will, I wondered what it would be like for you to inherit such a vast fortune from a man you had never even met."

As Robert continued, it was clear that he was speaking directly to Adam, but allowing all of the rest of us to listen in.

"It was during those moments of conflict and indecision that I happened upon the idea of a funeral banquet. Each of the persons that I invited could tell a story that would give you part of the picture. The parts combined would make a portrait of the man that I was, and the virtues and values that shaped my life. I chose all the people who are here today very carefully, not only because

I wanted you to hear their stories, but also because I wanted to honor each of them for their friendship. Well, I shouldn't say 'all of the people.' I asked Judge Johnston to be here for two reasons. First, I wanted you to hear the other side of the story, that I am a man like any other man, with plenty of faults, which I was sure that the judge would point out. The second reason that the judge is here is because I was sure that, if he thought I was dead, he would use the occasion to complete his attempted takeover of the Tyler Companies and Lynnmont. I knew that if he did that, he would expose himself, and in so doing, destroy himself. I would not need to destroy Alexander Johnston, he would do it.

"When I made the decision to invite the judge, it dawned on me that I would be worth far more to you, Adam, if I were dead than if I were alive. So, I made the decision that night that I would rather die for you than live for myself. After I had put together all of the documents that would protect your inheritance, I would expose myself to the judge and his cronies; like Daniel walking into the lion's den. Once I made that decision, a peace came over me that I can't explain. The Bible calls it the 'peace that passes understanding.'

"The next morning, I went into the office and began to work. Without telling anyone what I was doing, I spent the first morning gathering copies of the deeds and contracts which made up the Tyler Companies. I began the painstaking process of copying each one. I knew that if I simply removed the existing copies, the judge would know that I was on to him and my plan to have him expose himself would fail.

"It took me three full days to copy all of the documents, write the will, put together all of the instructions for the funeral banquet, and finally to write the Letters of Emancipation which would set John Barnes and his family free. The letter to you, John, was essential, because without it, you could not have been the executor of my will. Early in the morning on the fourth day, Matthew Brown and I left Germantown to go to the bank in

Salem. I withdrew almost all of the funds of all of the companies and Lynnmont. Matthew and I then went to banks in Salisbury and Lexington, opened new accounts and deposited the funds. I wasn't sure if the judge had enough influence to raid the bank in Salem, but I was confident that the monies would be safer in banks outside of Surry County."

"It was late in the afternoon when we got back to the office in Germantown" Matthew interrupted. "Mr. Tyler had me go over all the documents. He wanted to make sure that every detail had been covered. After I had assured him that everything was, he fired me! He told me to get out of Surry County and to protect myself. I promised him that I would leave town the next morning. I left Mr. Tyler's office, thinking that I would never see him again." Matthew paused. It was Robert's turn to continue the story.

"I sent our office messenger, Willie, to take a packet of information to you John," he said, looking directly at me. "In the packet was your Letter of Emancipation and a note asking you to meet me the next day at Hanging Rock Mountain. I wanted to meet at Hanging Rock for two reasons. The first was that it was such a special place for me. I wanted to reveal everything that I could to my best friend in the place where I had fallen in love with Lynn. The other reason was that I was sure that it was such a remote location that we would be safe there and I would have all the time that I needed to tell you about Lynn.

"As I stepped out of the office, I was shocked that the temperature had fallen drastically. I stepped back in and grabbed a cape that had been hanging on the back of my office door. It had been a gift from one of my clients, and I had never worn it before. I was surprised at how warm it was. The hood protected my face from the bitter wind that was blowing. I had intended to get on my horse and go to Richmond to spend the night, but, on a whim, I decided to walk down the street and see you as you left the office as a Free Man of Color for the first time. My timing was perfect. You stepped out of the office, just as I came around the corner."

I remembered seeing the man in the cape and wondering who he was. Robert looked at me and said, "John, you did exactly what I thought you would do. You stepped out of that office and took in an incredibly deep breath. It was as though you were breathing air for the first time in your life. I had seen all that I needed to see. I slipped back around the corner, went to my horse, and rode out of Germantown for what I thought might the very last time."

"Let me interrupt," Matthew said. "I had left Mr. Tyler's office, intending to leave town, but when I saw him heading towards Richmond, instead of Lynnmont, I decided to break my promise. I decided that I would watch Mr. Tyler's back for several more days, but I would do so secretly."

"I had decided that I wanted to go to Hanging Rock the next day, following the route coming from the west that Lynn always took. It was a way of connecting with her. I had to make my way to Richmond that night. As I rode along, I was glad that I had the cape. Strangely enough, that cape saved my life. As I was riding along, I met a group of men on horseback who were also wearing capes and were headed in the opposite direction. We simply passed each other on the road. It was only later that I learned that every time Alexander Johnston's ruffians acted together in concert, they all wore hooded capes. I can only assume they thought that I was one of them who had been given a different task than they had that night.

"The next day," Robert said, still addressing me, "you and I met at the Hanging Rock and I delivered to you the documents that I had spent three days writing that would protect Adam's inheritance. I told you everything I could tell you that day, but I couldn't bring myself to tell you that I had made the decision to leave Hanging Rock and intentionally expose myself. As far as I was concerned, when I left you, I was riding to my death.

"I was about half way from Hanging Rock Mountain to Yadkinville, when suddenly a shot rang out. Startled by the loud gun, my horse reared, throwing me. I landed on my back in the middle of the road, the breath knocked out of me. Before I could regain my breath, the would-be assassin was standing over me. His hand was raised, ready to strike with a large knife he was holding. He swung at me, and I blocked the blow. When I did, I noticed a sharp pain in my shoulder and realized that I had been shot. I had intended to ride to my death, but when the moment came, I was fighting to stay alive. The desire to preserve my life was greater than my intention to die.

"I was still on the ground, flat on my back. The assassin had the advantage. I raised my leg and kicked, as hard as I could. I happened to catch him right in the chest, throwing him back. As I was struggling to get to my feet, I heard the steps of a horse, galloping to the scene. I thought that others were coming to assist the murderer. I was only half way to my feet, when the assassin struck me right in the jaw with his free hand, knocking me back to the ground. Why he struck with his free hand rather than with the knife, I will never know. He raised the knife again, ready to strike.

"At just that moment, he was tackled by another man. As the two men fell to the ground, the attacker fell on his knife. It plunged into his ribs. I was finally on my feet. As the second man stood, I realized that it was Matthew Brown!

"Matthew, what are you doing here?"

"I decided to break my promise, and to keep an eye on you."

"The attacker was lying on the ground, writhing in pain. The force of his fall had driven the knife in so deeply that even the hilt of the knife was inside the gaping wound. He was trying to pull the knife free, but it was clearly in too deep. He lay on the ground as blood gushed from his wound.

"Matthew knelt beside him and asked, 'Who are you? Why did you attack Mr. Tyler?"

"Between cries of agony, the man sneered at Matthew and said, "Why should I tell you anything?"

"Because you are dying! Tell us everything. It's the only way to get your soul right with God, before you meet him."

"After giving him a moment to think, Matthew asked him again who he was. 'Geoffrey Britt,' he said. Once he had answered that question, he opened up and told us the whole story. He was a member of a secret society named The Cause, a group of men who had been formed to protect freedom. They were an army of right, fighting a world of evil. The society met once a month in a barn on a plantation called Yadkin Oaks.

"Is Judge Johnston your leader?" I asked him.

"Oh, yes. He's a great man!" Geoffrey said.

"Can you tell us any of the other member's names? I asked him.

"I don't know all the members. But Sheriff Speight was always at the meetings. And I remember seeing Bruce Smithwell, nearly every month."

The fact that the sheriff was a member of the judge's secret society explained why the investigation into Robert's death had been so anemic. And Bruce Smithwell, the Registrar of Deeds must have been the person that Albert Schmidt had overheard meeting with the judge.

"Did Judge Johnston order you to attack Mr. Tyler?" Matthew asked him.

"Yes. He promised that whoever succeeded in killing him would be promoted to second in command."

Geoffrey was growing weak. He had already lost a lot of blood. And the knife had clearly punctured one of his lungs. His breathing was become shallow.

"Why did Judge Johnston want me dead?

"He said you were the most evil….." His voice trailed off. He took his last breath.

"Quite a dying declaration, wouldn't you say?" Matthew asked.

"Preposterous!" Judge Johnston yelled, as he rose from his seat. "I've never heard such a pack of lies in my life!" Lawrence Weeks pulled him back into his chair and said, "Sit down, Judge. You know perfectly well that a dying declaration is always admissible in court, especially when there are two witnesses to it!"

"Right after Geoffrey died, I said to Matthew, "Geoffrey Britt is dead. Albert Schmidt might also be dead. And you and I are still in danger. I wonder how many people will die before the judge's crusade will be finished."

"Matthew said, 'Maybe no one else needs to die. You and Geoffrey are almost exactly the same size; you have similar features, the same color hair. What if there was some way to make people think that he was you?' It was then that we devised the plan to substitute Geoffrey's body for mine. We retrieved my horse, found Geoffrey's nearby, put his body across the saddle and decided to hide in the woods near Hanging Rock until we could plant the body. Late the next night, we made our way to Lynnmont. I put my horse and saddle in my stall in the barn. While I was gathering the clothes and other things that I would need while I hid out, Matthew placed the body in the study. I went to the well and sabotaged it, cutting the rope and dropping the fire buckets. The fire needed to burn long enough so that Geoffrey's body would not be recognizable. When everything was ready, I lit the fire.

"As you all know, the ruse worked. Everyone believed that I was dead, including Judge Johnston. Now all I had to do was to stay hidden until after the judge crossed the line and exposed himself. Staying hidden was not too difficult. Matthew and I built a little lean-to in a camp on the hill above the church. I knew that it was an area that had been logged several years ago, and that it wasn't likely that anyone would be coming into the area. I carefully snuck into the kitchen pantry at Lynnmont late one night and got the food we would need for a two-month stay in the woods. And we waited.

"Everything was going according to plan until this morning. I had taken the precaution, in case I heard someone coming near the camp, of having Geoffrey's horse always saddled and having her tied to the tree which supported the lean-to. Fortunately, Matthew had decided to take a long walk and wasn't in the camp. I was lying on the makeshift bed that I had in the lean-to, when I heard the crunching of steps, not more than forty or fifty feet from the camp. I jumped up, untied the horse, and jumped on her back. As I galloped off, I glanced back and saw that it was John Barnes! John, what in the world were you doing?"

"I needed some time to ponder the story you wanted me to tell," I said. The judge had promised to be the most eloquent speaker at the banquet. I was trying to figure out how to make my story more impressive than the judge's. On the top of the hill, above your camp, there is a spot that has always inspired me, because I can see the entire Sauratown Mountain range, from Mount Ararat to Hanging Rock. I was on my way to that spot when you galloped off. At first I thought I had disturbed a deer. As I came upon your camp and saw the cape hanging there, I figured I had disturbed Robert Tyler's murderer."

Robert looked at me and smiled. "Did you give a more eloquent speech than the Judge?" he asked.

"I don't know. I didn't have time to think after I discovered your camp."

"Everything worked out. Matthew and I hid again and waited for the right time to make our appearance."

It was General Stanley who asked an obvious question. "Robert, how did you know when the right time to make your appearance would be?"

"By using this," he answered, as he pulled a small, folding, monocular telescope from his pocket. There is a place, about a hundred yards up the hill where I could stay hidden. With this instrument I could look right through the window, and see everything that was happening. I knew that John would follow my instructions and that Abigail Jordan would be the last person to speak. After Abigail's story would come your promotion, General. I needed to appear just after that. I couldn't let the law be broken by having John read the will of a man who wasn't dead."

The flash of light that I had seen earlier in the day must have been a reflection from Robert's telescope.

"Have I covered everything? Is there anything else that any of you needs to know?" Robert asked us.

No one said anything. For me, everything was crystal clear. In fact, it was like looking through the crystal snow. For the first time in months, everything made sense. Life was as beautiful as it was supposed to be.

It was Judge Johnston's voice that broke the silence. "I've got a question," he said. "What made you think that I would, how did you put it, 'cross the line'?"

"Judge," Robert said. "I have studied you all my life. I probably know you better than you know yourself. I knew exactly what you would do. You presented a fake will, and tried to claim Lynnmont and all the Tyler Companies as your own, didn't you?"

When the judge didn't respond, Richard Allen did. "That's exactly what he did, Robert. The evidence is on the altar."

There was silence for a moment. It was Mamie Smith who asked another obvious question. "If there isn't going to be a reading of a will, does that mean that we are about done here?"

"We may not read the will," Robert said. "But I can offer some gifts to some of my best friends. And that is exactly what I am going to do."

A Good Friend's Munificence

ROBERT WENT TO THE ALTAR AND PICKED up the large packet which contained the will. He laid aside the top few pages, which must have been the actual will. He turned and walked up to General Stanley.

"General, having watched through the window, I know that I am not the first person to offer you a salute." He came to attention and saluted the General smartly. General Stanley rose and returned the salute. Robert extended his hand, and as the General grasped it, Robert said, "Gilbert, I'm so sorry that it has taken the state so long to correct the wrong done to you. I'm just glad that I had a small part to play in righting the miscarriage of justice."

Richard Allen, hearing what Robert said, blurted out, "A small part? General, if it wasn't for Robert Tyler, the state would never have put things right!"

"I'm sure that you are right about that," Gilbert said, adding, "Robert, why don't you take credit for what you have done?"

"If I had been a better politician, it wouldn't have taken twenty years," Robert said. "Just know that I am really happy for you, and I wish we could have done even more."

Robert moved down the table and stood before Mamie Smith. "Miss Mamie, I can't remember a time in my life when I didn't know you. More than any other woman at Lynnmont, you have always been my mother. I have, and always will, love you for that. As of today, the dining room at Lynnmont shall be officially known as the Mamie Smith Hall. As soon as I can get it painted, a sign will be erected over the door." Robert handed her an envelope and said, "There is one more thing. In that envelope is a document stating that you are the owner of a savings account at Salem Bank. In the account is enough money to support you, comfortably, if you ever desire to retire. But, even if you decide to continue cooking for the rest of your life, the money will be yours to pass on to your children and grandchildren."

"O, Robert, mothering you has been one of the greatest joys of my life. You are every bit as much as son to me as my own children. You have honored me far beyond anything that I could have imagined." Mamie stood, reached over the table, and hugged Robert hard around the neck. "I love you, Son," she said and sat back down. She didn't open the envelope, but she stared at it as if it were pure gold.

Robert looked at the next envelope and walked over to Emily Gladstone. "In this envelope is enough money to fund Apple Blossom's operating budget for a year. If you and your brother would rather use the money to restore the building to its original splendor, you may certainly do that."

He handed the envelope to her and said, "I could never give you enough money to compensate for the love you lavished upon Lynn and Adam. I know that Adam will always cherish you and your brother John as his mother and father. I hope, in the years to come, that he may also come to love me. I assure you that I will do nothing to interfere with the love that he has for the two of you."

"Mr. Tyler," Emily said, and paused, searching for the right words.

"Please call me Robert."

"Robert, I can't accept a gift this large. I should be paying you for the privilege of having had Adam in my life all these years."

"I insist that you take the money. It's not for you. It's for all the other Lynn's that you care for."

"Well, when you put it that way, I'll be honored to accept. John and I will see to it that it is used very wisely." Emily sat down and leaned over towards Adam as she opened the envelope. Inside was a check, made out to Apple Blossom Sanatorium, for $15,000. Both Emily and Adam gasped. Robert Tyler was wrong. It wasn't one year's budget; it was three.

Before he could move on to the next person, Emily said, "Mr. Tyler, Robert, I have something for you." She reached under her chair, picked up Lynn's diary and handed it to Robert. "This was the diary that Lynn kept while she was at Apple Blossom. I think that you will come to cherish every word in it."

Robert simply nodded his thanks to Emily. He turned and placed the diary on the altar and moved on to the next person, Horace Hayworth. He spoke much more loudly than before. "Horace, I have wanted to offer you a job for a long time, but I knew that Judge Johnston would make your life impossible if you came to work for me. After today, though, I don't think that the judge will have the influence that he used to have."

"What job do you have in mind?" Horace asked.

"Head of Security at Lynnmont. The job comes with room and board and $8.00 a month salary. Are you interested?"

"I sure am! When can I start?"

"Why don't you plan to move to Lynnmont Monday morning? You can report to Franklin Campbell. He's going to be your boss." Robert and Horace shook hands, as Robert said, "Welcome aboard!"

"Franklin, as long as I'm here, I might as well talk to you next," Robert said to Franklin Campbell who was sitting just a couple of chairs away from Horace. "I want to thank you for the spectacular job that you are doing at Lynnmont. I knew that you were a good businessman when I hired you. And you have run the business side of the estate very well. Under your leadership, our profits have increased every year. As you have worked with us, you have learned something very important about Lynnmont that makes us different from all the plantations in the country. At Lynnmont, we are a family. We work, eat, live, and even worship together. And yet, we are all free to come and go as we please. You have learned what it means to be a part of the family and the family has accepted you and your leadership."

"Thank you, Mr. Tyler. That's very nice of you to say."

"The folks at Lynnmont tell me that you have a very special affection for a breeding pair of Percheron's named George and Georgia. Are they right?"

"Well, yes sir. They are the two most beautiful horses I have ever seen. I don't know what draws me to them so, but I do love those animals."

"I want to give you a bonus for all you have done to strengthen Lynnmont." Robert extended an envelope which Franklin took. "This is a Certificate of Ownership for George and Georgia made out in your name. What that means, of course, is that the foals that Georgia produces and all the stud fees from George will now belong to you. You're welcome to continue to board them at Lynnmont if you wish. I'll let you and Ben Randolph work out a fair fee arrangement, if you wish to do that."

"Mr. Tyler, you could never have given me a gift that I would appreciate more. I'm overwhelmed."

"Just make sure that you care for George and Georgia as well as you do Lynnmont."

"I will, sir."

Robert looked at the three envelopes he had left, but there were six people who had not yet received a portion of Robert's munificence.

He decided to go next to a person for whom there was no envelope. He approached Lawrence Weeks and said, "Lawrence, I don't have an envelope for you. But I do have a request. I would like to ask you to join me as a partner in the Tyler Weeks Law Firm. Are you willing?"

Lawrence was stunned. There were several other lawyers in the firm who had been with Robert much longer than he had and had never been offered a partnership. And not only was he offering a partnership, he was also offering to change the name of the firm.

Without waiting for an answer, Robert said, "We will have to sit down and work out a partnership agreement. I hope that you won't demand more than half, because, after today, the only income that I will have will be from the firm."

Lawrence smiled, broadly. "I'm sure that we can work out a fair agreement. Thank you, Robert. I am truly honored."

Sitting at the same corner of the table, with only the judge between him and Lawrence was Richard Allen. "Richard, as you know, the Educational Affairs Committee of the Senate launched an effort a couple of years ago to create endowed chairs for professorships at the University of North Carolina. As you also know, our efforts have been a complete failure. So far, we have received no endowments. Until today! In this envelope is the money to fund the first endowed chair at UNC, the Dr. Richard Allen Professorship of Law." Robert handed the envelope to Dr. Allen and said, "No professor deserves the honor more. You earned it by putting up with me for four years."

"Robert, I'm thrilled to accept the money on behalf of the university. But the professorship should be the Robert Tyler Chair."

"Absolutely not! I could never presume to be half as good a lawyer as the man who taught me! Besides, all of the legal papers to name the chair in your honor have already been drawn up. I am not about to go to all the trouble to change them."

Lawrence Weeks reached over the judge and touched Dr. Allen's arm. "Don't you know, by now, that it's impossible to argue with Robert Tyler? Just say thank you.

"Thank you," Dr. Allen said, "just seems so inadequate."

"It wasn't inadequate for Abigail Jordan," Adam said. "And I'm sure that it is all my father needs to hear, as well."

My father! It was the first time Robert had ever heard the words 'my father.' His first reaction was to run and hug his son, but, when he saw Adam's almost embarrassed grin, he decided that there would be plenty of time for hugs later. He simply smiled at Adam, and said to Dr. Allen, "Thank you is more than enough."

"I have only two envelopes left," Robert said, "and the first one goes to you, Miss Jordan." Robert walked up to her and handed her a very large envelope. Abigail could not begin to imagine what was in it. "Miss Jordan…Abigail," he said with a tenderness in his voice that seemed to be reserved just for her, "in this envelope are the deeds to the Salem Tavern and all of the properties that are contiguous to it, the carriage house, horse barn, corrals, smoke house, and all the other buildings, including the owner's cottage, of course. These deeds are now in your name. You are the new owner of Salem Tavern."

For only the second time in her life, Abigail Jordan was speechless. Her hands began to shake as she held on tightly to the envelope and began to cry.

"Miss Abigail, I certainly didn't mean to make you cry. I had hoped that I might see one of your smiles. Except for Lynn, you have the most beautiful smile of any person that I have ever known."

"I'm sorry, Mr. Tyler. I can't seem to stop crying. But I think these are tears of joy."

"By the way, Miss Abigail," Robert said. "Now that I am officially a widower, and you are a woman of some great substance, would it be permissible for me to call on you?"

She jumped up from her chair, wanting desperately to hug him, but the table was in the way.

"Now that's the smile I was hoping for! I assume that means 'yes'?"

"Yes! Yes! Yes!" she said, as the two of them reached across the table and held each other's hands.

I couldn't imagine that Robert Tyler had intended to have such a personal moment in such a public setting. He did not know, of course, that Abigail Jordan had publicly professed her love for him less than an hour before. As they held hands and looked into each other's eyes, everyone else broke into applause. It just seemed like the right thing to do.

In reaching out to take Abigail's hands, Robert had dropped the last envelope. After the applause ended, and they broke apart, he looked around for it. It had somehow ended up under the table near Abigail's feet. She knelt down, picked it up and handed it to Robert.

"Thank you."

"That's all I've ever needed to hear. Besides," she said, smiling broadly again, "that was a lot more pleasant than scraping boots." Robert's smile, in response, was nearly as beautiful as hers.

Robert came and stood directly in front of me. He only had one more envelope. I expected that whatever was in it would go to Adam. After all, Robert had already given me and my family our freedom and deeded us the house. I was about to tell him that I had already received far more than I deserved, but he spoke first.

"John, I can't remember a time in my life when you have not been my very best friend. But what you have done to show your loyalty and fidelity to me in the past few months is nothing short of miraculous. Like I said to Emily Gladstone about her love for Lynn and Adam, there is no amount of money that could compensate you for your friendship. I want to make a stab at it, though. In this envelope is the deed to the most prosperous of the Tyler Companies, Tyler Brick. As the manager of the Tyler

Companies, you know that Tyler Brick earns more than all of the rest of the companies put together. I am making you this gift, not just for you, but for John Thomas as well. I want him to have a great financial legacy to go along with the much more important legacy you have already given him. You have given the same legacy that your father gave to you. You have shown him what it means to be a man of integrity and faith. Adding money to the legacy will only make him wealthier than he already is."

"I'll never forget what Oskar Schoenfeldt said to each of us when our fathers died," I said. 'Live a life worthy of your father.' I know that you have done that Robert. I hope that I have, too." I didn't know what more I could say. I was so overwhelmed by his generosity that 'thank you' really wasn't enough.

Robert turned and walked over to Adam.

"Son, everything that I have, except the Tyler Weeks Law Firm, is now yours. It is ironic to me that I was about the same age you are when I became the owner of Lynnmont. You, however have one advantage that I didn't have. You have a father that you can go to for advice. I will not make any decisions for you, but I will always be here to answer your questions. I have only one request of you. Give me a chance to be your second father."

Adam looked, not at Robert, but at Emily Gladstone and asked, "Mom, would it be alright with you if I change my name to Adam Gladstone Tyler?"

"Certainly, Son. It honors both of your fathers."

"Sir," Adam said to Robert. "I have always called John Gladstone 'Father.' I would like to continue to do that. Would it be alright with you if I called you 'Pop'?"

"Yes! Yes! Yes!" Robert said. "Those words sounded mighty nice when Miss Abigail said it to me," Robert said with a laugh. He walked around the table to embrace his son. It was as though Robert was trying to collect twenty year's worth of missed affection. And it didn't seem that Adam minded one bit.

As Adam and Robert hugged, everyone rose from their seats and began to talk with one another. It was like the end of a good church service. The service was over, but people were hanging around hoping for just one more blessing.

It was Robert who reminded us that we were not yet done. "Everyone needs to be seated again," he said loudly enough to be heard over all our conversations. "There is one person to whom I have not yet given a gift."

I looked around. Everybody had received a gift. Except... Judge Johnston.

"Alexander," Robert said, "I am offering you, today, a gift more valuable than anyone here has received. I am offering you the gift, if you will receive it, of forgiveness. I cannot offer you absolution for the wrongs you have committed. If you choose, I will not press charges against you, or allow charges to be filed against you for any law that you have broken in your attempt to destroy me or to take over my estate.

"You may leave this church today as a free man, but in spite of this freedom, there will be many consequences that you will have to bear as a result of your actions. Everything you have done will become public knowledge. Your reputation will be destroyed. You will, of course, have to resign your judgeship. You will also have to name the names of the persons who were responsible for the death of Geoffrey Britt and, possibly, Albert Schmidt. Not even I will be able to keep the prosecutors from seeking to bring murderers to justice.

"I offer you forgiveness, not because you deserve it, but because you are the father of my wife and the grandfather of my son. I offer you forgiveness, not because you could somehow earn it, but because it is impossible to earn. I offer you forgiveness, trusting that forgiveness may help you turn from a life of hate, to one of love.

"I want you to remember the love that once dominated your life. I want you to remember the love that you and Martha shared.

I want you to remember how much you loved Lynn and how passionately she loved you. I offer you forgiveness so that you might find within your heart a kernel of goodness that would make it possible for you to love Adam. I offer you forgiveness in the hope that your life might be so dramatically changed that Adam might be able to, one day, love you.

"The life I offer you will be horrible. It would be far easier for you to spend the rest of your life in prison, hidden away from society, than to live a forgiven life; while bearing all the pain of your sin. I'm not much at quoting scripture, but I do remember Moses' words in Deuteronomy, 'I have set before you this day, life and death, blessing and cursing; choose life!'

"Alexander, I'll never be able to call you 'Judge' again. But if you accept the gift that I offer you today, there may come a time when I will be able to call you friend. After the worship service which will conclude our time together, you will be given a choice. You can walk out of this church, handcuffed by the deputy having chosen death and cursing, or as a free man, having chosen life and blessing."

I was sitting there, completely stunned. Ever since Robert's apparent death, I had been ready and eager for God to condemn Alexander Johnston to hell. It seemed to be the only fair and just thing to do. But now, if Alexander Johnston chose life, and accepted forgiveness, then all of us would have to choose it, too. What Robert Tyler had done was to make me look into my own soul and I didn't like what I was seeing. I was not even close to being the man that God wanted me to be. Robert Tyler had pierced me with the double-edged sword of the gospel. Oh how grace hurts, and how it heals!

At any moment, he was going to turn and ask to me to lead a time of worship. Never in my life had I felt so unworthy. Never in my life did I need the promise of New Salem more.

Evil Which Refuses to be Redeemed

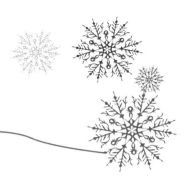

WAY TOO SOON, I HEARD ROBERT TELLING everyone that I was about to lead a closing worship service. A month earlier, when I had first read Robert's 'Letter of Instructions' for the funeral banquet, the Lord had laid on my heart what he would call on me to do. Every day for a month, I had fought the calling. I had reluctantly prepared to lead the service that God wanted me to do. But, even now, I prayed that I had heard the wrong thing. Sometimes, we are all guilty of deciding not to pray; because, when we do, we are afraid that we may hear the very thing we don't want to hear. That was exactly what happened to me. God's Spirit simply said, "Do it."

I stood up and heard myself saying, "It'll take me just a moment to get ready. If all of you will move to one of the front pews, I think it will make the service more meaningful." I walked to the back of the church and to the far corner. Under the back pew I had placed the things that I needed – a large pitcher of water, a basin, and a large towel. I reached under the pew and picked them up.

I had a momentary desire just to drop them and run from the church. After all, I was a rich man now. I didn't need to be obedient to God any more. I remembered then what my mother said, "If the devil ain't messin with ya, it's because he's already got ya." I quoted in my mind the scriptures, 'Get thee behind me, Satan' and 'Resist the devil and he will flee from thee.'

Even though I wanted to, I didn't flee. I looked up and saw that everyone had done as I had asked. I thought that it was really special that Robert and Abigail were sitting beside each other, much closer than they really needed to. As I headed back down the aisle, I was prompted by the Holy Spirit, not to go into the chancel. Instead, I went and stood directly in front of him. My feet felt like lead. It was the most difficult ten or twelve steps I have ever taken.

I laid the basin on the floor at his feet. I draped the towel across my shoulder. I poured the water from the pitcher into the basin. I knelt at his feet. But I could not bring myself to look at him.

"On the night that Jesus was betrayed," I began to quote the service from the Book of Worship, and as I did so, I reached to undo the buckle of his shoe.

Alexander Johnston jerked his foot away from me. "I'll never let a nigger wash my feet!" he yelled. He jumped to his feet; raised his cane high above his head, and, before I could get away or anyone else could stop him, he swung with all his might. Because I was kneeling, his cane struck my head, neck, and back and knocked me completely to the floor.

He raised the cane above his head, ready for a second blow. Lawrence Weeks ran and literally tackled him, before he could swing again. His cane flew out of his hand and across the chancel rail, coming to a clattering stop against the altar. It didn't take but another second for Horace Hayworth and Franklin Campbell to join Lawrence in jumping on the judge, helping to hold him on the floor.

Then everything seemed to happen at once. Robert and Abigail, who were the closest to me, came to my aid, helping me to my feet. Abigail was the first to see the blood streaming down my head and called for Emily to come and help. Gilbert ran to the door to get the deputy. Adam came forward, standing over his grandfather, and yelled angrily, "How dare you? How could you hit a preacher?" Gilbert came back with the deputy in tow; while Lawrence, Horace, and Franklin dragged the judge to his feet. It was Richard who told the deputy to handcuff and arrest Alexander Johnston.

"I'll go with you to the jail," he told the deputy, "and see to it that all of the proper charges are filed. Wait here just a second." Richard then went into the chancel area and picked up the fake will that the judge had brought. It would need to be protected as evidence.

Matthew Brown stepped forward and said, "Dr. Allen, I'd like to go with you too. There are some other people who will need to be arrested, including the sheriff. I'm not sure the arrests will be made with the word of only one witness."

"You're absolutely right, Matthew. I'll be glad to have you along."

As Emily and Abigail worked together to try to stem the flow of blood from the gash in the back of my head, we all watched as the deputy, Matthew, and Richard led Alexander Johnston out of New Salem Methodist Church and away from the new peace that had been offered to him there.

After he was gone, there was a stunned silence.

It was Robert who broke the stillness. "That was one of the most powerful worship services that I have ever attended," he said.

"But I failed completely," I said.

"Oh no, you didn't. It wasn't you who failed. Remember that evil which refuses to be redeemed must be destroyed. It wasn't you who failed, John. It was I. I wasn't able to convince him of the need to be redeemed. He, like so many others, chose death and cursing. No, John, you didn't fail. In fact, you did exactly what I asked you to do. You acted with your usual grace."

I didn't see anything 'graceful' about getting my head split open by a madman and getting the floor of my church covered with blood. Head wounds tend to bleed freely, but Emily and Abigail worked together to stop the flow of blood. Emily had grabbed the towel that I was going to use in the foot washing service and ripped it into several pieces. She wrapped them tightly around my head and the flow of blood changed to a trickle. Earlier this morning, I had been worried about picking my stockings as I walked in the woods. Now, every piece of my clothing was covered in blood. As Emily and Abigail worked on me, I wondered what Sally was going to say. How could her husband come home from a funeral banquet at a church covered in blood? It was going to be an interesting story to tell.

The funeral banquet had certainly come to an end, but the day was not over. Robert stood at the door, personally thanking each of the story tellers for being present and receiving their thanks for his generosity. As Abigail was leaving, I heard him promise to call on her soon. After everyone but Emily, Adam and I had left, he approached Emily and Adam and said, "I would like for the two of you to spend the night at the manor house. Tomorrow I will be thrilled to give you a tour of the entire estate, and, Adam, I'll spend as much time as you need answering your questions about Lynnmont and the Companies."

"I'd love to spend the night in the house. I can't wait to see it. I have been trying to imagine what it must be like," Adam said.

"Robert," Emily said. "It is very kind of you to offer. We will be more than happy to come."

"It's a little strange," Robert said. "Adam, I just offered you the opportunity to stay in a house that is no longer mine. I hope you will forgive me. It will take me a while to get use to the idea of you being the owner,"

"It's going to take me a while, too, Pop."

Robert turned to me and embraced me. He stepped back from the hug, gently touched the bloodstained towel on my head, and said, "John, you look awful. Do you feel as bad as you look?"

"I have to admit that my head is throbbing. That old man can really swing that cane."

"Why don't you go on home and let Sally give you a little compassionate care?"

"Are you sure you don't need me anymore this afternoon? Do you need for me to help explain everything to the crowd outside?"

"I'll be fine," he said. "I'll have my son with me. Once the people outside, who are mostly Lynnmont folk, meet him, they'll be a lot more interested in finding out about him than in hearing about me."

I really didn't believe that was true. But I was more than ready to go home. I really did need to hug my wife. Robert's hug had been special, and I had appreciated it, but I needed the kind of hug a mother would give her child. And since Sally always said that I was her oldest child, I thought she might be just what I needed.

As I was turning to leave, I noticed Alexander Johnston's cane lying next to the altar. I went and picked it up. I was amazed at how beautiful it was. Made of rosewood, the handle was carved in the shape of a loaf of bread. Down the entire length of the shaft was carved intertwining grape vines. The silver tip at the bottom was actually a chalice. All his life, Alexander Johnston had been carrying a cane that had the symbols of the Lord's Supper carved into it. I wondered if he had known. I also wondered at the irony of such a beautiful symbol of the grace of God being used in such a horrible way.

"I'd like to keep this," I said as I raised the cane. "I might need it to help keep you on the straight and narrow."

"If you ever try to punch me in the stomach with it like he did, I'll rip it from your hands," Robert declared.

"I'd like to see you try. You couldn't take the fool's gold away from me, and you'd be too weak to take this cane away, too."

It was like we were thirteen again. After all of the heaviness of the day, it was nice to banter with my best friend, even if his son did look confused. I wasn't really sure what I was going to do with the cane, but, like the fool's gold rock in my pocket, I thought that I would find a good use for it.

As I walked down the steps of New Salem, everyone in the crowd gasped. I really was completely covered in blood.

"Mr. Tyler will explain everything," I said as I made my way to Betsy. She had been tied to the hitching post all day, patiently waiting my return. When I got near her, she shied away. I don't know if it was the smell of the blood or the look of it. When I reach to untie her reins, she snorted at me as if to say, "I don't want you to touch me until you clean yourself up." I hung my new cane on the horn of the saddle. As I put my foot in the stirrup, I thought that Sally's first reaction might be exactly the same as Betsy's. It would be nice to clean up before I got home, but there wasn't any way to do that.

As I rode off from the church, I heard Robert say to the crowd, "I'd like for you all to meet Adam Gladstone Tyler, my son."

I dug my heels into Betsy's side causing her to take off at a fast trot. I was eager to see Sally and the children and Sally's father. There was so much that they needed to hear. As I rode into the yard, Anne Marie was sitting on the porch, clearly waiting for me. She ran up to me, and just as my feet hit the ground, she threw her arms around me and said, "Oh Daddy. Isn't he wonderful?"

"Who?" I asked. I was a little upset that she had not noticed that I was covered in blood and that my head was bandaged with a towel.

"Adam. Isn't he the most handsome man you have ever seen?"

"I, uh..." Fortunately, she didn't wait for an answer, but slipped her hand in mine, and asked another question, "Daddy, how do you know when you are in love?" We stopped as we were walking toward the door, and she looked at me and, for the first time, saw all the blood. I was glad that she did, because I could ignore her first two questions and answer the next one, "What in the world happened to you?"

I was about to answer Anne Marie when Sally, who had just come out of the door, saw me and all the blood. "Oh my God!" she said. I was so grateful that she didn't seem to care about my clothes at all.

I couldn't decide what to do first. I wanted a long hug. I wanted some of the herbal tea that she made for pain relief. I wanted to get out of these clothes. I wanted to get the strips of towel around my head untied, because they were too tight. I wanted to tell everybody that Robert Tyler was alive. I wanted to let everyone know that we were now rich beyond anything we had ever dreamed. I wanted to answer Anne Marie's questions.

I don't remember now exactly what happened when, but all of that was done in the next several hours.

As Sally and I were getting ready for bed, she checked the fresh bandage that she had put on the wound. The towels that had been tied so tightly had done their job, and stemmed the flow of blood. Sally had cleaned the wound and carefully washed the clotted blood out of my hair. Now she wanted to make sure that her new bandage would hold up through a night of sleep.

As she tended to me, I asked, "How in the world are we going to deal with Anne Marie? A child her age can't fall in love."

"How is it possible for you men to be so stupid?" she said, smiling. "She is about the same age I was when we fell in love."

We were both silent. There wasn't anything else to add. I crawled into bed and tried to find a spot on the pillow where my head wouldn't hurt. Being on my side, facing Sally's side of the bed seemed to be the most comfortable. Sally got into bed beside me. She blew out the candle, leaned over, kissed me and put her arm around me. After a couple of minutes quietly holding one another she asked, "By the way John, what are you preaching about tomorrow?"

I sat up straight in the bed. "Oh my God! Is tomorrow Sunday?"

I had been so caught up in getting ready for the funeral banquet and in telling my family everything that had happened that I had completely forgotten to even think about writing a sermon. But a couple of moment's panic gave way to confident assurance.

"I think I'll preach about Doubting Thomas tomorrow. I have a pretty good story that I can tell to illustrate our need to believe in resurrection."

I laid my head back down on the pillow and slept soundly all night.

Robert Tyler didn't sleep a wink that night. He spent the entire night in his bedroom at the manor house devouring a twenty-year-old diary. Every entry brought pain. He had not cried that deeply since the morning Horace Hayworth had released him from jail and brought him to Lynnmont. He was stunned at how many tears there were. It was early in the morning before he realized that the tears had not just been tears of pain and grief, they had also been tears of cleansing. It was as though God was washing him with them. He was being cleansed from the inside out. As dawn broke, he put the diary on the bookshelf beside his bed. He would never open it again.

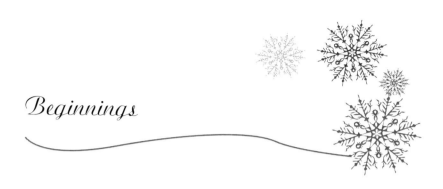

Beginnings

EARLY THE NEXT MORNING, ABIGAIL JORDAN PUT on her maid's dress, left the Single Sister's House, the building in Salem that the Moravians had built to house single women, and went to the tavern. Sunday was the one day of the week that she did not do the everyday heavy cleaning. All she would need to do is gather the chamber pots and wash them. After she had returned them to their rooms, she would be free to put on her Sunday best and head to church.

She had decided, on her way back to Salem after the funeral banquet, that she would continue to do the job of maid until she could hire just the right person to take her place. 'As long as I do the job,' she had said to herself, 'at least I know that it will be done right.'

It was only a three-block walk back to Single Sister's. She always enjoyed this walk because it took her by the bakery. She loved the smell of fresh baked bread. She also enjoyed walking across the town square and the change of scenery that came along with each season. Beautiful flowers in the spring and summer, the incredible beauty of the fall colors, and even all of the grays and browns of winter created an ever changing pallet on the square.

Today, because winter had come early, the grass was already brown and most of the leaves were gone. But there were two stubborn oaks which had refused to drop their leaves. The mixture of still green, slightly yellow, and even brown leaves on these two huge trees reminded Abigail of the subtle colors she had seen yesterday on the distant Sauratown Mountains as she had made her way to and from the banquet. On the way to the banquet, the muted colors had depressed her. On her way home, mixed with the subtle hues of twilight, and the distant sunset, they were the most beautiful colors she had ever seen. She was amazed at how looking at life through eyes of hope made everything seem so much more beautiful.

She was the oldest resident of the Single Sister's. She had been there for twenty years, and until yesterday, had assumed that she would live there until she died. It's always difficult being the oldest spinster in town. She had always handled the comments that town residents made, both to her and behind her back, with laughter. But under her laughter and beneath her smile there was a brokenness—a hurt that ran deep into her soul.

But today, as she walked back across the square towards the Single Sister's House there was no brokenness. Robert Tyler had healed her. He had touched the depths of her soul. He had made her a wealthy woman, probably the wealthiest woman in Salem. But it wasn't wealth that healed her. It was the promise of his calling on her. Today, when the offering plates were passed at Home Moravian, she was going to give the biggest offering of praise that she had even given. She didn't have a lot of money in her purse, but every penny of it was going in that plate.

She had only two Sunday dresses, but she picked out her best one. It was made of a mixture of cotton and linen, just the right weight for the cool morning. She had seen it in the dress shop and decided to buy it because its mixture of ivory and light blue matched the only pair of dress shoes that she had. It was the only thing that she had ever bought on credit. It had taken her six months of scraping together pennies, but it had proved to be worth every penny.

She sat in her regular seat at Home Church. She had been raised in Virginia where there were no Moravians. She had been raised in the Church of England, and, even though both Churches had formal worship, there was something different about the Moravians. Somehow, they lived the liturgy. They didn't just speak it. In her years in Salem, she could not remember a single Sunday that she had missed church. She also could not remember a single Sunday when she had enjoyed worship more than she did today. Every hymn was joyful, the Scripture uplifting, and every word of the sermon was just for her.

Abigail knew that joy produces joy. She was full of joy because of the anticipation of what she was planning to do after worship. She was not going back to Single Sister's. She was going visit the little house behind Salem Tavern. She had seen it many times, of course. It sat right behind the well house where she drew water every day. But she had never been inside it before.

When Church was over, she made her way past Salem College and crossed the square and the street in front of the tavern. She walked around the right side of the building, past the barns and carriage house, and well. She approached her new house. It was a small, plank house, built on a brick foundation. Brick steps led up to the porch which extended the full width of the house. In the center was the door, flanked by windows on either side. As she stepped on to the porch, she noticed that curtains still hung in the windows. She was glad that the previous owner had left them, because sewing was not one of her strengths.

She had gone into the office of the tavern earlier this morning and gotten the key. The previous owner had shown her where it was and told her to clean the house thoroughly before the new owner moved in. She slid the key in the lock, turned it, and opened the door. The door opened and she stepped into a parlor which was beautifully furnished. She had not anticipated the house being furnished and was delighted. She had worried during the night how she was going to raise the funds to buy furniture.

Through a cased opening on the left side of the far wall she could see a kitchen. To the right side, there was a door which led to two bedrooms. Every room had furniture—chests of drawers, beds, wing-back chairs, tables and chairs, wardrobes—everything that she could possibly need. The few things she had of her own in Single Sister's would easily fit right in. In fact, her one room there was smaller than any of the rooms in this house.

After eagerly looking in every nook and cranny of the house, she decided that she would move her belongings that very afternoon. There was no reason to put off, for even one second, enjoying her incredible new life. She went to the door and opened it. She stood there for a second, caressing the door. It was at this door, this very door, that Robert Tyler was going to call on her! She didn't know when he would come, but it couldn't be soon enough!

—⁓⦿⦿⦿⦿⦿⁓—

Adam had not slept very well. There were so many thoughts spinning in his mind. He was so stunned yesterday when he, Emily, and Robert had rounded a curve in the road and seen the main quad of Lynnmont for the first time, just as the sun was about to set. He could not believe his eyes. To his left were the lake and a pasture so large that he could not see the end of it. To his right, on the hill overlooking the lake were all the buildings! Right in the center of the quad was one of the most beautiful houses he had ever seen, even with one end obviously greatly damaged by the fire that his father had set. It was even larger and more beautiful than the Harrison's mansion in Harrisonburg. As beautiful as it was outside, it was even more elegant inside. There was nothing gaudy or even showy about the furnishings; they were simple, but elegant. Someone from the estate had gotten there before they had and every room was already candlelit.

Every bed in the house had been made with fresh linens and there was a pitcher of water, a basin, and a fresh towel in each of the bedrooms. A fire had been set and ready to be lit in each of the twelve fireplaces. The pantry in the kitchen was fully stocked, and the dining room table was fully set, as if a great banquet was about to occur.

If this house was any indication of what the rest of the Lynnmont was like, Adam could hardly wait to see it all. His 'Pop' had promised to show him everything. Adam was so eager he had woken up before dawn. It was while he laid there in bed, waiting for the sun to rise, that his mind was racing. Yesterday he had experienced every emotion that any person could possibly experience, and as he lay there, he experienced them all again. He cried as he relived the story of his mother's captivity, of her slow descent into sadness and her death.

He danced the Running Dance with Chief Joseph and ran, in his mind, as fast as he could into his future. He laughed out loud as he remembered Abigail Jordan's 'Yes! Yes! Yes!' And he seethed with anger as he remembered his grandfather raising his cane and striking Reverend Barnes. There was one other emotion that he had had yesterday. He had been intrigued with the pretty girl that had served his table. He hadn't asked anyone who she was, but, before he got out of bed that morning, he decided that finding out everything he could about her would be as important as finding out everything about Lynnmont.

⸻

Early Monday morning, Robert Tyler met with Franklin Campbell. He had a job that he wanted Franklin to take care of.

"I'd like for you to get some men to dig up the body of Geoffrey Britt and take it to his home. He lived on a small farmstead on the other side of the county, right where Abbott's Creek dumps into the Yadkin. I don't want my would-be murderer buried next to my father."

"Ill take care of it, Mr. Tyler."

Robert went into the office that day for the first time in two months. He didn't get a lot done. Too many people were dropping by to see the man who had been dead. Behind his back, people were calling him Lazarus. Robert knew this, of course. It didn't bother him at all. Robert Tyler had a new life. Once he was dead, caught in a never-ending battle with Alexander Johnston. Now that the battle was finally over, he was truly alive.

———

On the Tuesday morning after the funeral banquet, Adam left Lynnmont to escort his mother back to Harrisonburg. He had asked me to continue to manage the Tyler Companies until his return. After that, he said that I could turn my full attention to running Tyler Brick.

Four weeks later, Adam returned with his best friend, Edward Harrison, who was to be the new manager. Adam had run the idea by Robert and me before he left, and we both told him that it had certainly worked well for us.

Adam also decided to expand the office wing of the manor house. Instead of rebuilding it just as it was, an additional six feet was to be added to the end and two smaller, but more than adequate, offices were to replace the one that had been Roberts. A new outside entrance was to be added to the end of the house, so that anyone needing to do business with either Adam or Edward could enter the offices without having to go through the house.

Two days after Adam returned, a simple, flatbed wagon pulled up in front of the house. Adam looked out the window and saw the driver get down from the wagon and reach into the cargo section. He carefully picked up a large package, wrapped in brown paper and tied with string and brought it to the door.

"Massa," he said to Adam when he reached the door, "I'm James, the butler at Yadkin Oaks. Massa Johnston sent me a message to bring this here. He said that if I damaged it I would spend the rest of my life in jail. Would you please send him a note telling him that I did alright?"

Adam couldn't believe it. His grandfather had kept his promise. Maybe there was a kernel of goodness in him after all. He carefully cut the strings and unwrapped the portrait of his mother. He had wondered what she looked like. Emily and Robert had both tried to describe her to him, but their words had fallen far short.

"James, stay right here and guard this portrait while I write a note to Mr. Johnston."

Writing the note proved more difficult than Adam had originally thought. How should it be addressed? Should he include a word of thanks? Adam struggled. Every time he dipped his pen into the ink well and started to write, a picture of a slashing cane would come into his mind. The sound of the cane hitting John Barnes would echo in his ears. Finally, Adam wrote simply, "Sir, Your package has arrived in very good condition. Your servant, James, is to be commended. Adam Tyler."

He folded the note and took it to John. "Take this note to Mr. Johnston."

"Thank you, massa." James took the note, but he didn't leave. He clearly wanted to say something but was hesitating.

"Is there something else you need?"

"Well, sir," he began haltingly. "Are you Miss Lynn's son, like everybody's saying?"

Yes, James, I am."

That means you'll be our new massa, don't it?"

Adam was stunned at the thought. *Was it possible that he was about to come into possession of another estate?*

"I don't know, James. I just don't know."

"Massa Adam. None of us knows what to do. There ain't nobody in charge."

"James, you head on back to Yadkin Oaks. Tell everybody to keep doing the jobs that they always did, until I can figure out what to do."

Later that afternoon, Adam called Franklin Campbell into his office. "I need for you to move to Yadkin Oaks and take charge of running the plantation. Can you manage slaves?" Adam knew that Yadkin Oaks was not only on the other side of a mountain range from Lynnmont; it was a totally different world.

"I managed a slave plantation before I came to Lynnmont," Franklin said. "I much prefer working with free people, but I can handle the job. How long do you think I will need to be there?"

"I don't have any idea. I don't know if my grandfather will even allow you to stay. But I hope that he will. He may be an evil old cuss, but he is a good businessman. I don't think that he would want to see Yadkin Oaks, his empire, crumble or fall into the wrong hands. I have a note here that I want you to take to him. Just stop by the jail in Richmond on your way and see that he gets it."

"Who are you going to get to do my job here?"

"I thought that I would do it myself. Pop always needed help, because he had so many other irons in the fire. But, I think I might be a pretty good country squire. I'm going to need lots of advice until I learn the job. Is there somebody here I should lean on?"

"Ben Randolph. He can't do the work, but he knows what needs to be done. Besides that, everybody loves him. Except for me, you couldn't get a better man."

Later that evening, Adam was standing in front of the fireplace, looking above the mantle where he had hung the portrait of his mother. He had hung it beside the one of Robert. He had taken the silk ribbon Robert had given him, draping it over the two frames, linking them. He stepped back and looked at her. She had been a magnificently beautiful woman. He could certainly understand how Pop had fallen in love with her. She was almost as beautiful as Anne Marie Barnes.

⎯⎯⎯⎯ ∿∾෴ ⎯⎯⎯⎯

Lawrence Weeks had been working for days trying to come up with a partnership agreement that Robert Tyler would agree to. Every proposal he had made so far had been rejected. Robert kept insisting on a fifty-fifty split, an equal partnership. Lawrence kept insisting that Robert had built the firm, that it was Robert's name and reputation that brought clients, that Robert deserved credit for the years he had invested in the firm before Lawrence came on board, and that Robert's standing in the legal profession and North Carolina politics merited him getting the lion's share of the new firm's profits.

Robert had rejected every argument. "You are the only man that I have ever worked with who is as passionate about justice and fairness as I am. That means that you deserve an equal share."

Lawrence and Robert had another meeting scheduled for ten that morning. He was going to demand that Robert take a 65 percent share and that they agree to reduce Robert's share by one percent a year for the next fifteen years. If Robert rejected this plan, Lawrence had decided to announce to him that he was going to move back to Virginia, open his own firm, and go into politics. He wasn't sure what he would do about Betsy, who had announced that she would never leave Germantown. Betsy would be easy to deal with in comparison to Robert Tyler, who was turning out to be the most stubborn man he had ever known.

⎯⎯⎯⎯ ∿∾෴ ⎯⎯⎯⎯

Alexander Johnston was sharing the small cell in the Surry county jail with Sheriff Richard Speight and Registrar of Deeds Bruce Smithwell. Although the cell was intended to house just one prisoner, rounding up the members of the Cause had filled the jail to overflowing. Alexander had steadfastly refused to share the names of the other members of the secret society, but Bruce Smithwell had talked freely.

Alexander wondered what his fate would be. Robert Tyler had offered him forgiveness and freedom. After sitting in jail for more than a month, with no hope of bail because of the severity of the charges which he faced, he was thinking that he might have made the wrong choice.

But to accept forgiveness from Robert Tyler was unthinkable!

It wasn't long before I discovered that making bricks was a lot like running a church. It was a dirty, messy business. But, if you took the time, you could turn mud into something that would last forever. It seems that bricks and people are an awful lot alike.